Kate Simants was born in Devon. After studying English at university, she worked in TV production in London for ten years, specialising in undercover investigations (which was much less glamorous than it sounds), then moved from her little boat on the Thames to a bigger boat on the Avon to start a family and concentrate on writing. She holds two MAs in creative writing from Brunel University and the University of East Anglia, and has been shortlisted for the Crime Writers' Association Debut Dagger and the Bath Novel Award, and won the UEA Literary Festival Prize. Kate is now a land-lubber and lives between Bristol and Bath with her family and demented cat. She is a committed faddist, and her current interests include roller-skating, macrame, and Persian cookery. To get in touch, tweet her at @katesboat or visit her website at www.katesimants.co.uk.

Lock Me In

Kate Simants

OneMoreChapter

One More Chapter
an imprint of HarperCollins*Publishers* Ltd
1 London Bridge Street
London SE1 9GF

www.harpercollins.co.uk

This paperback edition 2019
2

First published in Great Britain in ebook format by
HarperCollins*Publishers* 2019

A catalogue record for this book
is available from the British Library

ISBN: 978-0-00-835330-8

This novel is entirely a work of fiction.
The names, characters and incidents portrayed in it are
the work of the author's imagination. Any resemblance to
actual persons, living or dead, events or localities is
entirely coincidental.

Typeset in Birka by Palimpsest Book Production Ltd,
Falkirk, Stirlingshire

Printed and bound in the UK by
CPI Group (UK) Ltd, Croydon CR0 4YY

For Tom, who never once suggested I give up this nonsense and get a real job. You're the best mate a girl could have.

Prologue

Y ou want to know fear?

Imagine someone there, every day when you wake. Imagine knowing, without even opening your eyes, that someone is watching you.

Take your time. Let your mind get used to consciousness.

A girl. There. Not in the passage, not at the door, or by the window. Not even at the end of your bed.

Closer than that.

She stares, unblinking, her eyes burning into yours even though you keep your eyelids shut tight. You move, and for a moment, she slips away from you. But she's not gone. You know that much.

You think, *please. Not again.* Your teeth tighten so hard they squeak against each other. You don't mean to do it, but this is real, right-now fear, and your body doesn't care what you want. Your heart starts firing out ball-bearings instead of blood. *Open your eyes*, you tell yourself.

You say her name, and she stiffens. You feel her do it, rigid and alert in your stomach. She is inside you. She is always inside you, listening under your skin.

When you were little, the doctors said this was a known disorder, that they could help. That this other you, your *alter*, the one who's always there like an unwanted imaginary friend, could be brought out into the light. That this other girl that you sometimes became was there because, at some point in your life, you needed to switch your reality off. There must have been something, they said, that brought her bursting out of you: some trauma, some incitement, some moment of quickening. You never found it. In the end they gave up, telling you she was nothing to fear, that she could be managed, medicated, contained.

The doctors were wrong.

You feel her rising. And it doesn't matter how much you know it's not a physical condition, that it's all in your head: when she fights you, it hurts. If you want your body to be yours and not hers, you have to fight back.

Now comes the tension, a thickening, swelling the marrow of your bones. You wrench the bedclothes in your fists, and you press your heels into the mattress. She is stiff and screaming in your veins, inside the cells of your blood. You try to cry out but your voice sticks behind your tongue, no breath behind it. She has her hands in the wet depths of your throat, bending the stiff cartilage of your windpipe.

And just like that she bursts into smoke. Goes quiet. You're left with the ragged sound of your breath, your heartbeat thundering in your ears. Even as it slows, you know she isn't gone. She doesn't go, ever.

You have learned never to trust the silence, never to let your guard down. Even as you sleep.

Especially as you sleep.

You want to know fear?

Fear has a name.

Her name is Siggy.

Chapter 1

Ellie

London, 2011

I woke gasping, the sheet dislodged and twisted tight around my limbs.

I kicked a leg out against the thin partition between my room and the kitchen. Through the wall I heard the radio being clicked off.

'Ellie?' Mum's voice, muffled through the plasterboard.

Siggy went still, and became a cold, thin layer at the base of my brain. She was quiet for a few moments, then she disappeared like a flame in a vacuum, leaving just the staccato sound of my breathing.

'Ellie, sweetheart? You awake?'

I let my eyes open, worked my jaw and mumbled a croaky, 'Yeah.'

It was later than I'd thought. A cold screen of early winter daylight sliced through the middle of my tiny room. Motes of dust danced in its blade. I spread my hand across the bare wall. All our walls were bare, in all the flats and houses we'd lived in since I was a child. We never stayed long, and whenever we left, we left in a hurry.

'She gone?' Mum called. She always managed to sound cheerful.

'Mm-hmm.' I untangled myself from the sheet and tried to swing my knees over the edge of the bed, but I couldn't do it. Too heavy. It was bad this morning, worse than usual. Soreness bloomed across my right shoulder and down my arm. I had to heave my breath in.

'Just doing coffee,' she said, her voice already moving away. She turned the radio back up. The track finished and was replaced by a DJ in an inoffensive, sing-song voice. I heard her unlock the crockery cupboard, taking out mugs, locking it again, setting them down.

I lay for a minute in the S-shape of warmth, trying to salvage what I could of the dream. There was a bright blue sky, and that building. Always that building, the one I'd drawn as a child over and over again: long and low, as unchanging and precise as a photograph, every time. Every night.

Slowly, under the duvet, I shifted. But as I moved to push myself up, bright, brilliant pain shot across my hand, bringing tears to my eyes.

Bisecting my palm, intermittent but extending right over to the base of my thumb, was a ragged tear. Deep punctures, red and swollen. I touched it and winced: it was exquisitely sore, the flesh not yet dry.

Gingerly, I pushed away the covers and looked myself over. Across the right of my pelvis, a blue-black mess of bruising. I pressed the tip of a finger to the centre of the darkest part. The ache, bone-deep, rose up to meet it.

Where had it come from?

A fine thread of fear started to tug at me, hard. I sat up,

planted my feet on the floor. Built up the courage to look at the door.

It would be locked. It had to be locked. Hadn't I heard Mum lock it? I played back the last moments of the day before. Matt had dropped me off after our quick trip to the pub near the narrowboat he was renting. Mum had made me dinner, a pasta thing we ate together in the kitchen. I'd gone to bed early to read for a while. Mum had locked me in before she left for her late shift. She had.

With my blood roaring in my temples, I turned my head. Opened my eyes.

It was only a fingerbreadth, but the door was open. There, on the white gloss of the frame, was something that made me shoot out of bed as if it had caught fire. I crossed the room in three steps and lifted my fingers to the dark marks on the paintwork.

Smears of reddish-brown, crusted at the edge. And on the backs of my hands – I saw it now – the same thing, the same colour, exactly.

Mud.

Siggy had taken me outside.

Mum appeared in the corridor, holding mugs. She stopped dead, then nudged the door fully open with her toe.

'What—?' she started.

I met her eyes. 'You locked it.'

She gripped her eyelids shut for a second, as if dislodging an image.

'You locked it,' I repeated, louder. 'You did. I heard you.'

She set down the two mugs of coffee and bent to touch the door. She was still wearing her cleaning uniform from the night-shift at the same hospital where Matt worked, the bleach-stained mauve tabard over blue scrubs.

'Holy shit,' she whispered, the blood sinking from her skin. She went back out, examining it from the other side. 'What the hell happened here?'

I followed her. In the hall, the bolt that should have been above the mortice lock on the outside of my door was lying on the floor, its two separate sections still secured together with the padlock. Torn paint and splinters of wood clung to the screws where they'd been wrenched out of place. Several inches higher was what remained of the sliding chain lock, the plug hanging uselessly, swinging on the chain. The force it would have taken to break it like that, wrenched inwards with enough power to break the locks on the outside ...

Siggy's little fingers plucked the fibres of my biceps. If I hadn't known her better I would have wondered if she was smiling.

'Do you not remember anything?' Mum asked.

'No. But ... look.' I lifted my hand, and her eyes went wide.

I let her take it, and she turned it over. Under her breath she muttered, 'Jesus,' then decisively, 'Bathroom. Got to wash it. Come on.'

Holding me by the wrist so she didn't touch the wound, she guided me through into the bathroom and pulled the cord for the light. She flipped the toilet lid down and sat me on it like a child, then yanked up her sleeves, exposing her ropey, muscular forearms, hardened from the years of push-ups she did to make sure she was stronger than Siggy.

'This'll sting, love.' The tap screeched as she turned it on, and a thick twist of cold water ran into the avocado-coloured sink. 'Stick it under here.'

I did as I was told.

Frowning at my palm, she pointed. 'My guess is barbed wire. Look at the spacing.' She was right: the punctures were even. Each a centimetre from the last.

She turned and angrily whipped the towel from the electric heater that hadn't worked in the eight months we'd been there. She dried her hands and kicked it into a bundle by the washing basket.

'*Fucking* Siggy,' she said, dragging her fingers hard across her scalp. 'What did she do with you this time?'

She wasn't expecting an answer. We called them fugues, and I never knew what Siggy made me do during them, where she took me. Or why. All I could do was piece it together from whatever mess Siggy left behind, crowbarring in cause by surveying the effect, trying to make sense of it. The fact that the fugues always happened at night had baffled psychologist after psychologist, neurologist after sleep specialist when I was younger until Mum got so frustrated with them that we stopped going altogether. It's a time in my life I have almost no memory of, but Mum kept journals: all the medicines, all the experts, all the sessions and techniques and homework. Nothing worked. The drugs they said would help with the dissociation made no difference. The fugues continued; the nightmares kept coming. Although I didn't get worse for a long time – I was plagued by panic attacks, but I never started 'switching' during the day, which had always been my fear – I didn't get better. Eventually, they ran out of things to try. We never got a cure, and we never got an answer: we were dismissed as an anomaly.

But this was back when Siggy was playful, doing small stuff, things that didn't matter. Like when she filled our shoes with milk while we slept or pulled all the books off the shelves and made them into colour-coded piles. Just the little things, things we could laugh about, almost.

This was before we started needing locks.

This was before Jodie.

My fingers were going numb with the cold, but the torn flesh on my hand was burning now and had started to swell. The mud darkened and flaked off under the water until soon there was nothing left, just clean, pink, angry skin. I turned to wash the mud from the other hand too, and found more of it, up my arm, as far as my elbow.

Where had I gone last night?

What had I done?

Eventually the cold got too much to bear, and I pulled my hand out of the sink and shook my hair back. Mum's eyes went to my throat.

'What the hell happened to your *neck?*'

I got up, dodging round her to get to the mirror. I lifted my chin.

'Don't freak out.' Mum stood behind me, put a hand on my shoulder. 'Control it. Do *not* freak out.'

Dark marks the size of grapes, with blue-white crescents indented at their outer edges. Bruises: four in a line on one side of my windpipe, one on the other. Just above the old, jagged scar from years before.

Four and one. Fingers and a thumb.

'Come on, sweetheart, try,' she said, angry now. 'Try to remember.'

I studied the bruises, touched my fingers to them, lining them up, then I stared at myself in the eyes in the mirror: one green, one blue. One for me, one for Siggy.

Think.

Mud.

Barbed wire on my hand.

And a handprint on my neck.

My breath turned solid in my chest as the thought bloomed, running its course.

'Mum. What if someone was trying to stop ...?'

I trailed off. Matt. I lurched out of the room.

My phone wasn't beside my bed, and it wasn't in the jeans I'd worn the previous night. I went to look for it in the pocket of the raincoat I was sure I'd left on the back of the door, but neither the phone nor the coat were there. I stumbled out into the living room. Spotting my phone charging in the corner, I yanked the cable out and dialled, pressed it to my ear, thinking, *answer. Answer, for Christ's sake.*

'OK, stop,' Mum said from behind me. 'Take a moment to think about this. Ellie. *Stop.*'

I turned to face her. 'What?'

'We need to think smart,' she said, reaching for the phone.

I ducked away from her before I processed what she'd said. I'd been thinking there must have been a fight, something I could fix. But my mother, she was already thinking of Jodie. Of what Siggy had done before.

That she'd done it again.

The fog in my head cleared suddenly and the gentle Scots of Matt's voice was in my ear saying *you've reached Matt Corsham. I'm probably in my dungeon* – the photo lab, in the hospital basement – *leave a message.* I hung up before the beep and dialled it again. Looked at the clock: 07:43. He was on earlies, started at eight, he should have been on his way to the hospital, on the 267. He should have his phone *in his hand.* I slumped onto the sofa. He should be texting *me*.

Mum sat beside me and took my face in her hands.

'What do we do?' she asked me gently. 'Things get tough, what do we do?'

'We deal with it,' I told her in a whisper.

'That's exactly what we do. You and me.' She sighed, took my good hand and peeled each finger from the phone, until I released it. It went on the table, out of reach, then she moved up next to me, pulling me close. I relented, sank my head against her chest.

'Please don't let this happen again, Mum.'

'Shh. He'll be OK, though. Probably just have worked late or started early or something.' She gave me a gentle nudge. 'Don't worry. Just a bit of mud. Just some scrapes.'

Even then, neither one of us believed it.

Chapter 2

Mae

Detective Sergeant Ben Kwon Mae stopped at the lights. He raised his eyebrows in the rear-view mirror and the kicking to the back of his seat immediately ceased. Bear, his 8-year-old daughter who was suspiciously engrossed in the palm of her hand, slowly lifted her chin to meet his gaze.

'*What?*' Eyes all wide, butter-wouldn't-melt incredulous. 'It wasn't *me!*'

He laughed. Thirty quid a pop, the drama lessons his ex-wife made him shell out for and look what it bought.

'You're a terrible actress, Bear. Really bad,' he said, returning his attention to the school-run gridlock. Should have walked.

The kicking resumed, and he swung around. 'Oi! Stop it!'

She laughed, but then he clocked the crisps all over her almost-freshly-laundered school sweater. Busted, she started to brush at them, scattering them into the footwell.

He blew out his cheeks. Didn't say anything. Didn't need to.

'I'm *hungry*.'

'But *crisps*, mate?'

He wanted to leave it, because the clock on the dash gave him eight minutes to get Bear to school and wasting one of those minutes complaining about her diet meant wasting them all. When the bell rang at 8.45 he'd be looking at a clear week and a half until he got her back. But Nadia had complained enough times about having to deal with what she called 'the BMI situation' on her own. It wasn't fair on her for him to just ignore it.

He shook his head. 'I did offer you a proper breakfast. I thought you loved scrambled eggs.'

'Not since I was like *three*. I hate it.' He could only see the top of her head now, but he was pretty sure she was holding back tears. 'You never have any decent food in your stupid flat. I'm always hungry at school after I have to stay at yours.'

'OK, well. I'll stock up next time.' The lights changed and he turned back to the road. 'Just have to make healthy choices, that's all I'm saying.'

'All you're saying is I'm fat and no one likes me.' She stared angrily out of the window, nicking at the raw skin around her thumbnail with her teeth.

'That's absolutely not true.' *Nice one, Superdad.* One guess what she'd remember about the visit with him now. In the mirror he saw her lean her head on the glass, and they finished the journey in silence. Could they bunk off for an hour? Take her to the park, make things okay between them so they'd part on good terms? No. Obviously not. Nadia would find out, for a start, and his approval rating was already on the floor. Things had eroded badly enough between them lately without him adding truancy to the list.

Only three minutes late, he swung into a space miraculously close to the school entrance. He got out and went round to open Bear's child-locked door.

'My tummy hurts,' she whined.

'OK. Well, let's get some fresh air and see how you feel in a minute.'

'But I've got a headache.' Her voice was quieter. He followed her gaze out across the playground to where two boys, older, were in direct line of sight. They turned away as soon as he made eye contact. Bear sighed and looked at her feet.

He leaned across her to undo her seatbelt. 'Friends of yours?'

'No! Get off, Ben,' she snapped, twisting away.

He made sure the sudden sag in his chest didn't make it to his face.

'It's *Dad*,' he told her, pulling her bag and reading folder out from the back seat. This *Ben* thing was new this visit. No way did she call Nadia by her first name. He hadn't even heard her shorten it from *Mummy* yet. He wasn't having it. 'You call me Dad.'

'Whatever.' She squeezed past him and stumped off towards the gate. Catching her up, he reached for her shoulder but let his hand drop before it touched her. Best not push it.

'Tell you what. If you don't give me a cuddle, I'll cave your head in with a fire extinguisher.' A bit too hopeful, the way it came out, but she let him draw level. He coughed, dropped his voice a bit. 'Gouge your eyes out with a soup spoon. I will. I've done it before. In Helmand.'

Which won him a very small smile. 'You haven't been to Helmand.'

'Flipping have.'

'And you've used that one before, too.'

'Right, right. Sloppy.' He shoved his hands in his pockets, thinking. 'In that case I'll just have to grate your nose off.'

'Yeah? How?'

'Cheese grater. Like I did in Operation Desert Knickers.'

A single sniff of a laugh, and she glanced at him. The shape of her eyes so almost-Caucasian, hardly a sniff of Korean about her. Like even his genes were being diluted, rinsed out of her life.

But her sideways smile was all his. She took a deep breath. 'I'll boil you alive and peel your skin off and sell it to the shoe shop so they can make shoes out of you.'

The realization that she'd planned that, rehearsed it, glowed like a coal in his belly.

'Nice.' He gave her a serious look and slow-nodded. 'What's the score? Seventeen-twelve?'

'You wish,' she said, appeased now. '*Nine*teen-twelve.' She cheerfully swung her bag at him, obliviously but narrowly missing his bollocks.

Bear started to skip but stopped when she got to the gate. She was scanning the yard for those boys.

Mae crouched. 'If there's anything you need me to deal with—'

She shot him a serious look. 'No. There's nothing. There isn't.'

'Because if—'

'Please, Dad.'

Mae shrugged, straightened up, committing those two lads to memory: bags, hair, sneery little faces. The last of the late-comers ran past them, ushered in by her classroom assistant (Mr Walls, 29, newly qualified last year, single, previously a gardener, caution for shoplifting aged 13). Mae bent to fix the mismatch of toggles on her coat, and she let him.

'Thanks for hanging out with me, Bear.' He squeezed her shoulders. 'See you next week.'

She ducked him and was gone, off down the path, trying to press into a group of girls he half-recognized. Flicking a hand up briefly as a backwards goodbye. He flexed his fingers a few times in his pockets and headed back to the car.

It didn't get to him. Saying goodbye and not even getting a

hug: it was no big deal. He dealt with assaults and suicides and RTAs, no problem, all the time. Cat C murders, child abuse, DV, the lot. All the fucking time. So, his little girl forgot to give him a hug before a whole nine days away from him, even though five minutes ago she was three years old, falling asleep in his arms as he read *The Gruffalo* for the eighteenth time? Christ! Take more than that to make *him* cry.

From the driver's seat he watched Bear disappear into the building.

Music. He reached round to dig a CD out from the pocket behind his seat, and his fingers closed on a disk in a square plastic wallet. She must have left it there by mistake. He brought it out: *Lady Gaga for Bear!* on the disk in sharpie, and then under the hole,

(not really, it's Daddy's very best CLEAN hip-hop mixtape).

And it was clean, too: he'd checked and double-checked each track, and there wasn't a single swear. It had taken some doing.

He tucked it into the glovebox, then tried again and found Snoop Dogg's *Doggystyle* under a fine layer of fried potato crumbs. It was scratched to shit but last time had played fine up to 'Who Am I (What's My Name)?', which would be long enough to get him to the nick. His speakers were almost as creaky as his brakes, but they were loud, and loud meant a clear head.

Ignition, arm round the headrest to reverse. And off.

All business.

Chapter 3

Charles Cox Psychotherapy Ltd.	
Clinical audio recording transcript	
Patient name:	*Eleanor Power*
Session date:	*14 August 2006*

CC: OK, I think that's recording … Good. Right, before we begin can we just confirm this because we've got a slightly unusual situation here. You have asked for your friend Jodie – our mutual friend, should I say – to be here during this first session?

EP: Yes. Please. If that's all right.

CC: Certainly, whatever makes you feel comfortable. OK. So, what I'd like to do to begin with is to have a chat about the dissociation, and the range of what you're experiencing on a daily basis.

EP: OK.

CC: And from there we can move on to having a think about where you'd like me to get you to. Does that sound OK?

EP: Yeah. Yes. That's fine.

CC: So. A normal day then. How does that start?

EP: OK well, it depends on whether I've had a fugue or not.

CC: Tell me about that.

EP: So, um, Siggy sometimes—

CC: Siggy is your alter.

EP: Yeah, sorry yeah my alter, she sometimes kind of takes over. I wake up at night sometimes but I'm not like, actually awake, it's not me, it's her. She talks to my mum sometimes, otherwise she'll just try to go outside, that kind of thing. Sometimes we'll only know Siggy was up because things will be moved, or lights will be on. Stuff like that. But I always know anyway because I feel her there.

CC: Physically?

EP: Not exactly. I mean, I always feel sick afterwards, sort of achy.

CC: OK, so let's say you've woken up, got up. What happens next?

EP: Well, she's always there. Just … like I can sort of sense her, whatever's going on. It's like she thinks things that I can hear—

CC: Does she speak? Does she have a voice?

EP: Well … no. Not really. But it's like she'll get scared or angry or whatever and I know it's not me feeling those things. Does that make any sense?

CC: Yes, it does. It sounds like what you experience is what I call co-conscious dissociation, which is when a person can feel that they have more than one identity at the same time.

EP: Right. Yes, that's what it's like. But the times she gets me up and does stuff with me at night, and … I just have completely no memory of that at all.

CC: OK. I'm getting from the way you're speaking now that it's quite distressing.

EP: I just … I don't know.

[pause: 32 sec]

CC: Would you feel comfortable going into a little more detail about the episodes you have at night?

[pause: 12 sec]

EP: Look, I-I don't know.
CC: OK: Eleanor—
EP: Ellie.
CC: Ellie. A lot of the people I see, they find it very hard at the beginning. They can feel like … well, they don't know if they can trust me. Or it might be that they don't trust that talking is going to help.

[pause: 27 sec]

EP: No. It's not that. I just know what's going to happen. We're going to go through all this, and then you're going to give up.
CC: Ah, OK. Tell me a bit more about that.
EP: I'm just … like, I've tried. You know? I talk to Siggy, I talked to other people, tried medicine and everything. All kinds of stuff. I don't want to do all of that again. Just tell you all of it and then have you just say that actually you can't help. Or that you don't believe me.
CC: Who does believe you, Ellie?
EP: My mum.
CC: She's always believed you.

EP: *Yeah. She's-she's seen what happens. The fugues, and — everything.*

CC: *Anyone else close to you? Other family?*

EP: *I'm an only child. My dad's dead.*

CC: *OK.*

[pause: 11 sec]

CC: *OK. And was that a long time ago that you lost him?*

EP: *Yes. Before I was born.*

CC: *I see. It can be challenging, growing up without—*

EP: *No. It wasn't.*

CC: *You don't want to talk about your father.*

EP: *No.*

[pause: 31 sec]

CC: *OK, Ellie, there's a couple of things I'd like you to know. Sometimes therapists can be a bit mystifying. They can wait for you to work things out for yourself even if they have a good idea of what's going on and what needs to shift in order to improve. But that can take a lot of time. In my experience I think it's best to be up front and tell you what I think is happening, and what we're going to do to put it right. Seems more honest, that way. Does that sound OK?*

EP: *Yes. I just want her gone. I want to be better.*

CC: *I hear you. So the first thing is, the aim of the psycho-therapeutic work I'm going to do with you is to understand what's happened. What I want to do is reduce the conflict between the different parts of your identity, help them coop-erate.*

EP: OK. I mean, I can't see that happening, but OK. We can try.

CC: Good. So, the second thing I need you to know is that the kind of issues you're having with Siggy, they're something that almost always stem from quite a significant trauma, often something in early childhood.

[pause: 34 sec]

EP: OK.

CC: And so at some point in our sessions we're going to need to talk about that. What you yourself think is at the bottom of it, how it all started.

[pause: 19 sec]

CC: Would you like us to come back to this at another time?
EP: No.
CC: OK. I understand. The reason I'm—
EP: I just … look, nothing happened, OK? There's no deep dark secret. She's just there. I don't know why. I'm not going to come along here and just suddenly remember some massive, buried … it's not going to happen. She's always been there. I just want her gone. OK? I want her to leave me alone.

[pause: 22 sec]

EP: I just want her to leave me alone.

Chapter 4

Ellie

It felt like she was gone forever. I called Matt again and again but there was no answer.

I checked the time on the wall clock – three hours gone – and then saw the streak of pink highlighter on the calendar. I was supposed to be doing a shift that afternoon, volunteering in the children's ward in the hospital where Mum cleaned, and Matt worked in the imaging lab. He'd set the whole thing up for me, sorting all the stuff out with the permissions, after I told him how one day I'd like to work with children. But after his effort, I'd manged to miss my slots twice in the last few weeks. The HR person had already come to see me about it, but I couldn't explain to her what had really happened: that if I went back to sleep after a fugue, I was impossible to wake.

Matt said I should just come clean about it, explain that I had a mental illness. It was a hospital, he said – how could they *not* understand? I didn't dare, but I knew then I'd made the right decision in confiding in him.

At first I'd been careful to stick to the rules, to censor myself. Mum knew how serious I was about him, and in his company at least, she approved of him. I'd come home once to find them roaring with laughter over a game of cards: he was genuine, polite, reliable, she said, and nothing like my father. She made me promise not to let myself fall asleep with him, no matter how tired I got, but she was still worried. There wasn't a man alive who was patient enough, understanding enough, to be with someone who'd always sleep alone. *Even good guys can break your heart*, she said.

To begin with I said nothing at all about Siggy, but I couldn't keep the secrecy up for long. There was no boundary where I stopped and she began, and after a few months, I realized I couldn't be myself without telling him.

Matt had listened to it all. We'd been sitting in front of the log burner in his narrowboat, sharing a bottle of wine. I sat propped against his chest, and I told him the whole story. From the first time Siggy had got me up at night and taken me outside, until Mum, frantic at 4 a.m., found me lying underneath the car. I told him about the exhaustion I got the mornings after a fugue, the grinding headaches, the ten-tonne limbs. I told him everything.

No. Not everything. I didn't tell him about Jodie.

After my very long monologue, there was a very long silence. And then he'd lifted my head from his shoulder and looked right into my eyes.

'I'm not going to lie to you,' he said. 'I don't understand this yet, but I'm going to. We're going to make you OK.'

I told Mum later, and she was silent for a long while. Eventually, she just hugged me. 'It's your life,' she said. 'Remember to be careful, though. He's a good guy, but I can't protect him from *her*.'

The very next morning, there were bruises all up her arms. I had no memory of what Siggy had done – what *I* had done. How I had slammed my own mother against a wall and thrown her out of my way.

Like I was an empty coat, Mum said. But it wasn't your fault.

I heard a sudden movement and I froze, listening, but it wasn't Mum coming back. Just boxes being moved around downstairs, from what I guessed was the stock room. Our flat was above a shop, an off-licence, and from the way sound travelled it seemed Mr Symanski's ceiling, our floor, was made from little more than cardboard.

I gave a start. Thin floors.

If I could hear *him* …

I pulled on my shoes and was at the front door before Mum's warnings about him sounded in my head. *Don't talk to the neighbours. It only takes one person to suspect us.*

What was I going to say? Did you hear me leave the flat in the middle of the night? Because I've got a whole load of unexplained injuries and I don't remember what happened? I stood there for a moment, my forehead resting on the cold glass of the door. Then I took my shoes back off and kicked them sullenly away.

In the kitchen, next to the sink, Mum had left a beaker for me and a carton of orange juice. Forgetting the damage to my hand, I made the mistake of trying to twist the cap. I recoiled and knocked the whole box to the floor where it slopped out across the lino.

Irritated, I opened the safe cupboard under the sink and took out the homemade cleaning fluid and some latex gloves. We didn't take chances anymore: everything harmful was locked away. I couldn't even be left alone with a bottle of bleach. I tried all the other doors, out of habit. All locked. Knives, matches, bleach, all beyond my grasp. I snapped on the gloves and clenched and stretched my hands, feeling the thin scabs on the wounds split, reasserting myself over her.

My pain, Siggy. Not yours.

After I mopped up the juice I carried on cleaning, using the soft scourers to attack the rest of the floor, the dented metal sink, the wood-effect laminate of the worktops. I scrubbed until my jaw ached from gritting my teeth. Folded in a corner, Siggy eyed me.

My phone rang, and I pulled off the gloves, my heart leaping as I recognized the first few of digits of the number on the screen. It was the hospital.

'Matt?'

'Oh, hi,' said an awkward voice, a man. Not Matt. 'Ellie, right?'

I let my eyes close. If someone at his work was calling me, that meant—

'Listen, do you know where Matt is? Only, we were expecting him in, and he hasn't shown up.'

I told him – after swallowing the lump of lead in my throat – that I hadn't. 'Who is this?'

'Leon. From the hospital. The imaging lab?'

'Oh, OK. Leon.' Matt had mentioned Leon: they'd been working together for a couple of months now and he'd gone for a pint with him after work once or twice, though I didn't get the sense they were particularly good friends.

'Did you see him yesterday?' Leon asked, concern in his voice. 'Like, in the evening? Because I can't get hold of him on the mobile, and the guy at his moorings says he's not there, and with yesterday being a bit ... you know.'

'A bit what?'

The wet sound of him opening and closing his mouth told me he was choosing his words. 'No it's ... it's nothing. But look, if you hear from him—'

'It was a bit *what*, Leon?'

'Nothing. Just, you know. Busy.'

Matt hadn't mentioned anything unusual. Had I even asked? I told Leon I'd call if I heard anything and hung up.

I went to the window, pulling the net aside. The thick cloud of the early morning was gone now, swept clean to expose a sky of cold blue, scarred all over with sharp shards of white.

Wherever Matt was, he wasn't OK. He wasn't OK at all.

My eye was caught by movement. I recognized Mr Symanski's son, Piotr. Maybe a little older than me, mid-twenties and already paunchy. He was a sullen figure, shuffling up the road. I watched him bend to scratch a passing cat behind the ears, and let it weave between his ankles a few times. When he stood, he saw me. Stock still, nothing on his face, staring straight at me for five seconds, ten. More. Then as if he'd suddenly come to his senses, he looked away, got out his keys, and went inside.

I dropped the corner of the net curtain, and stood there blinking, thinking only of that stare. Did he know something? I thought again of going down, speaking to them. But before I could make a decision, I heard movement on our steps outside and the clatter of fumbled keys against concrete.

Chapter 5

Mae

The Snoop Dogg was damaged worse than he'd thought, so he felt around in the side pocket for anything CD shaped and slipped it in. Turned out to be a demo from a mate of a mate, who Mae vaguely remembered wanting to punch. White guy, gangster lean, called everyone *bruv*. Mae gave it until after the first refrain, pressed eject, checked for witnesses, and windowed it.

He took a little detour and got a coffee from a new Cuban place on the corner by Acton Central. He ordered short and black on the grounds that it would be fastest and bounced on the balls of his feet as the barista made it up, feeling the snip of unspent energy amassing in his blood. A muted newscast on the screen above the counter was wringing the final drops from an American school shooting, a week old and almost forgotten.

After paying, he got out of there, and had emptied half the scalding caffeine into his mouth before he'd even pulled away. Needing the buzz, needing the lift, because there hadn't been a chance for a run that morning, either.

He tolerated the flack he got about his thing for exercise. If it made his colleagues feel better about themselves to call him vain, call him a poser, that was their business. But to Ben Mae, exercise had never been optional. Without a run in the morning, without an hour of circuits or weights or anything else in the evening, the noise in his head got too much and he knew where that ended. These days, he could trust himself to recognize that inevitable build-up of whatever-it-was and burn it off in the gym. But age as he might, those years after his dad died of finding himself prowling, angry without provocation, skulking around for a fight or a fuck never seemed that far behind him.

Objectively, he thought, as he slowed for the barrier and flashed the fob at the reader, it was doubtful that coffee helped. Objectively, the right thing to do was to deal with the anger, understand it. Go right back to that dark six months when he changed from a normal teenage boy and into a thug, to the point where his life could have gone either way. Tear the thing out by the root.

But who would he be then?

Leaning back in his desk chair, Mae transferred the phone to the other ear, then rubbed the stubble on his head up and down hard with the palm of his hand. Around him, the office was already in the full throes of post-briefing activity.

'But he's still missing,' the woman at the other end of the line was saying, her voice rising towards the inevitable crack. 'He's still gone. We can't cope with this not knowing. My poor *kids*—'

Her name was Charlotte, wife of Damien Hayes. Widow, almost certainly, of Damien Hayes. Mother of his four kids. Six months previously, Mr Hayes had left the final shift of his job at the vehicle plant just outside Uxbridge, driven his car half the way home, abandoned it, and disappeared. He left no note but, as it unravelled, it was a tale that told itself. The poor bastard had been in the red by almost forty grand, had defaulted on his last half a dozen mortgage payments and then, just to kick the man while he was down, the plant had laid him off. Mrs Hayes had only discovered in the weeks following his evaporation that he left behind no savings, no pension, and no insurance.

'Mrs Hayes I promise you we've done everything we can—'

'Done? *Done?*'

Mae winced. 'Doing. We're doing everything—'

'Are you? Like what? What have you done, since you made this call a month ago? On our last *weed date*,' she said, bitterness curling at the term.

He lifted the top sheet of the stack of paper in front of him and stifled a sigh. Four more calls exactly like this one, scheduled for today, but there was no news, no concrete developments in a single one of them. Thing was, in this business no news was bad news, even if – especially if – it wasn't the kind of bad news that had an event attached, a clear and obvious trauma that could at least heal cleanly. In the majority of the cases he had the misfortune to head in his current role, the misper was *there* and then they were *not*. No stages of grief to work through, no ritual to mark the end of the life. The family around them remained in stasis until eventually, secretly and ashamedly, they started to long for news of a body being found.

'I'm afraid without new information, there's really not much else—'

'So you've *given up?*' And right on cue, the sob. 'If you had any idea of what this is doing to us.'

Mae pressed closed his eyes. They always said that. Every one of them, and not just in Missing but in everything he'd ever been assigned. Murders and rapes and robberies, beatings, the lot. Nearly always, they were right. No, he'd never been sexually assaulted. Hadn't suffered the violent death of someone he loved. Since he'd been leading Missing, though, the accusation that he didn't know how it felt had been harder to take. But he never let it out, never put them right, not even to McCulloch when she'd given him the gig. Especially not then.

He was going to need that run, he decided.

'Look, Mrs Hayes,' he said, quietly. 'Charlotte. I'll put some calls in to the charities again, OK? See if there's anything new there. Sometimes there are delays with them putting stuff through to our systems. I'll see if I can extend the hospital checks a bit. I'm not promising anything,' he added as he heard her intake of breath, but the hope had already returned to her voice.

'Yes. Please.' She paused to delicately blow her nose. 'Anything you can do.'

A red light started blinking on his desk phone. Mae straightened, dispatched Mrs Hayes as sensitively as he could, and answered it.

'Should I send down a written invitation?' The gentle Hebridean lilt of DCI Colleen McCulloch.

Mae glanced at the time. *Shit.* 'Sorry, ma'am. On my way.'

He bombed it up the back steps and made McCulloch's floor in about thirty seconds flat. He slowed to a stroll as he passed her glass-fronted office for the sake of some semblance of cool, then went in.

'Sorry ma'am,' he muttered, 'difficult call to a—'

'Spare me,' she said, nodding over her glasses to the door, which he dutifully closed. Standing at ease the other side of the room was a statuesque, stony-faced uniform, a woman. He nodded an acknowledgement: he'd seen her swinging kettlebells around in the basement gym. She had cropped, bleach-blonde hair and had to be a good 180 lbs and rising six foot. The kind of woman who occupied every inch of herself. Lot of tattoos, he'd noticed: not that they were visible now.

McCulloch cleared her throat. 'How's it been going downstairs these past few weeks, Ben? Haven't seen you since I went to Egypt. Ooh, talking of which,' she said, turning to dig something out of a drawer, 'got you one of these. From the pyramids.'

He caught the paper bag just before it struck him on the head – she was nothing if not a good shot – and opened it. Inside was a small, stuffed camel, made from some kind of felt. He closed the bag. 'Uh, I'm honoured?'

She shrugged. 'Don't be, it's cursed. Paid the extra, thought why not.'

The uniform bit back a grin.

McCulloch had arrived on the force six months after Mae: they'd both started out in Sussex, albeit at very different levels of seniority. She'd been a hard sell to the whole department, straight in from civvy street to detective inspector, leapfrogging not only a whole generation of CID sergeants who'd been waiting in the wings – some of them – for literally years, but also sprinting past the two long years of uniform service. She was part of a new *Philosophy of Recruitment*, they'd been told, which *recognized outside skills* and *combatted red tape*. Translated: stuffed suit. Decoded: clueless leg-up wannabe. The entire team had been rooting for her to fuck up her first major job, but she'd steered the investigation to a solve with the cool, effortless ease of a seasoned skipper. Those who still remained unconvinced waited, hoping for a trip up to ratify their prejudices. It never came. Problem was, she might have come from some woolly sounding NGO background, but she was also bulletproof. She was bright as a supernova, knew her PACE back to front, her Murder Manual inside out and recited her CPS guidelines with her eyes closed. She bit only when antagonized, and she called every single decision with blistering speed and perfect judgement. What made all of that worse was that she was the most eminently likeable boss any of them had ever had.

And after Brighton, when his immediate superior had been sacked and Mae himself had been given a month's suspension, she'd moved to the Met to take the helm at Brentford and had been in the role ever since. It was McCulloch who'd encouraged him to relocate, to come and work in the capital with her, and with nothing on the coast to stay for, he'd eventually relented.

McCulloch pushed aside the wireless keyboard to make room for her tailored-shirted forearms and took a sip from a steaming mug of her ubiquitous mint tea.

'Detective. *Ben.*' She gave him a broad smile that pushed the plump cheeks into freckled bulges and exposed the quarter-inch gap between her front teeth.

'Ma'am.'

'I have a job for you.'

'That's very kind, Ma'am, but I have seventeen open—'

'Call it an expansion of your already impressive burden,' she said, waving his reluctance away. 'Tell me, how long have we been in the force?'

She knew the answer to this. She knew everything. Where he'd been to school, his bench press PB, and the name of his first pet. Not for the first time, it occurred to him she probably even knew about the dark years after his mum disappeared, even though he'd always managed to keep a half-step ahead of the law.

'Eight years, Ma'am.'

She pulled the keyboard back over. 'I've had some applications.

Some of your colleagues putting themselves forwards for inspector.' She was looking at her screen now, scrutinizing it for his benefit. 'But I'm not seeing your name here.'

'I'm happy where I am.' He glanced at the uniform, wondering where this was going.

Ignoring him, McCulloch folded her arms and leaned back in her chair, addressing the ceiling. 'You see, Ben, when we rank people up, we like to see people proving themselves as leaders. Showing managerial qualities.'

'I'm not looking to rank up. Sergeant suits me fine.'

'I see. Well anyway. Detective *Sergeant* Mae, this,' she said, gesturing at the mystery uniform, 'is DC Catherine Ziegler.'

'Right.'

'And she,' McCulloch went on with a twinkle of the eyes, 'is going to be your new TI.'

Mae took the hand extended towards him, met her eyes, and briefly returned a rough approximation of the broad, open smile she gave him. Thinking, *shit*. Trainee Investigator meant a shadow. Constant company.

'Hate to say it, Ma'am—' Mae started, but he was silenced with a finger held aloft.

'Then don't.' McCulloch folded her arms across her chest, assessing the two of them like a mother at a playdate. 'I understand that Catherine—'

'Kit,' the younger woman put in.

'I understand that *Kit* passed her NIE with stand-out results,' McCulloch was saying. 'So when HR asked me for a mentor, I looked around the floor and I thought to myself, Colleen, who have you got with the kind of skills and characteristics to drive a talent like that? I thought, who's willing to take the time to make opportunities for a new generation of detectives?'

My arse you did, Mae thought. Try, who have I got who's been coasting for getting on for half a decade, without a foot of movement in any direction? Who have I got *spare*? Not that he could begrudge it. If it had been DCI Anyone Else, this would have been a punitive move. But she'd called it right, he couldn't deny it. Sure, he'd sat the exams and taken the promotion to sergeant when he came back from his absence, even though he was fairly sure she'd swung it for him. After that, he'd kept his head down. He'd gone where he was sent, done the courses, gone through the motions. But it didn't take an HR review to see he'd been treading water since ... since before ... since before it had all gone wrong. He pumped his fists tight and loose, tight and loose at his sides, dispelling it.

'I thought Missing would give Kit a nice easy start,' McCulloch told him, 'and you can get her used to the juggling.' Turning, she added, 'Ignore the grumpy exterior, Kit. They're all the same: like to pretend they're brooding mavericks but buy them a bacon roll and they're anyone's.'

DC Catherine Ziegler glanced at him to gauge his reaction, and he conceded a reluctant twitch at the corners of his mouth. Might as well be decent, because he could see he wasn't going to win this.

'Squirt of HP and we can talk.'

'Then that's sorted,' the boss said. 'And don't forget your camel.'

McCulloch was already pulling the keyboard close, on to the next thing. She started typing, then looked up. 'What are you waiting for, lollies? Run along.'

But he could tell from the meaningful, encouraging look on his boss's face as she shooed them out of the door that there was nothing malicious about this. He wasn't despised, he was *pitied*. This was intended to aid his personal development. She thought this was what he needed.

And as Mae left the office, with his new TI following behind like a rugby-shouldered Valkyrie, he hated McCulloch for always being right.

Chapter 6

Ellie

Mum's outline was distorted through the bumpy glass as she bent to retrieve the dropped key. She cursed, but it was the weakness in her voice that made me certain that something was not good.

She came inside, her hair stuck across her face in muddy streaks as she unbuttoned her coat.

I took it from her and asked, 'Did you *find* him?'

'I'm sorry, baby,' she said. 'No luck.'

'So where have you been?'

'Just down to the boat, but he's not there. I thought I'd get a run in on the way back.' She started stripping off, moving quickly, her T-shirt slopping to the floor where she dropped it. Leggings going the same way; socks, the tube-bandage support she used on her dodgy knee. The bare wet flesh of her arms and torso was paling from the cold and stiffened with goosebumps, ropes of muscle tensing underneath as she moved.

She found a plastic bag and shoved the clothes inside. 'Don't look so worried, love. He'll be ... I don't know. Out for a walk? Or out taking pictures?'

'He's supposed to be at work. They called, Mum. He's not there.'

She was suddenly serious. 'What did you tell them?'

I shrugged. 'Nothing.'

'You didn't say ...' she started, her eyes drifting down the hall, to my bedroom door.

'That I smashed my way out of my room in the middle of the night and I don't remember it, and I've woken up covered in bruises? No. I kept that to myself.'

'OK. Stupid question. I'm sorry.'

I followed her into her room. She unlocked the box beside her bed where she kept tools, matches, things she couldn't leave lying around. She removed a pair of nail scissors and started cutting her nails down.

'So where is he?'

She sighed. 'I don't know, Ellie.' Finishing her own no-nonsense manicure, she gestured for my hand, which I gave her. 'There's nothing to say you had anything to do with it,' she said, trimming the white from the tops of my nails.

I tried to pull away. 'Mum, if you found something—'

'I didn't. It's nothing.'

'But it's not, is it?' I said, disentangling. 'What if Siggy ... what if it's happened again?'

'Don't. Please. Just don't think about it.' Mum took a deep breath, held it, as if bracing for something. 'And even if something *has* happened. We should definitely sit tight,' she said at last.

I broke free, stood up, went into my room.

'Where are you going?' she called.

'I'm calling the police.'

It took her about half a second to come after me. 'No.' She grabbed the phone out of my hand. 'No. That's not the right play. Not at all.'

I stared at her. '*Play?* He could be—' I stopped myself from saying it.

'But he's not. OK? He'll be fine. There could be any number of explanations. He might have just gone on a trip.'

I folded my arms. 'Right. A trip.'

'Maybe he wanted a break.'

It took me a moment to process that. 'From me?'

She shrugged apologetically.

'You're saying this is just him breaking up with me?'

'Men. They eat your pies and tell you lies,' she offered. It was our joke, the phrase with which every conversation we'd ever had about my father would eventually end. But I wasn't in the mood, and she saw it. 'I've got to get to work, sweetheart.'

'Me too. I've got a shift with the kids. What?' I said, when she made a face.

'Maybe best call in sick?'

'What? Why?'

She spread her hands but didn't answer my question. Didn't need to. She didn't want me to go because she wanted to keep me out of sight.

She thought I'd killed him.

Had I killed him?

After she left, I stood in the hall, taking in our dingy home. Nothing to mark it as ours. Our rent paid in cash – everything always paid in cash – so we could leave at a moment's notice if anyone came knocking on the doors, asking questions about me, about Jodie. Mum used a different name, Christine Scott, wherever she could. She chose agency work over proper contracts because it meant wages in cash, and there were always agencies with a relaxed approach to background checks.

Our whole existence, Mum's jobs, everything we did, was built around Siggy. Everything in her life was about me: boyfriends had been dismissed when they started to ask too many questions, jobs abandoned when demands were made that took her away from her duty to me. She'd given up everything just to cover my tracks and keep me happy, or at least keep me safe. Even before Jodie, we'd never put down roots, but since? I'd lost count of the number of times we'd moved. Always in a hurry when someone recognized her. It made her curse herself for ever having had success: if she'd never been on TV, it wouldn't be half this hard.

I padded back to where the calendar hung on the wall: my shifts marked in pink highlighter.

It's not like it's actually a job.

I was coming up twenty years old. I was the same person I'd been at fourteen. Afraid of everyone and everything, locked into the bedroom in my mother's flat every night for fear of what I might do if I was free. Whatever she said about my value in the world, I was jobless, dependent.

But I had Matt. Loving, understanding Matt. Patient. Blindly at risk.

I made a promise right there and then, that if Siggy had hurt him in any way, that I was ending it. I'd take her with me. I didn't care.

Nobody wins, Siggy. Do you hear me? This ends here.

Siggy heard. Her black eyes flashed wide, but she shrank back, flattening into the shadows. Didn't move, not a moment of a challenge. She'd been around me long enough to know when I meant what I said.

Chapter 7

Mae

Mae arsed the access door open and climbed the steel steps, steep enough to make the toe of his size twelves clang on the underside of each one as he ascended. The fire door at the top swung open and banged against the wall. He squinted as he went out. Bright. Stretching his arms out, opening his chest, he made a circuit of the flat roof then leaned out across the suicide bars, looking down to the street below.

He bit into his bacon roll. He'd lost DC Catherine Ziegler shortly after she'd handed it to him in the canteen. Or maybe not *lost*, exactly, more turned and walked away from, without checking she was behind him.

He rarely ate in the canteen. The food was adequate, but the place was rammed full of cops. For him, up here was the place to be. He chewed slowly, felt the cold on his skin, had a stretch. Movement at the edge of the roof caught his eye: from the door of the shed-like block that housed the steps came his new TI. Striding out across the felt roof like an uncaged animal.

'Sarge,' she called, 'got a sec?' She carried a sheet of paper, the other hand visored across her forehead against the sharp November sunshine.

Mae jerked his chin to greet her, then chased a dot of brown sauce from the corner of his mouth with his tongue.

'Love it up here, too,' she said, tilting her head back to the open sky and filling her lungs. An exchange of car horns sounded, and she glanced over the edge of the building.

She laughed softly. 'Funny little bastards.'

'Who?'

She shrugged. 'I don't know. All of us.'

Mae followed her eyeline, down to the stop-start of traffic by the junction of Boston Manor Road. Tiny faraway people pottering around, in and out of shops and cars and offices, fluid masses of them sloshing out of buses and onto the streets where they dispersed easily, innocuous as peas from a split bag. When he looked back at her, a smile had risen over her face.

'Did you need something, Ziegler?' he said, popping the last mouthful of the butty into his mouth and balling up the bag.

'Please don't call me by my surname, Sarge. Makes me feel like I'm at boarding school.' She followed him back out towards the steps and passed him a printout. 'Got a new one in. Misper.'

Mae glanced at the sheet she was holding out, swept his eyes over the first couple of lines. Just a log from a triple-9. He handed it back, frowning.

'Give it to uniform. If it's already marked as low-risk they'll do the work-up. They hand it over as and when.'

'Usually, yeah. But I thought the name might be of interest,' she said.

He sighed, took the sheet back. They went down the metal steps into the blue-walled normality of the nick. 'What was the name?'

'Matthew Corsham,' she said, peeling the top sheet off, handing it to him. 'White male, twenty-six, some kind of technician at Hanwell Hospital. No history of missing, not a pisshead or a junkie.'

He nearly choked. 'I think that's supposed to read, *no history of drugs or alcohol abuse.*'

She shrugged and moved on. 'The workmate who called it in said he's worried because it was the guy's last shift yesterday, dismissal was a bit out of the blue and he was distressed. Corsham promised to take his work computer back, and didn't show, which is very out of character because he swore he'd be there and he's very reliable. So the workmate calls, but it goes straight to voicemail, so goes round to his place – he lives on a boat, just up towards Isleworth – and he's disappeared.'

Mae scanned the text for dates. 'What timescale we talking?'

'It's only half a day. Leon, the colleague, says he spoke to him yesterday and he was really agitated about having lost his job.'

'Half a *day*? Give the bloke a chance, Christ! They never heard of a bender?'

'I think that's supposed to read, excessive period of alcohol consumption.'

Mae gave her a look. 'And anyway, I don't know a Matthew Corsham. Am I supposed to?'

'Not him. The girlfriend.'

Mae returned his eyes to the document. And his heart skidded to a stop. Eleanor Power.

Kit leaned against the doorframe. 'Rings a bell, right?'

It wasn't a question, and they both knew it. He gave her a quick glance. 'You like your homework, then?'

He read the whole thing en route to his desk, walking on autopilot. Not taking his eyes from it until he was in his chair, screen on. A dull wince, the kind that sits there for years until it's so familiar it almost goes unnoticed, tightened in his chest.

Yeah. It rang a bell.

Mae pulled the keyboard over, put the name through the PNC. Fourteen Eleanor Powers in the country, three in London.

Could it really be her?

'I've run her already,' Kit told him, reminding him of her presence behind his chair. 'No records on her, DWP, electoral roll, nothing. Hasn't had contact with a GP in five years.'

It figured. Five years meant 2006. The year everything fell apart. Eleanor, *Ellie*, who had seen Jodie Arden getting into a car the night she went missing. Ellie Power, whose mother held her hand and finished her sentences for her when she was too upset to speak. Who was consumed with the irrational belief that her friend's disappearance – her *death*, Ellie believed – was her fault. To the extent that, one afternoon, after the session of questioning that would end up being replayed and dissected in the tribunals that lost DS Heath his job and nearly destroyed Mae's career, she decided that her imagined guilt was unbearable. She followed that conviction through with such brutal decisiveness that Mae was unable to hold it together at work the next day, or the day after that. He'd never gone back, not to his old job, not to any of the spots they'd offered him in Traffic or Custody. Not to anything in the Brighton and Hove district. Not to anything on the Sussex force at all.

But there was one other tiny detail. One minor footnote that he hadn't come across before or since and would happily never come across again, not least because it was this that discredited her in the eyes of the CPS and collapsed the entire case against Cox: Ellie Power suffered from Dissociative Identity Disorder. He felt the fine hairs on his arms lift as he recalled the specifics of it. How according to her own testimony, sometimes she did and said things, went places that she couldn't remember. Stopped being Ellie Power at all and became – someone else.

Siggy. The name sounded like a whisper in his head, crept like insects on his skin.

He rubbed his palm over the stubble on his scalp and willed his heart to decelerate.

Kit, oblivious, reached over for the mouse and clicked through the pages. 'Coincidence she turned up here, on your patch. Nothing on her since your missing prostitute, and now—'

'Jodie Arden was a fucking *child*.'

She lowered eyes. 'Sir.'

Mae sighed. He leaned forward, started lifting the various notes and notices pinned to the blue hessian-fronted panel at the back of his desk. Under several sheets of stuff he'd been meaning to read, there was a photo. He pulled the rusting pin out.

Kit leaned close. 'Is that her?'

It was a head-and-shoulders of a dark-blonde girl in a dress that fastened at the neck: Jodie Arden at her cousin's Bat Mitzvah. It was the shot they'd used in the police press packs, but the media had rejected it in favour of a racier snapshot taken by a friend on a night out, that showed her in an altogether different light. The papers had treated her like an adult, which meant printing whatever they wanted. She'd missed the social media explosion by a hair's breadth, but the hacks had got hold of everything, nonetheless. Including the drinking, including the drug use. And including the fact that she had been sleeping with a much older man, a psychotherapist by the name of Charles Cox, who just so happened to be treating her best friend Ellie. Worse still, Cox also just so happened to be dating Jodie's own mum. It was this man who owned the car Ellie Power saw Jodie climbing into before she disappeared off the face of the planet. Her disappearance had been news for all of two days, after which another girl in another part of the country had gone missing. A nicer girl, Aryan and clean, a girl who'd volunteered in Uganda and had a place at Cambridge and played the oboe or whatever. With no new information, Jodie Arden had just become another statistic, one among thousands of almost-adult runaways who slipped through the cracks.

'She was a week off eighteen when she disappeared,' he said, carefully. 'I don't know what you were like, but I sure as hell wouldn't fancy being judged for life at that age.'

Kit put her hands up. She ventured a tentative laugh. 'You always this heavy first thing on a Monday?'

'You just wait till end of the week,' he said, replacing the photo. 'I'm an unstoppable gag machine by Thursday lunch.'

'Right. Well, apologies.' She gathered up the paper she'd delivered, giving him a sideways look that he couldn't interpret. 'Just saw the name and thought you'd be interested. Given your involvement.'

'Ancient history, to be honest.' He stood up and straightened his shirt. 'Come on.'

'So we *are* looking at it?'

'You're the trainee, so I'm training you. Got to start somewhere.' Good thing about rank was how you didn't have to explain yourself to anyone under you. He swept his jacket off the back of his chair and felt in his drawer for a tie, then remembered something. 'You got a change of clothes?'

Kit frowned, shook her head. 'Not apart from my gym stuff. Why?'

'Best ditch the uniform. There's a plain-clothes store down by the armoury, you can get the key from the guy in Evidence. Find something there, OK? Meet me in reception in five.' He flipped the collar of his shirt up and gestured an *after you*.

Chapter 8

Ellie

I stood back from the door, head on the side, to admire the result. Cosmetically at least, my doorframe was OK now. Between the tub of wood putty and a few scraps of sandpaper I'd found, I'd rebuilt the splintered section back up and shaped it to match the contour of the rest. There had been an inch of gloss paint left in the tin from last time it had needed repairing, and I'd done a fair job. I was proud of it. Mum would be pleased.

I felt my shoulders drop as I thought how Matt would be proud, too. I'd managed to convince him I was pretty handy with repairs the first time I'd gone to his narrowboat. It was about a month after I'd first got talking to him at the hospital while I waited for Mum to finish her shift. For weeks, we'd accidentally-on-purpose bumped into each other before he properly asked me out. Our first real date was on a Saturday afternoon: a lazy lunch at a riverside pub. Matt invited me back to see the boat afterwards but had forgotten that he'd been halfway through laying new floorboards until we went inside.

'Oh god, state of the place,' he said, shoving the mess of cushions on the built-in sofa up to one end to clear a space for me. 'Sorry, not a great start.' He started lugging the new boards across from where they were propped by the log burner, roughly laying them into place to give us something to stand on.

I sat where I was shown, but raised an eyebrow, flirty from the wine. 'Start to what, exactly?'

He glanced up, embarrassed, 'I meant, I—'

Nudging him with a toe, I put him out of his misery. 'Kidding.' And he laughed, and it felt good. Then, seized with the urge to show off, I got to my feet, rolled up my sleeves, and picked up a hammer from a pile of tools in the corner.

'Let's do it, then,' I said, indicating the boards. 'I'll help you get this floor down.'

He bit the corner off a wry smile. 'You don't strike me as the woodworking type.'

'Stronger than I look.'

'Oh yeah?' He grinned, ran his eyes over me. I let him do it, my hands on hips, weighing the hammer in my hands. After that, it was a matter of pride to prove it.

The memory of it split like a burning frame of celluloid the moment I heard the front door. I glanced at the time: Mum wasn't due back for another half hour.

She burst into my bedroom. 'Has he rung?'

'No. I'd have told you—'

'OK. All right,' she said, slumping slightly.

'What's happened? How come you're early?'

'I swapped cleaning sectors with Angie so I could leave early,' she said, then she told me how she'd gone to the photographic lab where Matt worked, to see if Matt had been there. 'There were two blokes talking outside his office, one of them said Matt's name, so I hung around. He said he'd been to find Matt, hadn't got anywhere, so he'd called the police.'

It was probably Leon, I thought, the friend who'd called me before. 'But the police weren't actually *there*.'

'No, but—' she made a gesture with her hands, flustered.

'Look – I just – are we still OK here? I mean, you've been careful, even with Matt, right? They're not going to find the address?'

I tried to hold her eye, but I couldn't.

She gaped. 'Oh no, Ellie. What did you do?'

'I'd been meaning to tell you,' I said weakly. 'It was when we were applying for the volunteering.'

'You gave them our *address*?'

'No, he did it. He didn't know not to. I could hardly tell him not to, could I? How would I explain it?'

'Well, fuck!' She threw her free hand up. 'Great! Wonderful, good work!'

I wanted to say sorry, but she hated me apologizing.

'I said this would happen. I said, the first time you brought him round. It was too big a risk. Didn't I *say*?' She went into her bedroom and started to rush about, pulling off her tabard and stuffing it into the washing basket. Then as if remembering, she went out to the kitchen and returned with the bag containing the wet clothes from that morning.

As calmly as I could, I said, 'Mum. Tell me what's going on.'

'Nothing! I just want to be prepared.' She roughly pulled a shirt on and went to the dressing table, plonked herself down and pulled out her make-up. 'They're going to come here, aren't they? The police. And they're going to ask questions.'

'So we answer them.'

'Yeah?' She spun round, a blob of foundation balancing on fingertip halfway to her face. 'With what?'

'How about the *truth*?'

'We don't know what happened! We've got no fucking idea what the truth is, have we?'

I bit into my cheek until I tasted blood. I wasn't going to cry.

Mum applied the make-up, sighed and got up. She went to the bed and patted the place beside her.

I sat, and she put an arm around my shoulders. 'Come on then.' She squeezed. 'They're going to come, so let's think what we're saying. Where had you been, last night?'

'The pub, but—'

'Which pub?'

'Mum, why are we even—?'

'Which *one*?'

'The Windmill. He had an IPA; I had a lemonade.'

'And people saw you.'

'Yes. No. Not people we knew.'

'You weren't arguing?'

'No! Why would we be?'

She sighed heavily and went back to the mirror, flipped open a compact. 'They're going to ask you this, Ellie. You need to get this right. If they get a whiff that you might be hiding something, we've got trouble. They're already going to have linked you to ... what happened before. You do understand that, right?'

'I'm not hiding anything!'

She raised her eyebrows, then moved her gaze pointedly to my neck. Gave a loose, open-handed gesture to my shoulder, my hip. Siggy shuddered in the aches, as if she was part of them, like they were hers.

Quietly, I said, 'I'll just tell them what happened.'

'About the bruises?' she said, incredulous.

'He might be somewhere right now needing help, Mum!'

'You can't talk to them. Not yet. Not until we know what's happened.'

'But that's what they do! That's what the police do, they find out what happened!'

She said nothing to that, but the rise of her eyebrows said, *not always*. I looked away. If there was one thing I did not want to be talking about right now, it was Jodie Arden.

My eyes lighted on the bag of wet clothes from the morning. 'What are you going to do with that?' I asked, nodding to it.

She peered into the mirror. 'I am going,' she said, lifting her lashes now with the mascara wand, 'to incinerate it.'

I waited for her to face me, to grin. But she wasn't joking.

'What did you find, Mum? This morning?'

An infinitesimal pause. 'Ellie—'

And then, from outside, we heard a woman's voice. 'This one. Over here.'

We both stood up, fast. She had turned towards the sound but swung back to face me, hands on my shoulders, pulling me into a hug.

'Listen to me,' she said, her voice dropping to a whisper. 'Let me talk to them. We can make sure they look for Matt properly, and maybe it'll all be fine. But it wasn't before, with Jodie, was it? And if something has happened to him, and if you – Siggy – had anything to do with it, we need to control this as best we can.'

Three knocks at the door.

'You are a good person, Ellie. We are *good* people. We've done our bloody best. I will not allow that *bitch* to ruin your life, or mine.' She brought her mouth right against my ear, and in a vicious whisper she said, 'Do you hear me? *Siggy? You're not having her. You're not going to take my daughter.*'

From the other end of the corridor I could hear a second voice, a man, calling through the front door.

My mother touched my face. 'Not. A. Sound.' And then she left the room, closing the door softly behind her.

Chapter 9

Mae

Mae knocked again.

Cold spiked in the morning air, and the sky above Abson Street was a flat, formless grey. Kit, looking distinctly uncomfortable in a borrowed pinstripe skirt suit, took a step back to assay the building, intermittent clouds of breath forming in front of her face. She stretched, then pressed her fists into the small of her back, wincing.

He cocked his head. 'Been fighting?'

She let out a small grunt and straightened up. 'Roller derby.'

'You're kidding.'

Kit grinned. 'Nope. You're looking at west London's fourth-finest blocker.'

He'd seen bruises on her legs before, at the gym, and wondered what her sport was. Hockey, he'd guessed, or rugby possibly. But roller derby was something else. Explained the tattoos, too. He tried extremely hard not to think about her in war paint and fishnets. Extremely hard wasn't hard enough.

'You play round here?' he asked, bending to call through the letterbox. 'Ms Power? Ellie?'

'Sure. Another reason that I'll hate you forever for making me wear this—' she gestured at her skirt, 'monstrosity. I look like I'm selling insurance. I've got a rep to protect. This is my "hood".'

She accompanied that with some kind of gesture that he guessed was supposed to be gangsta.

'Straight outta Acton,' he offered, but she just frowned, too young for the reference. 'Never mind.'

There was the scrape of several locks, and the door opened to reveal a lean, serious woman in her fifties. For just a moment, she gave them a warm smile that didn't match the restless eyes, and he remembered her in her entirety: the feeling that she always had a mask up, was always trying to calm herself down, keep something in.

Christine Power.

'Can I help you?' she asked. Then she recognized him. 'Ah. DC Mae.' The finest splinter of ice in her voice.

'It's DS now, actually. How are you, Christine?'

She didn't answer the question. This was the moment to say she looked good, that she hadn't aged. But the truth of it was that every minute of the five years since their paths had last crossed was in stark evidence in each crease of her face, in the near-complete greying of her hair.

Kit cleared her throat.

'This is DC Ziegler,' he said. 'She's a Trainee Investigator.'

Christine pulled her gaze away from Mae and greeted Kit, turning on the smile that reminded him how she'd been semi-famous once. A reporter, back when women covering international stories were vanishingly scarce.

'We've come for a chat with Ellie. Is she in?' he asked, taking in what he could of the corridor behind her, given the lack of light. 'We're concerned about the whereabouts of a Matthew Corsham?'

Christine gave a tight shake of her head. 'She's not here right now, I'm afraid. Can I help?'

'If you have a few minutes,' Kit said, stepping forward.

The door opened a little wider as Christine stood aside, and Mae followed Kit into a square, magnolia-coloured living room. They were offered tea. Mae declined with a smile, but Kit groaned with relief.

'Could murder one,' she said conspiratorially. 'Coffee would be great, if you have it.'

Christine nodded and turned away, closing the door behind her.

Mae turned slowly to face Kit. 'Ordinarily we avoid using words like *murder*.'

She rolled her eyes. 'Figure of speech, man. Lighten up.' She shoved her hands in her pockets and looked around.

The place was as tidy as it could have been, but everything was shabby. The carpet was in tiles, worn down in places to the foam backing: decades of service had left the curtains with vertical streaks sun-bleached almost to white. Elsewhere: chipped paintwork, bare lightbulbs, no photos, no clutter of any description. And it was cold in there. He touched a radiator. Hadn't been on that morning, and the dust on the control tap at the bottom said it had been longer. Like last year. This was more than slumming it.

'They just moved in?' Kit whispered, looking around. 'I've been in homelier bus stations. Who doesn't even have a single photo on the wall?'

She turned to the single line of paperbacks, standing on the deep sill of the single-glazed window, and bent her head to read the spines. Mae looked, too: *Dissociation and Me; A Child of Many Parts; Fugue State: A Carer's Guide*. She glanced back at him, confused. He knew what was coming.

'Yeah. Ellie's ... she's not well. Mentally.' Said it casually, like he was telling her Ellie was fond of horses.

'OK. Like how?'

He lifted a shoulder, dropped it. There wasn't time to explain properly. 'Complicated.'

'Try me.'

Mae checked round the doorway, then said, quickly, 'It's called DID. Dissociative Identity Disorder.'

Kit nodded. 'Makes sense she still lives with her mum, then. Poor bastard,' she added with a shrug, an unfazed gesture that made him suddenly conscious of how diametrically different their back-and-forth was from the relationship he'd had as a TI with his own mentor. One sniff of mental illness back then would have been enough to release a feverish tirade – sometimes delivered out of earshot of the target, sometimes not – about *snowflakes* and *limp-wristed millennials*. It would all be easier to stomach now if Mae could have convinced himself he'd stood up for the victims of DS Heath's vitriol. But it hadn't happened like that, had it?

And wasn't that why he was here in this flat, right now?

He turned back to the books, ran his finger along the titles until he came to a slim paperback, cheaply made, well-thumbed. Its spine was peeling away to expose the glue beneath, but Mae knew it immediately. He handed it to her.

'"A Splintered Soul: Collected Essays on Dissociation, Fugue and Recovery",' she read, whispering.

'Chapter seven is Ellie.'

'Seriously? What does—?' Kit started, but she was interrupted by the sound of Christine coming back with the drinks. Kit put the book back and affected a smile.

The coffee was distributed, and Christine perched on the arm of the angular sofa. She folded her arms over her chest, crossed her legs at the knee. Mae thought of a Transformer toy he'd had as a kid. Bend and fold and click and *bam*, suddenly you had something totally different.

He cleared his throat. 'So where's Ellie right now, do you know?'

'She's not feeling good. Gone for some air.' Then, to Kit, in a woman-to-woman tone, 'She has anxiety.' And to Mae: 'As I'm sure you'll remember.'

Kit nodded, sympathetic. 'That's no fun.' She glanced at Mae, who gave her a slight tilt of the head: *go ahead, your interview*. 'Mrs Power, we—'

'Ms,' Mae corrected her.

'Ms Power, my apologies,' Kit said. 'We received a call from a workmate of Mr Corsham's saying that he's potentially gone missing, so we wanted to talk to Ellie about him.'

'I see.' She ran her hands over her face, stretching the skin under her eyes for a moment. She looked tired, but not the kind of tired that went away with a good night's sleep. 'I'll ask her to call you, if you like? Although I'm not sure how much she's been seeing him lately. She's young. Keeping her options open.'

Kit smiled. 'Do you know Matthew at all yourself?'

'A little. We both work at the same hospital.'

Mae pulled out his notes. Frowned. 'Really? Because I—'

'Yes. Hanwell. I'm just a cleaner there. He's in the photographic lab.'

'That how Ellie met him?' Kit asked brightly.

'She was waiting for me in the canteen one day. They got talking.'

'Sweet.'

Kit made a note, took a long slug of her coffee, then stood. 'We'll need to speak to Ellie as soon as possible. Could you give her this card, ask her to call?'

'Of course.'

Kit thanked Christine and opened the door, making to leave. She made small talk as they passed to the hall, but it dried up at the front door. There was an awkward silence as Kit tied her shoes.

'Christine,' Mae said. 'What happened before—'

She held up a hand. 'It doesn't matter. All I need is for you to treat her carefully. All right?'

He nodded, handed her a card. There was nothing else to say. 'Could you have Ellie call us as soon as possible?'

Christine Power looked Mae full in the face. 'Be gentle. Do you understand? My daughter is not like the rest of us. If one good thing came from the ...' she paused, skewering the word, '*mess*, back then, I hope you at least learned that.'

Chapter 10

Ellie

I waited in Mum's room, too scared of making a noise to even move.

I would have known that voice anywhere. Ben Mae. I could make him out clearly as they came down the hall, but the moment they closed the living room door all I could hear was low, muffled and intermittent, and I could hardly catch a word.

Siggy breathed static in my head, watching me. She knew exactly what had happened last night, but she would never tell me. All I could do was imagine, and that was the worst part: the inability to differentiate between mine and hers. Between real memory and my own terrified imagination doing its best to fill in the gaps.

When I lost Jodie, I told the police the same story every time they asked, the story that Mum and I had gone over and over. What I saw that last night before she disappeared. *Jodie got into Cox's car. It was red. They were fighting. That was the last time I saw her.*

I'd rehearsed it so many times by the time I told the police, I'd almost believed it was true.

Dr Charles Cox had been in his mid-forties when they'd got together. She was seventeen. It wasn't illegal, as Jodie reminded me almost every time we talked about him, even though it was never me who complained about the age gap. What I was bothered by was the fact that he was dating her mother. But even that was something I could overlook, under the circumstances. The fact was that, apart from my own mum, Jodie was the only friend I'd ever had.

Our friendship lasted four months. From the day I met her to the day she died: 121 days. It was a Tuesday, the first time we met. I'd seen her around before, but she went to the big comprehensive the other side of Hove and wasn't around much. But that Tuesday morning in April, colder than she was dressed for and drizzly to boot, she was there in the stairwell outside our flat like she was waiting for me. Legs draped widthways across the step, smoking. I tried to go past her and when she didn't move I turned to go back the way I'd come, backing away from confrontation like I always did. But then she held out the cigarette. Hand-rolled, lipstick on the filter.

'You're the home-school kid.'

I nodded.

'Missing your GCSEs?'

My GCSEs, if I was going to take them, would have been two years off, but I didn't correct her. Looking at her I knew she had to be sixteen, seventeen at least. If I told her my real age, she'd have been up and out of there. So I just folded my arms, affecting nonchalance, and said, 'Whatever.'

She smiled, blew the smoke in a thin, elegant stream from the corner of her mouth. 'Just you and your mum in there?'

'Yeah.'

'Your dad turn out to be a bastard, like mine?'

I shrugged, but the answer was an indisputable yes: he'd only been with Mum a few months when she found out she was pregnant, and promptly disappeared when she told him the happy news. The news that he'd died of an overdose found its way to her a week before I was born. I used to ask her about him, what he was like, but I learned to accept her reluctance in the end. From the shadow that came over her face whenever I mentioned him, I guessed *bastard* didn't even come close. But somehow, I'd never quite given up hope that she was wrong: that whoever told her he was dead had made a mistake. I still found myself checking the eyes of every man I saw who could, conceivably, have been the right age to be my dad, looking for the mismatched irises that Mum said I'd inherited from him.

Jodie waved the cigarette again, offering.

'No thanks,' I said, almost inaudibly.

She looked at it and shrugged, then tossed it into the void at the middle of the stairwell. I gasped, leaned over the railings to see if there was anyone down there, and she laughed.

'Fuck 'em,' she said, getting to her feet. 'Going for a walk. The pier. Coming?'

She was on a suspension from school – *one fucking joint and they reckon you're Amy Winehouse*, she said – and things were brittle with her mum. Jodie drank, she smoked, she did drugs occasionally. After she disappeared there were even claims that she'd sold sex, though I'd never heard that from her. For all these reasons, I kept my friendship with her from Mum. Although I knew it was an unthinkable betrayal, lying by omission over and over: having a secret was the most delicious liberation, too. Jodie and I saw each other nearly every day, always at hers, always arranged the day before, to coincide with Mum being out.

Everything was easy with Jodie. I was happy. I'd never had a friend like her, someone I could truly be myself with. So, despite the promises I'd made to Mum, despite her warnings, eventually I told her about Siggy.

I told her everything. All of it. Not just the fugues but about the dreams that repeated until I knew every thread and wisp of them: the long, low building, just flashes of it; being trapped, a fire; the little boy bleeding on the ground; the cell-deep of the man in a uniform. These dreams – nightmares – were so vivid, their details so constant even in my waking thoughts that they felt like memories.

I explained to her about the panic attacks: terrors that would burst out fully formed, whose triggers I could pin down no more easily than puffs of smoke. Over the years, Mum had helped me understand that these fears lodged in my mind weren't *mine* but Siggy's, and that was a distinction that helped me make sense of them. And even though it couldn't have made sense to her in the way I wanted it to, Jodie had *listened*.

The next day, she took me to see her mum's boyfriend. Dr Cox. *Charles.*

I didn't want to go, of course. I refused all the way along the prom to his office in east Brighton. 'It's not going to make any difference,' I insisted.

'Oh yeah? How do you know? You psychic, too?'

'No,' I said grumpily. 'I've done psychotherapy before.'

'When?' She clunked her jaw, trying to perfect her smoke rings.

I shrugged. 'I don't know. I was a kid. Little.'

'Can't have been great if you don't remember it.'

'Well yeah,' I said, making an effort the way I tried to back then to give as good as I got. 'Obviously, it wasn't *great*, because it didn't work, did it?'

She pulled on my sleeve, rolling her eyes. 'He's *gooood*,' she wheedled. 'You'll like him. Come on. It's got to be worth trying again.'

We found a way of me going to sessions with him, and she came along. I ran with the lie I'd told Jodie about my age because it meant that Dr Cox would see me without parental permission. He waived his usual fee too, claiming I was an interesting case, though we all knew it was really because I was Jodie's friend. To start, she'd sit in and listen, not saying anything. No one, not Mum, not Cox, not even Matt, ever listened to me like Jodie did. Like she was storing it all away, cataloguing it, fitting the pieces of my fragmented pasts together. I believed she would solve it.

Maybe she would have done.

There was a click from the living room door, and the voices were clear again. Right outside the bedroom where I was hiding, crouching like a shamed dog. I mouth-breathed, absolutely silent, quiet enough to hear Ben Mae's deep breath before he said, 'What happened before …'

What happened before. I pressed my hands against my temples, and Siggy grinned.

Don't think about it, I told myself.

The only images I have in my head of the night my friend died are Mum's, just hand-me-down mental pictures appropriated from her description. The problem was that these appropriated visual details are lodged so close to my own memories – of the endless summer before it and the black-hole horror of the months after – that I sometimes feel that it was me who was there, not just Siggy. But that would mean the lines between her and me had started to blur, and if that could happen …

Just don't think about it. Calm down. Breathe.

Mum found her down by the river, where we go on Cherry Tree Day, to mark a special day for Siggy. I'd never taken Jodie there before, and it's a secret place, inaccessible, overgrown and wooded. But I – or Siggy – had taken her there that night. It was days until Mum admitted to me what she'd found.

The missing belt—

I can't breathe.

The missing belt from my—

Shit. I can't breathe!

The police were still in the hall, just a couple of inches of plasterboard separating us. I tried to force myself to think about something else, because this couldn't happen, not with them there – the police! – right outside the bedroom door with my mother *lying* to them.

Breathe. Breathe. Please just breathe.

Everything rotated. A slow, dark tornado, twisting around me, and the vacuum in my chest got harder, tighter. My vision darkened at the edges and my skin started to burn, and the insides of my lungs started to curl up from the heat and *this was it* but right at the last second, the pressure broke, and I was breathing but

Calm. Calm down.

Too fast now. I couldn't stop.

Deep breaths. Slow. You are having a panic attack. Slow down – breathe slowly – but I couldn't stop. In and out and in and out and too shallow, not enough, not enough air, and all the time the only thing I could think was all the things Mum had eventually told me—

The missing belt from my coat, sodden and caked and wrapped twice around Jodie's neck and

her fingernails broken and her hair bloodied and studded with broken leaves and

not enough air!

the skin of her throat pressed white and her mouth slack and her eyes wide and glazed and the rain falling against their bulging, panicked, unblinking surfaces

Because of me.

Movement in the hallway. I felt myself lighten, losing consciousness. Were they, were they coming in? They were coming in.

They know what you did.

The last thing I heard was the front door opening, and then everything went black.

Chapter 11

Charles Cox Psychotherapy Ltd.	
Clinical audio recording transcript	
Patient name:	*Eleanor Power*
Session date:	*21 August 2006*

CC: So let's start by checking in. How are you feeling today?
EP: I'm OK.

[pause: 32 sec]

CC: I'm sensing some anxiety.
EP: No. I'm fine.

[pause: 22 sec]

EP: Can you – why do you leave these huge long gaps all the time?
CC: OK. I'm glad you asked. Sometimes we find that when we're not rushed, when we're given the time to go into greater depth, we discover things that really help our journeys.

[pause: 23 sec]

EP: I haven't got anything to say.
CC: Sure.

[pause: 35 sec]

EP: OK, look, fine. She came. Last night.
CC: Siggy came?
EP: Yeah.

[pause: 19 sec]

CC: Would you like to talk about the episode you had?
EP: Well I don't know, do I? That's the whole fucking – sorry
CC: That's fine
*EP: That's the whole problem. I don't know anything about it.
It's like I go to bed every night and I'm me but then this
other person I don't know or like or want there, this other
me climbs in. She moves me about, says things like she's
me, like I'm, I'm, I'm just this, this puppet. I don't think you
can possibly know what that's like. It's terrifying. I'm terrified,
and I can't even think about it without ending up – look, like
this – ending up shaking. Do you see that, my hands?*
CC: I do.
*EP: It's like, and I know that I shouldn't say this and that it's
not the same thing but having someone else in your body,
someone you, you hate, who is there without permission,
it's like waking up and finding you've been … I can't say it.*
CC: You feel … let's say, you feel violated?
EP: Yes. Yes. Even if she's just got me up and walked around

*the flat. I can't remember any of it. [crying] Anything, at all.
And just – my mum, the way she describes it – I just-I just
[crying] I want to just*

[pause: 1 min 6 sec]

EP: Sorry. I'm sorry.
*CC: OK. Ellie, can you look at me? I know it's hard, but just
look at me just a moment. Thank you. There is no judgement here. None at all. Anything you say will be heard and
believed.*

[pause: 56 sec]

CC: OK. Do you need some water before we go on?
EP: I'm OK.
*CC: It's extremely difficult for you to talk about; I can see that
these episodes affect you very deeply.*
*EP: Yeah. Yeah, they do. I'm scared. I never know when it's
going to happen. Like, I had this fight with my mum last
night, because I wanted to try school. I mean, like sixth
form. I haven't had a fugue for, I don't know, a couple of
weeks? She just kept saying I wasn't strong enough and
about how last time we tried, my panic attacks got worse
and everything, and we fell out big time because I just want
to do normal stuff. Go out and live my actual life, you know?*
CC: I do.
*EP: And then I went to bed and I wake up and this has happened.
She said – my mum said – Siggy was really angry last night.
Like, she was scary, Mum couldn't get near her to talk to
her without her lashing out. Then she went out—*

CC: Siggy went outside?

EP: Yeah went out and Mum had to follow me ... follow her round the block until she'd agree to go back in again. Here, look this is where she fell over at one point when she was running. Look can you see on my elbow—

CC: That's quite a scrape—

EP: Yeah. Yeah it-it really hurts.

[pause: 20 sec]

CC: What I'm hearing is a lot of conflict between you and Siggy. It's a battle.

EP: Yeah. That's exactly what it is.

[pause: 22 sec]

EP: The days after the fugues, I can feel Siggy kind of ... there, all of the time. Like she's got to rub it in, make sure I know she's won, you know? Like last night was her telling me ...

[pause: 27 sec]

CC: You feel she's telling you something. Can you say a bit—

EP: It was like she was telling me to stay scared. Like it was a warning.

Chapter 12

Mae

They said nothing until they were back at street level, outside the Powers' flat. Fine rain sieved across the street, and Mae shrugged up the collar of his pea coat. Kit strode back to the car, heading for the driver's seat.

'Well that was weird,' she said, when Mae was in beside her.

'In what way?'

Kit frowned into the middle distance. 'I spoke to the guy at the hospital, Leon, right? The dude who called it in.' She turned to him. 'And he gave me Ellie's name as someone who knows Matt and said how he'd said she volunteered there. So I called the HR office and got them to find her address. He searched for Power on the staff system – he spelled it out loud as he typed it in – and he said "Here it is, one entry, first name Eleanor". Hers was the only record they had. Which means Christine isn't on their system, even though she works for them.'

'Maybe she's agency staff?'

'That's what I thought, but everyone needs clearance at a hospital, surely? Kids and vulnerable adults at a hospital, you need a DBS or whatever.'

Mae frowned, went to get his phone out, but Kit was eyeballing something in the rear-view.

'What?' he asked, turning in his seat to see.

On the pavement, staring into the car, was a young man. Caucasian with black, tightly curled hair, a faded band T-shirt under a checked flannel shirt. Early twenties, but already a little old for the gloomy, emo vibe he was projecting.

Kit was out of the car and coming round the front before Mae was even out of his seatbelt. 'Help you?' she asked him, brightly.

Mae joined them on the pavement.

'Doing surveillance?' the guy said. His voice was scratchy, something Mae immediately put down to the yellow plastic wallet of rolling tobacco protruding from his top pocket.

Kit already had her pad out. 'How do you mean?'

'The people in the van!' His jittering glare ricocheted endlessly between them. 'I'm not stupid.'

Which may or may not have been true, but what Mae knew with a reasonable level of certainty was that he *was* a nutcase. Kit, on the other hand, needed maybe a little more field experience.

'We're the police, CID,' Kit said, and gave their names, proper by-the-book. 'We're checking out a possible missing person. Do you live round here?'

He nodded across the road to the rear access of a shop that sat underneath the Powers' flat. Mae had clocked it on the way in, a Polish place.

'I see a lot.' The young man pointed enigmatically to his eyes with the V of his index and middle fingers, then turned the gesture on the street. 'But what I want to know is, what are you doing *with the van*? You want to listen to what I'm saying in my own house?'

Kit glanced around. 'Can you see this van now?'

'I'm not *imagining* it! It's just *gone*, right now, obviously!'

Kit nodded diplomatically and tucked her pad away again. Mae couldn't fault her professionalism: she gave him the non-emergency number, closed the conversation, stayed polite and respectful. The guy was still talking when Mae swung his own door shut.

'... *parabolic* microphones, serious kit, and if it's not you, it's MI6, or SO-15, or whatever, and I know about it. I know, OK, man?'

Kit waited until they were around the corner before she took her eyes off the road. 'Jesus. Get that a lot?'

Mae laughed, and got out his phone.

By the time they hit the Boston Manor Road he'd found what he expected to find. Not only was Christine not on her employer's records – at least not under her own name – but there were no records on Christine or Eleanor Power at that address anywhere else. No entry on the local government system, NHS, banks, credit agencies, nothing.

Didn't happen by accident.

So, what? Were they hiding? Why?

Kit turned on the radio, flicked quickly away from Heart, found nothing, turned it off.

'Christine Power was pleased to see you though, yeah?' she said, biting the edge off a wry smile. 'Big DS Mae fan. Ker-azy pheromones coming off that one.'

'Kit. Please.'

She lifted her hands from the wheel in surrender. 'Just saying. But what did she mean about—?'

'Can we leave it?'

She blew out her cheeks. 'What's next then? Open-door search then grade it? I couldn't get hold of the guy at the moorings, but I can go down there now, sure I'll find someone to let me in. Won't take long.'

The open-door search was the first point of call usually, checking the missing person's home in case they'd got sick or stuck or injured anywhere. But if it was a narrowboat it was going to be a pretty quick job.

'After lunch,' Mae said, suddenly aware of the chasm in his stomach. 'I'll go to the marina, you hit the phones. Talk to his manager about what he got sacked for.'

His phone buzzed against his leg and he pulled it out, checked the screen: Nadia. Turning in his seat for whatever privacy he could get in a five-door, he hit the green button.

'Are you OK to pick Dominica up from violin?' his ex-wife wanted to know. 'I've just been asked to go to this meeting.'

No *hi*, no *how's things*. And it was *Dominica* now instead of *Bear*, like they couldn't even agree on the name of their kid. 'Sure.'

'And bring her back at half eight?'

'Yep.'

'Mike'll be here, OK, so … just so you know.'

Mike. Who had ten years on Mae, twelve on Nadia, although a stranger could easily place him in his mid-sixties because the guy was utterly, relentlessly grey. It wasn't like Mae hadn't *tried* to find something interesting about him, something likeable. Mid-west American, drove a Citroen, played badminton three times a week, with a record that couldn't be cleaner if it had been formulated in an aseptic lab. Never so much as a day late with his TV licence. There was, of course, more than a slim chance that Nadia's attraction to Mike was all Mae's fault. That ten years with *him* had turned his funny, brilliant, game-for-anything wife into a reliability junkie. Or maybe it was just that maybe Mike happened to be hung like a centaur.

'Mike. Sure.'

Nadia sighed. 'Try to do something fun with her after, OK? She always comes back from you so ... I don't know. Flat.'

He took the screen from his ear and thumbed the red circle until he could feel the casing start to bow.

'Touch-screen means you only have to touch it, you know,' Kit told him.

'Uh-huh. And advanced driving means keeping your eyes on the road.'

Chapter 13

Ellie

Quarter of an hour passed before I felt halfway normal. After the police left and the panic subsided, Mum brought me sweet tea, made herself late waiting until I could convince her I was fine. She fetched the duvet from the bedroom and tucked me in on the sofa, then checked the time and swore softly under her breath.

'I have to go and make up for that shift.' She bent to kiss me goodbye. 'Just stay put. Don't let anyone in.'

'All right, Mum.'

She tapped her fingers on the edge of the mug, running something through her mind. 'They'll go to his boat next, I should think,' she said, almost to herself. 'Maybe they'll find something there.'

'How do you mean?'

'I don't know. Nothing.' She found a brief smile, shrugged her shoulders.

When she finally left, I got straight up from under the duvet and went into her room, pulling a corner of the curtain aside to watch her through the window. She paused at the car, glanced up at me, and touched her fingertips to her lips. Then got in and drove away.

Maybe they'll find something.

She meant a note.

Was there a note?

I wasted no time. I pulled some shoes on, and looked for my raincoat before remembering I'd been unable to find it earlier. I dug around in a drawer until I found the fleece-lined zip-up hoody I'd borrowed from Matt and refused to return. I left the flat with Siggy still tiny and shuddering in my chest.

Chapter 14

Mae

Mae bit into his bagel. Pinned to the fabric-covered room divider behind his workstation was a page from a set of ACPO guidelines, thoughtfully printed out and displayed by whoever had last occupied Mae's desk. IF IN DOUBT, THINK MURDER, it read. It had been there so long that the drawing pins had gone rusty, and snagged on the cloth when Mae pulled them out. He balled it up to lob, with flukily perfect aim, into the recycling, just as Kit walked in.

'Like things spic and span, don't you?' she said, looking around, holding a pen drive and standing in a strict at-ease. 'Speaks of a need to instil order.'

Mae held out his hand for the drive. 'Spare me the amateur mind reading. What have you got?'

'Apart from a first-class honours degree in psychology?'

He laughed, then stopped. 'Really?'

She narrowed her eyes at him. 'I can see into the very blackness of your soul,' she said, before breaking into a grin. 'No but seriously, tidy people do tend to crave reliability and control, and you tend to crave the things you didn't get as a kid. Just saying.'

He opened his mouth, shut it again, totally at a loss for what to say. What to even think. 'You do remember that I'm your boss here, right?'

She shrugged. 'Fluid thing, though, hierarchy, isn't it? Anyway,' she said, leaning over him to slide the drive into a port and commandeer his keyboard. 'Headlines. I couldn't get hold of the person who dealt with Corsham's contract but the HR person I spoke to said it looked like he was on short contracts and just hadn't been offered a new one. I'll keep trying for his direct line manager though, see if there's any more to it.'

Mae nodded, scanning the document she'd opened. 'Any more workmates?'

'The guy he shared an office with said he was talking about buying some vintage lomo gear.'

'Lomo?'

'Kind of cult photography thing. Analogue, retro stuff. Apparently Corsham had been reading up on the ones where you take the picture and they spit the thingy out, and you ...' she mimed waving a wet photograph, 'you remember?'

He scrolled through the rest of the notes, ticking off the lines of investigation. Matthew Corsham was an only child, estranged from his father since infancy; mother dead from cancer a few years previously.

'DVLA have a 1989 soft top Golf Cabriolet registered to him,' she told him, pointing it out lower on the page. 'I'm going to run a search on that in a sec. He'd been for a few after-work drinks but no particular mates – sounds pretty shy – and he hadn't been in the job that long.' She lifted her hands, dropped them, underwhelmed. 'Not much to go on though. He'd signed up for a few socials with a local photography group. I've emailed the guy who organized it to see if he made any friends there.'

As Mae read, the picture emerged of a quiet, unremarkable man. He'd moved from Glasgow to Edinburgh a couple of years before, then down to London only a few months ago. From what

Kit had managed to trawl in a couple of hours, they were looking at an average twenty-something bloke, without a particularly vibrant social life, with good, normal, healthy pursuits. Vintage cameras. The gym. Batshit crazy girlfriends.

In the pause, Kit moved her feet a bit before telling the floor, 'So I found that book online, *A Splintered Soul*. That chapter on Ellie.'

Mae looked up from the documents. 'OK. And?'

She gave him a look. 'You could have told me, you know.'

'Told you what?'

'Her phobia. Why you wanted me to change into plain clothes.'

'OK. Well,' he said, holding his hands up, 'not everyone's as well-versed in mental health as you are.' Back in 2006, if he'd suggested DS Heath wear plain clothes because a uniform was a known trigger for a vulnerable witness, he'd never have heard the end of it.

But Kit was still looking distracted. 'Maddening though, isn't it? I mean, I know it's none of my business what happened when she was little but, even in the book, there's no mention of the trauma.'

'Trauma?'

'Yeah. The cause of the disorder she's got.'

'I think he just couldn't work it out?'

She shrugged, but the nonchalance was forced, hiding something. 'Just – frustrating. I mean, this is an extreme thing, DID. It gets diagnosed like, practically never, and when it does … well, they say the mind can do literally anything, but there's going to be a bloody good reason for it to do *that*.'

Mae squinted. 'You really have got that degree, haven't you?'

But she waved it away. 'What I'm saying is, the trauma you'd have to experience for something that extreme to happen would have to be chronic, for one thing, and fuck-off massive, for another. But he never even offers a guess. Do we even know if she knew her father, for example?'

'Christine had been single for a long time. That's all I know.'

'See, that's waaaay suspicious, isn't it? Surely there has to be some context about her dad? Early years with him, or *something*. And I get that Cox had to anonymize it,' she said, holding up her hand to pre-empt the next thing that Mae was going to say, 'but it just seems like a massive missing piece. I mean, there's the mention of these scars of hers but it says that was because of an accident, right? I mean, I'm no expert but I don't think a one-off accident is going to be enough to cause something as serious as a dissociative disorder.'

Mae had noticed it too, way back when. The other cases in the book were fleshed out, the abuse or trauma that triggered the disorder in the first place forming part of the story. As per the title, they were stories of successful treatment. The book had been funded by a charity, so the message was fairly consistent: funding + excellent care = positive outcomes. The exception was the part dealing with Ellie, which was just a snapshot of the middle of her story, the few months she'd spent under Cox's care. There was no background, and no happy ending.

'Guess maybe he wanted to talk about the treatment part of it? To be honest it wasn't exactly the focus of our investigation.'

Kit seemed to take offence for half a second before delivering a hearty smack on the arm. 'I'm just interested.' Then, 'Maybe I should ask him.'

'I'm going to assume you're joking,' he said, before remembering something. 'You'd be wasting your time anyway.'

'Because?'

'It was something Lucy Arden told us – Jodie's mum,' he

explained. 'Apparently Jodie had asked him for copies of his research, a few weeks before she disappeared. He had transcripts done from the audio recordings of Ellie's sessions, all her medical notes, loads of data, but he lost it.'

Eyebrows up, incredulous. '*Lost* it? How did he manage that?'

'Apparently. He was still using floppies. Useless things. Lost your data all the time.'

Kit retracted her chin. 'What the hell is a floppy?'

Mae rolled his eyes in reply. Kids. He turned back to his screen.

Kit was staring ahead now, through him.

'What?' Mae asked.

She shook herself and looked at him. 'Just doesn't ... I don't know.' She mimed cogs with her fingers, not quite meshing. 'Doesn't fit. He spends all that time with her, recording her, everything, then the whole lot disappears? It's fishy.'

'Be that as it may. It's her own business, not our remit.'

Kit dropped her hands, reddening very slightly.

'I *know*. I'm just *interested*.' She cleared her throat. 'You going to get that?' she asked him, raising a finger towards the desk phone.

Mae laughed and shook his head, then took the call he could see was from the switchboard.

'DS Mae, Mr Jupp on the line. Says he's returning your call about visiting a boatyard.'

Chapter 15

Mae

Jupp's boatyard was only a couple of miles away, so Mae borrowed one of the force pushbikes. It was late afternoon, the light was sparse through a heavy ceiling of cloud. Spotting the marina entrance, he swung a leg over the crossbar and sailed it standing on one pedal, then hopped down and secured it in a single practised movement against a lamppost.

Mae had discovered the wharf earlier that summer, when he'd talked Bear into a walk along the towpath. He'd pointed out where he'd dealt with a burglary at one of the warehouses that backed straight onto the river, and he'd seen the boats on the towpath that extended from the yard. That was back when it had been warm enough for the residents to still be sitting out on their decks as the sun went down, drinking and barbequing. Different story now, at the arse-end of November. He smelled the smoke of the little log burners they used, the diesel emissions. There was the rumble of generators, punctuated by the honking of a pair of Canada geese. Scraps of laughter from outside a nearby pub lifted and cracked in the air.

He took the steps built into the sloping wall down to where a shabby prefab cube of an office sat precariously levelled on bricks. He knocked and went in. Cheap, functional furniture was laden with papers, notes scribbled on envelopes, and a jumble of polystyrene cups. Behind the desk, a fat guy in a shirt made for a thinner one.

Mae put out a hand. 'I'm Detective Sergeant Mae. We spoke on the phone.'

'Jupp,' the man said. He was puffy and goutish, the kind of clean-shaver who should have considered a beard. Waving a hand vaguely behind him, he said, 'My yard.' Strong Bristol accent. He didn't get up, and only shook the hand reluctantly when it became clear Mae wasn't going to put it away unshaken.

Jupp listened while Mae gave him the basics, then rummaged in a drawer and brought out a key. 'Take you down to his boat, shall I?'

Standing, Jupp was short enough for Mae to see the shiny top of his head, lit up with the reflection of the flickering single-bar strip light. Then again, everyone was short, to Mae.

Outside, a half-hearted drizzle had started to fall, blown across them by a brisk wind. A tang of lager and used nappies was emanating from three overfilled wheelie bins. They stopped at a gate where Jupp paused to key in the code, angling his thickly padded shoulders to block Mae's view of the keypad. Mae saw it anyway: 2580, all four numbers in a vertical line down the middle. Nice one, Mae thought: unbreakable. The gate buzzed and clunked open.

They went down the sloping pontoon towards the water, Jupp confirming on the way that he hadn't seen Matt since the morning of the day before.

'Said he was going to go down to the pump-out.'

'Where's that?'

'Mile or so.' Jupp indicated with his arm: downriver, east.

'Did you see him go?'

Jupp shrugged. 'Nope. But he came back, didn't he? Must

have come back last night on the big tide. Boat was in place when I did my patrol.'

'But you haven't seen him today?'

'It's not a prison.' Jupp eyed Mae with obvious dislike as they approached the bottom of the slope. 'They come and go as they please. Lot of us boaters just want leaving alone, tell the truth, not so keen on people coming round, poking their noses—'

'Left or right?' Mae asked with a smile, aware that life was short and he wasn't getting any younger.

Jupp sniffed and turned, leading Mae left along the metal gridding.

'How does it work then, mooring here?' Mae asked. 'Your tenants pay in advance?'

'Invoice them on the twentieth, payment due first of the month. Month's notice either way.'

The first of the month was coming up in a few days. 'People rent these boats then, or own them?'

'Bit of both. Matt rents his off my brother.'

Mae followed Jupp along a floating pontoon stretching maybe thirty, forty metres along the river. The walkway dipped and bounced as they moved along it, their footsteps causing the sections to clank together.

'Watch your step, boy,' Jupp said, glancing at Mae. 'Dangerous if you're used to nice safe driveways.'

'Don't worry about me. Spent my childhood fishing.'

Jupp frowned. 'Din't know your lot fished.'

'Police?'

'Chinese.'

Mae blinked. 'Korean.'

He shrugged. 'Same difference. Thought it was snooker. Gambling.'

'OK, yeah. We're all ninjas, too.'

Jupp frowned, but Mae raised a hand to dismiss it. Just could not be arsed.

The pontoon bouncing under their feet, they passed an assortment of boats. Traditional narrowboats; flimsy-looking fibreglass cruisers; wide, curvy-bottomed things with wheelhouses and Dutch-sounding names painted along their bows. *Twe Gebroders, Derkje, Ziet Op U Zelve.*

'Mr Corsham been here long? Regular with the rent? Any problems?'

'Moved down from Scotland somewhere a few months ago. Pays on time.'

'No wild parties, anything out of the usual?'

Jupp cast a look over his shoulder. 'People call us gypsies, you get that? Pikies, river scum.'

Mae waited, unsure where this was going.

'We get it in the neck, is what I'm saying. Brick brigade making their judgements. So we stick together, yeah? You're not going to get us dishing dirt on each other.'

'I'm not after dirt. I'm checking on his safety.'

'Yeah, well.' Jupp stopped, flipping through a bunch of small keys. 'This one.'

Matthew Corsham's boat was a red and green narrowboat, last on the stretch, past a mains hook-up board. Reasonable nick from the outside. Through a window in the front end – the fore? – the place looked tidy, nothing immediately suggesting forced entry. Moving along he tried the next window when the boat suddenly listed, the water slapping underneath the pontoon. Jupp had grabbed the thin handrail running along the edge of the roof and was hauling himself up, keys in hand. But after an extended fumble with a circular padlock, he grunted and gave up, huffing and stepping down clumsily from the gunwales.

'Changed the bloody locks. Supposed to supply the management with a working key at all times.' So much for the Anarchists' Manifesto of three minutes previously. 'You can have a look through the windows, but I'm not breaking the door without my brother's say-so.'

Jupp turned to head back the way they'd come.

'Do you have CCTV here?' Mae called after him.

'No. And I've got jobs to do.' He paused to light a cigarette, then stumped off back towards his office.

Mae stepped up onto the deck. The smooth metal was slippery under his feet as he braced to shove back the hatch. It wouldn't give, so he ducked down to the level of the two tiny doors that came up no higher than his thighs. Cupping his hands between his forehead and the glass, he peered inside.

Bear would have given her thumbs to live in there. Not that there was enough money in the world to pay *him* to endure what looked like several inches of negative headroom, but the attraction of the cosy, simple lifestyle in evidence there wasn't hard to imagine. Shallow shelves tucked under the windows held books and a few video games, secured against the inevitable rocking with taut lengths of curtain wire. A crocheted blanket was stretched neatly over the back of a sofa, and the few feet of wall space between the single-glazed windows were covered in mismatched picture frames holding photographs.

He was about to leave when something caught his eye. A single sheet of paper on the table opposite the wood burner and a pen next to it. Mae went along to the window next to the table, to get a better look. Carefully bending into a crouch on the narrow ledge beneath the glass, he wiped the rain from his eyes and squinted in.

It was a list. Toothpaste, toothbrush, razor. Blue holdall, phone, charger, wallet, tickets. Camera, film, batteries. All the items on it crossed off.

He read to the end. Footsteps approached, and he waved Jupp away with his free hand as he brought himself up to standing. 'All right, I'm coming.'

But when he turned, Mae saw that Jupp was long gone. The person who had passed him, who was now on the back deck and unlocking the door with her keys, was Ellie Power.

Chapter 16

Ellie

The dirty remains of the afternoon sun quivered in the puddles at my feet as I approached the marina. The office was closed up, but as I headed down to towards the boats I saw Mr Jupp. He threw his cigarette on the ground like a dart when he saw me, and came lumbering up the gangway.

'We've got the bloody police down here, looking for Matthew,' he said, passing me. 'You've got keys, you bloody let him in.'

Shit. Fear swelled in my chest, inflating in seconds. But I made myself go down before I could change my mind. Before I'd had a chance to think through what I was and wasn't going to tell him, there was Ben Mae, hanging off the side of Matt's boat.

'All right, I'm coming,' he said, waving me away without looking up.

I cleared my throat, and he turned.

'Ellie.'

'DC Mae.'

He smiled. 'Been a while. It's DS now. I'm the lead on Missing Persons, so that's why I'm ...' he trailed off, gesturing at the boat, the yard. Me.

'Congratulations,' I said.

We stood there for a moment, before I remembered what I

was doing. I climbed up, got both locks open and swung the tiny doors open and slid back the hatch.

'Coming in?' I asked him.

'Are you inviting me?'

'That's vampires, isn't it?'

He laughed and gestured at the door. 'After you, then.'

The familiar smell rose up around me as I went down, a woody warmness with the slight tinge of damp. I half-expected him to be there but the boat was empty. I stepped down into the cabin. Mae started to follow me in, but paused on the steps. He gestured at the four coat hooks next to the door.

'Should these have anything hanging on them?'

'It depends.' I frowned, thinking of the last time I'd been there, when I'd hardly had room to hang my own raincoat. Matt loved being on foot, but winter was forging on and he was skinny. Usually, those pegs were draped with his layers.

I went in and sank into the built-in sofa. It was as if the place had been exorcized. So *cold* in there. The few square feet of hearth under the wood-burning stove had been swept after its last use, and the shallow pile of the fabric of the upholstery was sticking up unevenly, recently vacuumed. Usually the windows wept condensation, but now they were dry. Which only added up if there had been no breath to wet them. I unzipped my rain-soaked top and hung it above the stove. Mae came in and abruptly slammed his head on the ceiling.

'*F* ... lipping hell,' he said, rubbing his scalp where he'd hit it. I almost wanted to laugh: Matt had a permanent bruise on his hairline at the front where he continually banged his head coming in. Unscrewing his eyes Mae said, 'This is not sensible for a man of his height.'

I fiddled with the keys, rolling the cork float-ball keyring around in my palm. Mae nodded at them.

'Mr Jupp couldn't get his to work. Reckons the locks had been changed.'

I nodded. 'First time I've used these ones. The old locks had just got rusty.' Matt had said he'd been meaning to change them for ages, and had given me the set of keys as an afterthought, less than a week ago. He'd rolled down the window of his car and called me back after we'd already said goodbye outside the flat. *Keep them to yourself*, he'd said. *You never know who might want to break in and swipe my dirty underpants.*

'You know why? Security worries?'

I gave it half a moment's thought, and shook my head. 'Not that I know of. No. He would have said.'

'Sure? His colleague said the hospital had been expecting his laptop back, so—'

'He's lost it.'

'OK,' he said, his notebook out now and pen poised. 'Details?'

'I don't know any more than that. He asked me to check around the flat.'

'But you didn't find it?'

'No,' I said, irritable. But now I thought about it, Matt hadn't found it and I hadn't asked. Guilt pecked at me as I ran that phone call back: he'd sounded really worried, but I hadn't offered to help. 'Does it matter?'

Mae made a *search me* face. 'It wasn't … stolen, or anything? You're sure?'

'Look, I really don't—' I started, then I broke off. Processed what he was saying. 'Why did the hospital want it back?'

Mae took a breath before he answered me. There was a look

on his face that I couldn't interpret. 'West London NHS Trust had him on rolling freelance contracts,' he said, watching for my reaction.

'Yes.'

'Until the end of last week.'

I blinked. Thinking, *no*. He'd have said.

'Did he not tell you he'd lost his job, Ellie?'

I said nothing.

'I have to ask, do you have any problems in your relationship, would you say?'

'No.'

'Because that would seem like a rather big omission, if you know what I mean.'

'We're fine.' It came out hard and loud, and he blinked at me. I felt Siggy spark at the base of my skull, goading, satisfied.

Were we fine?

Mae nodded solemnly, appraising me for a moment, then went to the table.

'So there's this.' He handed it to me.

I took it. A list, printed out. Things you'd take if you were going away. I held it with both hands, the burn of tears starting up in the corners of my eyes.

A bloom of hope spread across me. Did this mean he'd just taken a trip? But if it did—

Toothbrush, toothpaste, razor

then he'd left. He'd left me.

There was a blue-biro tick next to every item. I scanned it again, a storm started spinning in my head.

'Anyone could have written this,' I said eventually. 'Where's the pen? Huh? Are we looking for the pen, for fingerprints?'

Mae spread his hands. 'Ellie—'

'No. He wouldn't have just disappeared.' Not without telling me. He loved me. He *loved* me. I brushed the hair out of my face and handed the list back to him, defiant. 'This doesn't mean anything.'

'Why do you say that?'

'Because we're happy, that's why.'

We *were*. There was no way Matt had been planning to go away. A few weeks ago we'd been talking about a trip, a long weekend. Mum was so worried, wouldn't say why in front of Matt even though she knew he and I had talked about it all, but she went on and on about the locks on the hotel doors. Matt hadn't flinched. When she got emotional, demanding to know how he planned on dealing with Siggy, asking did he really understand what he was getting himself into, he put his arm around me. *I love your daughter, Christine. Nothing is going to change that.*

'What if he didn't write it?' I went into the kitchen and turned on the tap to fill the kettle. 'I mean, it doesn't prove anything, does it?'

Neither of us spoke for a moment, and I realized the water pump was rumbling, but nothing was coming out. The tap spat droplets and air. His water tank was empty.

I turned and checked the fridge: a Coke would do just as well. I opened the door, and looked inside. Dark.

Mae was standing next to me. 'It's been switched off.'

Meticulously cleaned and emptied, too. Mae paused for a while, then gently shut the door, leaving my hand to drop down to my side.

'Sometimes I go away in the winter,' he said, in a slow, quiet voice. 'Take my little girl snowboarding. I turn the water off in my flat and run all the taps until there's no water left in them. In case it freezes in the pipes, and the pipes burst.'

I opened the breadbin. 'He wasn't going away.' The breadbin was empty.

'And I use up everything in my fridge,' he said, as if I hadn't spoken, 'and give it a good clean.'

I pushed past him, cursing the lack of space, the fact that there is nowhere to go on a stupid tiny boat, nowhere to escape to. 'I've said he wasn't going away.' I dropped onto the sofa and drew my hands over my face. I wanted my mum.

'Ellie.'

When I opened my eyes, he was looking at my neck. I pulled my chin down fast, but it was too late.

Slowly, he asked, 'What happened there, then?'

He wouldn't have asked about the scar. He meant the bruises. 'It's nothing.'

'No. It's not.'

'I don't want to talk about it.'

'No?' Mae came round and sat next to me, the other end of the sofa. 'Doesn't look like nothing.'

I let all my breath out at once. 'Well, it is.'

Leaning forward, he said, 'Was it Matt? Did he hurt you, Ellie?'

'No! God, no! He would *never*. He's not like that. No.'

Mae looked away, placed his hands on his knees. 'Someone reports someone missing, we need to look at everything that might be suspicious. And to be honest,' he said, indicating my neck with a nod, 'mystery bruising might look a bit suspicious.'

I stared down at my feet. 'It's not mystery bruising.'

'OK.' He waited.

'I was ... sleepwalking. Mum tried to steer me back to bed. I was agitated. She had to be ... forceful.'

'And this was, when? Last night?'

I nodded, my heart hammering. Mae inclined his head to get another look.

'Looks like she fought pretty hard.'

'I was just confused,' I mumbled.

'Confused. OK.' There was a pause. 'See. Ellie, I get confused all the time. Sometimes I can't remember if I've left the oven on. Or I lose my car, or, you know, I annoy someone and I get confused about what I might have said to upset them. But I can't remember a time when confusion has ever ended up in me being held by the throat.'

'I'm telling you it wasn't *him*.'

Mae stayed where he was for a moment. Then he got to his feet, steadied himself against the motion of the boat under his feet, and turned to me.

'So for now, we're classing this as a low-risk case—'

'Low risk. What does that mean?'

'It means that we wait and see what happens. This is still very early days. To be honest it's only because I saw your name on the information that it's me dealing with this and not just a bobby making a couple of calls. But look, you have to realize that everything we have here is pointing to Matt having just *gone away* somewhere.' He tucked everything into his bag. 'It's a dynamic thing, though. If anything changes—'

'But what does it mean you will *do*?' I interrupted. 'You have to do *something*.'

He pressed his lips between his teeth for a moment, measuring his words. 'Look. Men are weak. Sometimes they are really shitty. I'm sure he's been great to you, and break-ups can be awful but—'

'No. It's not a *break-up*. He is the most honest, the most grounded person you'll ever meet. He is a good man, and I can rely on him. I can. You're making a mistake.'

He watched me for a second, like he was trying to find something in my face. 'I'm sorry. I've got a hundred other jobs stacking up and this is just,' he gestured around the boat, to me. The whole thing. 'It's just not a police matter,' he finished at last. 'I've already done more than I am supposed to.'

'Fine. Then go.' I turned away. He would not see me cry.

On the deck, he crouched and turned back to me. 'This isn't about you, you know. Men are shits. He didn't deserve you.'

I watched him swing himself down onto the pontoon, and I thought about how much Matt had given me. How bottomless his patience was, how hard he'd tried to help me believe in myself.

Mae was right. Matt didn't deserve me. He really, truly did not.

Chapter 17

Mae

Mae had just swung his leg back over the crossbar when he heard the blip-blip greeting of the siren. Kit, in a squad car, a heavy shade of pissed-off darkening her face.

'You planning to answer your phone any time soon?' The window was wound all the way down and her shirt sleeve was rolled all the way up. The pointed toe of the 1950's pinup girl tattooed on her bicep peeked out just above her elbow.

He dug his phone out, failed to wake it, showed her the screen. 'Dead. Sorry.'

'No deader than you are.'

He unsnapped the fastener under his chin and took the helmet off, leaning an elbow on the roof of the car. 'How do you mean?'

Kit turned to speak into the radio clipped onto her lapel. 'Got him,' she told it, then, 'I'll deal with it, Ma'am.' To him, she said, 'Get in.'

'That'll be, "get in, *Sarge*",' he corrected, then gestured to the bike, opened his mouth to argue that he couldn't, but she cut him off.

'Get in the car, *Sarge*, right now. You forgot to collect your daughter, and she's gone missing.'

Chapter 18

Ellie

I sat still for a long time on Matt's sofa, listening to the boats bump and creak. Thinking about the list. I'd looked for all the things on it, ticked them off one by one. Every single one of them was gone.

My phone rang: it was the hospital.

I didn't even say my name when I answered. 'Have you found him?'

There was a pause. 'Sorry, Ellie, found who?' the caller said, and I placed her voice. It was Helen, who managed the volunteer schedule at the children's ward where I worked. 'I was calling about the session you were going to do with the kids this morning.'

'Oh god, I'm sorry, I—'

'Look, I'm afraid to tell you that we can't have you volunteering here anymore.'

'What? Why?'

'We need reliability. We can't have the children disappointed.'

'You told me you were crying out for volunteers! That's why Matt got my forms rushed through, so I could—'

'Nothing was *rushed*,' she said. 'Look I'd love to keep you but the children have to come first, and if you can't keep your promises to them—'

'I'm sorry, I just—'

'No,' she said firmly. 'I'm sorry too, but that's where we are.' She said goodbye coolly and hung up.

I stood there in the kitchen, blinking, not believing it. Matt was going to be so disappointed. He'd suggested the volunteering in the first place, had set up my interview, helped me with the application. I'd loved it, too. I'd even started to believe maybe it could lead to an actual job, one day. And now I'd lost it. I slumped down onto the arm of the sofa.

Something caught my eye. A big metal bulldog clip hanging on a hook next to the sink, and between its teeth a wedge of scraps of paper. I reached over and took the clip down. Just receipts, mostly: a few postcards. But right at the back, with a fold of card across the top to protect it from being marked by the pressure of the clip, was something else. A faded, square-shaped photo, the old-fashioned instant kind that came straight out of the camera, ready-developed to be waved around and blown upon impatiently until the image slowly appears and definition emerges like a fog lifting. The colours were vague, less saturated, as if they were trying to fade back to a sleepy sepia.

A little girl. Less than a year old, probably, hair already thick and black. Even with the colours muted by age, the eyes clearly distinct: one eye sky-blue, one green with a narrow slice of brown in the iris. Her cheeks rounded with health and happiness.

Me.

As a child. The only picture in existence. What was it doing here?

I rubbed my thumb across the top of it, the two rust-stained puncture holes where a staple must once have been. We'd had a burglary when I was two and a half, a few days before we were due to move house. Everything we owned was in boxes by the door of the one-bed flat we'd been renting. *Might as well have gift-wrapped it*, Mum always said afterwards. All of my baby stuff, a whole load of Mum's old things, but worst of all, all the photos of me as a little kid.

Maybe because I didn't have any family, the absence of the pictures felt like a huge hole as I grew up. I used to make up pretend photo albums, drawing pictures of my dead grandparents, my dead dad. In my pictures, he was just like me, dark and broad-shouldered, each of us with one green and one blue eye, standing either side of petite, yellow-haired Mum. I pinned those pictures everywhere, but what I wanted more than anything was a photo. But they were all gone.

All but this one.

I'd found it inside a book. I was ten, and we had just moved flats again. I remember the swell of excitement when it fell onto the floor and I realized what it was. I'd never seen this one before. I ran into her room, beaming with pride at the discovery of such a coveted treasure. I had expected tears of joy.

None came. Just a request not to snoop in her things, and a dark, brittle silence for the rest of the afternoon. Confused, I apologized, and she put her arms around me and said the same.

'It was a dark time with your dad,' she'd say, by way of explanation. 'I've got my memories of you, baby, and they're good enough.'

The next day I found it folded into four, in the bathroom bin. So I saved it a second time. But this time, I kept my secret to myself.

In the picture I was smiling. I looked into the eyes of my infant self and tried to see Siggy. Was she there, in my head, when I was that small? Lurking, waiting for my eyes to close and for the dummy to drop out of my pink little mouth so she could show me all her horrible things?

But more importantly, why did Matt have it? I'd dug it out and shown it to him, maybe a month ago, after we'd gone through an old album of his. I hadn't given it to him, though. I'd tucked it back into the book where I kept it. He knew how precious it was to me. So why had he *taken* it?

I tucked the photo into my pocket and looked around. I had come to look for a clue, and all I had was a photo and a printed-out list. Outside, a solid darkness was starting to fall. I noticed Mr Jupp's light on, and realized he'd be locking up soon.

He snorted and hurriedly took his feet from the desk as I opened the office door. A thread of dribble hung sleepily from the corner of his mouth, which he noticed only when it hit his wrist.

'You, is it?' he said accusingly. 'Police gone, have they?'

'For now,' I said, forcing a smile. His eyes swept down to my chest and up again, like a kid reaching for a sweet they knew they weren't allowed. 'But I'm still a bit worried, to be honest.'

Not waiting to be asked, I brought over the only other chair, a faded green, moulded plastic thing, and perched on its edge, leaning towards him with as much warmth as I could muster. 'I know he liked the chats he had with you,' I lied. 'I was just hoping he might have said something about a trip somewhere. Anything about being away from the boat?'

He blew his cheeks out. 'Love, listen. Sometimes us blokes have got to blow off a bit of steam.'

'He hasn't fallen out with anyone here or anything?' I said, knowing Matt would have told me if that was the case. 'Or got behind on his rent or anything?'

He leaned back importantly. 'That's confidential.'

'Please, Mr Jupp.' Genuine desperation cracked my voice. 'I don't know who else to ask.'

He let out a big sigh. 'Look, leave your number, sweetheart,' he said, handing me an opened, empty envelope. 'Anything occurs to me, or he misses the payment, I'll be sure to let you know. Now if you don't mind, my missus is waiting for me, so I'm going home for my tea.'

I wrote my name and number on the envelope, with PLEASE CALL IF YOU HEAR ANYTHING underlined beneath. 'Anything at all,' I told him, handing it over and getting up to leave.

'Oh, while you're here, get rid of that lot, will you?' he said, indicating the moorers' postboxes on the wall, a grid of open-fronted pigeonholes. 'He got a parcel the other day and I had nowhere to stick it.'

I pulled out the stack from Matt's box and flipped through it. Bills, circulars. Everything machine-franked.

'Can I have the parcel?'

'Fuck knows where it is right now,' he said. 'I'll drop it over if I find it.'

I thanked him, shoved the post into one of Matt's huge coat pockets, and went back down to the boat. I shook the hoody off and used the chemical toilet. On the inside of the bathroom door was a full-length mirror. I stood in front of it, remembering.

Once, months ago, when Mum was on a night shift and I didn't have to be home until almost dawn, Matt and I spent hours in front of this mirror. He took my clothes off slowly like he was peeling an exotic fruit. I stood there now, in the dark, the reflection of my body lit just by the moon. Matt had made me look. The fine hairs on my arms bristled with the memory of his fingertips, stroking down my naked sides, kissing each one of the constellation of tiny puckered scars across my shoulder and down my back, from the accident when I was small.

I let my eyes flutter shut, recalled the way Matt raked the backs of his nails softly up my sides, then reached around to hold my breasts, tucking his hands underneath them. How he brushed his thumbs across my nipples, not letting me look away. The light had been just like this, an identical blueish monochrome. He had placed my hands high on the mirror so I was bent forwards, and took me like that. Slowly. Telling me to look myself in the eye, saying it again and again because I wouldn't, until his insistence took hold and he wasn't laughing, he meant it. He really meant it. When I eventually looked, he slid his hand around and pressed his fingers against me, making me gasp.

'Look at who you are,' he whispered as I came, shuddering hard against his hand. His breath hot and low and liquid against my neck. 'You are beautiful.'

I blinked the memory away, avoiding my eye in the mirror, and went along to his bedroom at the far end. I lifted the duvet and got into his bed, wriggling down with the covers over my head. I'd been in this bed dozens of times, but never to sleep. Closed my eyes and inhaled deeply.

Damp and woodsmoke and sex.

I slipped my good hand inside my jeans. I held the sense of him, built him up from the smell of his skin, his hair. I started to move, small circles, conjuring his mouth on my mouth. His fingertips on my breasts. I imagined the feel of his chest under my hands, my fingers moving along his shoulders, sliding across to his throat. Glimmers of his face, darts of memory, coming faster.

But then

the skin on his neck, glistening gathering and twisting, pink then white against the pressure of my fingers, and

his face suddenly panicked tight, and his hands on mine, grabbing,

and

his eyes starting to bulge, looking at me, not understanding, and

a creaking sound from his open mouth, no air going in or coming out,

and

his hand, coming up to my face, his eyes still locked onto mine. Stones in the ground under my knees digging in to me as I kneel over him. Sticks and leaves the same as when Mum found Jodie and something sharp against my shin. The smell of the wet leaves and the roar of a jet engine descending, low, and his eyes wild with horror, knowing now that I am not going to stop.

I scrabbled out of the bed and stood, panting, in the middle of the tiny room, my arms brace-position around my head, eyes open. A thin, cold trail of sweat slipped down my spine.

Was it real?

I pressed my fists into my eyes to make the images go away, to scrub them out, but it persisted. I wanted to get behind my eyes and pull them from their sockets, to wipe the images away. One thing I had learned from Siggy: once something goes in your head you can never get it out again. The shaking was in my knees and everywhere.

All I could think was, let me not be the last thing he saw.

Chapter 19

Mae

No sign of Bear. With Kit at the wheel, Mae was free to make the calls: dozens of them. The pool, the cinema, the school again, and any other mates he could think of that Nadia hadn't already rung. Phone to ear, he watched the pavements. They were heading out towards Acton, driving slow enough for Mae to check the side roads as they passed them.

'Thanks,' he said to the school secretary who had agreed to stay late in case Bear went back there. 'Call if you hear anything.'

Kit was under instruction from McCulloch to stay until Bear was found. She leaned over the wheel, scanning the streets ahead of her. 'Dark coat, you're sure?'

'Yes.'

'Dark what, though? Blue? Dark grey?'

'I don't know, it's very dark!'

'But not black. You're sure?'

'Yes!'

'Didn't have any other clothes in her bag when you dropped her off this morning. Something she might have changed into?'

Mae sighed. 'Not that I know of.'

'Gym kit? Wasn't a PE day?'

'I don't know.'

'Drama?'

He slammed a hand on the dash. 'I *said* I don't know, all right?'

'Just trying to help.' Kit indicated left with a sarcastically casual flick of the lever. Mae's phone – charging now – lit up and buzzed again.

Nadia.

Where are you? Tried Molly Zach Jess Anisha Freya B Freya M and Janade, nothing.

He fired off a reply, that he'd done the school, the two closest parks, was heading to the shops. Sending it, he looked up and spotted a newsagent he knew Bear went to sometimes, where they let her leaf through the magazines. 'Pull over,' he said, 'just here.'

Without wasting a second, Kit pulled in onto a bus lane, eliciting a heavy honking from a double-decker and almost causing Mae to break his nose on the dash.

He snapped off his seatbelt and launched himself out of the door. Fine rain was falling, and the temperature had dropped enough to instantly lift the hair on his arms. Bear would be cold. She hated the cold.

The shop door let out an electronic beep when Mae went inside, and the guy behind the counter at the end glanced up from his paper. Mae got out his phone, flashed the picture of Bear.

'I'm looking for my daughter.' He indicated just below chest-height and added, 'About this high. Dark coat.'

The shopkeeper eyed him. 'Dark what? Dark is not a colour.'

'Just – *dark*. All right? Have you seen her?'

The shopkeeper peered at the proffered phone. Bear, grinning, holding an ice cream, from a few months back. He'd sent it to

Nadia at the time, with a line about how they were having a good time, and she'd replied seconds later with 'FFS, diet? What's that, 300 Cals?'

On the bright side, at least *that* little fuck-up was no longer on the top spot.

The shopkeeper nodded. 'Oh yes, I know her. Cherry Coke, and—' he squinted at the ceiling as if trawling his memory, 'ah, big Twix. On her own, like usual. Maybe half an hour ago?'

The bus was still there behind the Focus, horn blaring, when he got back in the car.

'Well?' Kit asked, moving back out into the traffic before he'd got his seatbelt on.

'Try the park over by Acton Station. Just down there, right at the—'

'Yep, I know it.' She swung a uey and took a direct path. Dark now, almost. The wipers sped up automatically. Kit opened her mouth, but he cut her off before she had a chance.

'No, before you ask. She didn't have an umbrella.' He was sure of that, at least.

They drove in silence.

Kit tapped her fingers on the wheel. 'Just the one kid you've got?'

'Yeah.'

More silence.

'Any yourself?'

'Nope. Can't have them, it's a genetic thing,' and then, hurriedly and without a trace of any baggage, 'and that's totally fine. It's not for me.'

The traffic slowed along The Vale and she blipped the siren at a van blocking the flow, and they emerged along the eastern edge of the park. Scrappy huddles of naked trees obscured the swings and slides, and they both craned to see through the bushy perimeter.

'She'll be over there in the playground if she's anywhere.'

Kit slowed to park. She flipped an arm around the headrest, using the heel of her hand to spin the steering wheel, sliding the squad car into a perfect parallel.

He ran, scanning the whole park as he went, a cursory check of each bush and hedge. Because she liked dens, his little girl, she liked making little houses for her soft toys still because she was eight.

She was only *eight*.

The playground was demarcated with a low red fence of tubular bars. Hard to work out where the gates were, but easy enough to vault. No one on the swings. No one on the pyramid she'd fallen from aged four, breaking her arm, leaving her with a narrow, puckered scar near her elbow that would be there forever. No one on the slide, but under it—

Under it was Bear.

Mae shouted her name and was there in a heartbeat and lifting her off the ground, holding her, pressing her against his chest with both arms. *Thank you*, Mae said in his head, as if he believed in something to thank. *Thank you thank you thank you.*

'You're hurting me,' she mumbled, and he looked down at her. She smelled of rain and bubblegum. The slack in her arms as they hung inert from her shoulders damn near broke his heart.

'Not as much as I'm going to hurt you when you get home.'

'What?' Panic on her little face.

'With my special axe I just got sharpened—' he said, making himself smile, but it missed its target.

She pushed the heels of her hands hard against her eyes to stem the tears. 'You *forgot* me. I was all on my own.'

He set her down, knelt right in front of her, gravel biting into his knees. He took her face in his hands.

And for the first time since she was born, he looked into her face and he saw himself. Seven years old, sitting outside the flat in Leeds when he still lived with his mum, waiting for her to come home from wherever she was and let him in. Nine years old, after he'd gone to live with Nopa and Jobu, his grandparents: staring out their living room window on a Friday evening and hoping that this time, his mum really would be coming to get him for the weekend. By ten, although he'd still sit by the same window, he'd sit with his back to it like he wasn't even waiting, like he didn't even care.

He looked his daughter in the eye. 'I promise you, Bear, that we're going to do better than this. OK?'

'You deserve better than this,' Mae said, edging it around the choke in his throat. 'I'm not letting you down again.'

Bear looked at the floor.

'Let's get her dry,' Kit said, standing a few feet away. Bear looked up at Mae and he nodded, held her for another second and then released her. Kit took off her own jacket, knelt down and draped it over Bear's shoulders, then jogged ahead to get the heaters running in the car.

Chapter 20

Ellie

Full dark now. I'd checked every cupboard in the boat, gone through every shelf for a note, for a letter, anything, but there was nothing there. Frustrated, hungry and freezing, I locked up and left the boatyard via the shortcut, a hidden, muddy slope at the other end of the pontoon where Matt had shown me how to scramble down one time when he'd forgotten his key. I picked my way over the barbed wire, then paused just before emerging onto the pavement, remembering what Mum had said about the punctures on my hand.

Gingerly, I rolled up my sleeve and peeled open the dressing and turned on the torch on my phone. The skin all around the wounds was saturated and white from the lack of ventilation. But I hardly noticed the colour. What I saw was how, when I reached over to the wire to compare the spacing of the darkening, exquisitely sore craters on my palm and the barbs of the wire, they matched.

Of course they matched.

I'd just finished rewrapping my hand when my phone rang. Mum.

'I'm on my way,' I told her, eager to hang up to conserve the last of the battery.

'Wait,' she said, 'I just got back, looks like there's something going on round the front of the estate. Police everywhere. Probably best you cut through the back way, all right?'

I said I would, and headed home, walking fast. A few streets from home, I turned right instead of the usual left, and started the loop through the Axmouth estate. It wasn't a route I took lightly. There wasn't a week went by without half the place being shut off with police cars and tape, then the local press alive with outrage about the almost non-existent CCTV. I put my head down and slotted my housekey between the knuckles of my fist the way Mum had shown me.

Creeping poverty and years of neglect clung to everything in the Axmouth. Tired scales of white paint peeling off the timber balustrades, and single-glazed front rooms yawned blank and curtainless onto the walkways. Potholes, graffiti, smashed and defunct lighting: even the gutters were cracked and unkempt, choking with rotting leaves no one was going to clear.

I took a wide arc around a gang of kids huddled on a low wall, their faces monochrome against the glare of their phone screens, then jogged the last few poorly lit paths until I emerged into the relief of where the roads opened out on the western edge. Home was around the next bend. Before I crossed, I checked both ways.

And then I stopped dead.

Tucked in beside the entrance to a garage was a white Volkswagen Golf, with a black roof you could fold back, a doer-upper that had never been done up. A Greenpeace sticker, the glue perished and peeling at the edges. Expired parking tickets clogging up the vents behind the windscreen.

Matt's car.

Heart thundering, I went over, circled it slowly. Matt had driven away when he left me the night before. He dropped me here, then he was going home. So what was it doing back here?

Coming round to the driver's door, I saw the lock pin was up. I tried the handle, and the door scraped open. Casting a quick glance behind me, I pulled myself inside, swung the door closed. I smelled bleach, cutting through what remained of the familiar mustiness.

His things were here. I reached over to pick up a dismembered newspaper, half a pack of chewing gum, a plastic fork. I listened to the emptiness inside. Held the steering wheel, closed my eyes. Rested my feet on the pedals, the way Matt had showed me to do in the ten, fifteen lessons he'd given me. They creaked and resisted just a little under my soles.

It took a moment for the implication of that to hit me. I opened my eyes, dragged my gaze up to the rear-view. It was a perfect frame of the back window.

Matt, at six foot three, had almost ten inches on me. Every time I'd had a lesson in his car, I had to make half a dozen adjustments before I even turned the key. But the mirrors were all perfectly angled to my eye level, my hands were resting at the right height on the steering wheel. My feet were on the pedals.

The car was parked a minute from my home. And the seat was set for me.

I stared at the wheel under my fingertips. Then, like an answer to the question I hardly dared to ask myself, something caught my eye. I lifted my hands, unable to believe what I was seeing. There on the steering wheel, at two and ten o'clock, were two smudges. Brown. Mud.

There was only one explanation. Siggy could *drive*.

I arrived at our flat, breathless. The door swung open before I got to the top step, and a man came out, thanked Mum, and jogged down the steps.

'Locksmith,' she explained as she hustled me inside and closed the door. There was a new, brass-coloured deadlock and an extra steel reinforcement higher up. 'Got one you can't open from the inside without a key,' she told me. Then, seeing my face, she took a step back. 'Shit, Ellie, what?'

'Matt's car. I just walked past it.'

'OK?' she said, missing the significance.

'He said he was going straight home.'

She went immediately into her bedroom and pulled open the curtain and looked out onto the street. 'Where?'

'You can't see it from here. But it's that way.' I pointed. 'Back through there.'

She dropped the fabric. Looked me full in the face, scanning my eyes. 'Does he usually park there?'

I shook my head, mute.

Mum nodded, slowly. 'OK. I guess we've got to tell the police then. Maybe this is good news.' She pulled me in and hugged me. But when she let me go her face changed. 'Baby, what?'

I told her about the pedals, the position of the seat. 'It was *me*, Mum. It was Siggy.'

'Siggy can't drive, baby. You're overreacting. *You* can't even drive.'

I looked away.

'Ellie,' she said, ducking a little to hook my eyeline. 'Oh my god. You can *drive*?'

In a voice I could hardly hear myself I said, 'He gave me a few lessons.'

She threw her hands up. 'Tell me you're joking. Ellie! I can't believe you lied to me about that!'

'I didn't *lie*—'

'Withholding is the same bloody thing,' she said, her jaw tense, furious now.

'Mum, look, I'm sorry. Please don't be angry.'

She sighed and took my hands. 'This has to stop. OK? We can't do this to each other, there has to be trust. OK? There *has* to be.'

'He just thought I needed more independence. Thought it would be best if—' I said, dropping to a whisper, 'if I kept it between the two of us.'

She let her eyes close for a minute like she was composing herself. 'Listen to me. He does *not* understand what you can do, Ellie. He hasn't seen it. Good lord, if he knew what I know about Siggy there is no way he would have even thought about teaching you to *drive*. I cannot believe you made a decision like that without consulting me.'

I said nothing. Waited for it to pass. There was a long pause. 'OK,' she said eventually. She flexed her fingers. 'I suppose I'll have to call them. Only thing we can do.'

I couldn't say no. I didn't even want to say no, because I wanted Matt found, and anything that might help them find him had to be a good thing. But still, right down deep ...

'But what if—?' I started.

She touched a finger to my lips. 'It'll be OK. OK? We deal with it. I'll call them in the morning.'

In the hall, she took the hoody as I shrugged it off. 'So. Where have you been?'

'Matt's,' I told her, taking the post from his pocket, laying it on the radiator shelf.

She glanced at it, then back at me. 'You said you'd stay here.'

'I know but—'

'If anyone sees your neck, love—'

'Has he just left me, Mum?' I whispered.

'Oh, sweetheart.' She sighed like there wasn't enough air in the world. 'I don't know. I wish I did.' She wrapped her arms around me, then, after a while, squeezed and let go. 'Come on, got to eat.'

On the kitchen table there were two plates ready, salad with tuna and hard-boiled eggs. She ate in silence, but I just pushed mine around.

She gave me a look. 'Eat the eggs.'

'I'm not hungry.'

'Eat the eggs, you need the protein.'

I folded my arms. 'Really? For what?'

She sighed wearily at me. 'Everything? Healing, to start with.' She waved her fork, indicating my hand, then took another mouthful. 'Blood sugar. Muscle growth.'

'Muscle growth?' I nodded towards my bedroom. 'I practically took a door off its hinges with my bare hands last night.'

I hadn't meant it as a joke, but we stared at each other for a moment, and then we were laughing. She kept trying to stop but she couldn't, and it set me off again, and then she came around the table and she hugged me.

We were going to be OK.

Right at the back of my mind, Siggy glowed a little warmer.

Chapter 21

Charles Cox Psychotherapy Ltd.	
Clinical audio recording transcript	
Patient name:	*Eleanor Power*
Session date:	*1 September 2006*

CC: *OK. Good to see you again, Ellie. How have you been getting along?*

EP: *Fine, I guess.*

CC: *You mentioned last time that there had been some conflict between you and your mum, about giving school another try. How has that been this week?*

EP: *Yeah, well. She's worried about me seeing Jodie, and she knows that I'm hanging out with her still ... but. Yeah. It's OK, most of the time.*

CC: *OK. Is this something ... does this happen when you spend time with other friends?*

EP: *I don't have any other friends.* [laughs] *Bet you think that's a bit tragic, right?*

[pause: 18 sec]

EP: *She's just worried I'm going to talk about Siggy.*

CC: *Your mum doesn't like you talking about her.*

EP: *No, I mean, we talk about her, at home. It's just, other people can be really, um, freaked out.*

CC: *Freaked out?*

EP: *Yeah.*

CC: *Tell me about that.*

EP: *I mean, like, when I was six or seven or something we had this neighbour who said he was going to report us to the police because Siggy kept getting me up and wandering off at night and Mum had to go out looking for me. We moved away because of it.*

CC: *That must have been very unsettling for you.*

[pause: 15 sec]

C: *You're shrugging. It wasn't?*

EP: *I don't know. I was just a little kid. My memory's always … it's pretty bad. Like, this kind of thing, this therapy stuff: like, I know I've had therapy, but my memory of it is … it's just, not there.*

CC: *That's entirely understandable. The kind of dissociation you've been experiencing, that often comes with periods of amnesia, of not remembering. This is something that we can work on here.*

EP: *But there's whole loads of stuff I remember perfectly.*

CC: *OK, tell me about that.*

EP: *What, anything?*

CC: *Sure. If I was to ask you to tell me the first thing you remember about growing up, what would you tell me? I mean, aside from things like the fugues.*

EP: Moving.

CC: OK. You remember moving house?

EP: A lot. We moved house a lot. Like, I think where we live now, it's like the twelfth, or the thirteenth maybe? I don't just mean round the corner, whatever, I mean like different towns, whole different places.

CC: You never really settled.

EP: No. But, it was … normal. It was just what we did. Everywhere was just where we lived for now. It kind of never occurred to me that we would stay anywhere.

CC: Were these moves planned? Did you know in advance that they were going to happen?

EP: No. Mum always said that was part of the … fun.

[pause: 27 sec]

CC: And was it fun, Ellie?

[pause: 17 sec]

CC: Is that shrug a no?

EP: I-I don't know. Sometimes.

CC: OK. Why do you think it was that you moved so often?

EP: Well … like that time, that I was saying about, it was because of Siggy. We'd decided we didn't want any more, um, intervention from anyone and, you know. If anyone involved the police it would have led to social services, doctors, all of that.

CC: And you didn't want that.

EP: No. We'd had enough. Nothing worked, nothing made me better. Like I said.

CC: OK.

[pause: 28 sec]

*CC: And the other times you moved. Was that all because …
there was a concern that people were going to find out
about your condition?*

[pause: 32 sec]

EP: I-I don't know.

*CC: That's OK. That's fine. The reason I ask is that moving
house, and especially moving to and from different areas
the way that you're describing, when families do that it's
usually because of a pull or a push factor. So, if you're
pulled somewhere, you're making a conscious effort to get
to the new house or the new town. Let's say like a new job
in a new area, that would pull you towards a particular place.
Or moving to be closer to something or someone, like a
relative, someone who needed looking after, for example—*

*EP: No, that was never it. There isn't anyone. My mum doesn't
have any family.*

CC: None at all?

EP: No. Her parents died.

*CC: I see. And do you talk about these relatives much, at
home? No? OK. Or your dad, you talk much about him?
That's a no? Never?*

EP: No. We never do.

*CC: Do you think we can learn anything from that? What kind
of a person he might have been? I'm saying this because
most mothers would want to keep the memory of their child's
father alive, if there was a bereavement, unless the father
was—*

EP: I don't know what he was like. I've asked. I don't ask any more, she doesn't like me doing it. He wasn't great, would be my guess.

CC: OK. OK, look, we can come back to that. But, right … where were we? Ah, yes, regular upheavals, moving house. So, there was no pull effect. But with a push effect, that's when the emphasis is on leaving. So that's when it doesn't matter so much where you end up, as long as you don't stay where you are.

EP: OK … I mean, I don't know, like what?

CC: Well, for example, what you were saying about this neigh-bour. Or sometimes it can be that there's not enough work available, or housing is problematic for whatever reason—

EP: Mum always found work, and we always rented, it wasn't like we were homeless or anything.

CC: I see. But sometimes a push factor can be social. Sometimes a person, or a family, will feel they have to leave where they are, to get away from something dangerous.

[pause: 29 sec]

CC: Or someone.

EP: Like who? We don't have any … we don't know anyone. Look it's not, it isn't like that with us.

[pause: 18 sec]

EP: She would have told me if there was someone … I don't know, who wanted to hurt her.

CC: Or hurt you.

EP: Yeah.

CC: *You have a very close relationship, and she takes great care of you.*

EP: *She does. She really … yes.*

CC: *That's not in any doubt. But it's possible, isn't it, that … let's put it this way. If a mother had a child who was already struggling with … feeling anxious, being very concerned about their own safety. If that mother loved that child very much and knew that there was a threat of some kind, is it possible that she would try to keep that threat a secret?*

EP: *I don't know.*

[pause: 28 sec]

EP: *I suppose so. But, what kind of threat? What do you mean?*

CC: *Well, let's start with the things that Siggy is afraid of. Fire, for example.*

EP: *Everyone's scared of fire.*

CC: *Right, but—*

EP: *We read once that fire is like, it's a metaphor. You know, like it destroys everything, it's just a – what did they call it – a cypher. Like a metaphor for losing the stuff you care about.*

CC: *You read this with your mum?*

EP: *Yeah.*

CC: *That's an interesting idea. Sure, all right. But what about the man?*

EP: *From the … from Siggy's dream?*

CC: *Yes. You said he wears a uniform? Can you say anything else about it?*

EP: *Why?*

CC: Why? Well, because it might help us to isolate the source of the—

EP: But it's just a dream, though.

CC: OK. But, tell me anyway.

EP: Fine. OK. It's, um, it's kind of green, so like a soldier? But I don't know any soldiers, though. He's not a real person, he's just like, kind of like the fire, you know? A man with a gun is scary. Fire is scary. He's just a … just a symbol, you know?

CC: OK

[pause: 17 sec]

CC: OK, Ellie, I think that's something we're going to have to take a look at.

Chapter 22

Mae

Mae offered to carry Bear inside, but she wasn't having any of it. She stormed out of the car and off across to the gate and waited there, not looking back at the adults.

'Give her time,' Kit said, falling into step beside him.

'I don't have any. Got to take her back to her mother in an hour.'

They walked across the threadbare lawn to the front of his building and went inside. The smell of urine hit him the moment he opened the stairwell door.

'Wow!' Kit said, wrapping an arm across her face. 'Is it usually that bad?'

'No,' Mae said.

'Yes,' Bear said.

Kit raised her eyebrows at Mae. 'OK, well. Good to know things are looking up for me when I hit your paygrade.'

'I've nagged the management,' he said, although if he was honest with himself he'd mentioned it only once, and that was more than three years back when he'd moved in. As long as the inside of his home was clean and decent, he supposed he wasn't bothered about the outside. He wasn't exactly big on entertaining: in all honesty the majority of his good friends were still in Brighton and contact had pretty much faded away when he left. As for here, although there was five-a-side and a handful of colleagues he'd happily spend a night in a pub with, the only person he regularly had over was Bettina, who lived above him and was seventy-two years old.

He unlocked and they followed him inside. The twenty he'd left for his cleaner on the sideboard was gone, and the whole place smelled of artificial pine. Bear shed her coat and bag, and Kit stood taking the place in, amused.

'What?' he asked her.

'Well. You'll never hear me say anything about a *woman's touch* or anything—'

'Yeah, yeah,' he said, rolling his eyes. But he knew she had a point. Nadia had kept most of the stuff they had bought together, and although he'd bought the furniture he needed, it was true that it wasn't exactly – homely. There was nothing decorative, no pictures in frames: apart from the windowsill that was home to the growing collection of houseplant cuttings from Bettina, there was nothing to signal to a visitor what kind of person Mae was, what he cared about. He'd somehow never got round to unpacking the tubes of old gig posters and N.W.A. merch that even Bear would probably have had to admit was kind of cool. But it wouldn't exactly kill him to pick up some paint for her room.

He found Bear a clean pair of pyjamas to change into, then remembered his promise that he'd call Nadia as soon as they were home. He dispatched Kit into the living room to get something for Bear to watch, then dialled her number.

It rang just once. 'This,' his ex-wife told him, 'is the lowest point. OK? It doesn't get any worse than this for her.'

He wasn't sure if that was an accusation or a threat, but he said, 'Yeah. I know.'

'Put her on, Ben. I'll have a chat and then I'll come and get her.'

He nudged the living room door shut with his toe. 'She's tired, though, Naddy.' He crossed the fingers of his free hand. 'I think it might be best if she stays here.'

Nadia exhaled, and he waited for the immediate *no fucking way*, but as the seconds ticked by, he knew she was thinking it over.

He tried again. 'She's all right, honestly. And I've got dinner started so—'

'What are you giving her?'

He hesitated, tucked the phone between shoulder and ear and opened the fridge, crouching. Half a chorizo, some parsley, and there were tins of beans and chopped tomatoes in the cupboard. The ingredients assembled themselves in his head until he could almost see it bubbling on the stove.

'Cassoulet?' he said, about two-thirds confident.

'Let me check with Mike,' Nadia said eventually, and ended the call.

Bear came out, rubbing her eyes. 'I'm hungry.'

He picked her up, taking care not to make the *oof* noise that said something was heavy. She laid her head on his shoulder and yawned as he stroked her hair.

He hadn't done anything to earn her forgiveness, but he was forgiven, all the same.

The text came through from Nadia giving Bear the unexpected green light to stay over. Kit said she'd deal with the food and sent them both into the living room, where Mae sat with his little girl bunched up beside him, watching some animated thing Kit had streamed from her phone. He didn't realize pizza had been ordered until it arrived fifteen minutes later, eliciting a yelp of glee from Bear. She strategically avoided his eye as she opened the lid, filling the room with the calorific fumes of melted cheese and pepperoni.

'Daddy?' she said, a slice halfway to her mouth.

Mae didn't even blink. 'Sure. Go nuts.'

*

It was gone ten before the movie finished. Mae had left halfway through, mumbling vaguely about getting some work done, and Kit had wordlessly taken his spot, wrestling an extra cushion from Bear and settling in for the long haul.

For the next hour, Mae methodically entered alternative spellings of the guy Matt had been in touch with from the photography meet up. He found a couple of hopefuls and sent them messages to call him. When the familiar credits music started up, Kit came out into the kitchen. She was carrying the empty pizza box in one hand and two tumblers in the other. Theatrically soundless, she placed the empties beside the sink, half an inch of milk in the bottom of each.

'Asleep,' she whispered. She raised a knee, bent the pizza box across it and folded it in half. 'Recycling?'

Mae pointed to the corner cupboard then crossed to the living room door to peer in at Bear. Her arm was hanging limply off the edge of the sofa, but Kit had draped her with a blanket. On the muted TV, the credits were rolling. With her eyes shut, his daughter's face bore no sign of the probably irreparable trauma of the afternoon. He clicked the door closed.

Kit had her head in his fridge.

'Beer,' she said, removing a bottle. 'Want one?'

He was fairly sure that both the fridge and beer inside it were his, but he accepted her offer, nonetheless. She did something cool with her hand and the bottles were open.

After a long pull, she leaned against the wall, head back, bottle hanging loosely from her fingertips.

She jerked her head towards the living room. 'She'll be all right.'

'I know.'

'No, you don't. You think you're fucking it up, and that she'll be miserable because you and her mum aren't together.'

'Oh, I do, do I?' Mae halved the contents of the bottle in one go, and immediately thought of the fresh crate under the sink.

Kit went over to his kitchen table, pushed herself up and sat on it, feet on the seat of a chair.

'I'm one of seven.' A small smile played at the corner of her mouth. 'Third youngest. My biggest brother, bit of a wordy fucker, he's got this theory that I'm the *wilderness baby*.'

'Oh Jesus, is this the payoff for the free pizza? Listening to your life story?'

She drank, smiling at him as she tipped the bottle, swallowed. 'You're hilarious.' She cleared her throat and went on. 'So, my brother. He says the first kid's the biggest investment, to the parents. Everything's a big deal with child number one. New parents somehow manage to forget how they don't really give that much of a toss about other people's babies, and they fail to apply that to themselves. The kid is the only thing they think and talk about. What they're eating, how long they're sleeping, and the whole lot goes on Facebook, blah blah blah.' She dismissed infancy with a benevolent wave of her hand. 'Then number two comes along and stuff gets a bit more normal, no one goes apeshit if the kid gets a scraped knee or misses breakfast once in a while. Third one, the mum's still trying to hold the fort—'

'What about the dads?'

She skewered him with a look. 'You know many dads of seven kids staying home?'

'Well—'

''Course you fucking don't. But listen. Four kids in, the mum – *or dad* – is aware it's a sinking ship now and it's all about getting through it. The last kid's going to be the baby, always, and when the mum sees that one off to their first days at school or whatever, she's going to be all weepy and she'll spend the rest of the time wanting to keep them close and wishing they were little again.'

'Hold on though, you missed some out.'

'Number five?' She upended the bottle into her mouth, swallowed, pointed at herself. 'Want to know how many times I got left at school?'

And so they arrived at the point. 'More than once.'

She laughed, threw her head back. 'Try once *a week*. Reception onwards. Easily once a week, standing there like a dick, everyone going, *poor little Catherine, where's your mummy and all those brothers and sisters?*' She rolled her eyes but smilingly, no trace of sadness about it. 'There was a special seat outside the school office, and I used to think it was mine. Just for me. I used to hide a comic down the back so I had something to do while I waited for my mum to remember me.'

The rest of Mae's beer was gone. Just for a fleeting moment it occurred to him that he could open up a bit here. He could tell her he knew about this, that what she said before about craving order and control was probably pretty much spot-on. But he couldn't say that, could he? Couldn't say anything of the sort, couldn't really even drop the expression from his face that told her that this was all a bit heavy and personal. Because if he did *that*, then he'd need to talk about his mother. And that was not something he was prepared to do.

'What I'm saying is …' Kit started.

'I know what you're saying.' He felt the atmosphere change as he said it, but it was like his tone had a mind of its own. 'There's always going to be some tragic kid who everyone feels sorry for.'

She raised an eyebrow, hopped down from her perch on his table and handed him the empty.

'Nope,' she said, shrugging on her coat. 'What I'm saying is, case in point. I turned out fine. Mistakes get made, life goes less than perfectly, and you cope. Shit happens and you move the fuck on. She'll be awesome. Give yourself a break.'

*

Long after Kit had left, around midnight, there was a familiar thump from the floor above. Mae checked the time: just gone eleven, meaning Bettina would have finished moderating the chat site she worked for and was ready for her glass of rum. He looked in on Bear, who was sound asleep in her bare-walled room, the side of her perfect face illuminated by the nightlight she'd had since she was born. He softly closed the door, transferred half a dozen tin trays of casserole from the freezer into a plastic bag, then went upstairs, locking the flat behind him.

Bettina was waiting for him with her front door opened just a crack. She undid the chain and ushered him in. Her flat, although structurally identical to his, could not have been any more different. Every wall was covered in paintings, photos of the places she'd been, even letters and notes that she'd been sent over the years. There were scores if not hundreds of plants of all kinds, flourishing in buckets, trailing from pots stacked high on shelves the way Nadia stacked books.

'You OK?' Mae asked, handing over the bag and taking the tumbler she handed him. 'Can't stay long, I've got Bear with me.'

His neighbour thanked him for the food and narrowed her eyes. 'I thought she was off with her mum now.'

'She was. We, uh, changed the plan.'

'You did not,' she said simply. 'Something happened.'

He smiled, took a sip of the mahogany liquid, and told her the truth, because it was the only thing he could do. It was possible that one day, some kind of artificial intelligence would be able to edge a lie past Bettina, but it wasn't something he'd ever managed.

She listened, finished her rum, and got up. 'Do you know who else comes up here?'

Mae, caught off guard and wondering if she'd been listening at all, shook his head.

'No one.' She smiled. 'I speak to my family in Jamaica on Skype, you know?'

'That's—' he looked for the word. 'Sad. I'm sorry, Bett.'

'Hah!' she said and reached for her tobacco. 'That's not what I mean.'

He waited, glancing at the door, conscious that Bear would be freaked out if she woke up alone.

'I mean, *you* come. You don't have to come. I never ask for your presents,' she said, waving a hand towards the frozen meals. 'Do you know why you come?'

You listen, he wanted to say. You're always here. Your place smells like my grandparents' place. But he couldn't say that, so he said nothing.

'You come because you're good. You're a good father. I saw you, arriving earlier, you know. With the woman?' She flashed him a smile, nodding. '*Beautiful* lady.'

'No, look, she's—'

'Hush, I don't care. I saw you only caring for Bear. Eyes on your little girl, the whole time. See? So you make a mistake. You're a human being. You must not only count the things you do wrong, Benjamin.'

*

In his own kitchen, he rinsed the three beer bottles and put them in the recycling. He checked his messages: one from his friend Rod demanding a pint, and a few about the CID five-a-side match next weekend. He knocked out holding-pattern replies to both. Then, while the kettle boiled, he went into his bedroom, retrieved the box he kept on the top shelf of the built-in wardrobe, and carried it into the kitchen.

He allowed himself to do this only occasionally now, but when he did it, he did it comprehensively. He lifted the lid and unpacked the box onto the table. Copies of every document from the Arden investigation: statements, photographs, reports, transcripts, the lot. He made a cafetière of decaf, brushed away the mud Kit's shoes had left on the seat of his kitchen chair. The he sat down, and he read.

*

By the time he responded to the triple-9, Jodie Arden had been missing for almost two days. Her mother, Lucy, called it in. Mae had been at the end of his shift. He was hoping to get home in time to bathe Bear, who had just turned three. But DS Ian Heath, whom Mae had been shadowing, insisted on taking it. Needed the overtime, he said. Had four girls at home. There had been a slap on the back, Mae remembered: *and anything to avoid doing bloody bedtime, eh?*

So they'd driven over, Heath chuntering all the way about some long-running war of attrition he'd been having with another detective, a woman he thought was getting preferential treatment because of what he liked to refer to as 'the D-cup effect'. Mae, who'd been a substantive DC for all of a month, did his best to zone his mentor out until they got to the address. Heath was known among his colleagues not only for his hot-headedness but also for his grudges, and Mae knew better than to challenge him.

They swung through the door to the complex and up the stairwell. 'You can lead on this one,' Heath said, half-heartedly stifling a burp with a fist and thumping himself on the chest. 'See if you've been paying attention to the master.'

Mae hadn't had the luxury of experience, but if he had, he would have seen right away when Lucy Arden opened the door that this was something worse than missing. Something about the flat, its laid-back, careworn warmth. Possibly it was Jodie's room, where Lucy insisted he followed her the moment he arrived. The teenager's walls were covered with murals which Lucy was quick to tell him were Jodie's own work.

'And she's brilliant, isn't she?' Lucy said, when he'd compli-mented the artwork, the agony red in her eyes. 'Hates school, but loves art, so that's what she does. She paints.'

Lucy had already emptied the contents of her daughter's handbags and schoolbags and drawers and folders and pockets onto the floor and was trawling for some kind of clue. The room was plastered with posters of grunge girls, Courtney Love and Doll Squad, but also demo placards.

'Wouldn't catch my girls with these sluts on the wall,' Heath said under his breath, curling a lip. But Mae wasn't interested in Jodie's musical taste. Without even having to look for it, there was evidence all over the place, in every room, of a stable family home, albeit a two-person one. She'd had a so-so relationship with school, had been off for the preceding week, Lucy told him as he looked around.

'She does that, decides she's had enough of education, refuses to go in, then comes round again for a while.'

'And things are OK at home? Between the two of you?' he asked, examining the photos wedged between the vanity mirror and its frame. Several of them were of the mother and daughter: thin strips of photo-booth images. Fun stuff, moments of real happiness, nothing forced.

'We've had a few fallings-out. She's just pushing the boundaries at the moment. You know? Teenage stuff.'

Mae nodded, replacing the photos, thinking, fallings-out or not, this wasn't a home from which you ran away without a very good reason.

When he finally ushered her back downstairs and settled at the kitchen table, the first major, quantifiable alarm bell rang.

Lucy suspected Jodie had a boyfriend. Which would have been fine, except Lucy was concerned that the boyfriend was much older. When he asked her how much older, she gave a sudden sob, just one, and looked away.

'I don't even know who he is,' she told him. 'I just know there's someone.' She proceeded to explain how her daughter had been out a lot, late, how she'd had money. How there had been that row, when Lucy had discovered her daughter had been taking explicit photos of herself on her phone. With Heath hovering in the background doing nothing more useful than helping himself to the biscuits, Mae asked her to write down the names of friends, places Jodie liked to go. As she hunched over the notebook Lucy pulled unconsciously at her eyebrows, and when he took the pad back, he had to brush away a little drift of crescent hairs with the back of his hand.

He wrote down each version of the events of two nights before, increasingly aware of the inconsistencies.

Jodie had been alone, or with her friend, possibly, when she left the house.

She had been wearing a coat, or it might have been just a sequinned dress, but almost certainly Doc Marten boots. But maybe, actually, the Hi-Tecs.

Jodie had been out from six, or eight, or possibly while Lucy was on the phone to her brother, which might have ended at seven, or could have been closer to nine.

Mae tried another tack, already thinking CCTV, door-to-door, phone records, because there was unreliable and there was *unreliable* and then there was this poor woman, and unless Lucy's total loss of certainty was down to shock, he was going to be struggling here for much to go on.

'Let's think about who else might have seen her since Wednesday then,' he said. 'Are there people who visit you guys here often? Friends, family?'

'A good friend, yes. She's coming over in a minute.'

'OK. Anyone else?'

She hugged herself. Eyes downcast. 'I've been seeing someone. Charles,' she said, looking up with a look of awful realization. 'I've been neglecting her,' she whispered, her eyes filling with tears. 'That's why this has happened. Have I been neglecting her?'

As softly as he could, Mae assured her that he doubted it, that teenagers were hard, that he was sure she was a great mum. 'But look, do you think Charles might be able to shed any light on her movements?'

Even years later, Mae could remember the chime of the doorbell that interrupted her, and the sound of sobbing as Lucy met whoever it was who'd come in.

Because as he politely sipped the tea he didn't really want, into the kitchen and into his investigation walked a fourteen-year-old girl and her mother who would change the course of his life as surely as a fallen boulder changes the path of a stream.

*

He awoke to find Bear standing next to where he sat at the table, her little hand on his shoulder, hot through the fabric of his T-shirt.

'Daddy,' she was whispering. Freezing cold in the kitchen. 'Dad.'

Lifting his head from the table, he wiped his mouth and pressed the heels of his hands into his eyes for a moment. He moved a wedge of papers from his laptop and nudged the mouse to awaken the screen: 03.34. He closed the lid of the laptop and stood, taking her hand in his own.

'I had a bad dream.' She rubbed her eyes, and he pulled her into him, started stroking her feather-soft hair. 'The room was full of water. Grandma was there—'

He stopped stroking. 'Grandma?' She'd always called Nadia's mother *Nanny*.

'*Your* one, Daddy. *Your* mummy.'

Something clenched inside him, remembering her, but he

forced himself to resume the movement of his hand on her head. 'What was she doing, sweetheart?' Not, *what does she look like? Not, how is she even in your dreams when you've never even met her? When she doesn't even know you exist?*

'I couldn't swim. And she was there, at the edge, but-but she wouldn't help. Mummy couldn't hear, and you were—' she said, but her voice choked, and she shook her head, crunching her eyes shut.

'Shhh, Bear.' He made his shoulders drop, held her close. 'You're OK. It's only in your head.'

'I'm scared, Dad,' she said simply.

'What of, sweetheart?'

There was a long pause, and he had to fight the urge to interrogate her, ask her again about those mean-looking kids he'd seen at school, about whether Mike really was all right to her, as she always claimed.

But he gave her time to form her answer herself. After a long pause, she just said, 'Sometimes I'm scared of everything.'

Mae took her back to her bed and smoothed her fine black hair away from her face. She was asleep within seconds, but he sat there beside her for a long time. Watching her breathe, telling her in a low, soft voice that things would OK, there was nothing to be frightened of because Daddy was there. And she slept and slept, too deep and still to argue.

Chapter 23

Ellie

The regularity of the planes descending above us was decreasing, and the noise from the pubs at kicking-out time had died down. I'd been in my room for hours, but there wasn't a chance of sleep. I checked the time on my phone: 02.15.

Twenty-seven hours since Matt had disappeared off the face of the planet. Mum must have called the police about the car by now. I guessed it would be the morning by the time we heard from them though. There would be fingerprinting, CCTV. Maybe that would be the end of it all.

Giving up on sleep, I got out of bed and padded across my room for my dressing gown. I pulled it down from the back of my locked door and came face to face with my mirror. Full length but always distorted, made of some kind of plastic so it can't shatter, because everything in my room has to be safe. I don't even have a pair of tweezers. I lifted my chin to see my neck. The inky bruises were ringed now with the first bloom of green. There, just below them, was my scar.

Sometimes I forget it's there. I touched a fingertip to the hard, knotty skin, following the length of the damaged tissue and marvelling that I had gone through with it. It is from when I was fourteen. Three weeks after Jodie. I cut my throat with a knife. I used the serrated one, laser-sharp but scalloped on the edge for gripping meat, slicing through the fibres. I remember weighing it in my hand thinking it was best because it was biggest. It made an awful mess, but it didn't kill me. I watched myself do it in the mirror. In the last moment, when I dragged that blade across my neck, more than anything I had wanted to see Siggy. I stared myself in the eyes because I wanted her to watch and know she hadn't won. All I could think, at the time, was that if I wasn't alive, Siggy couldn't hurt anyone. I'd just wanted her gone. She had taken my friend, and I wanted her to suffer for it. I didn't care that it meant me too.

I hit my head on the side of the bath when I lost consciousness, and Mum heard. She broke the door down. Days later in the hospital, a nurse was changing my bandage and he thought I was asleep. He said to whoever was helping him that he'd have to get his wife to carve the roast lamb that weekend in case he got flashbacks. It was a joke, I thought, but neither of them had laughed.

It was all in vain anyway. Siggy never did reveal herself to me that night, anymore than she revealed what she'd done to Jodie. For her part, Mum never told me what she had done with the body. One day I had a friend, the next day she was gone.

Turning a circle, I lifted my top, looking over my shoulder, I could just about make out all the other marks. Half my body covered in a sea of small rucks and troughs, as if the skin had been pinched but not recovered. The swathe of damaged tissue across the skin of my buttock, between my legs, the inside of my thighs.

I'd tried and tried to recall the accident from when I was small, but it was as if someone had taken an eraser to that chapter of my life. I couldn't remember anything about it: not the accident itself, not the pain or the recovery, not the hospital, nothing. It wasn't uncommon, Dr Cox said, for that to happen with trauma. *The mind can do anything*, was what he said. Even obliterate the very thing that causes a person to fall apart.

Mum had told me the story many times though, and I knew it by heart. I was four, just about to start school. Mum had already given up her career in journalism and was working from home doing marking for a local college. It was exam season and she had a lot of work on: she was overworked, couldn't have eyes everywhere, and I was bored, restless. There was a pan of pasta cooking on the hob, and she had been in the other room. She said that she knew what had happened when she heard the crash, before she even heard the screaming.

Apparently there had been talks of skin grafts, but in the end it was left to repair itself. For a while, it seemed I would make a full recovery. Physically, at least, I did.

It was, Mum said, a few weeks after the bandages came off that Siggy started to visit.

I traced the edges of the scars in the mirror, knowing every twist, every ruck. I thought it made sense that Dr Cox wanted pictures of them. He said it was for his records, so he could show his colleagues if he needed to. Because I was an interesting case. A single incident of physical trauma didn't usually cause dissociation to the extent that I experienced it, and so he was going to write about it, a full paper at one point.

When he started taking the photos, just the arms and the calves and my shoulders, that was OK. I got nervous about the other ones, where I had to take everything off. But every fourteen-year-old wants to be an interesting case. I couldn't ask Mum what she thought, because she didn't even know I was seeing him. Both he and Jodie believed I was sixteen and that meant the decision had to be mine.

Mum found out eventually though, when it all went wrong. I felt as if I'd been turned inside out when she explained to me the real reason he'd taken them, what he was probably going to do with them.

They were still out there, somewhere, those images of me.

Chapter 24

Mae

The next morning Nadia was there as arranged, at the school gates. She was retying the belt of her camel-coloured trench coat, and he was struck how slim she was, edging now into skinny, thinner even than before the baby she'd had with Mike two years earlier. He wondered about that baby, Yolanda. Bear's half-sister. There were pictures of her in school projects Bear had shown him, but that was as close as they got. He'd never even met her.

Bear broke into a run and launched herself into a waist-level hug with her mother, who whispered something in her ear, hugged her back, hard, and ushered her ahead.

To Mae, she said, 'I've already been in, you're off the hook.'

'What? Why?' The plan had been that both parents would go in and speak to – or, more likely, receive their bollocking from – Bear's headteacher.

'Because I didn't want it escalating. You can get ... defensive.'

Mae, instantly defensive, gritted his teeth and summoned every ounce of calm as Bear looked back and waved to him.

'Remember about the school trip,' she called back, by way of goodbye. 'You are still helping, right?'

He rolled his eyes – *like I'd forget!* – making a mental note to write it down the moment he was back in the car.

Once she was out of sight, Nadia turned back to him. 'I'm sorry. I was here early, and I thought it would be best to get it out of the way.'

He shrugged, knowing he looked sulky. 'Doesn't matter. What did they say?'

His ex-wife rubbed her hand over her pixie cut. Years had passed since her rolling brown curls had been abbreviated to a severe crop, but he'd never got used to it.

'I told them it was a miscommunication, that we both thought the other was picking her up, and that we would double-check from now on. They're not happy though. They're making an official record.' She saw him bristle, and added, 'It's safeguarding, Ben. It's their job.'

He opened his mouth, thought better of it, closed it again.

'Oh,' she said, dropping her bag from her shoulder, 'before I forget. I found this.'

She held something out to him and dropped it into his hand. A watch. Slender gold-coloured strap, a crack through the disk of glass. He slid his thumb over the casing, knowing every nick and scrape of it, the exact trajectory and length of the break across the face.

His mother's watch.

'I was unpacking some boxes,' Nadia was saying. 'Think it must have got mixed up in my stuff.'

He looked up, and she was frowning, her head tipped to the side. 'You OK, Ben?'

Forcing a grin, he dropped the watch carelessly into his pocket, like it was nothing, just an old bit of jewellery. 'Fine. I'm fine.'

Nadia shrugged, taking him at his word, then muttered something vague about being busy, getting going.

The watch sat heavy as an iron bar against Mae's thigh. 'Yeah sure, me too, yeah. I'm parked over there,' he said, gesturing, 'so—'

'Oh, me too,' she said, so there was no choice but to walk together. There followed the kind of silence that precipitated their collapse in the first place. Freeze, thaw, freeze: it was the instability that caused even formations of granite to crumble, in the end.

'So,' she said, 'did she mention any other kids to you, last night?'

'No. What other kids?'

A shrug. 'There's been some suggestion of kids picking on her.'

He stopped. 'Bullying?'

Nadia exhaled heavily. 'Look, no one's used that word—'

'No? What do they want us to call it, then? What's it about, race?'

'No! Look, it's nothing like that—'

'What is it then, her weight, then? Or is it because of me? Because I'm old bill. Is that it?'

She took a step back, sighed. 'Ben.'

'She's still my daughter. Right? I need to know, OK?' He sounded truculent, he knew he did, but he didn't care.

'I don't think it's like that. You know what Bear's like. She gives twice as good as she gets. More.'

But Mae wasn't listening. 'And why am I only hearing about this now?'

'Ben. *Stop.*'

And then, because what was the point holding it in when it was inevitable: 'Presumably Mike knows all about it? He been in to talk to the head yet, has he?'

She nodded, lips a tight line, then dug in her bag for her phone, tapped something in, looked up. 'Right. I've sent you the number of the person dealing with it. Call her if you want filling in, Ben. I don't need the aggression.' She shoved her hands into her pockets. 'Please don't forget the school trip, OK? The zoo. You said you would, so ...'

And then she turned and walked away.

He took a deep breath, let it all out. 'Nadia.'

She ignored him. He jogged after her, drew level.

'Look, I'm sorry. I messed up.'

'To which mess are you referring?'

He didn't bite. 'Last night.'

She agreed it with a shrug but didn't slow. Not a single calorie of warmth in her face. 'You did.'

'And it won't happen again.'

'It never does.'

He slowed to a stroll, then stopped. Then, a few yards away, his ex-wife, with whom he'd really and truly thought he'd grow old, stopped too, and turned around. Her eyes were wet.

'Where were you, when you were supposed to collect her last night? I just don't ... I don't get it. What was important enough that you forgot?'

Just for that second he saw a years-younger Nadia. At home, alone except for a baby constantly rooting for milk, her atom-fine fingernails like shards of glass. Mother and daughter having grown incrementally further from him by the end of every shift, never to return. He'd known how it looked: if both time and care were finite resources, it followed that his laser-beam focus on every detail on every case back then meant he had nothing left for his family. But even though he'd sworn to himself that he would back off at work, just do his contracted hours, the horror of the world he saw from inside a stab vest trumped his good intentions every time.

This was the thing he could never have told Nadia. Everyone knew about that primal, protective force-field that some men got when their babies were born. But he'd been dealt a mutation. It was a terror. An inability to look into the wide-open face of his daughter without the fear – the absolute *certainty* – that if he couldn't do his job, Bear would be doomed. If he couldn't solve the murder, put the rapist away, find the missing woman, it meant he'd failed her. It would mean he was unable to protect her, this tiny, gossamer-haired child for whom he would die in a single heartbeat. It had been as if there were no rungs for him on the way down from that realization, until, right at the bottom, there was his wife. Desperate in the doorway of their chaotic rented flat, half-dressed and holding an arching, howling, months-old child as her chosen life partner left her alone again after a half-hour pitstop at home. Saying, *I'm not doing this. This wasn't the deal. You need to choose.*

Nadia cocked her head, waiting for the reply. 'Well?'

'Just a case,' was what he told her in the end, and she paused, shook her head, and walked away.

Chapter 25

Ellie

I woke up with the sense of a sudden fall. The shell of the familiar dream cracked and disintegrated: it was Siggy, trapped by a fire, too scared to shout for help. Dull embers of pain leapt into flame across my hand and I remembered. *Matt.* I grabbed my phone but there was nothing from him, or from anyone. Siggy scraped along the insides of my ribs. An ache to her, a calm I didn't trust.

'Can I come in?' Mum was outside my door, speaking through the locked door.

I croaked a yes and heard the sound of the top bolt sliding open. Then there was a pause.

'And ... it is you, yes?'

I cleared my throat. 'Of course.'

From the other side of the door came the sound of the other bolt, much lower, and then the key sliding home for the third, the mortice lock under the handle.

She walked in holding two mugs in one hand and offered one to me.

'He hasn't called, Mum.'

'No.' She sat on my bed, freshly showered and smelling of citrus, with her grey-rooted hair dripping dark marks on her violet sweatshirt.

I sipped my coffee. 'You all right?'

'Fine. We still on for this afternoon?'

''Course,' I said, thinking, *shit*. Today was Cherry Tree Day.

Every year since I was little, Mum and I marked the twenty-seventh of November. One of Mum's books said that it could be useful, therapeutic, to allocate some special time for the nondominant 'alter'. The idea was that we gave Siggy time to come to the fore, to express herself. The thing was, I didn't 'switch' like most people with my condition, so it never worked the way it was meant to. But Cherry Tree day became a tradition anyway, and we would spend the time talking to her like she was a separate person, like she was a friend. Wish fulfilment, after a fashion.

We'd planted a tree in a secret place that she'd loved as a kid, beside the river, a mile or so from Hampton Court. Even when we lived in Hove we'd travel every year to visit it. The exact spot was hard to find, along what looked like a dead-end path that would have been entirely overrun without our annual trip. I doubted the tree was seen by anyone but us from year to year. To me and Mum, though, that place was sacred. But this time, I'd forgotten.

She noticed, of course. 'I mean, we *can* leave it, if you're not keen. But—'

'No, it's fine,' I said, cutting her off.

'Good.' She shot me a thin smile, but then immediately winced. Her hand went up to her face, cupping her jaw.

'What's up?' I asked.

The hand stayed on her face. 'It's nothing.'

She went to get up, but I stopped her. 'Show me.'

Taking a deep breath, she lifted her face. On her jaw, a fist-sized swelling. Pressing up and out as far as her bottom lip, the skin discoloured darker along one edge of the bone and then blooming red towards her cheek.

Siggy tightened through the length of my backbone as I realized what I was looking at.

'Look, don't worry,' she said, her voice low, muffled by the swelling. 'It was my fault. It was just – you sounded – I thought it was you.'

'It wasn't me, Mum.'

Her watery blue eyes locked on mine. Neither of us said it, but we were thinking the same thing. If Siggy could convince Mum, who knew her better than anyone, better than even *I* did, it meant something had changed. It meant she was winning.

'I should have known.' She reached for my hands. I felt limp, like I'd been winded, or hit by a car. 'But it was how she *spoke*. I just couldn't tell the difference.'

'What did she say?'

Her eyes flittered shut. 'She said, "Mummy, let me out".'

I went cold. 'Just that?'

'Pretty much.'

'Mum. What else?'

She wouldn't meet my eye.

'Mum?'

'She *laughed*, sweetheart. Looked me in the eye and laughed.'

I sat heavily next to her, mute. Slowly she put an arm across my shoulders, and we sat like that for a while, silent with our thoughts, until she gave me a squeeze and got up.

'Come on. I've got to do the early, but I swapped with Brenda from eleven,' she said, gathering her things into her bag. 'Meet you at the bench and walk down together then, about twelve?'

I followed her out to the front door, where she had paused by the mirror to retouch the make-up over the bruises on her jaw. Closing the compact, she paused.

Tucked into the rim of the mirror were all the pictures of the Cherry Tree Days. All in order: the first showing the two of us muddy-gloved and serious, standing beside the sapling we had just planted. I am six, in tiny red wellies and a woolly hat. In each one Mum is a little greyer, a little more lined, and I am growing out of my awkward adolescence and towards adulthood.

Only one image is missing: 2006, when Mum went alone. She didn't take a picture that time, didn't feel like smiling for the camera, because that year, on the twenty-seventh of November, I was only just out of intensive care.

'Is it a fruiting year, this year?' she asked, touching last year's image lightly with a fingertip. 'Can't ever remember.'

'Me neither.' In each photo, the tree between us is a little taller. A little thicker in the trunk and wider in the branches. Stronger.

She sighed. 'I'd thought maybe Matt would come with us this year.'

I turned to face her. 'Really?'

'Why not? You seem serious enough.'

'You don't like him, Mum.'

She looked genuinely confused. 'Like him? Baby, I think he's lovely. I just—' She sighed heavily, frustrated. 'I just want him to be careful with what he's taking on. That's all.'

'I'm not a bloody Battersea dog.'

'I didn't mean it like that.'

We said goodbye and she got up and went to the door, smiled before she left. Or tried to. There's no such thing as a smile that can conceal fear in the eyes.

As she closed the door, something of Siggy's settled behind my heart: half satisfaction and half dread. Because she had seen the fear, too.

Chapter 26

Mae

Mae sat in the moulded green seat, number two in a bolted-down line of six outside Matthew Corsham's manager's office. He was about to bother the woman at the desk again – he'd already been waiting five minutes – when the door opened and a youngish, efficient-looking woman in a crisp skirt suit emerged, patent navy-blue heels clacking on the concrete floor.

'Detective,' she said, holding out a slim hand. 'Helen Williams, HR.'

He gathered the folder and his backpack, shook hands and he followed her into the office. Closing the door, she gestured to a seat on the passive side of an orderly desk, onto which she then perched. On the phone she'd sounded brisk and judging by the smile that now remained unwavering throughout her recap of the situation with Matthew Corsham's employment, he decided that his initial estimation was pretty accurate.

'As I explained,' she was saying, 'Matthew was a freelance lab tech. We use a lot of freelance contracts these days, just a way of keeping costs down, and—'

'I don't really need to know about your management strategy,' he said, interrupting. 'I just want to understand why he left.'

The smile tightened. 'As I say, he was a freelancer, on a rolling contract. The contract came to an end.'

'But it says here,' Mae countered, flipping open the folder and scanning down Kit's notes, 'that his contract *technically* ended every week.'

'Technically, yes.'

'But in reality, he'd worked for you for several months. On that rolling basis.'

A curt nod conceded it. 'And then by mutual arrangement, we allowed the contract to default.'

'Mutual ... arrangement ...' Mae parroted, writing it in his notebook.

'I mean, we did sort of find ways to reduce the workload down there, too. So someone had to go, if you see what I mean.'

'Sort ... of ... find ... ways ...' He could do this all day. Finishing the sentence, he looked up. 'I understand his girlfriend works here too. Do you know her?' Kit, again, who'd dug that out. A background inspection in the form of a DBS check had been done on Ellie, and it linked back to the hospital. 'Reads to the kids on the children's ward, something like that?'

She stiffened and relaxed so fast that he wasn't entirely sure he'd read it right, but the smile didn't move. 'Yes. She volunteered.'

'Past tense?'

'Yes. She was unreliable.'

'So ... you're firing her, too? Or is her one-week-stroke-three-year contract going to be, uh,' he checked his notes, '*mutually defaulted*, or whatever?'

Helen Williams sighed heavily.

Mae softened. 'All I want to know is—'

'All you want to know is, why did we not renew Matthew Corsham's contract this time.' She spoke with her eyes closed, as though the thought of answering the question caused her physical pain.

He closed the folder, crossed his legs, and leaned expansively against the back of the chair. 'Exactly.'

'Fine.' She stood, went round the back of her desk, and opened a drawer. She withdrew a zip-topped plastic bag containing what looked like vials and a couple of plastic bottles, lifted it up for him, and gave it a shake.

'This. This is the reason.'

Mae stood and took it from her and read the names of the bottles.

'They were discovered in his locker. We had an anonymous tip-off from someone who'd noticed him putting them in there. They thought it looked suspicious.'

'Really?' He turned one of the bottles over in his hand. It was just a glass bottle, nothing particularly fishy about it. 'Suspicious how?'

'Well, for a start, they're not domestic volumes. That one,' she said, gesturing to the bottle Mae was holding, 'is a 500 ml bottle. Dosages are tiny, you'd never need a quantity like that for one person.'

'All right,' Mae said, still not getting it. 'But what *is* it?'

'This one,' she said, pointing to a bottle of clear liquid, 'is lidocaine. This is propofol, and that one you've got is haloperidol.'

'But let's say I primarily speak English.'

Pointing to the items in the same order she said in clipped syllables, 'Lidocaine is a surface anaesthetic used to numb the site of injection alongside general anaesthetic. Propofol is a non-barbiturate general anaesthetic. This one, haloperidol: the velvet hammer. Antipsychotic, muscle relaxant, tranquilizer. For use in acute presentation, for urgent sedation. Used in prisons, from what I understand.'

'So it's not a personal prescription.'

She paused, let out a sudden laugh, then dragged her hands down her face. 'No,' she said wearily.

Mae dropped his shoulders and cocked his head. 'Hard day?'

'Could say that, detective, yes.'

'Ben. Hard in what way?'

She sank into her chair. 'We've had to review security across all our sites. Press office shitting themselves, and you don't even want to know about *that* lot,' she said, gesturing to the ceiling, the echelons above.

'The brass?'

'I've had the PCT area director leaning on me, it's been hell.' She sighed and glanced out of the window, and her hand fluttered to the V of her crisp, white blouse and loosened the top button. Tight, tanned skin. The twitch of a flirt at the corners of her mouth when she turned to face him again.

He made one hundred per cent sure he looked her in the eye, and only in the eye. 'Leaning on you about what?'

With her enormous reluctance written into each furrow of her face, she told him the thing that would breathe sudden, unexpected life into the image Mae had been creating of Matthew Corsham, in his mind's eye.

'He'd stolen these medicines from our pharmacy.'

Mae thought of Helen Williams's top button – that and the insistence as he left that he should ask for her by name if he needed anything else – all the way down to the ground level, and out to his car. He thought of it as he turned the key in the ignition, and as he turned the engine off again and walked back into the building and down to the basement and Matthew Corsham's photographic lab.

By the time he was knocking on the door and being shown into the bright, sterile room in which Matt had worked, Helen Williams's top button had been overtaken in his mind by something else. Something Ellie Power had told him twenty-four hours earlier.

He is the most honest, the most grounded person you'll ever meet.

He is a good man, and I can rely on him.

I can.

A check-shirted lab tech with a little Dave Grohl beard walked him through the workspace. There were several large, white machines spaced down the centre of the room, each looking as if it had been cast in a single piece. Wheeled stools stood under the continuous desk system that skirted the entire room at waist height. There was a weird, inorganic feel to the place, like it could be any day of the year and the temperature would be the same, ditto the odourless atmosphere, the unrelenting, shadowless bright of the LED lighting. It was the opposite of what he imagined photographic labs had been twenty years previously: dark, red, chemical.

'We kinda hot-desk,' Grohl told him, stopping in the far corner of the room, 'but Matt mostly used this corner here.'

There was a blank section of smooth white table, with several plug sockets where it seamlessly met the wall.

Mae ducked under the table, came back up. 'No filing cabinet, nothing like that?'

Grohl smirked. 'Oh sure, yeah, 1998 is just next door.' Mae kept his gaze level until the smirk withered. 'No. No filing cabinet, we're pretty much one hundred per cent digital.'

'Right. About his computer?'

'It's not here. The chick I spoke to not mention that?'

'I wouldn't call DC Ziegler that to her face, mate. But yes,' Mae remembered, 'she did. You were expecting his laptop back though, right?'

Grohl shrugged. 'Just not like him to forget something like that. He's – what's the word – conscientious. But then, what happened with the drugs they found wasn't like him, either.'

'About that. Was there a reason you didn't mention that when you reported him missing?'

Suddenly interested in his shoes, he blew out his cheeks. 'Matt just … you know. Asked me to keep it on the down-low.'

'Right.' Mae made a note, then looked up. 'HR said something about a locker?'

Grohl nodded. 'Yeah, but it's not like high school, you don't have one allocated just for you. You just pick whatever's free in the morning. They're they kind you put a quid in. Surprising he used one at all, really.'

'Yeah? Why's that?'

He chuckled. 'Pretty easy to jimmy them open. I mean, if you had a baggy full of notes, wouldn't you keep it down your sock, or something?'

Mae lifted his eyes, very slowly, from the pad. 'Notes.' He waited. 'I'm assuming we're not talking Post-its.'

'Oh,' Grohl said slowly, the air visibly leaving his body. 'You didn't know about the money.'

'I did not. But I do now. Keep talking.'

'Last day Matt was in here – Monday? – he came back in to say cheers, you know. Bye. He came over here for his coat, and when he put it on, this baggy falls out of the inside pocket.' He rubbed his first two fingers and thumb together, international sign for cash. 'Twenties, all stacked up, like when you get them out the bank.'

'How much are we talking?'

He made a *pfff* sound and shrugged.

'Roughly? A grand? Five grand?'

'How the hell am I supposed to know? I work in a hospital, not a cartel. It's not like they pay in cash.'

Mae went for his phone, did a search for an image. He turned the screen round. 'This,' he said, 'is five grand, in twenties.'

'More than that. Maybe ten, then?'

'And do you know where it came from?'

A flick of the eyes then, decisively, 'No.'

'You're sure.'

'I could only guess.'

'But you do *have* a guess,' Mae encouraged, because the reluctance was coming off the bloke in clouds. 'Just speculation and conjecture. Won't tell a soul.'

Grohl leaned on what had been his colleague's favoured desk and rubbed a hand around in his stubble. 'You already know about the drugs.'

'The ones he lifted.'

'Yeah, those. I only know about that from my mate who works in the central pharmacy. Rutherford Wing. It's not being talked about, and Matt left quietly. Really quiet. No one's pressing charges.' He raised a meaningful eyebrow. 'Know what I mean?'

'You think he was paid off?' Mae turned it over in his mind, but stayed far from convinced. 'Surely it would have been in Matt's interest to keep quiet about it if the hospital was happy to let it go? Avoid a criminal record, for a start.'

'Maybe. But also, the big story really is how he managed to do it in the first place. Shoddy security. Tabloids love that sort of shit, right? And he's quiet, but he's also pretty smart. Why walk away empty-handed when you can use a secret to your own advantage?' He shrugged, just putting it out there.

'You're saying Matt threatened to spill the beans on his own crime? He *blackmailed* the hospital?'

'I'm not saying anything,' Grohl told him, dipping to pick a thread of lint from the immaculate floor. 'Speculation and conjecture, like you said.'

Chapter 27

Ellie

We met at the usual bench on the boundary of the estate, then went down to the path. It was always a little overgrown at this time of year, but it was no match for us. We both had our cuffs tucked into Gore-Tex gloves, and Mum had a machete. I'd always loved this part as a kid, scrambling after her as she swung the blade through the brambles. It made us fearless explorers, battling the jungle.

'Big one there,' she said over her shoulder and I ducked just in time to avoid a thick thorny vine swing back towards me.

The hems of my trousers were soaked by the time we were out the other side of the overgrowth. We stood together, brushing leaves and thorns from our clothes and breathing hard, our exhalations drifting on the cold air like fog into the clearing. The clean, woody scent of wet sang out everywhere: from the vegetation, the dew, the rain, the river.

Beyond the little clearing was a thicker perimeter of birches where the land gave way to the water. A newcomer might be surprised by the sudden majesty of the Thames, but I'd been there, on that exact route, so many times that I could pace the steps to the water's edge blindfolded. This place was ours.

We spread out the blanket and sat down, our backs against the bough, and she gestured for the bag and got out the flask.

'You going to start?' Mum asked me. 'You need to talk to her.'

I got up. 'Siggy,' I started, and I felt her watching me. 'I know you're angry. But we've come because ... because ...'

I gripped my eyes shut, feeling her blooming darkly inside me. When I opened them, Mum was standing in front of me. She took my hands, and searched my eyes.

'We come here because we want her to know we care about her.'

I folded my arms. 'We've been doing this for years. It doesn't make any difference. She's not going away, is she?'

Mum unscrewed the lid of the hot chocolate, poured a capful and handed it to me from her spot on the rug. 'We don't know that.'

'No? So where's Matt?'

She looked away. 'I don't think you should worry.'

'Really? Why are you pretending it's all fine when he's gone, and I'm covered in cuts and bruises and you're—' I gestured to her face, but couldn't articulate it. 'Look what she did to *you*.'

'I've had worse, love. I'll be fine.' She'd thrown the entire make-up arsenal at her damaged face before she'd gone to work but it was almost back to its natural state now. The swelling had maybe receded by a fraction, but the bruise was purple and intense. It was going to last her weeks.

I stared out to the river. 'She's getting stronger. We're losing.'

'Don't be dramatic. He's probably fine,' she said, reaching up for my hand.

The wind was picking up now, lifting the tendrils of steam from the plastic cups and dispersing them.

'I should have stayed well clear. Told him I was nuts and just walked away.'

She let the hand drop. 'You're not nuts.'

'No? Have you looked in a bloody mirror, Mum?'

'OK.' She shifted on the blanket, settled into an easy lotus. 'Let's go with your version for a minute. Let's say Siggy did take you there, down to his boat. He would have seen it was a fugue. He knows about the fugues.'

I shrugged miserably.

'And he would have stopped you.'

'How?'

'I don't know, but look at it realistically. He's what, six foot?'

'Six two.'

'And he's not a weakling. He goes to the gym.'

'So what? You work out pretty much every day of your life and look how that ended up!'

She got up again and came to me, hugging her arms over the top of mine, holding me in. 'Oh baby, OK. Calm down.'

I'd been trying so hard not to cry but something just juddered and broke and I lost.

'If she's done this, done the same to Matt that she did to Jodie—'

'Don't sweetheart. We don't know anything yet.'

'Yes we do.' I pulled away, wiped my eyes roughly with my cuff and swallowed. 'We do. It's what we both think, isn't it?'

'Come on. You're just assuming the worst.'

'... and you keep saying it wasn't me, but you're scared of me, Mum!'

The moment in which she could have told me it wasn't true came and went. We both saw it. She held me by the shoulders, looking into my eyes. 'I'm never, ever going to abandon you to this. I'm not.'

'What are we going to do?'

'I don't know. I mean – we *can* just start again. No,' she said, holding up a hand to stop me from interrupting. 'No. Listen to me. If you're that worried, let's just go. Move.' She gestured expansively. 'We can go anywhere. We've got nothing keeping us here.'

'So you *don't* think he's coming back.'

Her shoulders dropped. 'I'm not going to lie to you: there is a chance it's not good news. But we still have options. We still have each other.'

I opened my mouth, closed it again. I couldn't say it.

But her sad smile told me I didn't need to. 'I know I'm not enough, baby.'

'It's not that—'

'I get it. You're a grown woman. You need something more than your mum. But Ellie, love, sometimes people have to lead different lives. Some people aren't meant for normal relationships, you know? It doesn't mean we can't be happy. But maybe, until we figure out how to control her, we'd be safer keeping to ourselves.'

I picked up a stick and scratched in the dirt. 'I'm not just disappearing without finding him.'

There was a long silence before she spoke again.

'OK, fine. I understand. But maybe we're going to have to prepare ourselves for finding something we don't like.'

Chapter 28

Mae

McCulloch stuck her head into the corridor as Mae walked past and called him over.

'How's the baby bird?'

'Kit? Fine.'

Dipping her head to deliver a meaningful look she said, 'You're being nice?'

'I'm being exemplary.'

'Good.' Her phone started to ring, and she made to go back in to answer it, before changing her mind. 'Any developments on the misper? You weren't exactly garrulous in the briefing.'

Matthew Corsham's disappearance, or whatever it was, had been an AOB item, and half the shift were already getting up and heading off. 'We're just doing some background work on the bloke. Looks like he was caught thieving at work and got himself summarily P45'd, so there might well be a charge, if we find him.'

She nodded, her chunky curls bobbing around her face. 'But he's still low-risk, you think?'

'Yep.'

McCulloch was confused. 'You're on a decent slab of cases, aren't you, Ben?'

It was one way of putting it. He hadn't put the promised calls in about Damien Hayes, and although Corsham was the only new one this week, there were follow-ups due for a dozen other actives.

'But this one's been top of your to-do? How come?'

Her eyeline shifted to the door, and Mae turned to see Kit Ziegler standing behind him.

'Catherine. We were just talking about your missing person. Progress?'

Kit cleared her throat. 'Main problem is he was a loner, so we've hardly anyone who knew him, apart from the girlfriend.'

Mae tightened his jaw. *Don't say the name.*

McCulloch nodded. 'And the mother. Anything useful from her?'

'No, can't get hold of either parent. It was the *girlfriend's* mother we spoke to, actually,' Kit corrected her.

Don't say it. Please.

Kit shoved her hands in her back pockets. 'But neither of the Powers have yielded much yet, to be honest.'

Bollocks.

Mae opened his eyes as McCulloch slowly moved her gaze over to his.

'*Powers,*' she said. Delivered it with a stare that turned his fingernails blue.

Kit nodded, then looked to Mae, and back again. 'Something wrong?' she said, then she glanced into her boss's office. 'Ma'am, your phone's ringing.'

McCulloch blinked, pressed her fingers against her temples, then crossed to her desk. 'I'll come and see you in a moment,' she said, before lifting the receiver.

Kit waited until they were in the corridor before she voiced her confusion. 'What was that all about?'

'No idea.'

She paused at the coffee machine. 'Want one?'

'I like my goats' piss seasonal and organic.'

Laughing, Kit slotted her coins in to the machine. 'Seriously, though?' she went on, pressing the buttons for what was promised to be a latte. 'She looked like she was going to take your head off.'

Mae shrugged, spread his hands like he was fucked if he knew, but it wasn't without a sheen of guilt. Protocol had little to say on the matter, but he knew he should at least have cleared it with McCulloch. From the outset she had been supportive, even when, after the Arden case fell apart, the brass were just as happy to let him go as they had been to hang his DS out to dry. But McCulloch had fought his corner: it was DS Heath who'd been responsible for the misconduct, not Mae. She repeated it whenever the cause arose: to him, to her peers, even to Internal Affairs.

Not your fault, Ben. She was very unstable. DS Heath – she never called him Ian, not anymore – DS Heath messed up. It wasn't because of you.

'You all right, Sarge?' Kit asked.

He unclenched his shoulders, forced a smile. Kit shrugged, satisfied, and retrieved the brown plastic cup from the machine and took a sip.

'Holy actual fuck,' she said, grimacing. 'It literally does taste like goat piss.'

Mae started filling her in on the deal at the hospital when her phone rang. She took it, speaking in *yeahs* and *rights* followed by a few *thanks* at the end. As she hung up she turned to face him, her expression buzzing.

'One of my buddies on Traffic,' she said. 'I had them run a VIN search, and guess what it turned up?'

'Corsham's car?'

'Corsham's car. 1989 Golf Cabriolet. Burnt out round the back of the old cinema site in Feltham.'

Charles Cox Psychotherapy Ltd.	
Clinical audio recording transcript	
Patient name:	*Eleanor Power*
Session date:	*10 Septembert 2006*

CC: Welcome again, Ellie.

EP: Thanks. Hi. Should I … do you want me to lie down this time?

CC: Well, it's up to you. I've put these cushions here so you have the option if you feel that you'd be able to get into more of a relaxed state by … yes, there is fine, I just move this over … here. OK. Comfortable?

EP: Yeah. Fine.

CC: So today we're going to try a bit more of a guided session, if you're still happy to do that.

EP: I wouldn't exactly call it happy but OK.

CC: [Laughs] All right. So in a minute we're going to listen to a recorded relaxation guide. What we're trying to do is calm your mind and see if we can connect in some way with the sort of feelings that Siggy tends to have.

EP: OK.

CC: So let's start by naming a few of those feelings. You've said before that Siggy often feels very angry, is that the right … would you describe her that way?

EP: I think so. But probably even more scared than angry.

CC: Scared. Tell me about that.

EP: She kind of … she always wants to check everything, make sure things are safe, kind of. She doesn't trust people.

CC: OK. Good. So we're going to listen now to the guide, and see if we can create a very safe, calm place for her to surface. Let me just stop this a moment—

[recording paused] [recording resumed]

CC: All right. I want you to stay as relaxed as you are now. We're not forcing Siggy to do anything, and we're not fighting her.

EP: Mmm.

CC: So when you're ready, I'd like you to let me know if Siggy is feeling anything particularly. Just let it come, let your body do nothing at all.

[pause: 12 sec]

EP: She's frightened.

CC: OK. That's all right. So just bring that feeling to the front of your mind. No rush. Let's very gently try to bring this fear into focus. Keep your eyes closed. See if we can help her find what it is she's frightened of. See if we can locate the danger.

[pause: 41 sec]

CC: I'm noticing your breathing is getting faster.

EP: It's like, uh, tightness? Here.

CC: In your chest? OK. Can you tell me anything else that you're feeling, any other sensations?

[pause: 23 sec]

EP: Like everything getting small. I want to be small. Hide.

CC: OK. Let's stay with that feeling. There's something or someone that you want to hide from. If you can, I want you to take a step back now from yourself and tell me what else is near you, what else is around that might be adding to this feeling of fear.

EP: It-it hurts.

CC: It hurts. You're feeling pain.

EP: Everywhere. All across — all down my — down my back and my legs.

CC: Is there anything you can say about where this pain came from?

[pause: 32 sec]

CC: I'm seeing you still trying to make yourself small, and you're closing your eyes very tight there.

EP: I-I don't want to look. I-I need help.

CC: Yes. You need help, you're hurt and need someone to be there to help you. Is there anyone there to help you? Is there anyone you know there?

EP: No.

CC: You're on your own? If you can try to slow your breathing now, try to make your face relax a little. Can you do that?

EP: I can't see my mum.

[pause: 24 sec]

EP: I can't see anyone else.
CC: Can you tell me why you're whispering?

[pause: 27 sec]

CC: Ellie?

[pause: 23 sec]

CC: Siggy?
EP: [whispers] Because if I scream, he'll find me.

Chapter 30

Ellie

It was gone three by the time we got back to civilization. Mum had to get back to relieve her colleague, so I took the bus home alone. The afternoon had only got colder, and I was soaked from the trip to the woods, cold hardening in my feet as I sat shivering on the top deck.

I got off the bus and crossed the dual carriageway. I didn't see the girl until she was nearly on top of me.

'Ellie! Oh my *god*!'

It took me a moment to place her, because she was wearing spray-on jeans and a bobble hat, instead of the pyjamas or hospital gowns I'd always seen her in.

'Natalya.' She had been on the kids' ward, one of the oldest there. 'How are you doing?' I shoved my hands quickly into my pockets to hide the bandage.

'Waaaay better,' she said, rolling her big eyes. She was beautiful in an unselfconscious way, with a bouncy Barbie figure that must have had all the boys slouching after her like wolves. She was what, fifteen? She'd always reminded me of Jodie, the energy that shone out of her. 'How are you? Still help out in the hospital?'

'Yeah, kind of.' I made a vague gesture and tried to leave, but she grabbed my sleeve.

'Listen, I'm so glad I saw you.' She pushed her hair back from her face and I caught a glimpse of the reason she'd been on the ward. A boiler had burst in the flat above her family's. Her face had avoided the torrent of boiling water, but her body would tell the story of it for the rest of her life.

'All right,' she said, self-consciously smoothing her hair back over her scars, 'you don't need to stare.'

'I'm ... sorry,' I said, horrified that I'd been caught. 'I thought it would be ... nothing. Sorry.' It was the first time I'd seen her injuries unbandaged, and I was struck by their vivid colour, their smoothness: nothing like the colourless alien landscape of my own burns, but then, I suppose, mine were more than a decade older.

She straightened her shoulders, a little indignant. 'Look, you know Matt, right?'

I nodded uncertainly.

'Cool!' she said, brightening. 'So look. He said he'd show me the lab some time, and I lost his number.'

'He gave you his *number*?'

'Sure! He's awesome. I met him in the cafeteria one time, and he came up to the ward once or twice, after you started coming.'

'You do mean Matt. Matthew Corsham. Tall guy?'

'Oh god I *know*. Really cute! So, do you have it? His number? Or his address, actually? He said he'd show me the boat. He lives in a boat, right?' Then, 'Are you OK?'

I walked away, fast. I broke into a run. She shouted after me, telling me to stop, then shifting into insults.

'Jesus! Fucking *nutcase*!'

I ran until I couldn't hear her anymore.

He said he'd show her the boat?

My heart was thudding fiercely by the time I got to the door, fumbling with the new lock. I slammed it behind me, hard, and closed my eyes, trying to get my breath back. I was furious.

Natalya had already been on the ward for a month by the time I started volunteering. Our chats were never exactly heart-to-hearts but I knew I'd mentioned her to Matt. I searched my memory. Had he ever told me he'd spoken to her? No, I was sure of it. Not a peep.

So what else did he keep from me?

My eyes lighted on the radiator shelf, where Mum had put his pile of post, and I remembered that it had been bills. There was a phone bill.

I needed that bill.

I checked the pockets of the big hoody in case I'd imagined taking it out, but it wasn't there. Would Mum have tidied them? I checked the living room, but the table was clear, nothing on or under the sofa or the cushions. The bins? Not the bins. Not magneted to the fridge, not in my room. I searched Mum's room, feeling a twinge of unease as I did it. But still I found nothing.

I exhausted everywhere I could think of and ended up back where I had started, confused. Maybe she'd already spoken to the police about the car, and given them the post in person? Surely not. She would have told me. I pressed my palms against my temples – think, *think* – and when I opened my eyes, I was looking at Mum's coat, her blue duffle. I pulled it off the hook, felt in the pockets. There was loose change, an eyeliner, bus tickets. In the inside pocket, sealed with a zip, was the post.

I spread it out on the floor and found the phone bill. Having nothing sharp handy, I tore a hole and slit the envelope open with my finger. Quickly, before I bottled it. I slid the sheets out and read. In an instant, the anger disappeared.

I saw him shake his head at me, despairing, that I could be moved to tears by a phone bill. But I saw him – his quiet care, his reliability – here on this sheet of paper. A £15 contract, every call made consciously so he wouldn't spend money he didn't have. The lengths of calls varied, but the costs were always billed the same: £0.00.

Except – except *that one*, on the eleventh of November – £6.88. An international call, a prefix I didn't recognize. I pulled out my mobile and punched the number in, checked it, pressed green. A recorded voice told me I had insufficient credit. I grabbed the list stared at it again, willing something to leap out at me. But nothing did. I'd just have to do it the hard way.

Starting from the top, I rang the numbers. Those I recognized I skipped, and those I called I hung up on when I realized what they were. He'd called the same few numbers: his work, the Chinese place we used sometimes, the number of the camera shop he'd been to-ing and fro-ing with about a repair of his Rolleiflex. Nothing of interest, nothing revealing.

Until – *there*.

I straightened, muttered the number under my breath: it was *beyond* familiar. He'd made a twenty-minute call to it, the same day, the same afternoon as the international call. Seven days ago. Then again, two days later, eleven minutes. I had to be sure. I tapped the number into my keypad and pressed the phone to my ear. As the tone sounded, a siren in my head, I flipped back over the bill. In the course of the month, he'd rung that same number fourteen times.

The same number that Matt shouldn't have known at all.

The call connected.

'You've reached the mobile of Dr Charles Cox,' the recorded voice said. 'Please leave a message.'

Chapter 31

Mae

He'd dispatched Kit to check out what was left of Matthew Corsham's car, and taken the lull to get started on the backlog. He checked in with his counterpart at Thames Valley, who was stressed to his eyeballs dealing with the press over a family on the run from social services, But half an hour in, Mae's stomach remembered lunch. He unfolded himself from the chair and jogged down to ground level, against the tide. The canteen was out of pretty much everything, but he settled for a tuna sandwich washed down with tea. As he pushed his tray away, his phone rumbled gently on the tabletop: a text from Nadia about a Parent's Evening, which in turn reminding him to call Bear's teacher.

The office answered on the first ring, and put him through to the staffroom.

'I'm calling about Dominica Kwon Mae,' he said, his daughter's proper name sounding more alien than ever in his mouth.

There was a long, low sigh. 'Ah yes. I did wonder when I might hear from you.'

She'd have to try harder than that if she wanted to wind him up. He explained that he had only just been made aware of the problem his daughter was experiencing at school.

'Let me just stop you there,' the woman said. 'We're not

discussing a one-way street, here, in case you're under that impression. Dominica has been very – ah – vocal in her descriptions of the year six boys in question.'

'Oh yeah?' He stood up, swept the crumbs into the sandwich box, and drained the last of his tea.

'More than one of the children has been repeatedly called a ...' she paused, dropped her voice to a whisper, 'a *dickhead*.'

Stifling a chuckle, he balanced the tray on his free hand and took it over to the rack. 'OK. Well, is he?'

'Is who, what?'

Out to the corridor. 'Is the boy in question a dickhead? Because what I'm hearing here is an adult defending a bunch of kids who've singled out a girl, a much younger girl, and focusing on the fact that she's fighting back. To be honest, Mrs—'

'Collins,' came the tight reply.

'Mrs Collins, it sounds to me like Dominica is reacting like this because the adults that her mother and I have entrusted to care for her are letting her down. Big time.'

There was a pause that suggested she was unused to being spoken to firmly. 'Well,' she said at last, 'I'm sorry you feel that way, but I can promise you we do our best to create a reliable environment. Especially for our students whose home life is ...' she paused, as if choosing her words, 'a little rocky.'

He gave up on the diplomatic bullshit after that and demanded a parlay with the head, for which he was perfunctorily booked in. Just before he hung up, Collins delivered her parting shot.

'I assume you do know, Mr Kwon Mae, that Dominica has expressed a preference for the surname Marston here, the same as her mother. I understand it's not her official name at this stage but it might avoid confusion to use that.'

Mae ended the call with maximum efficiency by throwing

the phone at the floor. It bounced once then, naturally, skidded under a water fountain.

A run, he thought after he'd retrieved it, heading to his locker in the basement without a second thought. The only solution. Still enough time to get a few K in, if he rushed the shower. He pulled on his trainers, laced them up hard. Needed to get out of there before he fucking burst.

Marston. *Fuck's* sake.

He snapped his headphones on, found some early Dre on the iPod and ratcheted it up until the base shook straight through to his spine. He filled his water bottle, then dressed: vest, hoodie, tracky bottoms.

And out.

A grey drizzle dusted his face as he stepped outside the building. He headed right, out of the squat, cramped grids of suburbia and towards the North Circular, dropped his gait and picked up the pace.

He ran past the fifteen-minute cut-off he'd set, knowing that any further would mean a late return. But he kept going, twenty minutes, twenty-five, ignoring the rain that got harder as he went. No real plan in his head, just lefting and righting, the same as how he'd learned the city when he'd arrived from Sussex, weaving a nice mess to untangle on the homeward leg. But he couldn't shake it, the feeling that Bear was lost somehow, that he hadn't fought hard enough and now she was hardly his anymore.

Somewhere past Willesden Junction, his phone rang. He silenced the music and dropped to a jog. It was Ellie Power.

'I've found something,' she said. 'I've got his phone bill. Matt was talking to Dr Cox.'

Mae stopped jogging. '*Your* Dr Cox.'

'Yeah.'

'Did you know they were in contact?'

'No. But it's the date. The last time they spoke. I looked it up and I remember something: I heard Matt arguing with someone, on the phone. He said it was someone from back in Scotland, but I've looked, and there's no other personal numbers from that day. I think it must have been him. Cox.'

Mae ran his hand over the stubble on his head. Then he remembered Kit's discovery. 'We found his car. It was up on some derelict land in Feltham, abandoned it, looks like. Do you know of any reason he might have taken it there, assuming it was Matt who drove it?'

There was no answer. He took the phone from his ear for a moment to check the call was still connected. 'Ellie, did you hear what—?'

'Yeah, I heard you.' Her voice was low and weak: she sounded terrified.

'Is there any reason you can think of that—?'

'*No*. He's never said anything about Feltham.' She was breathing hard now. 'But you're going to follow this up, right? About him speaking to Cox?'

'Ellie, what were you doing with his bill in the first—?'

'You said you wanted to help me. So help me.'

He kissed his teeth thinking, *bloody hell*.

They agreed that she would send over a copy of the bill to his phone. Mae brought up the maps app and set the GPS to find his quickest route to the nick.

His footsteps echoed wetly as he entered the empty shower area. He chose one and turned the squeaky tap, bracing himself for the few seconds of icy cold before the hot came through. He turned his face to the water, opening his mouth, filling, spitting.

Cox. Everything Mae remembered about him – the man whose very credentials he had suspected right from the beginning – came crashing back as the water sluiced away the sweat.

The fact that he had been seeing Lucy Arden, Jodie's mother. That he had admitted, days into the investigation, that he had been screwing Jodie, too.

Bollock naked and dripping, Mae dried his hands on a towel and checked the inbox on his phone. The photo of the bill was waiting for him: Ellie had highlighted the number every time it appeared. A quick google just to make sure Ellie wasn't mistaken led him to Cox's surprisingly basic website. It told Mae he still had the clinic space he'd had back then, the first floor of a smart Victorian redbrick just off Highbury Fields. There was a landline number, but Mae went straight for the mobile that matched Matt's bill. The call was answered on the third ring.

'Dr Charles Cox,' he said, a subtle lilt of laughter just trailing from his voice. Mae was, he guessed, supposed to infer that he had just finished delivering a hilarious anecdote to a saunaful of dressing-gowned admirers.

The lilt disappeared completely once Mae introduced himself, of course. He had that way with people.

Chapter 32

Ellie

The moment Mae hung up, I ran outside. Across the road, down the alley, out towards the estate. I saw, with my heart clanging in my chest, that he was right: Matt's car was gone.

I walked back along the pavement on autopilot, trying to piece it together. The way he'd spoken about it, it couldn't have been Mum who had called it in to the police. So had the car been *stolen*, then? Or had Matt just come back for it? As I turned into our street I stepped off the kerb without checking the road. A silver van slammed on its brakes and missed me by about a foot. I jerked back, put my hands up to apologize, but the driver, unseen behind tinted windows, accelerated away from me.

An hour later, Mum came back. I told her about the car. Calmly, she took off her coat, hung it up, went into the kitchen and unlocked the cupboard for the kettle. I asked her the question about the car directly, and I got a direct answer.

'No,' she said. 'I didn't call the police.'

'What? Why?'

She didn't answer.

'So, what … I need to know what happened, Mum! This is just—' I stopped, scrunched my eyes shut for a second. 'It's driving me nuts. I nearly got run over earlier, I'm not thinking straight.'

She put the kettle on the worktop, unfilled. Looked at me.

'What?' I asked her. She looked different than she had before. Beleaguered.

Her eyes stayed on me for a long time before she said, 'We both know what happened.'

'What? I thought you said—'

'I've been thinking about it all. What you said earlier, about Siggy getting stronger.' She leaned against the worktop and I saw for the first time how depleted she looked. Exhaustion pulled at the swells of skin under her eyes, and the slight distention behind the bruising on her jaw drew the shape of her face into something I couldn't look at. Something old. 'I'm worried you're right.'

'But you've been saying all along that—'

'I haven't been completely truthful, baby.'

I went cold. 'What do you mean?'

She looked up at the ceiling, sighed, and left the room. She came back carrying a bag, and pulled something out. Fabric, caked in mud. But not so caked that I couldn't immediately recognize it as mine.

'Your raincoat. I found it at the moorings.'

I shook my head, unable to speak.

'You were there. That night.'

She held my raincoat out, but I couldn't take it. Couldn't even look at it.

'I just really wanted to think that there was another explanation.' Mum set the coat on the worktop gently, like an unexploded bomb. She took my hands. 'It was me. I got rid of the car. I needed to buy us some time. But we've got to face facts.'

'Mum, don't. Please.' I felt for the back of a wooden chair and sat down.

'Here's what's happened,' she said, staying on her feet. 'We thought Siggy had stopped, but she hasn't. I thought, when you were little, that if we focused on being gentle and kind and letting you express whatever part of yourself you wanted to express, that Siggy would go away. It's my fault, love. I wanted so badly for it to be OK that I was blind to it, even after Jodie, and everything. Convinced myself, even though none of the therapy and the regressions and the exercises and all of that *stuff* that didn't work, I convinced *you* that as long as we were careful, maybe we could be all right. We did try, didn't we?'

I thought of all the sacrifices she'd made, the job she'd given up so she could take better care of me, how we'd had to move so many times. Then after Jodie, how even though the case was closed, we knew it would only take one witness, one new piece of evidence. So we hid. We kept our heads down, and resigned ourselves to a life of just the two of us. No friends, no partners. No exceptions. Because when we let people in, bad things happened.

'We *did* try,' she said. 'But it didn't work out that way for us. I'm sorry, Ellie.' She lifted one of my hands and I let her do it, and her kiss was cold on the backs of my fingers. 'But this is where we are. She has got bigger and badder than we thought she could get. Jodie is dead, because of her. And now Matt—'

She broke off, settled herself with a breath. 'We've got to leave, love. I really think we have to go. Really *leave* this time.'

'Go where?'

'I don't know! Away! Anywhere!'

'I can't. We have to know what happened. I need … I don't know. *Proof.*'

'What more proof do you need? Look at everything we know. Look at your hand! Look at your bloody *neck*!'

'I'm not just leaving, Mum. I love him.'

'He's gone, Ellie!' she shouted. 'For god's sake open your eyes!'

I'd had enough of her. I went into the living room and sank into the sofa. Try as I might not to catastrophize, the fact of the matter was that Mum, my one ally through all of it, had given up hope. I was bonetired, weary to the marrow, my thoughts clanging against each other.

'Right,' she said, coming in. 'You need to sleep.' She held her hand out and instinctively I took it, but then she was pulling me up.

'I just want to sit for a bit,' I told her.

But she got hold of my other hand. 'No. *I* need to put myself first for once. I need to have a bath, and a glass of wine, and to be able to relax.'

'You can, Mum, go ahead.'

'No. Come with me.'

'What are you doing?' I said, confused, trying to pull my arms back.

But she held tight. 'I need to plan. I can't do anything if you're still out here. You might fall asleep, and I don't want to get punched again.'

Her eyes flicked up suddenly to meet mine, shocked at what she had said, but then she hardened. I hadn't seen the line in the sand, didn't even know there was one. But I had crossed it now. We had both crossed it.

'Do you know what? I have given everything to you.' Her voice was controlled and firm now, but her face was flushed, and tears balled against her lids and broke down her cheeks. 'I love you so much. *So* much, and you give *nothing* back. All I'm asking is to have one, *safe* evening in my own home. OK? So you're going,' she said, tugging me hard towards my room, 'to come. With. Me.'

Then, loud as a shout, Siggy sounded in my head.

STOP IT

'*Stop it!*'

When it happened, we both gasped, and stood rooted to the spot. Panting.

Something had propelled me forward. Something had lifted my hand, and hit her, hard, across the face.

Mum clasped her hand across her temple. 'Was that her?'

I opened my mouth to speak, but then I saw the blood. On the corner of her eyebrow.

'Was that *her*, Ellie?' The blood welled, the droplet split, and a thin, red trail crept down her cheek.

But it wasn't Siggy. I was wide awake.

It was me.

Chapter 33

Mae

Just before Hammersmith, the District line train descended into the tunnel system. Mae's window became a mirror in the darkness, his own eyes staring back at him where seconds ago there had been the terraced brick backs of houses. He looked away, massaged the aching masseter muscles on the angle of his jaw. A tube map near the curved roof of the train told him he had maybe a half hour journey. Seven stops to Green Park, change onto the Victoria line, short hop to Highbury & Islington, then a ten, fifteen-minute walk to the clinic.

The last time he'd been up there, it had been after the search team had taken the place apart. Cox had tried to fight the warrant, citing patient confidentiality as if it would stand up against a charge of child abduction. The search had been in vain in the end: nothing was found that hadn't already been established by the paper trail of Cox's furtive seduction of his girlfriend's daughter. What had started as just a bookending of Ellie's sessions deepened into something far more regular, far more intimate. Dozens of receipts, scores of notes, hundreds of text messages built up a hedonistic story of late nights in bars Jodie shouldn't have even been served in, hotels that should have raised the alarm, but whose receptionists invariably deferred to Cox's immutable charm.

Jodie never told her mother that she'd wound up sleeping with Cox. It had been up to Mae and Ian Heath to tell her that.

It was fair to say, he could admit now, that Cox's personality had contributed to the vitriol with which Heath had pursued him. The doctor was smug, arrogant, self-righteous even in the face of what most people would experience as crippling shame. But for every adjective Mae could fling at him, Cox's complaint against Heath – and, by extension, Mae himself – offered an opposite claim. The police had been aggressive, Cox had argued, even after the CPS dropped the case. *Insulting, personal, crass. Unnecessarily intimidating.*

Part of Mae said maybe Cox had a point.

The other part was louder and it said, *fuck him*.

Five minutes to six and Mae was emerging onto the black, rain-glossed pavements of N5. He kept to an easy pace, making the south corner of Highbury Park by the time the bells at the Christ Church a few blocks away rang the hour. Mae located the door, then depressed the buzzer next to the *COX PSYCHOTHERAPY* engraved in the polished brass plate beside the heavy-looking door.

The receptionist cheerfully answered the buzzer, but her demeanour changed when he gave his name.

'Oh, so it *is* you,' she said when he arrived at the first-floor reception.

'Samira, right?' Mae asked, her name coming back to him in a rush. He hadn't expected Cox to have retained the same receptionist – he seemed the kind to value anonymity over familiarity – but here she was.

She nodded, anxiety edging across her face. 'Yes, but, look. Does he know you're coming?'

Before he had a chance to answer, the door behind her opened.

'Detective.'

Unlike his receptionist, Cox had aged terribly. In 2006, he'd been the definition of dashing: all teeth and a smile that went from nothing to a hundred watts at every opportunity, as if he was expecting a film crew. Mae remembered him looking more like a corporate lawyer than a psychotherapist: silk shirts obviously selected to showcase the well-maintained pectorals beneath them; flashes of bespoke turquoise or violet lining to his charcoal suits.

Not anymore.

The blond in his hair was resigning itself to grey, and the former glow of his skin had abandoned him. His cheeks were hollow, his eyes dull, and as he brought his fingers up to rake across his scalp, Mae recognized the tell-tale tremble of the habitual drinker. It was true that the case against him had crumbled, but it only took a glance to see there were other ways to pay a price.

'Do come in,' he said, then, to the receptionist, 'Samira, you won't need to stay.'

He showed Mae into his office, a tiny room with none of the pomp and prestige promised by the exterior.

'What happened to the oak-panelling?' Mae asked, looking around.

Cox settled behind his desk in a high-backed leather chair that fitted the room even less in size than it did in style, and levelled him with a chilly glare. 'You mean the parlour. First floor: I sublet it. Same as all the other rooms in the building, actually.'

Mae folded his arms. 'Business not what it was?'

'Do you want to try that again without the glee?'

'Not really.'

Cox assayed him for a moment, then shrugged. 'Business has been catastrophic, since you ask,' he said, before pulling out a drawer of his desk. 'A few patients a week if I'm lucky. Samira comes for a day here and there, primarily out of innate benevolence, given that I miss her payments half the time.' He straightened, lifted a half-bottle of supermarket vodka on the table and without a hint of shame, unscrewed the cap and dumped a third of it into a mug. Then he sank it, eyeing Mae over the rim with a flash of defiance. Swallowing, he said, 'But I trust you haven't come all this way to exchange pleasantries.'

Something unexpected, uninvited, was eroding the sharp edges of Mae's contempt, and it took him until Cox had refilled the mug to work out that it was pity.

'I said on the phone why I was coming.' Mae took the other chair, a plastic swivel not unlike his own back at the nick, and tented his fingers.

Cox nodded. 'You do missing persons these days.'

'Looking for Matthew Corsham. You had a phone conversation with him shortly before he went missing.'

Cox positioned the mug in front of him, lined the handle up just so. 'You do understand, I hope, that I'm not able to divulge information about a client unless you have a court order demanding that I do so.'

'He was a *client*, you're saying?'

Cox gave him a weary look. 'We don't have to dance around the common denominator here. Eleanor Power. That's why he came to me, that's why *you're* here now.'

'No. I'm here to establish his whereabouts, Dr Cox.'

He leaned back. 'I can't help you.'

Mae reclined too, mirroring him. He wasn't in any rush. 'Let's look at this another way. Our mutual friend Ellie—'

'She calls you a friend now, does she?'

'Says she had no idea you and Matthew knew each other.'

'As it should be. This is what we in the trade know as *confidentiality*. It's a code of conduct thing. Oh,' he said with hand held up in mock apology, 'forgive me, jargon. A *code of conduct* is a—'

'I know what a code of conduct is.'

Cox refreshed his mug, swallowed. A silence followed that Mae could have chucked a fridge into and never heard a splash.

Eventually: 'What were you discussing with him, Charles?'

'I fail to see how that could be of interest to you. *Ben.*'

'No? Well, let me set that out for you. He wasn't a big one for talking on the phone. Girlfriend, work, takeaway: that was pretty much it. But he did talk to *you* a few days before he apparently vanished. And it so happens that you played a major part in a missing person case involving the same witness five years ago.'

After an admirable battle, Cox set his jaw and broke eye contact.

'So I'll ask you again,' Mae went on, 'before I have to go away and get your goddamned court order as you know perfectly well I will. What were you talking about? Ellie?'

'Eleanor Power has not been a client of mine for a long time. Years. There's a little breach in my confidentiality for you: she's not under my care anymore.'

'Is that so?' Mae leaned back. He had plenty of time. 'Because the way I understood it, when she was released from hospital she was discharged specifically to you.'

The bafflement Mae felt when he discovered Ellie's mental health section had been lifted had only been compounded when he discovered she'd been discharged from hospital, with

Christine's permission, into Cox's care. Cox, who'd seen Ellie for months without Christine's knowledge. Who had, in Christine's words, set Ellie's progress back by years. It made precisely as much sense now as it did then.

'That was a long time ago.' The doctor sighed and examined his hands. 'Even if I was predisposed to breaking my clinical oaths, I would have informed Matthew that the policy of this clinic is to destroy all patient records two years after discharge.'

Mae sighed. But there was more than one way to skin a cat. 'What I want to do here is eliminate you from my list of people to be concerned about. I want to go home, and say, right: Dr Cox isn't a red flag. But I can't do that if I've got you sitting here being obstructive about a fairly simple question, can I? That sort of thing means I have to get other people involved. I'd have to get a local bobby round to park outside your house in a police car and ask you a lot of questions, which would hardly be a good thing if you still live on that nice street. Which was it, Tongdean Road? Even worse if it happens while your neighbours are all out getting their kids into the car for school.'

A single note of a bitter laugh. 'I live in a one-bed above a Ladbrokes. I sold that house five years ago to pay my legal fees.'

'Right.' Mae clicked his neck.

After a wait: 'This sounds a lot like blackmail.'

'Does it now.'

Cox brought the items on his desk into orderly lines, then met Mae's eyes. 'And you'll go away if I give you the simple answer.'

'Yes. Yes, I will,' he said, trying not to sound too keen. 'What did he want?'

'Matthew Corsham had an interest in my field.'

'Dissociative disorders?'

Cox flinched, nodded. 'And I told him I no longer have anything to do with that.'

Mae frowned. 'How come? You're the country's go-to man, right? One of?'

'Was.' He refreshed his vodka, drank it off like it was milk. 'Ellie Power was my final case of that kind. Haven't touched it since.'

'That sounds like a very short conversation. What else did you talk about?'

'He was concerned about her mental health. He wanted access to her records, but I had to refuse. So we talked in *general* about symptomatology, causation, pharmacology.'

Mae's text alert sounded, and he brought the phone out to silence it. But the message was short enough for him to read on the home screen: from Kit, saying just:

Glug glug glug!

He supressed a smile – weird way of inviting someone for a drink, but he wasn't going to complain – and pocketed the phone. 'You spoke to him over the phone?'

'Yes.'

'And in person?'

'Yes.'

'How many times?'

'I don't know.'

'OK. *I don't know* isn't going to be enough, you see. Was it once? Twenty times?'

'A few,' Cox said, shaking the hair back from his forehead and raising his eyes to the ceiling. 'The last time would have been around week ago.'

'And that was where, here?'

'No. At my flat. I told you, he was persistent.'

'And you maintain that in these *few* conversations you discussed general psychology?'

'Yes. That and the principles of privacy.'

Taking the strategic decision to stand, unball his fists and lock his hands behind his back at this point, Mae said: 'Seems to me we're done here.'

'Seems that way.'

Mae made to leave, then remembered something.

'Did he bring a laptop with him, when you saw him?'

Cox frowned, touched his fingertips to his temples as if divining the answer. 'I don't know, possibly. Why?'

'Did he have it the last time you saw him?'

He squinted. 'Apologies, I—' he started, casting a glance at the bottle on the desk. 'My memory's not exactly ...'

'Fine. Never mind. But there's nothing else that you can think of that would help us? Nothing at all?'

It only took a split second, an almost undetectable movement of Cox's eyes, towards the floor and back up again.

Then, 'No. Nothing else.'

Mae could have not seen it. But he did.

Chapter 34

Ellie

In the end I went quietly. We didn't even say goodnight. It was far too early to turn in but by the time she'd come out of the bathroom, I was in bed. She glanced through my door long enough for me to see the butterfly stitches she'd stuck across the cut on her eyebrow, and then she locked me in. There was the sound of something heavy dragging across the hall carpet, its journey ending outside my door, and then silence.

I turned to face the wall and bunched my knees up, listening, knowing I was hours from sleep. I read, tidied, painted my toenails. Twenty minutes before ten, I heard the sound of the flush, her footsteps pausing briefly outside my door. Her bedroom door closing softly.

My indignation subsided, I was seized with a moment of terrible sadness for her: a bath and a glass of wine being her greatest vice. There had been no hint of a romantic relationship since my dad. Once, I'd suggested dating again, even with a false name if she was worried about our anonymity.

'I know everything I need to know about men from your father,' she'd told me darkly, and that was the end of the conversation, full stop.

I played around with my phone for a while, trying out possible passwords to get into Matt's email, but without success. After a while, the battery died, and I flipped the covers back and got up to hunt for my charger before remembering it was in Mum's room. No way was I going to ask.

Suddenly aware of the cold, I went back to my bed. I reached out to pull the duvet back over myself when a noise made me freeze. Quiet, urgent knocking. The front door.

A squeak, and then 'Miss', whispered loudly through the letterbox.

I put my ear to my door, breathing shallow and silent through my mouth. My first thought: the police. They'd found Matt. But the police don't whisper through letterboxes. Fingers flat against the door, I weighed up my options. If I shouted, would they hear me? And even if they did, what would I say?

'I need to talk to you,' the voice said again. A man, but I couldn't place the age. Not a native Londoner. 'Miss. Are you there?'

Then I got it. It was Piotr, Mr Symanski's son.

I was about to call out when I heard the slam of the letterbox's metal flap against the door, and feet on the steps. Another voice, a low-voiced exchange further from the door that I had no chance of deciphering, and after that, a door closing. Mr Symanski's door.

I stayed where I was, unmoving, listening. Movement in the flat below, a door slamming, and muffled bursts of voices. I dropped to my knees, lay down with my ear against the carpet. I could make out what I guessed was Mr Symanski's voice and that of his son, but though I could hear the heat in their alter-cation I couldn't understand a word.

I went to my window.

A low, single-story addition to Mr Symanski's place below meant there was a narrow, flat section of their roof just beyond where I stood. At the edge of that roof, there was a drop to the street, and there was no railing.

If I was careful and dangled at full length before I let go of the edge, I could reduce that drop to a couple of feet.

I dressed fast. Jeans, bra, shoes, jumper, hoody. I opened the window, and I climbed out and along to the edge of the roof without looking back.

I turned, brought my legs and the lower part of my torso over the edge, then eased myself down. The impact jarred hard on my knees and I fell back onto my bottom, scraping my hands when I instinctively flung them out behind me. But I was on the ground. I took a step back, gave half a thought to the window I'd left open in my excitement, and I laughed out loud.

Chapter 35

Mae

As he rounded the final corner before Kit's street, it occurred to him that maybe this was a bit weird. The heat from the takeout boxes burned as they brushed against his leg and he longed for a table to set it down on. He slowed up. Reassessed.

It was gone ten o'clock. He'd left a message replying to hers, and he'd texted, twice, to ask where they should meet. But no reply. So he'd looked her up remotely on the system and found her house. Discovered that it wasn't beyond the realms of possibility, even, that he could be dropping round to hers on his way back home. With a bottle of Chablis and a few boxes of food from the best takeaway in the borough. Casually.

But now, thinking about it as he walked, looking for number 128: she'd probably have already eaten. Or, what if she just plain couldn't stand Indonesian. Or had meant another night, or had gone to bed. Or changed her mind.

A few doors ahead, the garden lit up and laughter tumbled out. Four, five voices, women's voices, the sound pausing as the heads dipped, then a collective cloud of smoke as cigarettes were lit and the laughter resumed. Counting the doors as he passed 120, he realized the gathering was at Kit's place. She had company. He'd come all the way here, and he'd brought wine, and fuck. She hadn't meant tonight.

It was too late to turn back. Was it? He passed 122. Yes. No. He would just walk straight past. No way she was a smoker herself, so maybe she would be inside still, he'd get away with it, she wouldn't see him, it would be fine. Or he could just pop in and claim that he was ... no.

He kept his gaze straight ahead: 126 ... and 130. He breathed out, kept walking.

'Sarge?'

He stopped. Turned. Kit, in an unreasonably short and low dress made entirely from gold sequins, her bare arms resplendent with anchors and roses, was walking down the path. She wore both a smile and a frown, and from her fingers dangled the neck of a Corona, complete with lime.

'Sarge! It *is* you.'

There was a hush across the garden, the other women pulling on their cigarettes, glancing at each other with eyebrows raised.

'Oh, Kit,' he said, half-heartedly feigning surprise. 'Hi.'

'You live round here?' She asked him, benign confusion furrowing her face.

'Shortcut,' he said, then, because she'd noticed the bag, he raised it slightly and said, 'taking this for a mate.'

One of the women snorted, laughing, and turned her back.

'Right.' Kit nodded, but her eyes narrowed. 'It's a dead end.'

A mere second of giggling from her mates before she shot them a look, then silence.

He was a dick. He *knew* he was a dick. Would it be better to tell her, there and then, what a massive dick he was? Would acknowledging it help?

One of the smokers, a short, solid woman with cropped black hair, sauntered down to stand next to Kit. 'Evening!' she said, brightly, before squinting at him, then Kit, then back to him, through a pull of her cigarette. 'Who's this then?'

'Ben,' Mae said, putting out a hand, which the woman shook with the grip of a docker.

'Beer?' she suggested. 'We don't bite.'

'Actually Pain does, doesn't she?' one of the others muttered. More laughter.

'Well, yeah,' the docker conceded, 'I meant the rest of us. Pain bites like a bastard, don't you, sweetie?' she cooed at Kit. Then cocking her head, 'though maybe *Sarge* already knows that.' She blew a thin jet of smoke from the corner of her mouth.

Kit elbowed her friend, then, tossing a thumb towards her front door, said, 'Do you want a drink, though? I've got a fuck-load.'

So he didn't really have a choice, in the end. He followed her inside, past her amused friends, and put the food down discreetly just inside the kitchen door. Her hall was bedecked in kitsch: 7" records mounted on screws all over the walls, and strings of mismatched fairy lights. Nothing, *nothing* like any other police officer's home he'd ever seen before. In the kitchen Kit opened a fridge and stuck her head inside and brought out a bottle.

'It's my derby name, by the way,' she said, doing the flicky thing with her fingers that popped the beer cap off without any discernible effort or discomfort.

'Sorry?'

'Pain.' She handed the opened beer to him and watched him drink it, folding her arms. 'Roller derby thing: everyone gets a name. I'm PC Pain.'

He swallowed. 'But you're a detective. DC.'

'Yeah,' she said, stretching her arms above her head and loosening her neck. 'Should've future-proofed it really.'

He took another mouthful of beer. 'I tried to call.'

'Shit.' She made an *eek* face. 'Where's my phone? Sorry. I had a bout. A match.'

'And she fucking killed it,' one of her mates added in a singsong voice, coming between them and making a grab for a pitcher of something colourful that looked way too strong for a school night. 'We left those bitches minced and bleeding.'

Mae watched as the friend downloaded a mugful of fluorescence, gripped her eyes shut, then gnashed her teeth and shivered, before sashaying back into the living room, where the music had just risen by a handful of decibels.

'Well, that's good to know,' Mae said, and he finished his beer in two swallows.

Kit located her phone, plugged in beside the kettle, and woke the screen. '"Wine or beer?"' she read, clearly baffled. Looking up, she said, 'Did I … did we have a plan?'

'Your text,' he reminded her, but her frown only deepened, so he added, 'Glug glug glug?' Slowly, he was getting used to the idea of having cocked up in a way that would leave him blistering with embarrassment for weeks to come. 'I assumed you meant …'

She grabbed his arm, creasing up. 'Oh! No! It's the sound of the plug being pulled,' she told him between hoots. 'Sorry, sorry.'

He waited for her to compose herself. 'Funny. I'd always thought of *the plug* being an electrical plug.'

She tilted her head, considering it, then shrugged. 'But listen, the point was I got a call from Colleen.'

'Coll— McCulloch?' Mae had never heard anyone refer to his boss by her first name. 'Saying what?'

'She wanted to know exactly what we had. So I told her, and she said she was going to speak to you. She wants us to hand it over to someone else, far as I can tell.'

'Why?' Mae asked, knowing perfectly well *why*.

'She was pretty vague. Something to do with "history",' she said, miming the speech marks. In her defence, the questions Kit was evidently desperate to ask stayed unspoken. 'Anyway,' she said, after a period of time that confirmed to the both of them that Mae was not going to offer further illumination, 'now you're here: I got out to Feltham. Where Corsham's car was, yeah?'

She tapped on her phone and turned the screen to him. The image was of a car with a lot of past and not much future. Although sections of the rear were more or less intact, the skeletal front end was entirely blackened, the plastic components melted and cracked.

He handed the phone back. 'You find out how it got there?'

'Nope. Fishy, though, isn't it?'

'Yes and no. There's no parking on the mooring, so it's likely he'd usually park on-street somewhere. Meaning anyone might have clocked the car not being used, so—'

'So could just be kids, joyriders? It's old enough to be hotwired without too much trouble.'

'Possible. I've got a contact in the CCTV room at the council. I'll see what he can get.'

Kit rubbed her face and groaned. 'Can't we just have a straight answer to anything?'

Mae gave her a consolatory nudge. 'Never know, though. Maybe your next job'll turn out to be a frenzied knife attack, bloody footprints leading back to the suspect's house.'

'No, no, that's not what I mean,' she said, suddenly serious.

'I really want to find him. I know he's an adult and everything, but he's someone's son, isn't he?'

Mae felt the smile drop from his face. Found his head suddenly crowded with images from the thing he had spent so long burying.

'What?' Kit asked, putting her beer down. 'What did I say?'

With practised calm, he forced the image of his mother away. The video she sent. *You'll always be my son. But—*

The most destructive word in the English language. Three letters that turn everything that comes before them to shit. Makes them not exist at all.

But.

'Mae?'

But I'm not coming back.

'Yes. Fine,' he said. 'Nothing.'

She eyed him, then upended the bottle into her mouth again.

Chapter 36

Ellie

I stood there on the lamplit street for a good ten minutes, but no amount of calling through Mr Symanski's letterbox or banging on the door had made him answer me.

I went halfway up our front steps, then stopped. I didn't have a key. There was no way I was going to get Mum up to let me in, not after what happened earlier. Left with no other choice, I started the long walk over to Matt's.

The pontoon was deserted when I arrived. There was an eerie stillness in there, as if it had been waiting for me. On the top step, delivered via the catflap, was a brown-paper parcel sealed up with wide brown packing tape. The package Mr Jupp had mentioned – he'd found it.

I turned it over. There was a return address, inked in little black capitals along the short edge. Brighton.

I realized what I was holding. Its shape and weight were as familiar as a favourite pair of shoes. I couldn't tear through the tape, so I grabbed a knife from a drawer and made a slit. The first thing my fingers found was a note. Handwritten. Short, with the address again in the lower case of the same small, rounded hand, and a number.

Dear Matthew, I read. *Here it is. Please, please promise me you'll keep it safe. Give my love to Ellie. She always was a lovely girl. My Jodie would have done anything for her. Lucy.*

Lucy Arden, Jodie's mother. *My Jodie* caught like a bone in my throat. Tearing off the paper, I sat down heavily, causing the narrow keel to lurch. The book inside, roughly A5, was covered in purple vinyl. Bent and damaged at the corners, the spine cracked. The thing that made this particular book different from any of the hundreds that would have been printed at the same time was the unmistakable smudging of fingerprint dust.

It was a diary, an old one, full of handwriting of two different styles. Half of it written by me, the other half by written by my dead best friend. Alternating entries, because we had taken it in turns to be the custodian and hand the book over next time we saw each other, to be read only later, alone, at night. I flicked through the pages, swallowing Siggy down into my clenched stomach. Here and there my words were carved deep into the paper, the pen conveying that early teen emotion – rage, love, sadness – that swelled us to bursting point.

Reverently I turned to the back. The last entries before the empty pages. In her wide, bubbly hand, her near-hysterical declarations of love. Her many exclamation marks anchored with tiny hearts instead of dots, the same ones that topped her i's and j's. She never named the object of her devotion in case her mum ever found the diary, but I knew it. Could hardly miss it.

Those first few days after Jodie went missing, Cox had called round every night. Wanting to talk to me, but Mum wouldn't let him. She didn't want him anywhere near me. She stopped working when it happened; she went with me everywhere. At first she'd insisted it couldn't have been Siggy. Tried to make me believe that the scrapes I had could have been anything, were nothing to worry about.

That intermission, between Jodie's disappearance and what Mum found, was short-lived. Although I wanted to help the investigation, and I knew the only chance we had was to tell the police the truth, it was in those few days that the lies began to take hold. All Mum and I talked about were the details of it, going over and over them. Did I even know we were making it up? Remembering it now it seemed like some grey limbo, but we certainly never said we were talking about lying to the police. The origins of those fabricated details were lost now: the broken streetlight above the spot where I said Jodie got in the car; the argument I swore they'd had about her shoes; Cox calling her a *fucking tart*. It happened so gradually that the seam was invisible: where what might have happened became what I definitely, honestly saw.

It wasn't until Mum found her that we put it all together. The real version. By then, it was too late.

I had been sleeping when she came in to tell me she'd had an idea of where Jodie might have gone. It had come to her out of the blue: that place she'd wanted to go camping, a few months before. Mum had tried to call Ben Mae about it as soon as she thought of it, she said, but he hadn't answered. It was late, and he had a young family at home. So she'd just got in the car and gone on her own.

As she walked around, something had caught her eye, something bright.

And when she got closer, she'd seen that it was a scrap of Jodie's hair.

Mum had cut her hands on the brambles when she pulled her out: she showed me the cuts, the spherical globs of dried blood. There had been a tuft of black hair in Jodie's hand, she said. I touched the sore spot on my scalp. There was nothing else to say, after that.

Cox wasn't an innocent person, but what I'd done to him, what we'd done, with that story when we'd known he hadn't even been there: it wasn't OK. What his life must be like now, after all that, was something I just couldn't think about. The case against him had fallen apart when I did what I did with the knife. Mentally unstable, they said. Unreliable witness. But the damage was done. And he knew I'd lied.

I folded the book shut and rested my fingertips on the cover. Not from a lack of appetite for it: after so long, I wanted to absorb the thing whole. But I needed to think. I traced a finger over the note from Lucy, who had begged me to stay in touch after her daughter disappeared, but whom my mother had banned me from contacting.

It's not safe for us, Mum said. It would only take one slip of the tongue.

But here was our friendship, preserved, and Matt had found it. He had found Lucy Arden, and she had sent him this. The only memento she had of her daughter's real thoughts and feelings before she died. The book she had hoped would prove Charles Cox's guilt, but which was, in the end, dismissed as just the witterings of two teenage girls. Unspecific, circumstantial, anecdotal.

So why did you have this, Matt? What did you want to know?

*

I read until I started to feel sleepy, then I got up, made myself stretch, get my blood moving. Outside, moonlight reflected in the still surface of the water, sending bright reflected ribbons up to dance and twine on the ceiling, and down the walls. I watched them, my lids hanging heavily, desperate for rest now, until suddenly I heard voices on the pontoon.

Out of the window I saw a family I recognized: residents, Matt's neighbours, out late. The dad carried the little girl, still in her school clothes, fast asleep against his chest, and the mum softly cajoled the toddler wriggling, a boy with eyes half-closed, in her arms. The man turned and I saw, draped across his shoulder, something that triggered a snap in my temple. A jacket, cut from camouflage fabric. I hadn't seen it before: he was in combats, too, and the T-shirt wasn't brown but khaki. The man was a soldier. I gripped the edge of the kitchen surface and Siggy turned to me, her lifeless eyes hooded.

My knees crumpled. I dropped onto the floor where they couldn't see me, and the whisky spilled all over my jeans. I heard them move off, the toddler starting to whine. A flash of that child, the little boy from the dream, ignited behind my eyes and I dug my nails into my palms thinking *no, not here. Come on, Ellie*

But it was coming whether I liked it or not. I couldn't do anything, and the panic and the noise rose up around me like I was there, like Siggy was right there and the boy was right there just looking into my eyes and I can't help—

he's crying because he's hungry
he doesn't understand and you mustn't

Breathe – breathe – in for seven

please leave him alone
please don't he'll be quiet he will he doesn't understand
he doesn't

                                                                  no
                                                               don't
                        someone make him stop leave him alone
                don't hurt him don't hurt him no no no no no NO

Cold liquid on my legs, seeping through my jeans

                                please I want my mum. Please

And my eyes were open, and the only sound was my own ragged breath. The image – that scene that was still there, somehow behind my vision – started to fade and then, with every lurch of my heart, the juddering panic slowed. My mouth was locked open, and I could still smell *him*, the soldier from Siggy's dream, the smell of blood, all of it thick in my nostrils. Tears cooled down my face as I worked my jaw free. I shuddered, waiting for it to clear.

When I eventually stood up, I poured what was left of the whisky down the sink. I moved slowly, with Siggy hanging like a smog around me, making me slow, dull, exhausted.

Midnight came and went. I found a book, not knowing what to do to prevent myself from drifting off. Then the boat shifted in the water and when I sat up again, bolt upright with a gasp, I realized I had fallen asleep. I didn't know for how long. Minutes? An hour? I was sure I hadn't moved, but I could feel Siggy, sparking between the layers of my skin. Our skin. I pushed myself up, jumped up and down a few times, flexing and clenching my hands and dispelling her, until I remembered that family, those children sleeping only yards away from where I was. Plenty of the boats had no internal locks at all.

I could not allow her to come to me tonight. Not here.

Under a panel of the foredeck I found a bunch of cable ties. I tested one, poking the thin end through the eye at the other, yanking it taut the way I had seen the police do it on something Mum and I watched once. I made a bracelet of one and slipped my hand into it, pulling it tight enough that I couldn't get it off again. Then I threaded a second tie through the loop on my wrist and was just putting my hand into the circle when a last spark of wakefulness kindled a realization.

If Siggy could drive his car, she could find her way out of a pair of plastic handcuffs.

I knew what I had to do. I grabbed an empty Ikea bag from the bedroom cupboard and started my collection. From the kitchen: all the knives, scissors, forks. His sharpening steel, the skewers. Then razors from the bathroom: an unopened pack of the disposables that he always managed to bloody his beautiful face with, which I found wedged in behind the sink. I checked every cupboard and drawer from bow to stern: hacksaw blades from the tool cupboard, a chisel, a hammer, screwdrivers. Wire coat hangers, two corkscrews.

And when I was sure I had everything, I crept onto the aft deck and slipped them one by one into the black water.

Chapter 37

Mae

His breath turning to steam, Mae stood shivering on the steps of Ealing Town Hall, checking left and right for any sign of the cab. Beneath the grand, castellated building was the Central Control Room of the area's council-managed CCTV, and it was there that Mae hoped to get some answers about the fate of Matthew Corsham's car.

He set the two coffees he was holding down beside his feet and checked his watch. On the face of it seven thirty was a fairly unsociable hour. But Rod, his good friend and contact at the council, was an ex-squaddie, so Mae inferred this meant he was not unused to an early bugle. Admittedly he hadn't been exactly *thrilled* to hear from Mae at 6 a.m., but a job was a job.

Mae's phone rang, and he retrieved it from his pocket. Colleen McCulloch. His thumb hovered over the green circle but didn't connect: *She wants us to hand it over to someone else*, Kit had said. *Something about history.*

He'd call her back. It would be fine.

On the opposite side of the road, a woman shepherding a cluster of hi-vis vested kids along the pavement. He watched their slow progress, lunch bags swinging from their fingers, and the feeling that he had forgotten something edged slowly from the back of his mind and into the front.

Shit and fuck.

School trip. Bear wanted him to do the school trip.

He got out his phone, realized he had a message from Kit, sent last night maybe ten minutes after he'd made his escape from the Hounslow Hellcats the night before.

All it said was: *Yum yum yum*

And then another one beneath it, sent seconds later: (*disambiguation: that's us eating the dinner you left behind*)

Mae smiled, the mortification softening slightly, then called the school office and left his message about helping with Bear's trip, wondering whether it might involve an introduction to the boy – the 'dickhead' – who'd been bothering his baby.

Eventually the big mobility-adapted cab came crawling into view behind a string of buses. The driver got out, lowered the ramp, and Mae straightened from his lean and went over to greet his friend.

'You, my dear, are a barbarian,' Rod told him once he'd wheeled himself clear of the taxi and paid. But his annoyance wasn't enough to come between him and the flat white that Mae held out to him, which he took with a flourish of fake indignation and deftly stowed in a holder at his hip. 'Also, your call woke the wife, and she's on nights. So if you see her you better watch your bollocks.'

Mae apologized and followed him up the ramp. 'New rig?' he asked, taking in the streamlined, brushed aluminium frame of Rod's wheelchair.

'This old thing?' Rod glanced down at it with evident pride. 'Worth losing one's legs all over again for.'

Mae showed his badge at the desk, and they headed up the corridor, strip lights crackling into life above their heads.

Inside the control room, Mae paused to acclimatize to the

gloom. They were the first to clock in. The room, about the size of your average primary school hall, was much like any other office – mess, paperwork, printers and desks – but much darker. The front wall was a bank of screens. First time he'd seen inside one of these rooms, he'd been struck by how they really did look the way they did in films. It couldn't be healthy, working five days a week in the semi-darkness, but it didn't seem to bother Rod, who had joined the council straight after his medical discharge after losing both legs to a landmine at twenty-two.

Rod propelled himself to his station front and centre, shook off his coat, and reached underneath the console to flick a switch. Ahead, twenty-five by about fifteen feet of screens fired up, illuminating the room.

Grinning up at him, Rod said, 'Love that bit.' All trace of the grumpy routine of the pavement was gone. 'What is it you need then, that's important enough to interrupt my favourite dream?'

Mae pulled up a chair. 'Need to trace the final movements of a car before it got burnt out.'

Rod heard him out and nodded. 'Time and date?'

Mae reeled it off, and Rod got to work. In additional to his military-induced love of order and precision, he knew the borough like the back of his hand. Mae had seen him follow cars on these screens in real time, switching between views, pre-empting direction like a seer, bringing up the next feed and the next as easily as dominoes.

'Problem you'll have is that your blocks up here and here,' Rod told him, indicating areas with a laser pen, 'aren't council anymore, got sold off about ten years ago. I'd've given you about fifty different views when it was ours, but now it'll just be a couple of cameras up poles to cover the whole stretch.'

It was a fallacy oft repeated that you couldn't go anywhere

without being recorded. Sure, there were a lot of cameras, but it was a rudderless patchwork of coverage, not the huge centralized network people imagined. Reality was, if you wanted exterior footage, your best bet was to literally *look up*. See what cameras might have caught anything, and then go round finding out who owned them. Maybe half of your longlist would be actually connected to anything, and of those, only a small proportion would have been recording.

Rod squinted at the screen embedded in the desk in front of him. 'This the place?'

'That's it.' The Feltham site had been earmarked for a major new leisure development in the nineties, and the cinema had been flattened, but the funding had been cancelled and the whole site had sat dormant ever since. It was still fenced off, a mixture of chicken wire and hoardings ringing the entire perimeter with the usual half-arsed warning signs about trespassing.

'Best I can do is this one,' Rod said, showing Mae a truncated shot of the top of the road leading up to the derelict site, 'or this one,' which was a higher angle and covered the gate, one half hanging open and unsecured.

Mae leaned in. 'Cue up the first one. My guy was last seen at about five o'clock, so run it from then and we'll see what turns up.'

Rod loaded the footage and set it to run at 10x speed, walked Mae through the controls, and headed off to the gents. By the time he'd returned, Mae was exactly fifty per cent less optimistic than he had been.

'No sign of it?' Rod said, reaching for his coffee.

Mae sighed. 'Try the other angle.'

On the recording, Feltham got dark. The streetlights came on, the frequency of the car stripped right back, and then ... nothing.

An hour of footage that could have been a still image, bar the occasional flash of a plane coming in from the east for Heathrow. The timecode flew along, and the on-screen midnight became one, two in the morning. Rod yawned, leaned his elbows on the desk.

And then, he abruptly sat up. 'Gotcha.'

Mae had seen it too. Tracking in from the left of the screen was the unmistakable two-tone of Matthew Corsham's soft top. Rod ran his thumb slowly over the control wheel.

'Right, 3.09 a.m.,' he said. They watched as the car turned into the entrance, then crept into the site and out of shot.

'Run it again.' Mae was on his feet now, peering up close. But even running it a frame at a time, there was little else to be gleaned from the image. 'Bloody glare,' he muttered: there was no hope of identifying the driver thanks to the light reflected off the windscreen. But the height of the wheel arch told him there was no great weight inside – one person at a guess – and the timing was something, at least.

'You said the car gets burnt out, right?' Rod asked him, looking up.

'Looks that way.'

'Right, so the driver's got to leave at some point.' He pointed to the shuddering freeze-frame. 'And that's the only exit, so ...'

'So let's wait.'

And wait they did. But by 5 a.m., when the blackness started to dissolve into a grey day and the traffic rose and shone, it became apparent that the driver wasn't coming out the way they'd gone in.

Mae scoured his hands against his scalp. 'Bollocks.' Then he thought of something. 'What about if we follow the car backwards?'

'Ah. Trace it back to the source.' Rod poked his tongue into his cheek, smiling, then turned back to the console. 'You might want to get us some refills, mind, it could take a while.'

All told it took Rod about an hour to put it together, but when he'd finished the job, it was a thing of patch-worked and slightly disorientating beauty.

'Try to just watch the car, instead of the environment,' Rod said, calling Mae back from where he'd been googling for ideas on decorating bedrooms for pre-teen girls. 'The shots vary a lot in height and orientation so it's hard to follow, but we get there in the end.'

They watched the car move backwards in space and time, exhaust-first out of the derelict yard and into the road.

'It backs up towards the Staines road here,' Rod said, narrating it for Mae, 'and then here, it cuts up north and goes towards the motorway.' A beat. 'Exciting stuff, surveillance, huh? Shits all over *Game of Thrones*.'

Mae watched as the car slipped under the M5 around Heston, then looped back down before finally turning off the Boston Manor Road just past Elthorne Park and disappearing.

'Afraid it basically peters out around there. Coverage is super patchy around the residential bits there.' Rod paused the sequence and turned in his seat. 'That help at all? This where the guy lives?'

Mae shook his head. 'Good couple of miles away.' He reached for the A to Z poking out of Rod's in-tray. 'What road is that, though, where it goes offline?'

Rod punched in a command and the map in the screen to the right switched from satellite to map view. He leaned in. 'Top of Abson Street,' he said.

Abson Street. Where Ellie lived.

'That mean something to you?'

Mae got up. 'Could do.'

'Hold on, big guy,' Rod said, watching Mae lift the coat from his chair. 'You're not leaving until you tell me when you're taking me out next. It's been months. I lie awake at night, dreaming of the day I get a call—'

'Yeah, yeah. Sorry. Been up to my eyes.'

Rod regarded him with something approaching concern. 'What's this one about, then?'

Mae weighed up telling him. Rod had been a colleague from way back, when Mae had worked security before he'd even started on the force. He was one of the few to keep in touch when Mae had taken what Rod euphemistically referred to as his *sabbatical*. He'd had some stuff to say about DS Heath, Mae remembered now: the two of them had served together, and Rod had a long memory for a grudge.

'You remember Jodie Arden?'

'Yes.' A slow nod. 'Yes, I most certainly do.'

Mae hesitated. It was an active case, confidential, but Rod was as solid as they came. 'Our misper is the boyfriend of Ellie Power, who was the—'

'... best mate, yeah, I remember,' Rod finished, frowning. 'Bit of a coincidence.'

'Tell me about it,' Mae said, shrugging on the jacket and downing the last cold inch of the coffee. 'And I don't know for sure but it looks like that fucker Charles Cox has got something to do with it, too.'

Rod's eyes widened, but before he could respond, Mae's phone rang.

It was Kit. 'I'm outside,' she said. 'Come down.'

He thanked Rod, said goodbye, and headed out to the stairs.

Kit was on the double yellows, engine running, with her phone to her ear.

'Are you there now?' she said into it as Mae got in beside her. She gestured urgently for him to close the door, then let the handbrake off and moved out into the traffic before she'd cut the call.

'Good,' she said. 'Be with you in ten minutes.' She laid the phone back in the recess above the stereo. 'Well, it's news, but I'm not sure if it's good, bad, or very fucking weird.'

'What happened?'

She kept her eyes on the road. 'That was Jupp. Matthew Corsham's rent's just been paid.'

38

CC: *I'd like to spend some time following up from the session last week, if that's all right with you.*

EP: *OK, I suppose.*

[pause: 21 sec]

CC: *I'm getting the sense from your body language that you're finding the idea of doing that distressing.*

EP: *It was … I can't stop thinking about it. I keep seeing it, sort of … feeling it, all the time. I don't want to feel it.*

CC: *It was a very difficult session.*

EP: *I'm fine.*

[pause: 31 sec]

EP: *Seriously, I'm fine.*

CC: *OK. Sure. So at the end of our last session we agreed that if you could, you would have a conversation with your mum about your scars.*

EP: *Yeah, all right, I suppose. If you think it'll do anything. But honestly, look, I don't remember it. I just don't. What you said last week, that you think my accident has to do with Siggy though? It's just not, I just don't think that's the case.*

CC: *You don't, you're saying you don't think there's any connection?*

EP: *I honestly don't. I had an accident.*

CC: *But you don't remember it.*

EP: *Well … no. I was really young. But that thing with – whatever we did last time, that was – something else. Siggy can … I mean, you don't have to believe everything she says.*

CC: *Except we ended up accessing something, that sensation of pain, and fear, that seemed to offer another explanation of the injuries you sustained when you were very young.*

EP: *No. What happened when I was a kid was a pan of boiling water. That thing last week – that dream, or whatever it is – that's Siggy in a fire. It's just a dream. A nightmare. It's not real.*

CC: *Ah.*

[pause: 31 sec]

CC: *But Ellie. Do you remember that you mentioned a fear that someone was coming? That it was necessary to hide. There was a man.*

[pause: 22 sec]

EP: It was a dream.

CC: OK.

EP: Look, this thing about her being scared of something, like the whole soldier thing: it's made up. I've asked my mum, we don't know anyone in the army or anything, never have. It's nothing to do with me.

[pause: 40 sec]

EP: OK, go on, then, what? Why are you just saying nothing about that?

CC: I just want to remind you that when we talk about Siggy is that she is essentially a part of your own identity that has split off from your dominant self.

EP: Yes, I understand that.

CC: She doesn't ... it's not as if she is a separate person. She doesn't exist outside of you.

EP: I know that.

CC: So any ... details, any fears she has that are in some way stuck for her, as if she is experiencing them all of the time, these are not random. There are experiences that have shaped her: moments that she's hanging on to because of how crucial they are to her identity, OK? Things like the dreams that you've told me about: the mention of a soldier, a little boy, and this long building that you've said about a few times—

EP: They're Siggy things, they're not me.

CC: OK. Listen, I do understand that if you haven't had therapy since you were a small child that you might not have had any frank conversations with any professionals about this. But you're coming to see me independently now, essentially

*as an adult, so I'm telling you what I know and what I believe
as frankly as I can: dissociation doesn't work like that.*

*EP: You said before that the mind can do anything. More than
once. That's what you said.*

*CC: I did. I did. But there are patterns, and … OK, look. What
we are talking about, these images and events, they have
been buried, split off from your psyche. Siggy is the identity
who's become like a gatekeeper to this … information.*

EP: No. No.

[pause: 1 m 12 sec]

*CC: OK, look, here's some tissues, here. Can you look at me?
OK, good. Ellie. What you talked about last week, that was
not your imagination. What you were describing, the pain,
being scared, not wanting to open your eyes: all of that.
This is a traumatic thing that happened.*

[pause: 23 sec]

EP: It's not.

*CC: All right. There's a lot at stake for you there, isn't there?
Letting it be real, admitting that there's a chance it could
be real: that's dangerous for you.*

EP: No. It isn't real.

CC: It's scary to even think about.

EP: No, because—

*CC: If you let yourself believe that the trauma is real, how can
you trust anything?*

[pause: 21 sec]

CC: How does that make you feel, thinking about that?

[pause: 33 sec]

EP: I can't do that. I can't. It would be better just to stay the way I am.

Chapter 39

Ellie

On the boat, sleep came fitfully. The dreams were a bloody, rolling blur, jumbled in chronology. I saw Matt, his neck crushed by a rope, and I was standing, uncaring, doing nothing. Then later again, but with his head twisted off but not yet dead, lying gasping for air beside his lifeless body. Then sprawled face down in a pit, a grave, water seeping upwards through the cold earth, getting in to him, somehow, through his pores, drowning him. He was still alive, and begging me to help him.

But in all of it, I didn't see Siggy, or anything of hers. Not the building, not the bleeding little boy, the uniform, the fire. Not once.

When I finally woke with the resolve to get up, I swung my legs out of the bed and went in search of something I could use to free myself from the cable ties. Having jettisoned everything sharp, I tried initially to cut through the bind with the teeth of my key, but I couldn't get the right purchase on it. I settled on the corner of the galley work surface and rubbed one of the cable ties against a section of metal edging that had come away from the chipboard. Eventually the strip around my right wrist was worn thin enough to pull open with my teeth. It gave a snap and broke. The others were much easier with my hands free, and before long I was gathering my things, not forgetting the diary, and readying to leave.

A pinkish dawn was just lifting into day when I slid the hatch back and emerged. I jogged some of the way home, but I was hungry and felt weak and had to slow to a stroll.

At the corner of our road, I paused, remembering the night before. Someone wanted to tell me something. I was going to find out what it was.

I knocked at my neighbours' door, but it wasn't Mr Symanski who answered.

'They're watching you.' It was his son, Piotr, his skin grey and the shadows under his eyes as dark as thunderclouds. 'I tried to tell you but—' he started, taking a step out towards me, but then his dad was there, moving in front of him, pushing him back.

'You go home now,' Mr Symanski said to me, and he pushed the door between us. But the door didn't close. He looked down. I was almost as surprised to see my foot, wedging the door open, as he was.

I stood firm. 'Piotr had something to tell me last night. I need to know what it was.'

'No,' he said categorically, and he tried to shift my foot with his own.

Obscured behind him, Piotr shouted out, 'The van!'

'What van?' I asked. 'Mr Symanski, what does he mean?'

'He means nothing. Piotr is a very troubled boy.'

I called back to Piotr, shouted it. '*Which one?*'

I just caught the answer, shouted from the hall, 'The van! That van in the street!' before Mr Symanski won the battle, and the door slammed in my face.

Breathless and baffled from the struggle, I turned to look at the street. There were only cars.

I couldn't go home, of course. I'd left without my key, and

Mum wasn't in. I sat on the steps for a moment deciding what to do. I wanted to see Lucy, but that would mean a trip to Brighton. I could call Mae, tell him about the diary, but not without my phone, which was also inside the flat. The only thing to do was swallow my pride and go to the hospital to get the keys from my mum.

The walk to the hospital took an hour, and when I got there I headed straight downstairs to where Mum's base was. I'd been down there only once before but managed to find my way: all the way to the back and then down until you got to the floor with bare breeze-block walls and the entire arterial plumbing system running overhead.

I found the door and went in. Mum's manager was a Haitian with a voice as huge as his stature was diminutive. I knocked and went in, expecting to have to introduce myself. But the moment he looked up he scraped back his chair, got up from behind his metal desk and came straight over, hand outstretched.

'Ah, what a nice surprise. Ellie Scott!'

I opened my mouth to correct him but then realized he wouldn't even have known Mum's real name.

'I'm just looking for my mum,' I said, shaking the hand. 'Do you know where I can find her?'

'No idea!' he said cheerfully.

'She's-she's not here?' I felt my spine turn to ice. She was gone. She'd found me missing from my room, and she'd finally decided enough was enough.

'Well, yes, she is here, *somewhere*,' he said, not noticing me almost collapse with relief, 'but it's the usual thing.' He ducked back behind his desk and opened a drawer. 'She picks up her task sheet and her gear and off she goes; I don't know where they are most of the time but the work gets done, so ...' He closed the drawer and opened another one. 'But she said you would be coming.'

I frowned. 'Did she?'

'Mm-hm. Ah! Here,' he said, pulling something out and bringing it over. It was my phone, and strapped across the screen with an elastic band, a brass key. 'Said you must have forgotten it when you left. I charged it up for you, should be fine now.'

I took it, thanked him. Back on the ground floor, I turned the phone on. The first thing to beep: a message from Mum.

I don't know what you're doing Ellie but you've got to go home.

I let my thumb hover over the screen for a moment. Another message, then another:

Baby where are you?

Please. I'm worried sick. Tell me you're OK, and then go home.

I deleted them all, without replying, then I went straight to Matt's office.

The door was a white slab in a white wall, the whole corridor strip-lit and sterile as a spaceship. I lifted my hand to knock but before it connected, a man, Matt's age but shorter, plump and bearded, opened the door and came out, almost knocking me over.

'Shit ... sorry,' he said, putting out a hand to steady me. Under the other arm he held a package, a padded envelope containing something the size of a heavy book. 'Help you?'

'My boyfriend Matt works – worked – here,' I said. 'I think he might have left some things behind and I was just passing so—'

'Ellie?' he said. 'I'm Leon. The guy he worked with? We spoke, yeah?'

'Leon. Right.' I wondered what he knew about me.

'So has he turned up now?' he asked, smiling. He leaned on the doorframe but didn't invite me in. I'd never been inside Matt's workplace but looking past him, I found that I hadn't missed much. With the scanners and expensive machinery elsewhere, it was little more than a crisper-than-usual office, with white vinyl walls and a few racks of screens.

I shook my head, and his face fell.

'Oh, really? I just assumed as he brought his computer back—' he said, lifting the package under his arm slightly and pulling out a sheet of paper from inside it.

'That's *his*?'

'Brought it back. Last night.' He unfolded the paper, scanned it, frowning.

'You *saw* him?'

'No. I just got a call a minute ago from the front desk saying they had a delivery. But actually yeah,' he said, waving the paper. 'Delivery note says it was someone else – Hamsworth? Harnsworth? – who delivered it. Courier, I guess.'

I couldn't take my eyes from that package. 'Listen, do you mind if I have a quick look at that?'

'Ah, not really,' he said with an apologetic smile. 'I was just taking it up to HR. Our manager up there wanted it pretty urgently when I told her it had arrived.'

I reached out a hand. 'Just for a minute. Honestly, it won't take long.'

'Sorry,' he said, tucking it tighter under his arm and sidestepping me. The door to the lab was closing very slowly. 'She said she needed it right away – she'll be down looking for it any minute.'

'Please.' I looked him in the eye, knowing I had one shot. 'He's still missing, Leon. I've got no idea what's going on, or where he is, or anything. I just need to know he's safe. I just need ... something. Anything. And that,' I said, indicating the package, 'is pretty much all I've got at the moment.'

He sighed, suspicion softening into sympathy on his face. 'OK. But literally two minutes, yeah?'

I smiled. 'Thank you, Leon. That would be wonderful.'

Chapter 40

Mae

As soon as they pulled up outside the boatyard, Mae got a call.

'You get started, I'll catch you up,' he told Kit, who was already halfway out of the car. Bringing his phone out, he recognized the number of Bear's school on the screen. He took a few steps away before answering it.

'I'm returning your call about the school trip in Dominica's class,' the secretary said.

'Right. I just need to clear it with work but should be fine. What time do you need me?'

There was a pause. 'That's the thing, Mr Kwon Mae, I'm afraid. We don't appear to have a Disclosure and Barring Service check for you on our system.'

'No. You won't, but I'm a serving police officer, you know that, right? I don't really need a criminal background check,' he said, rolling his eyes.

'Yes, I know. But we have a policy that we don't have volunteers who aren't DBS cleared.'

She did in fact appear to be serious. 'OK, fine. I'll come and fill in the forms so you can get one done, if you seriously need me to.'

'That would be great. Just remember to come to the office

for the paperwork and hopefully we'll have you cleared for next time.'

'Next – no. I need to come *this* time. Dominica asked me.'

'I don't think that's going to be possible. The checks take weeks. You need data from your former employers, all kinds of things. There's no chance it'll be cleared in time, I'm sorry.'

Pissed off but knowing how to choose his battles, he hung up. He caught Kit up just as she got to where Jupp was braced against a rope on the pontoon, swearing at an emaciated underling on the aft deck of Matt's boat.

'I said a bloody bowline!' Jupp growled. The boat was swinging out precariously into the river, at a right-angle to the bank.

'Is it supposed to be doing that?' Kit called out cheerfully, prompting a bright string of profanity from Jupp. They waited on the pontoon while the two men got the boat under control. Kit made a grab for a stray rope and lashed it expertly to a mooring cleat.

Wiping the sweat from his ample face, Jupp nodded his approval. 'At least someone knows what they're doing. Must have told this twat,' indicating the boat to infer Matt, Mae guessed, 'a hundred times that she's got to be portside in.'

'Because of the wash,' Kit said absentmindedly. Then, clocking Mae's surprise, 'The wash from passing boats. Your grey-water outlets in a narrowboat are close to the waterline, doesn't usually matter because they're mostly on the canal where you're limited to four knots. No wash. Different on the Thames. One big wave and you're an accidental submarine.'

Mae raised his eyebrows.

'Sea cadets,' she said, stooping to make an adjustment to one of Jupp's bowlines. Then, brushing her hands on her thighs, 'Have a word, Mr Jupp?'

He made them tea in his office. Kit got out the tablet and Mae led the questions.

'So, you said he paid his rent.'

'I did.' Jupp's attention was on the bulky screen in front of him. He stabbed a fat finger at the escape button on his keyboard a few times, folds deepening on his forehead.

'Could you be more specific?'

'If you like. His rent was owing, and now it's not.'

Mae folded his arms. 'Mr Jupp, this is important.'

Sighing, Jupp said, 'I got here this morning and there's an envelope through the door.'

'Do you have it?' Kit wanted to know.

Jupp lifted a few slabs of paperwork before finding it, then held it out for him. Kit whipped a fresh pack of nitrile gloves from her pocket and handed them to Mae, who put them on before taking the envelope. It had already been torn open, and inside was a thin stack of twenties and tens.

'Just this? No note?'

Jupp rummaged in a pile, withdrew a folded piece of A4 and held it out to him. 'Just Matt's name and the name of the boat, the date and amount.'

There was nothing else inside, Matt's name at the bottom. Typed and printed, no signature.

Kit said, 'Does he usually pay in cash?'

'Sometimes.'

'But you didn't see him? Didn't cross paths at all?'

'I would have said, wouldn't I? Haven't seen him since he left for the pump-out.'

Kit narrowed her eyes. 'You didn't see him go, though, or come back, after he'd emptied his tanks?'

'Like I already told you. I didn't.'

Mae clicked the end of his pen, noticing Kit digging in her jacket. She rounded Jupp's table with her phone in her hand.

'Mr Jupp, do you know this man? Seen him around?'

From his leaning spot by the door Mae could see Cox's face on her screen.

'Yep. Mate of Matt's.'

Mae blinked. Exchanged a look with Kit. 'You're sure?'

'Do I seriously have to repeat everything for you people? Yes, I'm sure. He came down here a handful of times and don't ask me for dates,' he said, holding up a hand, 'because I won't know.'

'Are we talking recently, though? This week?' Kit asked.

'Probably. Yes.' He smacked the screen. 'Fucking thing.' Then, slightly dolefully, 'Chose his bloody moment to go on his jollies though. Said he was going to help me with this.'

'Matt did?' Mae asked. 'Good with computers, is he?'

'He's all right,' Jupp said reluctantly. 'Not that you'd guess it, with the massive slab of a laptop he carries around with him. Even *I'd* be embarrassed by it. Size of a printer.'

'We haven't been able to find his laptop, actually,' Kit told him.

'No? Lent it to the guy in the picture, I think.'

'*That* guy?' Kit said, indicating Mae's phone.

'Yeah. Saw him leave with it under his arm. Came in a big padded bag thing with NHS on the side.'

Mae said, pad out. 'And that didn't look suspicious to you?'

Jupp shrugged. 'It wasn't like he was running off with it. Kind of waved when he saw me, you know?' he said, lifting a hand to demonstrate the casualness of it.

'When was this?'

Jupp glanced at the A3 calendar he kept taped to the wall. 'Few days before I saw Matt last. But actually, now you ask, there was a bit of confusion about it. Matt came in the next day, asking if he'd left it behind in here.'

Kit frowned hard. 'Surely the definition of lending someone something is that you do it by choice? I mean,' she said, glancing at Mae, 'I'm no lawyer, but I'm fairly sure that without that element to it, it's just theft.'

Mae nodded. 'Fairly sure that's how it works, yeah.'

Jupp shrugged. 'Matt would've said if it had been nicked. I told him his mate had it, described him, and he just said *okay* or something and went away.'

And that was all he was going to say. Kit thanked him for the both of them and headed back to the car.

'Well, fuck me rigid,' she said as Mae fired up the Focus and pulled away. 'And we know Matt changed the lock at some point too, right? Did he do that because he'd already been robbed? Or because he thought he might be?'

But Mae hardly heard. The questions were stacking up in his head like planes in a holding pattern. Did Cox really have the missing computer? Just how well *did* Cox and Matthew Corsham know each other? What did Ellie think about that?

Did Ellie even *know*?

'We've got to find that laptop,' Kit said, bringing out her phone. Once she'd dialled a number, she wedged the phone between her ear and her shoulder, then flipped open the glovebox. She dug around for a moment, pulled out someone's discarded half-eaten pack of Jammie Dodgers, and crammed one into her mouth.

'You're an animal,' Mae said, waving away her offer of a biscuit. 'Who're you ringing?'

'Hospital,' she said through a mouthful. 'Worth a check in, see if the laptop turned up. Yeah, Helen Williams, please,' she said, turning her attention to the call and wiping crumbs from her mouth with the back of her hand. 'In HR, yeah. It's Detective Constable Ziegler.'

It took almost the entire trip back to the nick to get through to Helen Williams, but when she did, Kit sat bolt upright, listening with eyes wide.

'It came in *last night*?'

Mae had slowed for the turning to the nick, but slammed his foot down on the middle pedal, reversed, and accelerated off towards the hospital.

'Why the hell didn't you ring?' Kit said urgently. There was a pause, in which she gripped the bridge of her nose. Then: 'No! Don't let anyone touch it!'

Chapter 41

Ellie

'Seriously, we have to be quick,' Leon said, letting the door close behind us. 'I'll get such a bollocking if she finds out.'

'I promise.'

He set the laptop down on the worktop and turned it on. The screen lit up and my heart leapt into my throat: he'd changed his screensaver since I'd last seen it to a picture of us. Matt's cheek squeezed hard against mine – I could almost feel the stubble, the press of his ear against mine. I found myself smiling, reliving that happiness for one fickle moment before it was tarnished by the reality of why I was here.

I rested my fingers on the keys and took a mental step back. What was I looking for?

Secrets.

I was looking for anything that Matt wanted to hide. But where? Apart from the default icons that you'd find on every desktop across the globe – My Computer, Explorer, Recycle Bin – there were only a dozen or so folders and none of them looked particularly personal.

Leaning across me, Leon took the mouse and pointed with the cursor. 'It looks like it's just going to be work stuff. These down here,' he said, moving the arrow across folders with names like *ONC. Lab TO DO* and *PAED. for review*, 'they link to the central server. Whatever's in them refreshes whenever you link in to the system.'

'Can I have a look anyway?'

He blew out his cheeks. 'I guess so, if you want.'

I took the mouse and opened one at random. It was empty.

Leon drew in his chin. 'That's weird.' A little spinning-ball icon appeared in the folder. 'There, you see? The system's repopulating it now.'

On the screen, files were pinging into place. But Leon's frown didn't lift.

'What are you thinking?' I asked. 'He must have been trying to hide something if he's deleted everything.'

'That's just it. I don't get why he would have bothered. He knows that they just repopulate like this.'

I clicked open another few folders. It was the same story for all of them. There were hundreds of files now, but it wasn't exactly helping. Every filename followed the same Surname/Forename/Date pattern, topped and tailed by some kind of code. The handful I opened at random were clearly patient-related. Even if there was anything in there, some clue, finding it would take hours, days probably. If Leon's increasing agitation was anything to go by, I was already on borrowed time.

I scrolled despairingly through the lists, unsure what to do next. There *had* to be something here. It occurred to me that if Matt had wanted to conceal something, hiding it under one of these maddeningly innocuous names would be the best way of making sure it was never found. Short of deleting it.

I straightened, thinking, *surely not*.

I opened the recycle bin, mentally crossing my fingers. There were a dozen folders in there. And between one he'd named

'Exhibitions' and another called, inexplicably, 'Corporal James Scott', was a folder called *Cox/Arden/Powers*.

Arden? I had never breathed a word about Jodie to Matt. Also: *Powers,* plural? My heart throwing itself around in my chest, I clicked it open.

The folder was completely empty.

I turned to Leon. 'Will this repopulate as well?'

'No, only the shared stuff. Deleting your recycle bin is a bit more permanent but ...' he tipped his head, thinking about it.

'But what?'

'Well, it's not *permanent* permanent. Something to do with bytecode: the tech guys explained this to me when I deleted something a while ago before they brought this shared system in. It's complicated but basically, unless you really know what you're doing or, like, you dissolve your hard drive in acid or whatever, deleted files can usually be restored without too much trouble.'

'Could *you* do it?'

'God no. But the police probably could,' he said with a sideways glance. Then, looking at a space just behind me, he jumped to his feet. 'I'm sorry, I was literally just about to—'

I turned. In the doorway and with a look of outraged horror on her face was Helen, the children's ward volunteer coordinator and Matt's line manager.

'What are *you* doing here?' she demanded. Then pointing at the laptop she said to Leon, 'Tell me that's not it?'

I got up, dodged her, and ran until I cleared the building, until I was out of the complex completely.

By the time I got to the bus stop the other side of the Hanwell shops, my lungs were burning with the cold air. But I wasn't thinking about my lungs. I wasn't even thinking about what Helen would do about finding me there.

I was thinking about what was in that folder. About the fact that Matt must have gathered enough information to warrant keeping it all together somewhere.

And about what could have motivated him to delete it.

Chapter 42

Mae

Helen Williams was applying powder to her cheeks when Mae and Kit found her in her office.

They sat without being invited, and Mae folded his arms.

'Right. Let's start from the bit where you promised you would tell me if anything that might be of interest came up. Did the return of his laptop not seem of sufficient interest?'

Williams dropped the compact into a large cardboard box sitting on her desk. 'Forgive me. I've been very busy.'

'So where's the computer now?' Kit asked.

She pulled out a drawer and laid the laptop reverentially on the desk. Looked up. 'I thought I better save it for you. That's why I got it sent up from downstairs. I was just about to call when you rang.'

'Is that so?' Kit raised her eyebrows, then tore open a packet of nitrile gloves from her pocket and put them on. 'Who brought it in?'

'Delivery note's in there. I don't know the name. It wasn't Matthew, anyway.'

'Has it passed through anyone else's hands since it got in the building?'

'Leon Baxter – he's in the imaging lab, where Matthew worked.' She paused, broke eye contact.

'Who else?' Mae asked.

'No one,' she said, a little too quickly.

Mae didn't have time for this. 'We'll talk to Leon anyway so if he's going to have something to tell us, you're going to want to have told us first, all right?'

She sighed. 'Eleanor Power.'

'What?' Mae and Kit said in unison.

'She intercepted it. Somehow talked Leon into letting her have a look before he brought it up to me.'

'Right,' Mae said, closing his eyes. 'Excellent.'

'She didn't mess with anything. Nothing was copied or deleted. He assures me.'

'Right, well, if he *assures* you, that's your due process sorted then.' Kit gestured to the boxes. 'What's the deal here, then? Moving offices?'

The smile stiffened on her mouth. 'Pastures new,' she told them stiffly. 'Private sector.'

'Coincidence,' Kit said flatly.

She batted it away. 'Not really. Everyone worth their salt is leaving. NHS is going to the dogs, haven't you heard?'

Outside, after sealing the laptop in an evidence bag and locking it in the boot, Mae gave IT forensics the heads-up, telling them he was bringing the machine in for a thorough combing. Hanging up, he thought of something.

'How about you go back to the front desk,' he said to Kit. 'If the laptop came in to the reception, they'll have a record of who brought it in, presumably.'

'Maybe surveillance?'

'If we're lucky.'

They split up. After settling himself in the car, he dialled Ellie's number. She picked up on the second ring.

'You better have a very good reason for doing what you just did,' he told her.

There was a pause. 'I was going to phone you.'

'Was that before or after you decided to try to intercept his computer? Ellie, I can't help you if you just go ahead and do things like that.' He hadn't even asked her about the car yet, what she knew about it. 'We need to meet. I've got things I need to talk to you about. Your mum, too. This is serious, OK?'

'Oh really? Because I thought it was all a big joke.' Anger in her voice. 'I thought you were convinced he'd just decided to skip town.'

'I never said that,' he said, knowing that the caveat was that he *had* thought it. But what did he think now? Cox was involved, stolen drugs, money. The hospital was telling him one thing and the evidence another. Cox admitted speaking to him about Ellie, but he was hiding something. The rent had been paid but no one had seen the guy for days. His phone was dead, the evidence was chaotic, his home was a dead end, and his girlfriend was ... well. His girlfriend was Ellie Power.

So, was Matthew Corsham missing? Was he fine?

Ellie breathed out a long breath. 'He'd been in touch with Lucy Arden.'

'*Matt* had?'

'Yeah. She sent him this book, this ... diary thing that we used to have. Me and Jodie.'

He remembered it. Remembered poring over with gloved fingers, hours and hours at a time, looking for an overlooked detail, a code, anything he could use.

'And I'm going to go and see her,' Ellie was saying. 'I'm heading there now.'

Mae almost laughed. 'No. No, you're not. This is a police

investigation, Ellie. You get that, right? I'll go and see her. Where is she, Brighton still?'

'Yeah, but—'

'But nothing. You need to keep clear of this. Let me do my job.'

Chapter 43

Ellie

I couldn't go to Lucy's now, but that was OK. There was something else I needed to do.

There was no need to check a map. Although when I was Dr Cox's patient I'd only ever had my sessions in Brighton, I knew exactly where his London office was. Jodie had been up there; she'd come home buzzing with stories of their illicit weekends. Mum had forbidden me to contact Cox after what happened, but I knew his website like the back of my hand, and when I approached the address on Highbury Park, I knew it almost as if I'd lived there.

Siggy lit up like a circuit as I mounted the stone steps. The intercom box crackled with an answer from inside.

'Hello?' A woman's voice. Instantly familiar.

'Samira? It's Ellie. Ellie Power.'

There was a small gasp, then the lock clicked. 'Come on up, sweetheart.'

I pushed the heavy door open, and went inside, up the wide, carpeted stairs to the first floor. On the landing, the door into Cox's suite swung open, and there she was. She had on a cardigan that looked impossibly soft, and it took everything I had not to let myself fall into the arms that were outstretched towards me. But I didn't do it.

Eventually the arms dropped, and she gave me a sad smile, pushing the glasses she hadn't worn when I'd last seen her onto her nose. 'No hug. OK.'

I shrugged, tightly. She was hurt, I could see she was hurt, but I didn't care.

Because whatever she said, Samira had never believed I was sixteen. She couldn't have done: she had kids of her own, girls. Even with the clothes I borrowed from Jodie, I was a little kid, barely pubescent. Although I hadn't seen it for what it was until Mum explained grooming to me, Samira was a key part. She *facilitated*. I trusted her, because she made me trust her.

'I need to talk to Dr Cox,' I told her, matter-of-factly. I didn't want to chat; I didn't want a hug. I just wanted to know what the hell he was doing talking to my boyfriend without my say-so.

'Come through,' said a stiff voice from behind me. I turned. He was standing in the doorway to his office. New creases on his face. Arms folded, his lips a tight, straight line like a No Entry across his face.

'I wish you'd called ahead,' he said flatly as he turned and went back in. 'Do close the door,' he told me as I followed him in.

I did as I was told, and stood there by the door, and stuffed my hands in my pockets so he couldn't see them trembling.

'It's been a very long time, Ellie,' he said, lacing his fingers into a knot on the desk in front of him. 'How have you been? Are you working? Studying?'

'I haven't come to talk about my education.'

A brief, joyless smile. 'No. You want to know about Matt.'

'Do you know where he is?'

He shook his head. 'No.'

'I know you were talking with him.'

'I did. He had a lot of questions about your condition, and your past. He was very interested in—' he paused, as if the word was unpleasant in his mouth, 'in Siggy. He wasn't sure he was getting the whole picture.'

I waited, pretending this wasn't news. But I felt as if I'd been punched, and Siggy recoiled, stung, leaving me fighting an instinct to wrap my arms around myself to soothe her. So what, he thought I was lying? Misleading him in some way?

Cox just sat there watching me like an exhibit of middling but familiar interest in a zoo.

'You're feeling anxious,' he told me.

'Don't you tell me how I'm feeling. You don't know anything about me.'

He sighed, picked at a loose thread in his cuff. 'You might be right, Ellie. But I tried.'

'No, you didn't. You exploited me.'

He winced at that, screwed his eyes shut for a moment. 'Ellie, I did not exploit—'

'Yes, you *did*. Both of us, me *and* Jodie.'

I had sworn I would not cry. But the shell I'd built around the sadness, the humiliation: it all suddenly felt very weak. Siggy enveloped me like a skin, holding me in.

'I made a very big mistake with Jodie. I should never have allowed myself to—' he started, but I bristled, held up both hands.

'I don't want to hear anything about what you did to her.'

'*With* her, Ellie. She was not a child.'

'She *was*. She *was* a child. I was a child.'

'I didn't touch you. I would never have—'

'You did worse. What you did to me was *worse*.' I flexed my hands out of the fists that had involuntarily formed by my sides, remembering what Mum said. *There is no greater scope for exploitation than in the promise of a cure.* Breathing a heavy sigh, he crossed to the window and poured himself a drink.

Swallowing, he turned to the window. 'Does your mother know you're here?'

'I'm nineteen years old.'

'Yes, of course you are. An adult.' He took another mouthful. 'Independent from her.'

I shrugged, not understanding, and tried to swerve it by getting to the point. 'There was a file on Matt's computer. All of our names in the title: yours, mine and Jodie's. Why?'

He paused with the glass halfway to his lips. He stayed that way for a breath, two, then set it noiselessly down on the desk. 'And you know this how?'

'I saw it.'

'Where did you see it, Ellie? The police told me his laptop was missing.'

'It doesn't matter where I saw it. I'm asking you—'

'If you've seen his laptop and you've seen a folder, how is it that you're asking me what was in it?'

'Because he'd deleted the contents. That's why.'

'So maybe he didn't want you to know.'

He obviously wasn't going to budge. I brushed at a non-existent speck on my shoulder like I didn't care one way or the other. 'Well, I guess the police will find out what it was, whether you tell me or not.'

'How could they? I thought you said it was deleted?'

'Doesn't make any difference if the bytecode is still there,' I said, like I knew what that meant.

There was a long pause. Cox went to the window, opened it, then lit a cigarette. His hands were shaking.

'I think you should leave now.'

'I'm not leaving until you tell me what you know.'

He didn't take his eyes off me. After a few long drags, he stubbed the cigarette out. 'Do you remember the last thing I said to you?'

I did.

When they discharged me, miserable but functioning and with my throat stitched and bandaged, my care was transferred to Dr Cox. He met me and Mum in the CAMHS inpatient unit. Right up until we got to the car park, I thought he and Mum had put their differences aside so that I could keep seeing him after all. I remember pulling my bag onto my knees in the back of our car, Mum reaching over and fastening my seatbelt. I thought he was coming with us, like they said he was. But he just stood there, hands hanging, and Mum drove us away.

And that was the last I saw of him.

The whole thing of him signing the forms was all just for show, just to get me out of there. A favour to Mum, to settle things, she said, so it could just be the two of us again, because after everything, and after what he'd done, I was just a little girl who needed her mum.

Even though Mum forbade me from contacting him, I'd been desperate to speak to him, wanted more than anything for him to explain. Because I just couldn't make it fit – the way he'd been with me, and what Mum told me he was really like. I had been so convinced that he had cared about me, and being wrong about that was just – catastrophic. Once she found out, Mum forbade me to contact him. I'd lied to her about it, seen him without her consent because she'd sworn off any more doctors after the endless, fruitless searching of years before. I'd made a huge mistake, she said, an error of judgement. I'd thought I could trust him, and I'd been wrong, and that was all I needed to know.

I remembered the last thing he'd said to me because it was a phrase Matt used, too.

Challenge everything.

'You betrayed me,' I said.

He sat back down behind his desk and rearranged his mug, bringing it to the exact centre of the desk with his forefingers, before repositioning his laptop, phone, pen, then lastly the flats of his hands.

'I did not betray you. That's not true.'

'No? Why did you need those images, Dr Cox?'

'It was professional documentation!' he shouted, bringing his fist down on the table and making the mug jump. Breathing heavily through his nose as if calming himself, he was silent for a moment. When he spoke again his voice was low. 'Let me tell you something, Ellie. What you did, the lies you told about my having something to do with Jodie's disappearance, it nearly ruined my career.'

'What you did to me, that nearly ruined my *life*. If it's a conversation about morality.'

He narrowed his eyes. 'Your mother made me swear I would never even *speak* to you again—'

'My mother?' I was on my feet and Siggy was there, turning in a tight, black coil of rage. But I wasn't afraid of it, that fury. It was something I could use, something uniting us. 'Without my mother I would still be thinking you were all right. That you were decent. But you're not, are you?'

'Ellie.'

This wasn't what I had come to say, but it was too late to stop it now. 'How many little girls have you had up here? Huh?

How many desperate kids who think you're someone they can open up to? Tens of them? Hundreds?'

'Ellie.' On his feet, hands up, eyes wide. 'Calm down.'

'You told me those photos you took were for my benefit—'

'They *were*.'

'But all the time,' I said, my voice trembling with the rage and the effort of holding everything in, 'all the time you were just thinking what you could do with them. Who you could sell them to.'

'OK. You need some deep breaths now.' Cox came towards me, hands out as if to take mine but I pushed him roughly away.

'*Don't* touch me,' I snapped, whipping myself away out of his grasp. 'Don't you *dare*.' I wiped my face angrily with the heels of my hands. What was I supposed to do? Leave? I knew I should leave but I couldn't.

'I just want Matt back. I just want him *back*.'

'OK,' he said. '*OK*.' He gave me an appraising look, and then appeared to make a decision. He went back around his desk, and slipped his arms into the jacket on the back of the chair. 'I'm going to get us some tea, and then we can talk.'

'I don't need tea. I need you to tell me the truth.'

'*I* need some. Just … just wait here.'

He left me alone in the room, his silhouette dissolving behind the frosted glass window. A moment later, Samira came in.

She said nothing for a moment then let out a long sigh. 'Dr Cox told me he's gone missing, Your Matthew.'

'Looks that way.'

'He seemed *lovely*,' she went on. Clasped her hands together to emphasize it. 'People are so much nicer when you meet them in person, sometimes.'

'He— you've met him?'

She nodded. 'Good few times he's been up.'

I opened my mouth. Closed it again.

'He's very sweet. Very concerned, I gather,' she said, before dropping her head into a sympathetic tilt. She went to the window to retrieve a stray scrap of paper, then stopped, frowning back at me and then peering down through the glass.

'Had you finished up here, then?' she said.

I crossed the room and followed her eyeline, down to the road below. The sound of the heavy door hitting its frame reverberated through the building and, at street level, a blond head emerged.

Cox wasn't getting tea.

I shot out of the office and down to the front door taking the steps two at a time, but I wasn't fast enough. By the time I got the door open, he was gone. At the bottom of the stone steps, my heart was tripping heavily over itself. The last I saw of him was a flash of grey-blond hair in the driver's seat of a battered, cherry-red three-door.

Chapter 44

Mae

Mae stood in a patch of sunlight in the living room of Lucy Arden's maisonette, while the whistle of a stovetop kettle sounded over the gentle voices of a radio drama in her kitchen. He'd left Kit to get to the bottom of how Matthew's laptop had found its way back to the hospital, leaving strict instructions to call with any developments.

'Milk?' Lucy called from the kitchen. 'Sugar?'

'Yes, and no. Thank you.'

He'd realized in the taxi from Brighton station that over a year had passed since he'd last been to the coast. There were still a handful of friends down here of course, and to start with he'd kept in touch, made visits. But after he'd changed forces, and Nadia had made the move up to London as well, their gravitational pull had dwindled into nothing. Little had changed in the town, but inside Lucy's home, *everything* was different.

He cast his eyes over the room, trying to reconcile the place with the way it had been. After Jodie disappeared, Lucy Arden's neighbourhood had rallied. They'd made sure there was enough food to fill both fridges in her kosher kitchen, with the surplus stacked across the worktops. Last time he'd been there, Mae had filled a couple of bin bags with some of the forgotten casseroles and foil-wrapped cakes, for the sake of her health. Mould crept unchecked across the Pyrex dishes, and there were ants. The sort of thing he was used to seeing in the homes of addicts.

The rest of the flat had been worse. She hadn't been able to stand the void her daughter had left behind, so she'd got everything from Jodie's childhood out of storage and brought it into the living spaces again. The whole place had exuded a pulsing sense of chaos, the kind of disorder that worms into your head and breaks your sentences in half. Belongings were piled everywhere, games and cartoon DVDs and books, school projects, dressing-up things, soft toys, building up and spilling out like a panic attack.

This, though, *this* was like being in a different flat, with a different person. Either mental health prescriptions had got a whole lot better since he'd needed them, or she'd found peace some other way. It was clean, hoovered, warm, orderly but lived-in. He touched an ornate branch of the traditional menorah sitting in the centre of the windowsill, its five candle spaces polished and ready for the Shabbat candles. It was something he'd seen many times in the homes of victims of serious crime: where some lost their faith, others immersed themselves in it with renewed vigour. Maybe her religion had been the ladder out of the hole: and who was he to judge? Things got bad, people needed to cling, just like boats needed anchors. What he wouldn't have given for some faith when Nadia left. God only knew what he'd turn to if something like that happened to Bear, if someone took *her*—

Lucy returned with the coffee, plus slices of a fruit cake on a tray. She sat, passed him a mug, wrapped her hands around her own.

'So what's this about?'

He settled in an armchair. 'I understand you were in touch with Matthew Corsham. You sent him something? A diary.'

Her smile solidified, and she touched her throat, where a thin silver chain caught in a slip of sunlight.

'He asked me not to tell Ellie,' she said after a pause. 'He said he was trying to work something out about her, but she was still very – what was the word he used? Fragile. He wanted to find out everything he could about her.'

'Like what? About Jodie?'

She shrugged, and the thing that had been bothering him suddenly came into focus, named itself. Acceptance. Lucy Arden was no longer at the mercy of grief.

'About all of it. How the girls had gone to see—' she paused, swallowed tightly before saying just the surname, '*Cox*, without us knowing. He wanted to ask about the terrible thing with-with what Ellie did. After. She's better now, though? He said she was thinking of moving in with him.'

Mae bounced the rubber end of his pencil on the hard cover of his notebook a few times before he spoke again, watching her face.

'Last time I saw you, you told me you'd found some things out about Cox. What he'd been doing since.'

She sighed, looked out of the window. 'That was a long time ago. I was still very angry about everything. I haven't been following him again, if that's what you came here about.'

'I'm not here to accuse you of anything, Lucy.'

A look of shame, embarrassment, clenched her features. 'I've put it behind me now. I've got a different job, I've moved on. Why are you asking about *him*?'

Pause. Phrasing. He needed to get this right. 'It seems Matthew and Cox were in contact.'

'Were they really,' she said, shaking her head with a look of disgust. 'Well. If I had known *that*—'

'And Matthew Corsham appears to be missing.'

'Oh, no.' She leaned forwards. 'Is he ... do you think he's ... all right?'

Mae spread his hands. 'I don't know. But anything you can tell us about Matthew might be helpful.'

She stood up and went to the window. Through the glass, above the flat skyline, a haemorrhage of dark pink and purple clouds, lit by the sinking sun.

She pressed her lips together. 'OK. Two weeks ago I got a call from him, wanting to know what I knew about Ellie.'

'Tell me about that.'

'We only spoke for half an hour. I had to get to work. We were going to meet up for a coffee, but I said I'd send him the diary. But he wanted to know everything, how we met Ellie, her relationship with Charles Cox, everything.'

'And what did you tell him, about Cox?'

She flashed a wire-tight smile that hardly even touched her cheeks and said, 'I told him he was a paedophilic bastard who I'd gladly see hang.' She finished her coffee and stared at the empty mug.

'I'm sorry to drag this all back up, Lucy. But if there's anything else you can tell me—'

'I followed him, before. Charles. Back when it was raw, you know?' She looked up, her eyes suddenly shining. 'I followed him a *lot*. Pretty much every day.' She shook her head. 'And he knew I was there; I didn't try to hide it. Obviously, he didn't do anything incriminating with me there, but I didn't care. I wanted him to be scared of me. The way I saw it, he'd ruined my life. But if it hadn't been for me, he'd have never met her. Can you imagine how that feels to know that someone you'd been—' she winced as she said it, '*sleeping* with, was grooming your baby? Worse? He'd just … *razed* everything.'

'But you didn't find anything, or you would have said.'

Lucy Arden stretched her head back, let out a long sigh above her. 'Every day for a year, I went to his house. It was like he'd turned into this robot, did everything the same as the day before, like he was on a schedule. Although I know he lost a lot of work. No one wanted to tell him all their dirty secrets, after what happened.' A short, dry laugh. 'So his mum has this yoga retreat place, out in East Molesey. I left a load of one-star reviews on her website.'

'His *mum's* website?'

'Yeah. I know,' she said, looking up at him and cringing. 'Disgusting behaviour. His mum might be lovely, for all I know. Not her fault.' She sighed heavily. 'I don't know why I'm telling you this.'

Mae shrugged. 'You went through a lot, Lucy. Not a lot of people understand what it's like, losing someone like that.'

'No.'

She held his gaze. For a few stretched seconds, it was as if his secret, his own loss, shifted and began to climb out of him. He could almost feel it, the sharp claws of it gaining traction in his throat, rising. But he forced himself to look away. He stood, he smiled his professional smile and made to leave.

His wasn't a grief to be shared. Certainly not with her, a victim. Not with anyone.

There was a smell of oranges cooking, layered with a little choke of burnt sugar, as he stepped out into the mosaicked hallway. He sniffed the air, and Lucy Arden laughed. It was a sound he had never heard before.

'Marmalade. I don't know if it'll work.'

It wouldn't, from the smell of it, but he wasn't going to ruin her fun. Though he'd certainly been the bearer of much worse news, he thought, as he tied the laces of the boots he'd respectfully left by the front door.

He stood and held out his hand to shake hers, but something behind Lucy's head caught his eye. He sidestepped her, peered at it. A painted portrait. Oils, faintly impressionistic, but he knew the face in seconds. He looked at Lucy.

'Is this …?'

'It's a lot like her, isn't it,' she replied quietly, picking at a fingernail.

He got up close to it. 'What is that, like an age progression thing?'

'Yeah,' she said. 'Like Madelaine McCann.'

'But it's painted,' he said, not taking his eyes off the young woman.

'Yes.' Lucy was at the door now, slipping the chain out of the latch. 'They did a good job.'

She wasn't kidding. All there had been back then were photos, a scrap or two of amateur video. Jodie sitting primly in her school uniform or drama-class costumes. Lady Macbeth, Blanche DuBois. He'd never seen the missing girl in the flesh. But, if Jodie had aged half a decade like the rest of them, she'd be in her early twenties by now. And she'd look a lot like that young woman wearing the cowl-neck grey sweater in the painting: the subtle nobility of her features; her thick, bark-brown hair twisted into a rope and tossed over the milk white of her clavicle.

'Where did you get that done?'

She glanced at it. 'Uh – online, somewhere,' she said vaguely, before pulling the front door open. 'Company went bust though, I think.'

Mae slipped his phone out of his pocket and framed the painting up for a photo, making sure he got the signature in the bottom right. Maybe that was someone Mae could use on his team.

She agreed to call him if anything else came to mind, and they said goodbye.

All the way back to London Victoria, something about that picture was bothering Mae, like a tick in his ear. When he stepped off the train onto the windy platform, Kit rang, telling him something fast and urgent.

'Say it again?' he shouted down the line, a palm pressed over his free ear.

'Hold on.' She was outside somewhere, having to shout over the beep of a heavy vehicle reversing. Then all of a sudden the line cleared, and he could hear her. 'I said, I've just finished at the hospital. They've got pretty good CCTV review, as it happens. I'm sending over a clip of when the laptop got delivered to reception. It's not a courier, I don't think, and it's not Matt.'

'You're sure?'

'Yeah. It's a woman. Dark hair, middle-aged, from the looks of it.'

'Any one you recognize?'

'I don't think so, but it's hard to tell. Sending it now. See what you think,' she said.

'Hold on,' Mae said. 'Before you hang up, I've got a job for you. If you get a chance before I get back, see if you can track down an artist for me.' He enlarged the corner of the photo of Lucy's painting with his finger and thumb on the screen and brought it close to his eyes. 'Looks like the name is ...' he squinted, trying to make it out. 'E. Shevah.' He spelled it for her. 'I'm sending you over a portrait.'

'As in a painting kind of portrait?' Amusement in her voice. 'None of us like the pay freeze, Sarge, but I'm not sure art dealing's the way forward.'

'Yeah? Same goes for stand-up. Get a decent printout of the picture, see if you can track the artist down for a chat.'

'Fine. Clip's on its way.'

Mae hung up and moved with the crowd through the barriers, phone in hand. The video clip arrived, and he found a free seat as it downloaded.

He opened the picture. It was grainy, from too high, he thought, to distinguish the face on the person standing on the public side of the desk.

Then he stretched it with his fingers. Leaned in. He paused the footage, spooled back, spooled forwards, did it again, a third time, until he was absolutely sure.

'Fuck,' he began, hardly able to believe what he was seeing, 'me.'

Because the face on the screen, the face of the person who had anonymously brought Matthew Corsham's laptop back to where it belonged, was none other than the secretary of the man Mae believed had murdered Jodie Arden five years ago.

Samira Anand.

Chapter 45

Ellie

Hand on her throat, Samira met me at the top of the stairs as I came back up from the street. 'Where did he go?' she said, bafflement on her face. 'What happened?'

I'd already decided how I was going to play it. 'He said there was some dry cleaning he'd suddenly remembered.'

'Really? But I only just picked his jackets up.'

I shrugged. 'That's what he said. He'll be back in a minute, he told me to wait.'

Suspicion clouded her face. 'I don't know, I mean, he doesn't usually—'

'It's only me, Samira,' I said. 'I'm not going to rob the place. He said he'll be back in a bit.'

Visibly buoyed by the change in tone, she acquiesced. 'I don't see why not. I'll make some tea.'

I closed the door behind me. She might have been a mug, but she wasn't stupid, and I probably had just a few minutes until she called Cox and realized that wherever he'd gone in such a hurry, it wasn't the laundrette.

Security, it turned out, was not his forte. The filing cabinets were locked, but the keys were in the first place I looked: the top drawer of his desk. I silently crossed back to the locked metal units and unlocked the middle one. I ran my fingers over the alphabetical tabs, from *Rutherford* at the back to *Leonard* at the front. *Payne, Petherham, Pienaar, Porter, Pringle*. No *Power*, not even an empty file.

Through the wall I heard an unseen kettle click off, footsteps, a cupboard door opening.

Fumbling with the keys, I opened the next drawers. *Ryder* to *Thatcher*, and *Thebo* to *Young*. There was nothing there at all. The thought struck me that he might have something on Matt, but there was no *Corsham* under the Cs.

Fuck.

Through the wall: 'Sugar?'

I never took it, but it would buy me some time. 'Do you have any honey?' I called back. 'Or sweetener?'

Carefully, I slid the drawers home, before spotting something right at the back of the last one. Past the end of the alphabet, to *Misc*.

Behind the divider was a single envelope. Brown, with a card back and an instruction printed in red: *Do Not Bend*. Cox's name and address on the front in a delicate, curling, script and a foreign postmark beneath a shield decorated with stars.

And in big, felt-tip capitals: *E.P.?*

EP – Ellie Power, maybe? But why the question mark?

I turned it over and lifted the flap, the glue long since dried to a brown sheen and the paper soft with age. Inside was a single document.

From the kitchen, I heard the tap of a spoon on china. I slid the document out, one eye on the door.

It was off-white, thick and watermarked, the text in black with red curlicues around the edges, a line of rust in one corner a centimetre long. It was an official document, like a certificate but not in English. Some of the words were filled in, handwritten onto dotted lines, and there was a date in 1989, two years before I was born.

I slid it back into the envelope with the starry-shield stamp, and read the postmark: 22nd September 2006.

Four days before Jodie died.

'Nice and sweet,' Samira said as she pushed the door open with her hip.

I didn't waste a heartbeat. In the time it took her to enter the room, set the mugs on the desk and turn, I'd slipped the whole envelope inside my sweatshirt, shoved the drawer back, and straightened up.

'I'm sorry,' I said, 'I can't wait after all. I have to be somewhere.'

'Oh, okay,' she said, looking crestfallen. 'Another time?'

'Sure.' I made for the door.

'Did you get in touch with that aunty of yours?'

'Aunty? What do you mean?'

'Your aunt, your mum's sister. Came looking for you, left her number. Very keen for me to pass it on.'

I blinked, baffled: Samira folded her arms, frowning. 'No? She not get hold of you? I dug out your mum's old email and sent the number. Thought at the time she might have changed her address but,' she shrugged, 'it was all I had. I did try to look you both up but you'd—'

'When was this?'

'Oh, good while ago. Couple of years? She'd been looking for you for a long time, she said. I think she eventually got hold of us through the hospital, after you were discharged to Dr Cox.'

An *aunt*? 'Must have slipped her mind. Did she leave a number?'

'I'll dig it out for you,' she said, as the phone rang on her desk. 'Leave your number and I'll call when I find it – sorry, I should take this.' She lifted the receiver and waved me goodbye.

I went down the stairs and out onto the street with one thought in my head. Mum was an only child. Both her parents had died, years back, but there was never a sister.

I didn't have an aunt.

Chapter 46

Mae

Once he'd identified Samira Anand on the hospital CCTV, things got moving pretty fast. While he waited outside Victoria Station for Kit to come and pick him up, he called McCulloch and filled her in.

'Bring him in,' McCulloch said. 'But when you're back here, Ben, we need a conflab, all right?'

'Sure thing, yep,' he said, cutting the call before she could say anything else. He knew what was coming: given his previous involvement, she was going to want to move him discreetly elsewhere. But the longer he could delay that, the better chance he had of getting to the bottom of it.

It wasn't hard to find Kit: she'd pulled in round the back of the station. Helpfully, she had a full-blast Bikini Kill playlist on that he could hear from a range of fifty metres, though she respectfully lowered the volume when he got in beside her.

He set the GPS to Cox's office: it estimated a forty-minute journey to the middle of Highbury. The visit didn't constitute an emergency worthy of the blues and twos but even without them, he knew he could rely on Kit to shave at least a little off that.

'What's the plan when we get there,' she asked, nosing the car out. 'Interview Cox and the receptionist separately?'

'If they're both there. I just called him and he's not answering. I've requested a unit to his flat just in case.' Cox's home address – which was exactly as salubrious as he'd described – was a shock even to Mae when he found it. He couldn't imagine much longer a drop from the palatial home he'd had in Sussex only a few years before.

He put on his seatbelt, sniffing the air. Something unseen smelled immodestly delicious. The lights changed as Kit swung the Focus into a box junction, blocking the oncoming stream of traffic. The driver of a shiny beamer honked her, with good reason, but she gave him the hairy eyeball as she slipped out of the minor gridlock she'd just caused.

'You are one lucky bugger, recognizing her from that image at the hospital,' she told him as she eased down on the gas.

'I'm one investigative bugger,' he corrected. He sniffed again. 'What *is* that?'

She reached into the back and produced a paper bag.

'Churros. Want?' She helped herself to a thin, piped stick of deep-fried doughnut batter, the kind that Bear begged him for at fairgrounds, before making a disparaging face at his hesitation and shaking the bag at him.

'Go on, go mad,' she said through a mouthful. 'Hear the call of the wild side.'

He declined, and she shrugged, sucking sugar off her fingers. 'Your loss.'

They headed over the river and north. Neighbourhoods changed fast as they passed the invisible social boundary line that bisected the borough of Islington. Packed-in social housing gave way to grand townhouses lining leafy, comfortable-looking streets as they came off the Holloway Road. The car slowed as they passed the old Arsenal ground, and Kit smiled out of the window. She'd navigated her way there with the deft precision of a cabbie, and now Mae saw why.

'Gooner?'

She grinned at him. 'You?'

'Nah. I'll watch the Bees when they're winning.'

A smirk. 'Not often, then.'

'Yeah well. Watching football isn't exactly my thing. Especially when I know what we spend on the clear-up.'

'Oh! So it's a *litter* problem.'

'I mean the social clear-up, obviously. Pissed-up fans. You never worked a match day? Seen the domestic spikes we get afterwards?'

She ran her tongue around her teeth, shaking her head. 'Yeah, but there's nobheads in every sport. You can't tar the whole game with that brush. What about Bear, though: she like going?'

Mae opened his mouth to reply, then closed it again, unsure how to phrase it.

She gawked at him for a second. 'You haven't taken her? *Sarge*. Seriously?'

He held up a finger. 'One word—' he started.

'Is it *Hillsborough*?' She rolled her eyes. 'Come on. *I'll* take her.'

'No, you bloody won't.'

Kit laughed, giving it up. 'OK, fine. Maybe she's a baby derby girl though? How about I take her to a bout? Think she'd like to come and see Daddy's new workmate get the shit kicked out of her?'

He changed his mind and reached into the back for a churro. 'There isn't a person alive who wouldn't like to see that.'

Highbury Park was an upmarket street, lined with 4x4s and shiny hybrids. Trees, already bigger and thicker than the pavement wanted them to grow, heaved through the tarmac, lifting sections of the high kerbs in places. But they were the only source of disorder. Hammerited iron railings gave way at regular intervals along the street to wide stone steps, old enough to bow in the middle from decades of erosion by expensive shoes. Cheap shoes, too, if you accounted for staff.

Kit tucked the car into a tight space and killed the engine. As she got out she whistled quietly, looking up. Mae knew what she was thinking: you didn't get opulence like this in Hounslow. Proper girl of her patch, he thought, watching her click her neck from side to side the way she did whenever she got out of a car. As if she was stiff from a cage: as if she was somehow a bit wild. A bit like him.

She turned. Caught him looking but didn't look away until he did. Mae ran his thumbs around the crease of his collar to straighten it and shut the door of the Focus, then went after Kit, who had cleared the steps nimble as a mountain goat.

He pressed the buzzer, then blew out his cheeks.

'You all right?' Kit asked him. 'Look antsy.'

There were footsteps inside, but no answer on the intercom. 'She's not going to be pleased to see me.'

'Oh yeah? Is anyone?' Kit asked as the deadlocks clunked inside. The door opened to reveal Samira Anand, a face on her like she knew exactly what was coming next.

'Come in,' she muttered, glancing behind them into the road and visibly sinking at the sight of the squad car.

The first-floor clinic was immaculate: neutral fabrics on the big, soft sofas; thick pile on the floor. Samira locked the door of the reception room behind them once they were all inside. She took the phone off the hook, perched nervously on the end of the polished mahogany desk, and gestured for them to sit.

Kit leaned against a wall, while Mae clasped his hands behind his back, uniform-style.

'So. The package you delivered to the hospital yesterday.'

Samira looked up to him, then to Kit, as if appealing for leniency. 'How did—?' she started, then cut herself off.

'How did we know it was you? When you signed it in from,' he made a show of checking the jpeg Kit had forwarded, '*Mrs Harsworth*?'

'Oh ... did I?'

Kit dropped her shoulders and sighed. 'You did, yeah.' She picked a spot in the middle of the expansive cream-coloured sofa and spread her arms across the back of the cushions. 'Look, we just want to find out what you know about the package, and why you tried to hide that it was you who dropped it off.'

Mrs Anand, looking like she was about to cry, whispered, 'I just ... I was passing. It seemed a waste to courier it, like he said, so I just took it in.'

Mae took an unoccupied seat and got out his notebook. 'From the top, if you wouldn't mind.'

She sighed, then fixed her gaze hard on a spot in the middle of the room. 'Dr Cox wanted me to send this ... parcel off to the hospital. He said it should go by courier but I shouldn't say it was from him.'

'Why?'

'I don't know.'

'Oh yeah?' Kit screwed her face up and shot Mae a look. Clearly didn't believe a word of it. 'And you're saying you didn't ask?'

'No.' She met Kit's eye, then got started on a staring match with the carpet. 'I've known Dr Cox a very long time. Know him better than I know my own husband, really. Thick and thin, richer and poorer,' she added with a thin laugh. 'He can be a little ... eccentric. So if he asks something out of the ordinary, I just go ahead and do it. He'll have his reasons.'

'Did you wrap the package yourself?' Kit asked, careful not to disclose or lead, her training still box-fresh.

Another shrug. 'I didn't even know he had another laptop.'

Mae glanced over to see Kit narrow her eyes. 'So you did know it was a laptop?'

The arrangement of biros and pencils in a glass desk-tidy suddenly became very interesting to her.

'Mrs Anand,' Kit said, leaning forward, 'I think you already know that we're investigating a young man's disappearance. We have reason to believe he may be in danger, and anything you can tell us to help find him is absolutely crucial.'

'And time-critical,' Mae added. Last thing he wanted was for her to get a pang of conscience this time next week.

Samira Anand cleared her throat. 'Dr Cox said he wanted it taken in, urgently. Right after you left,' she added, glancing briefly at Mae, 'yesterday evening. I don't know why, but it was very important to him that it didn't have his name on it. He said to book a courier, but I thought, well, I know the hospital. I passed it whenever I went to visit my sister, and I'd already planned to pop round after work. Dr Cox doesn't exactly have money to burn these days. I thought I'd just drop it in on my way.'

Kit leaned forwards, elbows on knees, head cocked. 'That true?'

'Yes.'

'So why'd you give a fake name?'

The older woman sighed. 'I-I don't know. I just suddenly thought, maybe I wasn't supposed to do this, maybe there was a reason he wanted the courier.'

'Not because you knew what you were doing was potentially assisting in the commission of an offence?'

She drew a sudden breath, her eyes darting between the two of them again. 'No! What offence?'

Kit spread her hands. 'I suppose we'll work that out when we find Mr Corsham, right? In whatever … *condition* he happens to be in when we finally do that.'

Just then Mae's phone went off. Two buzzes: a text. Ellie. He drew it out, read it.

Screwed his eyes shut. Opened them. Read it again.

Saw Cox a couple of hours ago, the message said. *He's hiding something, ran off while I was talking to him.*

He got to his feet, faster than sneezing. He excused himself, motioned to his phone, then left the room and had Ellie on the line before he got to the front door.

'What do you mean, ran off?' he hissed.

'I mean he *ran away*,' Ellie said, sounding defensive. 'He said he was going to make us tea. He left, got in his car and drove off.'

'What? Why?'

'No idea.'

'Well, think, Ellie. What had you been talking about? There must have been something that spooked him.'

There was a pause. 'There was a folder on Matt's computer. In the recycling bin, like he'd meant to delete it. It was called *Jodie Ellie* … no, hold on. *Powers Arden Cox*, or something. I told him I'd seen it. I wanted to know what he knew.'

'And what did he say to that?'

'Nothing. He wouldn't give anything away at all. I mean, I told him what Leon said, that the police can put deleted files back together, and that seemed to bug him. Then we talked about something else and then, well, he just vanished.'

'And have you called him? Cox, since he ran off?'

'Goes to voicemail. He's turned it off.'

'Listen.' He forced calm into his voice now. 'We need to talk. Where are you?'

There was a pause. 'Nearly home,' she said. She sounded exhausted, lost. 'I might have a walk somewhere. Have a coffee.'

'OK, look. We need to talk. If you're not going home, pick a café or something, then text me.'

'All right.'

Mae wasn't convinced. 'You'll do that, yes?'

She gave him her word, and as they said a sober goodbye, a second call came up on his screen.

It was Rod Stevens. Mae glanced back up the stairs: the door into the clinic was still closed.

'Twice in a day,' Mae said as he answered. 'What a treat.'

'Yes well. Not that I'm trying to guilt trip you into actually coming out for a pint with me or anything, but listen. I found myself with a few spare microseconds and had a little dig on your gentleman.'

'Cox?' He had Mae's full attention now. 'And?'

'Few hits of interest. He's got this silver VW Transporter.' Stevens reeled off the licence before getting to the meat. 'He gets about quite a bit, spends a good deal of time in East Molesey, but parks it mostly in a garage block in Haringey.' He gave the address, which Mae estimated to be maybe half a mile from the flat Cox rented above the bookies. 'Also seems to frequent an address in N5, the more bucolic subdivisions thereof,' Rod added.

'Somewhere around Highbury Park?'

A pause, then a disappointed grunt. 'And here I was thinking my honorary DI chevrons would be in the post.'

Mae laughed. 'I'm here now,' he explained. 'It's his clinic. Look, thanks mate, but I've got to—'

'Oh no you don't. That's not even the headline.'

'Go on, then.'

'Last few weeks he's been parked quite a lot on a few roads within a very small footprint in West 13, just off Windmill Road. Which is where the car ended up when we did our little retro-trace at kill-me-o'clock this morning.' He was silent for a moment, before he said, 'Ben? Are you there?'

'Yeah. Yep, I'm here, mate,' Mae said, trying to sound neutral while the adrenaline spiked holes through him. 'Which roads are we talking about, exactly?'

Rod cleared his throat and named a couple of streets. As he listed them, the place that formed their convergence point formed in Mae's mental map.

'And,' Rod said, 'right in the middle of those—'

'Is Abson Street,' Mae finished. 'Holy shit.'

'And not just that,' Rod went on. 'But look: the angle's a bit awkward and I could be wrong, but I'm looking at a live feed and I'm pretty sure he's there right now.'

Chapter 47

Ellie

The waitress in the café brought my tea without a word and left me in peace. It was warm in there, with the burble of a radio behind the counter playing innocuous pop. Mae's text told me to wait, but after forty-five minutes he still hadn't arrived. I was gathering my stuff to leave when I saw a police car pull up outside. Mae was driving, but instead of getting out the car I watched him take his shades off and squint through the café window. He scanned the place until he saw me, then turned in his seat, away from me, and said something to his passenger who then got out. It was a tall, muscular woman, full of that easy confidence that had always been so elusive to me. She jogged round the back of the car and slapped it twice on the roof. Mae flicked a switch near the rear-view mirror and the blue lights started to turn as he pulled away.

Why wasn't he coming in? What had happened?

By the time the woman swung open the heavy glass door, I was on my feet. She came striding over and slid into the booth opposite me waving me back into my seat.

'Have you found him? Matt? Has something happened?' I asked her urgently.

'Ellie,' she said, extending a hand when we'd both sat. 'Nice to meet you, I'm DC Catherine Ziegler, I work with DS Mae.'

'Why is he not here himself?' I wanted to know. 'What's going on, where was he going?'

'There was some ... urgent business to see to,' she said. Then, as I drew back from her, panicked, she added, 'it's not Matt. We haven't got whereabouts yet, I'm afraid. DS Mae sends his apologies, he's, ugh, he's got a lot of cases to deal with.'

I didn't believe her for a moment. She waved the approaching waitress away then leaned towards me, her hands clasped in the middle of the table between us.

'He wanted me to have a chat with you anyway though, Ellie. I'm afraid there are a few things that are causing us alarm at this stage, and I need to have a really honest talk with you about that.'

Siggy stayed quiet, but she was there, crouching. Not gloating, not judging me. I slid one hand over the other, and up the sleeve. Touching my fingertips against my bare skin. Needing the contact. The pain from my injured hand glowed secretly under the dressing, under the glove.

I glanced around the room. It seemed to me that every face was turned towards me. I got up, suddenly. 'Can we – would it be OK to do this – somewhere else?'

She got to her feet. 'Sure thing.'

Outside, the cold air bit through my layers. I felt Siggy slip down to the soles of my feet and turn away.

We headed north. The low light made the unbroken grey cloud look solid, a huge undulating shell hanging over the city. Last time I'd come through here it had been summer, with Matt. We'd got sandwiches from the Boots a few streets away, made a picnic of it. But the flower beds were empty now and the well-tended grass was slipping into winter patchiness.

DC Ziegler stopped at a bench, brushed someone's crumbs from the peeling green paintwork and sat. 'Take a pew?'

She put her hands on her knees, took a deep breath and said, 'The first thing to say is that we really appreciate you calling about Cox. Telling us what happened when you were there.'

I'd transferred the envelope I'd stolen from him into my bag, but I could feel it in there, and my cheeks burned with paranoia. Did she know? Could she?

'But we need you to stay clear of what we're doing, all right? Trying to get hold of his laptop like that before we got there. I mean, you knew we wanted to see that computer, right?'

I tensed my jaw, looked away.

'You have to back off. If we find that we're—' she paused, obviously taking great care over the words she used, 'we're not just looking at a case of a person going missing, anything we find might end up being used as evidence. We can't have you tampering with that.'

'I wasn't tampering!' I said, anxiety winding its shaking arms around me and sending my voice high. 'I'm just trying to find out what the hell is going on.'

'OK. I know. But we need to have an understanding, all right?'

I forced a smile, nodded. 'All right. Fine.'

'Good.' She got a notebook from her pocket and flipped to a clean page. 'So, let's have an amnesty here, yeah? Is there anything else you want to tell me?'

I blinked. I can't account for my actions the night he disappeared, and my mum destroyed his car because she thinks I killed him. 'No.'

She nodded, made a note. 'OK. Here's a question. How did you know to go to the hospital?'

'I didn't. Lucky break. I was there to pick something up from my mum.'

'Yeah? And how's she doing?'

'Fine, I think. I don't know.'

'How come?'

I shrugged. 'Haven't seen her since ...' I paused, thinking, how long was it? Had I ever gone this long without seeing her?

'Fallen out?'

'No,' I said urgently. 'No, nothing like that. I went to find her at work, but she was halfway through her shift, she could have been anywhere. And her shift pattern, you know? It's unreliable, and I didn't have my phone so ...' I trailed off, realizing I was protesting too much.

'OK. Sure.' She waited for a moment, watching me.

'So, how are you doing? You want to tell me how things are going with your mental health?'

I must have flinched.

'I'm not here to judge you about it.'

'I don't—' I started, 'it's got nothing to do—'

'Look. I know you lost your friend, before. I'm just saying, it doesn't take a PhD in psychology to guess that you're going to be struggling right now.'

She wasn't smiling, not in the conventional way, but there was something about her face. I could trust this person. I knew it instinctively.

'Her name's Siggy, right?'

My jaw tightened involuntarily at the mention of her name. I opened my mouth to reply but then I just shook my head. I was five years old, mute. My fists were balled in my lap and I just wanted to go home. I had to get home, because if I started talking to this woman, I might never stop.

I stood up. 'I've got to go,' I said, and I started walking, but she matched my speed. 'OK, I'm going out on a limb here. I'm speaking as a person who knows about trauma, and mental health, and not as a cop, OK?'

I didn't slow, but I was listening.

'Ellie, if the last contact you had with a psychotherapist was Dr Cox, all those years ago, I really think you might want to consider finding someone else for a time. Because I can spot how badly this ... this thing is affecting you, and I sincerely don't believe you have to suffer like this.'

Hot, angry tears split down my cheeks and I wiped at them roughly with the back of my gloved hand. 'You don't know what you're talking about.'

She took a long breath, like she was psyching up for something. Then she put her hands on my shoulders. 'You *can* get better, if you work at it.'

Siggy started to solidify in my arms, growing heavy but vibrating. I wrenched myself away, and in one moment the warmth I'd felt for this total stranger fermented, turned into indignant fury.

'You don't know a thing about me. Not a thing. You think it's just some silly little game I'm playing?'

'No. *No*, that is absolutely not what I mean.'

I was shaking now, fear and rage and bitter sadness seizing up inside the fibres of my muscles. 'Who the hell do you think you are, making judgements about me? About who I am?'

She folded her arms, gave a long, slow, nod. 'OK. All right, Ellie, I'm sorry.' But then she said, 'Last chance then. Whatever it is you're not saying. The next stop is a formal interview and I know you're not going to want to go there. *I* don't want to go there.'

It came into focus clearly then, right in front of me, the choice I was making. In one bowl of the scales sat the right thing to do, the real truth, and justice, whatever that would mean for me. All crammed into a dish the same size as its opposite, which held only one thing: my mother, and the sacrifices she had made for me, was bigger and denser and weightier than any and all of those things.

'Ellie.'

'Yes, I heard you. I haven't got anything else to tell you.'

'All right then. Have it your way. I'm going to have to call you in to the station, all right? Call this number,' she said, handing me a card, 'and we'll work out an appointment, today or tomorrow, latest. In the meantime, you need to stay out of our investigation. Is that clear?'

I said nothing.

Her head tilted to the side, she said again, 'Is that clear?'

'*Yes.*'

I watched her walk out of the park and cross the road. My teeth were chattering. The cold had got into me, it had threaded up over my legs and proliferated. All my fingers were numb with it, and I flexed them without thinking. A sickening bolt of pain crashed through my bad hand and I reeled for a moment, eyes shut, riding it like a boiling wave, and when it subsided, I was aware of a buzz in my pocket.

Two texts in succession. A message first:

Sorry for the delay, we've had the police here. But I found your aunt's number. Keep safe, Samira.

And then an electronic business card.

Power, Bernadette. Followed by a number.

I held it in my hand for a long time, after the screen went dark.

Thinking, did you lie to me, Mum?

Who are you?

Who are we, really?

48

Charles Cox Psychotherapy Ltd.	
Clinical audio recording transcript	
Patient name:	*Eleanor Power*
Session date:	*17 September 2006*

CC: So – come and sit at the table this time – how are things with you?

EP: Fine. What's all this ... [laughs] are we doing art this week?

CC: I wanted to try something new with you.

EP: Uh, OK?

CC: So a few sessions ago we did that piece of work where we held the space for Siggy to come to the foreground—

EP: I don't want to do that again. I don't ... no, sorry—

CC: OK, Ellie – just sit down a moment – we're not going to do anything you don't want to do. All right? Trust me. Do you trust me?

[pause: 21 sec]

EP: [whispers] *Yeah.*

CC: Good. Good, Ellie. So. I understand that you're reluctant to make these connections between what Siggy shows you, and your own experiences.

EP: Yeah.

CC: But … look, the other way we can look at it is that – and remember the mind works in some incredible ways, it really can do anything – we could see that possibly this part of your identity is creating a narrative, like a story, in a way. Like a way of understanding something that is traumatic, that it wasn't able to make sense of when it happened.

EP: Right.

CC: [laughs] OK, you don't sound sure. That's OK, it's a new way of looking at it, might sound a bit outlandish. But, so what I wanted to do with you was to have a think about some of the details in the dreams you've talked about a few times. Does that sound all right to you?

EP: I suppose so.

CC: Great. So … hold on, let me just find them. I made some notes from our previous sessions about the dreams. Here. So you've talked before about a dream that you're trapped – that Siggy is trapped – and there's a fire.

EP: Yes.

CC: And she won't cry out.

EP: No.

[pause: 41 sec]

CC: Ellie? I'm sensing some real reluctance about—

EP: No, look it's just … I just hate them. The dreams. Even

just talking about them, now, I can feel her right here—
CC: *At the front of your head?*
EP: *Trying to, I don't know, crowd me out. You know?*
CC: *She's very intrusive right at the moment.*

[pause: 23 sec]

CC: *This would be a great time to access some of the visual information that might be hidden there—*
EP: *OK give me the—*
CC: *Paper's here, OK, and the pencils—*
EP: *Right. Here's the fire.* [scribbling] *There's stairs or steps here.*
CC: *That's great Ellie. Is that Siggy there?*
EP: *Crouching. She crawls under something, like this, like a piece of wood or a door or something, I don't know.*
CC: *And she's on her own?*
EP: *In there she is, yeah but … out here—*
CC: *The other side of a wall, or a door?*
EP: *Yes, I don't know … out here, there's someone else.*
CC: *Who is it?*

[pause: 14 sec]

CC: *OK.*

[pause: 11 sec]

CC: *Ellie you can keep your eyes shut like that if it helps, but I'm putting just a plain pencil into your hand and the paper is right in front of you. If you can draw anything about this person—*

EP: *I don't … I'm sorry. I don't know. It's a man. Don't know him.*

[pause: 33 sec]

CC: *Shall we have a little break? Some water?*

[pause: 56 sec]

CC: *Ready to try again? Good. This is really great work Ellie*
EP: *OK. Can I-I want to draw to the building.*
CC: *The building from?*
EP: *The other dream. I see this building like, every night, pretty much. Can I have another piece of – thanks. So it's long and – like this – but there's a section right at the end here that's fallen down.*
CC: *OK. So what's this … out the front?*
EP: *Like … it's like a big field.*

[pause: 25 sec]

EP: *Not grassy though, something, darker, I don't know.*
CC: *Great. Is that – are you finished with that one? OK. So. What is the feeling that comes with this building?*
EP: *The feeling?*
CC: *How you … how Siggy might feel about this place. Is it comforting, seeing this picture? Scary? Something else?*
EP: *I-I don't know.*

[pause: 22 sec]

CC: Does this place have a connection with the fire, do you think?
EP: I don't think so. No I think the fire is somewhere else.

[pause: 35 sec]

EP: I don't know.
CC: You're doing great. Ellie? This is great, we're really getting somewhere. Can we have a think now about what this building might be for? It looks … I mean, I'm guessing it might be a little too big to be just one home?
EP: No, it's not a home. I mean, people live there but …
CC: Right … so is that a lot of people? Anything else you can say about this place?

[pause: 24 sec]

CC: I mean, might it be a … I don't know, like a hospital? A boarding school?
EP: No. I don't think so.
CC: Like a hotel or …?
EP: No, nothing like that, it's all broken up, you know?
CC: OK sure.

[pause: 14 sec]

CC: And is this where the little boy is?
EP: No. He's not … he's never at the building. He's … somewhere else.

CC: Do you think you could draw something——
EP: No.

[pause: 38 sec]

EP: I think I'd like to finish now.

Chapter 49

Mae

After dropping Kit at the café to talk to Ellie, Mae raced down to Abson Street. The patrol car he'd sent ahead parked round the corner, tucked out of sight the way he'd instructed. But when Mae parked up and tapped on the window, the constable inside confirmed what Mae had already suspected. There was no sign of either Cox or his van.

Mae thanked him and sent him on his way, then radioed Control for an update. Cox wasn't at his home address either, and the woman in the bookie's beneath his flat said she hadn't seen him since he'd left that morning.

He thanked the operator and got her to take Cox's plates and description again. 'Any sign of either, get back to me straight away,' he told her.

Back in the driving seat with a decent view of the flat, he cranked the window a bit to stop it steaming up. Christine wasn't going to like the news he was about to break to her. He'd wait for Kit, he decided, twisting in his seat to remove whatever was digging into his hip.

It was the bloody watch, obviously. What was he supposed to do with it? His granddad had made such a thing about giving it to him: his sixteenth birthday, when he hadn't seen his mum for what, three years?

He passed it from hand to hand now, snaking the links around his fingers, clicking and unclicking the clasp. *To remind you she loves you*, Jobu had said, not a hint of irony about it. It had been just the two of them that afternoon. Mae had discreetly nipped out for a cake to replace the blackened disaster his grandad had attempted, and neither of them had mentioned the switch. Jobu had lit candles, and they'd eaten the cake from paper plates and shared the bottle of Stella that had been bought especially weeks earlier. Once the festivities were over and Mae had helped Jobu to wash and get ready for bed, the first thing he did was ride down to Gipton to pawn the watch. After that, he scored a half-ounce of resin from his guy Paul and didn't resurface until he'd turned the whole lot into curling blue smoke.

It was a testament to humanity how, three weeks later when Jobu died, the pawnbroker had taken one look at Mae's swollen face and handed the unsold watch back to him without a word.

A car horn sounded, right next to him, and Mae jumped half out of his skin. It was a black cab: and Kit was in the back seat, laughing her head off. It pulled in just ahead of him, and she got out.

Mae dropped the watch into his jacket pocket and met her on the pavement.

'Having a bit of a snooze, Sarge?'

'No, I was just – nothing. Ellie OK?'

Kit shrugged, handed her driver the fare and slapped the roof. 'Lockdown, basically,' she said, folding the receipt into her wallet and pocketing it.

Something about her manner was off. 'Something happened?'

She tutted, as if at herself, shook her head at the sky. 'No, I just got a bit involved, you know? Tried to talk to her about her health. Turns out she doesn't really like talking about it to complete strangers.'

'Right.' Stood to reason, he supposed.

'Yeah. Then I read her the riot act and got her to book in at the nick. She wasn't happy. You?'

Mae shook his head. 'If he was here, he'd gone by the time we arrived. I've got an APB: nothing so far, but it's early doors.' He indicated the Powers' flat with a jerk of his head. 'Shall we?'

Christine opened the door to her home and invited them in without a word.

'Are you going to wait for Ellie?' she said, hovering in the hall as they went into the living room. 'I don't know when she'll be back.'

Kit shook her head. 'Couple of questions for you, actually,' she said.

Christine went through and perched on the arm of one of their threadbare sofas, crossing her hands and her knees. 'Go ahead.'

'We have reason to believe Matthew was in touch with Charles Cox.'

Her eyelids fluttered closed. She muttered something inaudible.

'Sorry,' Kit said, softly, 'could you—?'

'I said, I knew this would happen. I knew it.'

'What do you mean?'

A long sigh. 'Matt is very interested in Ellie's condition, but he can also be very controlling. He wanted to know everything about her. He wanted to keep an eye on her all the time.'

Mae and Kit exchanged a look, thinking the same thing, but

Mae was the one to say it. 'Why did you not mention this before?'

She touched her fingers to her temples and pressed. 'I mean, it was nothing ... dark, exactly. Just that Ellie has very specific needs, and Matt, lovely as he is, does like to challenge them. I did find out that he was speaking to people from her past.'

'How did you find out?'

She stared at him. She was measuring her words.

'I need to know this please, Christine. What you found out and how.'

She turned and spoke to Ziegler. 'I've heard him on several occasions call her *Siggy*.'

'The name of her—'

'Her alter, yes, exactly. That's very, ah, *triggering*, for her. I got the sense that he enjoyed her weakness. It's not uncommon.'

Ziegler did an admirable job of remaining impartial but he could feel the indignation coming off her in waves.

'It's why I wouldn't be at all surprised to find that he's manipulating her in some way. She's a naturally very dependent person, and if you're asking me, I'd say it has occurred to me that this, whatever it is, going missing, is some kind of game he's playing with her. I know he was speaking to Lucy Arden, for example. Jodie's mother.'

'Did he tell you that?'

'I overheard him. After that I ... well, it's not going to reflect very well on me but I'm not going to hide anything from you. I checked his phone. So yes. I knew he was talking to Cox.'

Mae nodded, giving nothing away. 'And what did you think of that?'

'What do you think I thought? I told him he might as well give her a rope and have done with it.'

'Ms Power,' Kit said, 'Have you seen him, at all?'

'Cox?'

'We understand he may have been in the neighbourhood recently.'

'Matt's neighbourhood?'

Kit made a face. 'This neighbourhood. Here, actually.'

Christine stood up abruptly. Eyes wide, looking between Mae and Kit. 'You're telling me he's *stalking* us?'

'Not at all. We wanted to know if you'd seen him.'

Christine pulled her jumper closer around her as if the room had suddenly gone colder. 'There is nothing I wouldn't do to avoid having to ever see that man again as long as I live.'

'So you haven't seen him?' Kit went on.

'No.'

'At work, or on your way home from work?'

'No.' Christine gave a slow shake of her head, confused at the question. 'No, of course not!' She gave an abrupt, brittle laugh. 'Do you not think I would have noticed?'

'Of course, I mean—'

'What was he doing, *watching* us?'

Kit consulted her notebook, but Mae knew she was playing for time, framing her statements to minimize alarm. 'So far we're just looking at the activity on his vehicle.'

'What car?'

'A van, actually. Charles Cox has a silver Volkswagen Transporter registered in his name.'

She got to her feet and pounded along the hall. Mae got up, saw her open the front door, scan the street. When she came back in, she was shaking.

'I know the one you mean. It's been there ... weeks.'

Mae nodded, and Christine visibly sagged.

'Does Ellie know?'

Mae cleared his throat. 'She is aware that there's a connection. She's been to see him.'

Christine pressed her lips between her teeth, nodded slowly. Eyes on him. When she spoke again her voice was low, controlled. Not addressed to either or both of them.

'Please understand this. After Jodie disappeared, we tried to find our balance again, to get back to normal. But Ellie has battles every day of her life that you and I can't begin to imagine. She doesn't know who she is going to be from one minute to the next. Just everyday life, things that we don't even notice, they send her—' she mimed an explosion. 'She is *fragile*. Not that she hasn't made a fantastic effort to conceal that, of course. The whole façade she does sometimes, the performances I've seen her give to strangers, to Matt, even.' She paused there to throw up her hands. 'Inspirational. But every time, she'll come back here at the end of it, and it's *me* who drags the blankets out to the front door to wrap her up when she can't take another step. *Me* who has to rock her back to sleep when she wakes screaming from the horrifying things she sees in her sleep. She depends *entirely* upon me. For safety, for comfort, for everything. I live *entirely* for her. Do you understand that?'

Kit's notebook was hanging lightly from her fingers, forgotten as she listened. Mae filled his lungs to reply, but Christine was addressing him now and he was unable to interrupt her.

'After what happened with Jodie, every little thing became a trigger for her. We spent years of our lives repairing the damage you and Sergeant Heath did. Oh, I know,' she told him, waving away the protest she could see he was about to make, 'there were other factors. Her friend had disappeared, the whole thing was awful for everyone. Of course it was. But the treatment she got from the police? The accusations, that-that *rage* your colleague had. And what did you do to stop it? *Nothing.* I don't suppose your new colleagues know about it, what you drove Ellie to.'

It took an effort of will to contain the flinch as she mentioned it, and Mae could feel Kit's eyes on the floor, pointedly not looking at him. What she was talking about wasn't in her case file, he'd made sure of it.

'DS Heath was sacked, Christine. I testified about what happened.'

'And then you walked free.'

He didn't need to justify it to her. But he found himself saying it anyway, the thing he'd told himself hundreds, thousands of times.

'I was a junior officer. It was my first case.' I should have stood up to him, but I didn't, and I will regret that until the day I die.

'You could have stopped him. It's your fault as much as his.'

'It wasn't my fault, Christine.' But the way it came out, no one would believe it, least of all her. Least of all him.

Christine watched them both, Mae's denial hanging there between them like the blade of a guillotine.

'This is exactly why we have tried to stay away from you,' she went on, her voice still in that groove of wrathful calm. 'You are poison. Do you understand that? And you come back and what are you offering to us? Help? Protection? No. You're drip feeding fear back into our lives and waiting to see what it will do to her.'

Seeing the rage building, Kit took a step between them. 'Christine—'

'No, get away from me. You have no idea what you're doing to her.'

She was shouting now, her hands balled in stiff fists by her sides. Mae turned his face to rubber, hard and impermeable. He couldn't hear it. Whatever it was she said, all the hate that she had been carting around for him for what he'd done, he would stand there and feel it ricocheting off the walls until it slowed and lost its power. All he had to do was wait.

But Christine didn't just shout. She lunged at him: fists on his chest, a hard slap on the side of his face, and then she was kneeling, with Kit next to her, holding her wrists.

'Christine Power, I'm arresting you on—'

'No!' Mae told her. Kit stopped, looked up at him, and he shook his head. Said it again, softly. 'No. We don't need to do that. I'm going to go outside, and we're all going to calm down. All right, Christine?'

She didn't answer him. As he left the flat, her gaping, hollow sobs followed him down the hallway.

'We just want to be left alone,' she was saying. 'I just want to look after my poor girl and for all of this to go away.'

Kit walked ahead of Mae back to the car. She'd already got into the driving seat, finding the ignition with the keys, before he'd even crossed the road. They sat staring ahead saying nothing, the engine still dormant, for a few moments before she turned to him. Whole torso. He wanted to face her, face it, but he couldn't.

'You want to tell me what that was about?'

'I don't know, Kit.'

Kit didn't grace that with a reply. She just waited.

For the first time he found himself wishing it was in the main file, not locked away in Professional Standards somewhere. That way, she'd already have read it, would have already judged him for his part in it on her own time. That way, he wouldn't have to sit there now in the knowledge that within a few short minutes, her opinion of him was going to nosedive beyond salvation. The car was silent apart from the soft sound of his lips parting, the rushing sound of the deep breath he took before he finally got it out.

He told her the whole thing. About Heath, half-cut from an intensive hour at the pub, losing the plot in the interview room. Blaming her. Telling Ellie she was a nutcase, that she might as well have killed Jodie herself. The FLO had first demanded Mae step in, but when he had idiotically, pathetically, *shamefully* deferred to his superior, still believing in chain of command, the FLO had run out into the corridor, calling for assistance.

But by then, the damage was done.

'And when Ellie got home, she took a kitchen knife to her throat. She lost a huge volume of blood, had to be put in a medical coma. Twenty-one stitches.'

There was no sudden intake of breath from Kit. She kept her eyes on him, listening, her face a mask.

Later, at his tribunal, Heath had claimed he'd been at breaking point, that the booze was killing him, his marriage was over, his kids ... All the sob stories at once. The fact remained that his excuses didn't make any difference to Ellie, who'd hung onto life after her suicide attempt by a thread.

The excuses hadn't helped *him*, either. A panel found Ian Heath grossly negligent and he was summarily discharged. Less than a month later he was dead, crushed in his car on an A-road central barrier, five times over the limit.

Kit didn't interrupt. She didn't ask questions. When Mae

finished, she carried on staring out of the window. She looked furious.

'You're not saying anything,' he said after a while.

She blinked, as if released from a coma, her face lined with the effort of formulating a response.

'Did it–did it seriously not occur to you to tell me this sooner? Prior to any of this?'

She met his eyes then. It held.

And then she wasn't pissed off. It had gone, evaporated. Just for that moment, a thread connected. The very edges of him, the raw ends that he'd thought too tattered to do anything but fray further, wound around something of hers and then, somehow, it didn't all seem so ruined. She looked away and sighed heavily: something that ten minutes previously would have sounded like derision, or frustration, or disappointment. But it wasn't any of those things.

It was forgiveness.

Kit turned the key in the ignition and lifted her left hand to the gearstick, but instead of moving to find first gear, she let it fall the other side, landing for a moment on his.

'I'm pretty sure you're not that man anymore.'

And then she lifted the hand again, the ringing of her phone snapping everything back into sharp normality. She straightened to take the call, but his own focus was slow to shift. The five soft patches where her fingertips had touched his skin shone into him, and he couldn't have turned them off if he'd tried.

Kit's call lasted less than a minute, her end of it supported mainly in monosyllables.

'Yep, right, good. Got it.' She met Mae's eye and mouthed *got him*. 'You're sure it's his? OK. Great. Be right there.' Finishing the call, she beamed at him. 'That garage your CCTV guy mentioned? Haringey? It checked out: Cox's van's there. They're just taking it back to the nick.'

'Fucking A.'

'Quite.' She pulled away from the kerb and grinned at him, and there was the sense, to Mae, of the ground levelling after a long climb. Of something like the sun coming up.

Chapter 50

Ellie

The sky was shot with charcoal grey, with a low pale sun bleeding wide across the cold stretch of cloud. I hadn't been to Richmond in years, but it was easy to navigate through its low-rise, high-rent streets and out towards the river.

Bernadette, who I was about to meet, had contacted Samira Anand out of the blue, and could be anyone. I had to keep reminding myself of that fact, and that this trip might be a total waste of time. But as I walked, moving against the flow of commuters and shoppers marching towards the station, I also thought of what Matt had said. That what I believed wasn't always the truth. I consulted him in my mind. Made myself pitch it, gauged his probable reaction.

She says she's my aunt, I told him.

> But you don't have an aunt.
> That's what Mum said. Always. Her parents were dead, she was an only child.

I imagined his eyes on me, forehead creased.

> Are you saying you can't trust her?

I waited for Siggy, expecting her to bait me. But all I could find of her was the glowing outline of her, a swirl of anticipation coming from where she usually lay glaring. I pressed on towards the meeting place, increasing my speed.

We'd lived near here once, along the river in Kingston, but it hadn't ended well. Mum had been noticed in the box factory where she worked nights, some guy saying one night how much she looked like Christine Power, *you know, the bird off the news!* Next night he'd worked out it really was her. Pestered her all shift. An hour after she got back we had everything in the holdalls, and we were on the night bus to a new hideout – a new *home*, she said – on the other side of the city before the sun rose.

On the waterfront, the cobbles were glossy under a sheen of recent rain, and the air was cut with metal. I stood with my toes edged right up against the wall that dropped suddenly away to the river below, and watched the water. High tide, almost exactly. A blistered willow leaf floating from the east slowed to a stop on the surface before turning a few lazy circles in the water and drifting back the way it had come.

A string of wrought-iron edged benches lined the stretch of grass set back from the waterfront and I chose one, brushing the worst of the wet away from its narrow planks and spreading out a discarded *Metro* to sit on.

I waited. A mist of finely sifted drizzle started up and when I shielded my eyes against it, there was a hand on my shoulder.

'Ellie?'

I squinted up into the rain. Beige wool coat, like she'd said in the text. A knitted hat. But what really identified her was her face: pale skin, intense blue eyes, bright like they were lit from inside.

She could have passed for my mum.

But she took her hand from my shoulder as soon as I lifted my head.

'Gosh,' she said, crossing her flat hands at her throat, 'I do apologize. I'm just waiting for ...' and she let the sentence drift off, running her eyes over my clothes. Confused, but I couldn't see why: I was wearing exactly what I'd described.

'Ellie Power. It's me,' I told her, rising.

But she took a step back, shaking her head in quick, worried movements.

'No,' she said. 'I-I'm sorry. I think there's been some kind of mistake.'

51

Mae

The car park of the station was floodlit and alive with activity when Kit pulled the Focus in. The two of them got out, but before Mae'd taken a step, McCulloch spotted him.

'Just the man,' she said, striding over. She steered him out of earshot of his colleagues.

For a brief moment he considered his options. But his boss was someone who appreciated directness, so he'd be direct.

He said it before she got a chance to say her piece. 'I want to see this one through, Ma'am.'

'Ah. So that's why you're avoiding my calls.'

There was zero point denying it. 'I know I should have told you the Powers were involved but—'

'Yes. You should.'

'But I promise you, I don't have skin in this game. I'm just treating it like any other case.'

She looked at him for a moment before softening into a gentle laugh. 'Come on, Ben. *No skin in the game.* You're not a fucking android. But I wasn't going to take you off the case, if that's what you mean.'

'You weren't?'

'No. I wanted to give you an out, if you wanted one. Nobody would have to know if you decided you'd rather—'

'I really don't.'

She assessed that for a moment, her eyes narrowed, then allowed it with a small wave of her hand. 'Remember I do actually care about you, Mae. What happened before was ... well, it was a tough thing. One of the toughest.'

He kicked a stone. 'Long time ago now.'

'OK, Ben. Received.' Then, happy to change the subject, she led him over to the secure garage. 'So. This van. Interesting bit of kit.'

A couple of gloved and shoe-covered CID newbies, same intake as Kit, were bagging and tagging out of the back of a silver Volkswagen Transporter. It looked expensive, pristine, not a mark anywhere, its windows heavily tinted. Kit appeared beside him.

'No. Flipping. Way,' she said, eyes wide.

Now Mae had never been much of a surfer, and he could safely say he'd never camped in his life, but from what he understood, when these vans were converted they were ordinarily kitted out like tiny homes: foldaway beds, miniature kitchens, cupboards for food and bedding.

Not this one.

This one was something else. There was a yoga mat rolled up in one corner and strapped to the partial bulkhead that separated the front seats from the main space. The rest of the van was given over entirely to what appeared to be decks and drives. There was a laptop, a deep little monitor with a needle dial on the front of it, and a couple of compact little decks, like baby versions of DJ equipment.

With extreme care, the guy in the van was contorting himself into the corner behind the driver's seat to get a picture of what appeared to be a dish, a couple of feet in diameter, standing on its edge and secured at the top and bottom so that the rim of the dome faced the blacked-out window of the van. At its centre was a stubby cylinder, and attached behind was a rod, bent down at both ends like handlebars.

Kit turned to her DCI with a face like she'd just struck oil. 'You know what that is?'

McCulloch shrugged. 'High-end divining rod? Dildo?'

'Parabolic microphone,' Kit said. 'Saw one on some spy thing, they were ...' But she trailed off, locking eyes with Mae, who said, 'That guy. The neighbour.'

What was it he'd said? Something about surveillance.

They'd laughed at him.

'Someone going to fill me in?' McCulloch asked. 'What neighbour?'

'The guy under the Powers' flat, he was pretty agitated about us being ... I don't remember, Secret Service, was it?'

'MI5,' Kit said, screwing up her face in apology. 'We, ah, we thought he was nuts.'

'Well, nuts or not, we'd better get a statement pretty quick.' Turning to one of the Tech Services civvies McCulloch said, 'How long until we can get our hands on whatever's on these drives?'

'Couple of hours?'

'Make it less.' Then to Kit, 'Bit more good news for you too, if you can call it that.'

'Is there?'

'You sent that laptop of Matthew Corsham's over to the nerds, bit of data recovery?'

Kit frowned. 'Yeah, but how do you know about—?'

'It's the content,' Mae muttered, realizing what this meant. He caught McCulloch's eye and she confirmed it with a sombre nod. 'Gets referred straight up if it's anything over three on the COPINE scale. What is it?' he asked McCulloch, crossing his fingers for a low number. The scale, a typology of child pornography, went from level 1 for non-erotic images to level 10 for extreme sadism and bestiality.

'Six, I'm afraid.'

'Shit,' he said under his breath. Then, blowing out his cheeks and preparing for the worse, 'Better go and see, I suppose.'

Kit appeared at his door, loaded with sandwiches and crisps, at the same time that Mae was opening the message McCulloch had forwarded from the guy at Data Forensics.

'Let me see,' Kit said, twisting the monitor and scanning through the email before pulling a face, '"512-bit algorithm",' Kit read, slowly and through a mouthful of bread and protein. '"Unlocked and mounted." The fuck's that mean? Do you think he's trying to get in my knickers?'

Mae snorted and called up the sender on Skype. The tech, a chubby dude going by the handle *GuildOfThieves1987*, did his best to put it into layman's terms.

'Basically, there were a large number of images on this machine,' he said, his face moving jerkily on the screen. 'We're working on cataloguing them, but the good news is, whoever deleted all the files didn't know what they were doing.'

'In what way?' Mae said.

'OK well, all you do when you delete a file is remove the index data: the list in the folder that tells you where the file is. But the files themselves are still there.'

'Really?' Kit said, incredulous. 'Bit scary.' She tore open a sandwich box – ham and cheese – and handed Mae a half without taking her eyes from the screen.

Encouraged by her interest, 87 went on, 'So with jpegs, the files themselves often get fragmented across the whole disk but what you have to do is find the bytecode—'

'Excellent work,' Mae interrupted. 'Can you just skip to the part where you tell us what you found?'

'Oh, OK,' 87 said, trying not to look offended. 'So, what's interesting is that your material here has come from two distinct sources. I'm going to call them Cache 1 and Cache 2. Most of Cache 1 are, as you probably heard, pornographic images of kids. We're going to be cross-reffing all of them against the CAID once we've scoured everything off the drive but the sample we've put through so far has come up with a lot of matches.'

Kit glanced at Mae.

'Child Abuse Images Database,' he explained. 'If you've got an image that's already got a lot of hits, it means it's done the rounds already, so whoever you've found in possession of it is unlikely to have made it.'

'Right,' 87 said. 'I'll dispatch those over in a bit. But I think it's the other ones you're going to want to see first, Cache 2. Totally different deal: it's a bundle with concurrent file numbers. It came to this machine encrypted, from another single source.'

'Send them over,' Mae said, then thanked him and cut the call. A minute later, 87 had sent an email with half a dozen files attached, with a promise of another batch shortly. Mae selected all six items and hit open.

There was a delay of a few seconds.

And then Kit was on her feet, coughing a mouthful of food into her hand, her chair crashing back onto the floor behind her.

'Oh, Jesus. Oh, f-fucking hell,' she stuttered.

Mae pulled a tissue from a box in his drawer and handed it to her. But he couldn't move his eyes from the screen.

At the front of the newly opened documents, a photograph. The lower half of a female body – a girl's body – hip to thigh. She was sitting, naked, with her legs apart. Stretching across the inside of her thighs was a swathe of knotty, bloodless scar tissue that reached to the left side of her labia. Slowly, Mae put the sandwich down and pushed it away.

'She's alive, right?' Kit asked in a small, flat voice from the corner of the room. 'She is *alive*, at least?'

Mae leaned forwards, zooming in tight to a section of undamaged skin on the lower thigh. The resolution was pretty good, and he could just make out what looked like the slight bumpiness of gooseflesh. 'There. Response to cold. Yes, she's alive.'

'But-but what the hell *is* that, though? Is that burns?'

'Don't know.' Apart from the scarring, the skin was olive-hued but livid. He minimized the image, and looked at the next, and the next. A small breast, disfigured with the same ridged, long-healed mutilation. Buttocks, shoulders, chest and throat, the back of a leg. Five images, all presumably of the same woman. Or girl: she was young, postpubescent, but not by much. Without getting a look at the face it was impossible to be sure if they were looking at pictures that could possibly have been consensual, or something far worse.

He waited for Kit to come back to the screen in her own time. When she did, there was stillness to her.

'Don't let it in.' He said it softly, his eyes still on the screen.

'What do you mean?'

'I mean, don't let this,' he indicated the image with a nod, 'in. It's not what people are, you have to just tell yourself that. If you let it in, it never gets out.'

'People? No, that's not—' she started, but she took the mouse out of his hand and put two of the pictures side by side. One focusing on the throat, the other on the shoulder.

Kit touched a finger to the screen.

'They're the marks Cox talked about, in the book. It's her,' she said, tracing the unblemished centre of the throat. 'It's Ellie. But before she … before Jodie Arden disappeared.'

And Mae, lifting his hands from the keyboard as if the whole thing was burning, saw that she was right.

52

Ellie

Her name was Bernadette. Bern. She'd lived here for a decade, just east, she said, in Hanworth. She was a PA in finance, no children, but had fostered for a while. Her husband Duncan had died young, a motorbike crash. And she'd spent a decade and a half looking for me.

'So how did she do it?'

'Do what?'

'Disappear off the face of the planet.' She fidgeted with the teaspoon as she spoke, glancing up at me only occasionally. 'I mean, I looked everywhere. Tried everything. I even paid an investigator at one point, but he gave up after a week. She just vanished.'

'I don't know,' I said, almost truthfully. I knew Mum used a different name sometimes, especially after Jodie, just to keep our privacy, but I wasn't aware she'd vanished – especially not from a family. But how she did it wasn't the question: the thing I wanted to know now was *why*. Because even though she'd always said Siggy was the reason, that we kept moving to avoid the doctors and social services and everyone else who wouldn't accept that I couldn't be helped, I found myself questioning that now. A scrap of a session I'd had with Cox suddenly resurfaced like a beachball released from under water: something he'd said about what made people relocate repeatedly. He'd called it the push factor, I remembered then.

Sometimes people leave where they are, to get away from something dangerous.

I eyed the exit, shifting in my seat. If it was true – if Mum *had* left her entire family behind – surely she would have had a very good reason.

Bern stirred her coffee. 'So what does she do now? For money.'

'She's a cleaner.'

She laughed, then stopped. 'You're joking?' I shook my head. 'That can't be right. She was a *war reporter*. She was fearless and-and *brilliant*. A *cleaner*?'

'She *is* fearless and brilliant.' I folded my arms. 'Nothing's changed.'

'No, no, I didn't mean that. I just don't understand. Any of it.' Everything she said was addressed to the cooling cappuccino in front of her. 'I don't understand what we could possibly have done for her to cut us off like that. Mum and Dad never got over it.'

'Mum and— You're talking about my *grandparents*?'

She glanced up, then away again, like she just couldn't sustain eye contact with me. 'They were so proud of her. Always telling people Chrissy this and Chrissy that, blah blah blah. I mean, it's fine, I get it. She achieved so much. Then when they got a grandchild, to them she was just … well.' She indicated an invisible level with the side of her hand, then raised it, way above her head. 'I remember this time we had a walk on Hampstead Heath. People kept coming up to her. She'd started fronting her reports, so she was a known face. She only came home from whatever war it was when she was seriously showing with … when she was pregnant,' she said, indicating her stomach. 'Dad waved his stick at them in the end. Chris was mortified. We laughed about that for ages.'

All of which would have been lovely, except for the fact that I didn't have grandparents. Not ones I'd ever met, anyway, because in the real version of this story they refused to talk to Mum after she became pregnant with me. They cut her off, and I hadn't even met them. We didn't talk about them.

But there had to be some truth in Bern's version of events, because there were no two ways about it – every feature of her face said she was my mother's sister.

'So what happened?' I asked. I wanted to hear the whole of her version of events before I challenged it. 'How did we lose touch?'

She sipped her drink, took her time over it, wiped the corners of her mouth. Haltingly, in a voice roughened with cigarettes, she started to tell me.

'There was a birthday party. Third birthday.'

'Mine?'

The slightest nod. 'Just a little gathering. Me and Duncan, Chrissy, and our mum and dad. I didn't see Chrissy again for a few weeks after that. Tried calling a few times but no answer. So I went round, and there was another family there, moving in.' A shrug, to signify the end of the story. 'I never saw her again. She took my beautiful niece away, and it was like they'd never existed.'

'So that's it? You just, what, forgot about us?'

She shot me a look that started fierce but crumbled quickly into immense sadness. 'I looked *everywhere*. Her old colleagues, friends we'd had at school, her doctor. Anyone who might know anything at all about where she'd gone. The police didn't help. Made a few calls, then nothing. She'd talked about living abroad before, so as far as they were concerned it wasn't out of character. She knew a lot of people in a lot of countries, she'd spent her life travelling. There was nothing worrying about her state of mind, anything like that, and there was the letter—'

'What letter?'

She took a sip of her drink, set the cup back on the saucer without a sound. 'Saying she was going on a trip. Just that, no details. It was hideous. Mum was distraught, she was already ill, getting worse and worse by then, and Dad was on his way out and ... you know.'

'No. Not really.' I didn't know *anything* about what she was telling me. A few hours ago, I'd never questioned the rock-solid fact that Mum was an only child. Bern's hands were shaking, and her eyes were crowded with tears. I pulled a napkin from a jug on the table and handed it to her.

'When you don't have children of your own,' she said, pressing the fabric to her eyes, 'and you want them, desperately want them but you can't have them ...'

I fumbled for something to say. 'I can't imagine what that's like,' was all I could think of.

'No. You can't. I know my niece wasn't my child, but I loved her so much. *So* much. I looked, everywhere, I spent every penny I had, and then I moved back in with my parents. Thirty-five years old, back in my old single bed.' She lifted her cup, stared at it, didn't drink, put it back down. 'And years later – years of not knowing if I'd ever see my niece or my sister again, if they were dead or alive – I found Chrissy's name mentioned in an article about that girl that disappeared. Jodie Arden. It took me weeks, but eventually it led me to Dr Cox. But his office wouldn't give me a number no matter what I said. I'd missed her again. She'd been *right there*, and then ...' she made a *pff!* sound, and made a miniature firework with her hands, 'gone. And now this.'

I didn't understand. If she loved me so much, where was the joyful reunion? 'But I'm here now.'

She shook her head. 'I don't know what's happening. I don't understand what you want.'

I glared at her. '*You* contacted *me*,' I told her. 'I came because *you* asked me to. I don't *want* anything.'

'Come on,' she said gently. 'Calm down.'

A woman on the table next to us threw a suspicious glance our way, muttering something to her friend.

Bern kept her eyes on me. 'Do you really not know? It's not your fault. But you're not … not who I thought you'd be.'

'No? OK. So, who exactly were you expecting?'

She didn't answer me. 'What did she tell you, my sister? About me?' Then, like it had just occurred to her, she said, 'Does she even know Mum and Dad are dead?'

There was no nice way to put it. 'Nothing. I didn't know you existed.'

She nodded slowly. 'What about everyone else, the rest of your family? I mean, I know you don't see Jim but—'

'Jim who?'

'*Jim*,' she said again. 'Your *dad*.'

'My dad's *dead*.'

She gave me a long, hooded look. 'I'm so sorry,' she said eventually, but it was mechanical, like her mind was doing something else. Like she didn't believe me. 'When? What happened?'

I shook my head, bewildered. 'Drugs. But it was before I was born.' How did she not know that?

Her eyes fluttered shut.

'What?' I said, angry now. 'What is it?'

She took a deep breath, trying to find a way of telling me something without upsetting me.

'Look, I-I think I should talk to your mum.'

'No. *No*, you're talking to *me*.'

'Ellie, please. I really need to talk to her.'

'Do you know what?' I said, suddenly running out of patience. 'I don't have time for this. This is bullshit.' What was I even doing there, listening to this? I had to find Matt, and this was getting me precisely nowhere. I got clumsily to my feet and the chair half-toppled behind me before I caught it and shakily set it down. I went to retrieve the hoody I'd left hanging on the back, but she stopped me. Half standing, she reached out for my wrist.

'OK, please,' she said. 'Sit. Please, look, we need to work out what's ... we need to talk about this.'

Her fingers were slim and pale and just like Mum's, nothing like mine. Her thumb rubbed the back of my hand and I pulled it back, not because of the pain. I didn't want to be soothed. She didn't get to do that.

But I couldn't leave without knowing what it was she knew. I stared at her for a moment before I did as I was told, heat rushing to my skin. She gave me a weak, sad smile before pulling her bag onto the table and unzipping an interior pocket. Brought out her phone, but didn't look at it, didn't turn it on.

'Fine. OK.' She took a deep breath, let it all out. 'I don't know what Christine has told you, but to be honest I suppose I'm not surprised. It was obvious they were having problems. Jim was—' she looked away. 'He was a very troubled man. Volatile.'

I wrapped my arms around myself, almost involuntary and Siggy flattened herself across my back, trying to make herself invisible, like she didn't want to hear. *I* didn't want to hear.

'He was a little older than her, and when they first got together – God, must have been ten years before you were born – she was still pretty young, still getting started in her career. She met him while she was working on a documentary after the war—'

'The war? What war?'

'The Falklands,' she said, trying and failing to hide her incredulity that I didn't already know this. She sighed, shaking her head. 'It affected him really badly, even years later. He was in specialist units for quite a while. That's how they met. Chrissy interviewed him about PTSD and it kind of went from there, they were—'

'So what? He was a doctor? A psychiatrist?'

'No,' she said slowly. 'Not a doctor.' She drew her eyeline from mine and brought her phone to life. 'Don't get me wrong,' she said, tapping something I couldn't see on the screen, 'he could be very sweet, very gentle, but sometimes he'd just flip, lose it completely. He'd get in trouble with the police, went to prison a few times. Couldn't adjust after what he'd seen out there, what he'd been involved in.'

I looked at my hands. 'Are you saying he was violent? With Mum?' *With me*, I wanted to say.

'Look, I don't know,' she said, cutting me off. 'Chrissy never said so. What I do know was that he was devoted to his family. Properly devoted, he couldn't bear being separated. *Hated* it.'

Obviously finding what she was looking for, she looked up. 'There's no easy way to say this but somewhere along the line, things have got ... twisted.' She looked me in the eye. 'Jim's not— they were just taking some time apart, and then Chrissy disappeared. He swore, just like I did, that he'd keep looking. Here,' she said, and turned the phone around to show me. 'This is him.'

I leaned in. It took a moment or two to register, to really see what I was looking at. She slid the phone over, carried on talking 'This was taken maybe a couple of weeks before – wait – are you all right?'

I shrank, gripped my eyes shut. Black panic crowded behind my eyelids, but I couldn't, I would not look at that picture. I pushed it away, covered my eyes.

'Please, I don't want to see it, please, that's not him.'

It couldn't be. I wouldn't let it. I didn't even get as far as looking at the face on the screen. I couldn't have said what colour his hair was, whether he even *had* hair, whether he was tall, short, thin – anything. All I saw was what he was wearing.

Green uniform. Green, khaki, camouflage.

He was a soldier.

What this woman was saying was that my *father* was a *soldier*.

If Siggy could have screamed, she would have shattered the sky.

53

Mae

Kit was waiting for the one decent colour printer to fire up when he found her.

'The tech at Brighton and Hove called back,' Mae told her, leaning against the wall. 'Those images of Ellie were definitely from Cox. They had someone get access to Cox's old clinic and took some pictures of the room he used to have. Background and lighting signatures match up. And with the timing on it, with the absence of the scar, means—'

'She was definitely well underage.'

Mae nodded stiffly.

'So, what we thinking, Cox sold them?' Kit asked. The copies of the pictures emerged like tongues from the machine, and she took care lifting each one between thumb and forefinger, like dirty laundry, turning them face down in her folder.

'Don't know yet. Possibly.'

'And no clues on where he's gone?'

Mae shook his head. 'We've had UKBA put a stop on his passport though, so he's not going far.'

She gave a cynical sniff. 'We hope.'

Mae waited for her to finish with the prints before walking with her to the lifts. They stood in silence, then emerged onto the ground floor, where the neutral décor of the upper levels was replaced by walls of wipe-clean blue and alarm buttons embedded at intervals along the mid-height bumper.

They paused at the snack machine, and Mae dug in his pocket for some change, fed it in, and punched in the code for a cereal bar.

Kit leaned against the radiator. 'These pictures. Do you think they're something to do with that money, the cash his colleague said about? Maybe Corsham ... I don't know, maybe he got off on young girls with injuries? Liked the idea of his girlfriend being degraded by someone else?'

'Quite possibly. We'll need to get Helen Williams in, and her manager, everything about this pharmacy theft: dates, specifics on what was stolen. Here,' he said, handing her the snack bar. 'Energy.'

'I've eaten.' Her voice was robotic, and her face was set, a one-way street. Not even looking at him.

'OK. Come on. Code 99, let's go.'

'What?'

He'd forgotten how new she was. 'Code 99: tea break.'

'Ah, no. Too much to do,' she said, waving her hand vaguely but not meeting his eyes.

He stood right in front of her, forcing her to look up. 'You OK? I need you present and correct.'

'I'm fine.' She pushed herself off the wall, walked off towards the lifts.

'Kit,' he said. She must have heard him, but she didn't respond. 'Kit,' he said again. '*DC Ziegler.*'

This time she stopped. Turned around. Walked back.

'One of my sisters, right?' Everything about her was tight. Fists, shoulders, jaw: even her stance was rock-hard, as if she was expecting an impact. She stopped a few steps from him and dragged her hands hard through her hair. 'Younger than me, twenty-four. She lives with my mum. When I say she lives there, I mean, she *lives* there. Stays in. All the time. Thank fuck for the internet and everything because as least she's got "friends",' she said, putting quote marks around it bitterly with her fingers, every word acid-sharp, 'but social life, real life stuff?' She turned the corners of her mouth down, shook her head. 'Nothing.'

If Mae didn't know her better, he would have thought she was going to cry. He kept his mouth shut and listened, because he knew the deal with these why-I-really-signed-up stories that not everyone had. If someone joined the force because they needed to believe in the whole *making the world safer* line: invariably, they'd have a pretty good reason.

She folded her arms. 'So, when she was in sixth form, she was raped.' Fissures appeared in her voice from the effort of controlling it. 'One of those stranger-in-a-park rapes, opportunist. Bad fucking luck. Up to that point, everything was going perfectly: straight As, football captain, ran the student newspaper, nice line in creative writing. Now? She eats. Just ... she can't stop. She has flashbacks. Panic attacks like two, three, four times a day. For *eight years*. You ever have a panic attack?'

He shook his head.

'No. She thinks she's going to die. She can't breathe, she literally can't—'

Kit cut herself off and tipped her head back, swallowing the rest of the sentence.

Mae waited.

She took a few long breaths, then looked back at him, creaked out a weak smile she didn't really mean. He hoped she wouldn't apologize, and she didn't.

'The fucker who took these pictures,' she said, tapping the

folder under her arm, 'he's why I'm here. He's why I spent two years of my life that I'll never get back, scraping drunks off pavements. So I could get here, get into a room with a fucker like that, and make him pay.'

Mae nodded. 'Good.'

'What?'

He unlocked his arms from across his chest. 'I said, good. I'm glad you're angry. I'm angry, too. A lot of people here, they're not, not really. They're complacent. Just here for the status, for notching up the shiny silver badges on their shoulders, the retirement after thirty years' service, or whatever. But people need us pissed off, we're no good to them if we're content. If I had it my way we'd all have to be fuming when we went on shift. There'd be like some kind of little monitor built into your radio. You're nice and calm, go home and – I don't know – watch some Britain First posts on YouTube. Come back when you're good and seething.'

She laughed, and the dam cracked. The tears that they'd both thought she was going to hold in broke across her face, and she turned, rubbing angrily at them, saying, 'Fuck. Fucking hell.'

He let her cry. He didn't look away. 'What I'm saying is, you've got this far being you, coping the way you cope. But separating the anger out like it's something to be ashamed of? You don't have to do that. There is a middle way. The anger isn't going away, so you just use it, make it sing for its supper. Don't hide it.'

From a pocket she produced a tissue, smiled sadly as she unfolded it. 'You practised that little spiel on Bear?'

He opened his mouth, closed it again. Because he suddenly found himself ashamed that the answer was no. The pep talks he gave Bear were all about being tough, keeping it all in. Why?

After noisily blowing her nose, she asked him the question he should have seen coming.

'So what got you into the job? And please spare me the "giving back to the community" crap.'

He shrugged. 'The pay?'

They both laughed at that, but not for long. Eyes still red, Kit asked it again. 'Really, though. Something bad happened, didn't it?'

The gold watch hung like a bar of solid iron in his pocket. He opened his mouth, unsure of what was going to come out of it, but then his phone buzzed.

He pulled it out, checked the screen: a voicemail. Mike.

'I'm going to have to call this one back,' he told her, waving the handset. He turned back the way he'd come, bringing up Mike's number to call him back.

Kit called back after him. 'You're wrong about one thing.'

Pausing at the double doors, he took the phone from his ear, glanced back.

She shook her cropped head as if clearing long hair from her face. 'About the rage.'

'Oh yeah?'

'I don't hide it. I just save it. You want to see what pent-up means, you're going to want to see PC Pain in action.'

'It's a deal,' he told her, and laughed as the double doors closed behind him.

Finding Mike's number busy, Mae went straight to the CID kitchen. After filling the kettle and sticking it on to boil, he checked through the window that he wasn't about to be disturbed, and rang the voicemail.

Mike's nasal voice, its warmth as artificial as a two-bar fire.

'Ben. Hi.'

Mae held the bridge of his nose and realized that deep down, he already knew what was coming.

'Listen, Nadia asked me to make this call to you because she didn't know how you would, uh, take it.' The unsaid things jostling against each other behind every word, stacking up against each other. 'So I know it might be hard to hear this, but we're, um, the plan actually is, ah—,' and there was the jar in his voice now, confirming that Nadia was with him, gesturing, pulling his little puppet strings, 'we're going to be putting in an application to move back to the States. Make a go of it, the four of us.' Mae listened to the pause, his heart jolting under his ribs like a series of sobs. 'Yeah. We, ah, we thought it would be better for Bear – for Dominica – to just, to make a clean break. Nadia asked me to call because she was worried you'd be – uh – you might not take it that well.'

More broken, stilted, clichéd non-information followed: that they'd already sorted the visas; that they were hoping to *find their feet* and then *work out the detail* regarding his contact with Bear. That they'd already chosen a nursery for the toddler, and they'd seen a school for Bear that was *just perfect*. What a great opportunity it would be for her, what *great experiences* she'd have.

They'd talked it over with her, he said. She couldn't wait, he said.

'So yeah. Exciting times. But it all rests on you, now.'

Mae listened to the whole thing. He listened to the voice after the message, telling him what options he had. To listen again, press 2. To delete, to save. None of them good options. None of them involving making it right, being his daughter's dad. Her real dad, not just the guy she got her almond eyes and her temper from, who would call her from the other side of the world. Who said he loved her, but somehow never managed to show it.

The main menu repeated in his ear, several times over.

This was him being written out of her story. *My real dad lives in England*, she'd tell her new friends when they asked how come her parents were both white. *No, I don't see him much.*

The coffee was stone cold by the time Kit came bursting in, excitement was firing out of her in all directions. She was on her radio, but grabbed him by the sleeve.

'Abson Street, the names are Eleanor and Christine Power. Don't let them leave.' Then, after signing off, 'Where have you been?!'

He waved his phone. It wasn't something he was going to go into.

'It doesn't matter, come on,' she told him, pulling him into the corridor. 'Big fucking news.'

'Where are we going?'

'AV room, now. You're going to want to hear this.'

54

Ellie

Bernadette had hailed a cab for me and sent me home with a twenty for the journey and a promise to be in touch very soon. But I stopped the driver and got out a few streets before ours, and walked the last bit. I walked past slowly. I couldn't be sure she was out, but I didn't want to risk knocking, risk seeing her. Having to talk, having to lie. I found a small stone, checked around me, got a bit closer and threw it at the window. Retreated. Waited a minute, two, but she didn't respond. Threw again. Nothing.

I went in.

There was a note for me on a sheet of A4 on the hallway floor.

I'm out looking for you, if you come back, stay here, will be back by seven.

I glanced up at the clock. I had half an hour to find something, anything at all that would prove or disprove what Bernadette had just told me.

I balled the note up, tucking it into one of the three black binbags queued up along the wall. Then, starting in her room, I made a search. If Mum really was lying to me about something as big as this, there had to be a clue, some evidence of it. A letter, a card, a photo I didn't care what form it took. I just wanted answers.

I opened drawer after drawer, using just my good hand because the other one was so sore. Everything was already packed. Under her bed, where there had been crates of paperwork and other stuff, there was nothing. If it hadn't been for the suitcases and boxes on the bed, it would have looked like we'd already left.

Into my room. Clothes folded and stacked onto my bed. Everything else, books and notebooks, keepsakes, make-up and jewellery, the lot: gone.

The kitchen door, which Mum usually left locked, was open. I soon saw why. It had been scrubbed and emptied, the fridge was bare, the food cupboards the same. Plates and mugs and knives and forks: the locks had been removed, but so had everything we owned.

So she'd made her mind up. We were leaving.

I stood in the hall and tucked my hands in my armpits, which reminded me in no uncertain terms about the damage to my palm. I unwrapped the dressing: the injury no longer burning, but it was numb, and I didn't dare look at it. I went back to the suitcases. I opened the first one: it contained just clothes, but just underneath the lid was an A4 envelope.

Inside were passports, one for Mum, and one for me.

I didn't even know I had a passport.

I took mine, and replaced the envelope. In the next case was the first aid kit. I picked it up, felt its weight. I'd seen it before of course, many times, but it was always locked away until Mum needed it: I'd never held it, certainly never opened it up. But as I unzipped it and rifled through, looking for something for the pain, the first compartment I tried held none of the usual things, plasters, bandages, ibuprofen. Just an unmarked bottle of pills, half a dozen glass vials with their labels peeled off. Under that: syringes.

I rocked back on my heels.

Syringes?

I zipped it back up, and tried the other side, where I found what I'd been looking for. I took a double dose of painkiller, the last four tablets in the blister pack, then closed the whole thing back up and put it back where I'd found it. I took the empty packaging to the bin. No bin liner. The bins were in the hall.

Three black sacks. I nudged one with my toe. Paper inside, loose, dry things: not a kitchen bin.

I got down on my knees, and I undid the knot. As fast as I could I went through the first two bags, checking each item as I took it out, putting it to the side until I almost gave up: there were only so many old free papers and till receipts you can sift through before you lose heart. But I made myself open the third: *if a job's worth doing*. There, crumpled up inside an oversized receipt for our new locks, was a letter, addressed to Mum's other name, Christine Scott.

It had been sent to a PO box, not our address. Dated a week and a half ago, from a storage company called Logic Storage near the Hanger Lane tube. *As a valued storage unit holder here at Logic, we'd like to inform you of some changes*, it started.

I flattened the letter, smoothing out the crumples, and read it through. Just a circular, but it wasn't junk. She was a customer. At the top was her name, the PO box again, a customer number, and the unit number: 003/27.

Folding the whole thing along its original crease lines, I pocketed it and went back to sifting through the bag.

I stopped. Froze. Someone at the door.

And through the narrow pane of glass beside the door, I could make out the unmistakable colour of a police car.

Banging on the door. A man.

'Miss Power? Eleanor?'

Not Mae, and this was a squad car, not CID, which meant ...

'Eleanor? Christine? It's the police. We need you to answer the door, please.'

It meant they'd found something. They'd worked out it was Mum who'd moved the car – or something worse. It could be something much worse.

The reality of what this meant came quickly into focus, like someone had turned a dial in my head. If I opened that door, it would be over. Whatever the truth was behind the things Bernadette had said, and whatever Matt had been trying to find out: if I got arrested, I would never have a chance to unearth it. So I made my decision. I grabbed the letter and with my back flat against the hallway wall, I edged swiftly along until my fingers connected with the handle on my bedroom door.

I already had my shoes on, but grabbed an extra top and tied it around my waist. I didn't waste another second. From the extreme right of the window, I had a full view of the car on the street, and I could see it was empty.

The window was still open from the last time I'd needed it. And although I couldn't be sure I could get down to the street without being spotted from the door, now was as good a time as any to try.

55

Mae

Mae and Kit waited for McCulloch on the CID floor. Mae had called her – interrupting her evening run – the moment Kit had finished playing him the recording the data team had found in Cox's van, then he'd listened to it another three times. It didn't get any less incredible.

When she arrived, their boss was flushed and out of breath. She leaned against the doorframe, finished a plastic bottle of water, binned it, and nodded at Mae.

'Hit me. You found Cox?'

'Not yet. We're trying various—'

'Got something out of the Powers?'

Kit resisted the instinct to look at Mae and said, 'We were expecting interviews with both of them, but – uh – we're—'

McCulloch's bloodhound instincts kicked in at the pause. 'Don't tell me they've gone AWOL.'

Kit grimaced and inspected her hands.

McCulloch turned to Mae. 'Do not fucking tell me they've gone AWOL. *Ben.*'

He held up a finger and a thumb, an inch between them. 'Teeny chance. Probably fine.'

'Mae sent a car round,' Kit chimed in.

'Why are you not there yourself?' McCulloch demanded. But

then something dropped and she narrowed her eyes. 'There's more, isn't there? You didn't call me away from my constitutional just to tell me that you've lost our two key witnesses, or whatever they are?'

Mae and Kit exchanged a glance, then Mae said, 'Yeah ... there is something else, Ma'am.'

They went back down to the AV suite, Mae explaining the *something else* as they went.

'Rough estimate is something like fifteen grand's worth of equipment,' he told her, 'and my guy at the council CCTV puts Cox on site for between six and eight hours a day for the last month.'

'Every *day*?'

'Apparently.'

'Recording them the whole time?'

'Quite possibly. We corroborated that with records from his clinic – his assistant's being rather helpful – and it checks out.'

He pushed open the double door and waited for the women to pass. Approaching the suite, McCulloch stopped, turned. 'You're telling me he spent fifteen large to listen to these two *through the walls*. Is that right? Just listening to them? There's no visual element? Are we not thinking covert video bugs, anything like that?'

Mae had thought the same thing. 'We'll be checking.'

'But what else could he have been after?'

Kit opened the door to the darkened suite. 'I think I'll let the recordings answer that one.' She sat at the desk and handed her boss a pair of headphones. Off to the right they had a Civilian Support logging the sections that Cox had digitally earmarked into folders named things like 'For Backup' and 'Do Not Delete'.

It was going to be a long job, but from what they'd heard already, it was going to be worth it.

Kit snapped her own headphones on and got out her pad. Mae sat between them both and cued up the clip that McCulloch needed to hear.

56

Charles Cox Psychotherapy Ltd.	
Clinical audio recording transcript	
Patient name:	*Eleanor Power*
Session date:	*30 September 2006*

CC: *So, I'd like to start this session by saying how incredibly brave you're being. We've had some very tough sessions, and the fact that you're coming back is something you should be really proud of.*

EP: *Yeah well. I don't feel very brave.*

CC: *You don't feel brave? Tell me about that.*

EP: *No, I … look. I wanted to say this in person because you've been really good about giving me these sessions for free and everything, but I don't think I can come any more.*

CC: *OK. OK, I'm listening. Let's talk about it.*

EP: *No, look, I can't.*

CC: *Has something happened? Something at home?*

EP: *No.*

[pause: 33 sec]

CC: *It's hard, coming here. Talking about this is really tough.*

EP: *Yeah.*

CC: *It's distressing, going over it. Poking at it, raking it over. You're questioning what the benefit is.*

EP: *Yeah.*

[pause: 19 sec]

EP: *All of that. Yeah. Look the more I have to think about her, the more she's just there, you know? And that's the opposite of what I wanted to happen.*

CC: *Can I ask how it's been for you this week with your fugues?*

EP: *Two more.*

CC: *Two? Ah, OK. That's … that is more regular than you had been—*

EP: *Yeah. That's what I mean. And my mum's on my back, wants to know what I'm doing all the time when she's at work and I just really, really hate lying to her.*

[pause: 40 sec]

CC: *What's the fear about that, Ellie?*

EP: *How do you mean?*

CC: *Well, you talk about your mother finding out that you're in therapy, and you've talked before about this feeling that you're betraying her by talking to me, and to Jodie as well, about your dissociation. So I suppose my question is, what is it that you're worried is going to happen?*

EP: *She'd go mental.*

CC: *OK.*

EP: *I mean, we spent so long, so much effort trying to find a cure, and it just took over her life. So we promised, we made a proper promise to each other that we would stop, just try to get used to Siggy and just live with her. Going against that, behind her back, it would be … it would just be … I mean, I don't know what she'd do.*

CC: *What do you fear she would do?*

EP: *I don't know.*

CC: *I think maybe you do. What is it, what's the worst thing that you're worried might happen, if your mum finds out you broke that promise?*

[pause: 54 sec]

EP: [Inaudible]

CC: *That … sorry Ellie, say that again?*

EP: *That she'll-she'll give up on me. Kick me out.*

CC: *OK. Your fear is that you'll be abandoned.*

EP: *Yeah.*

CC: *OK. What does Siggy think?*

EP: *She doesn't care. She hates us both. She doesn't care what happens to us.*

CC: *She hates you, and she hates your mum.*

EP: *Yeah.*

CC: *We need to look at that. Why do you think she hates your mum?*

EP: *I don't want to look at it! Looking at it is just making it worse! I've been having panic attacks like every day now!*

CC: *OK. All right.*

[pause: 22 sec]

CC: There's a problem there, isn't there? On the one hand, you, your dominant identity, you're worried that if you get help, you'll be abandoned. But the more afraid you are, the more distressed and triggered you're going to feel, and – this is my reading of what's been happening lately with you – the more stressed you are, the more conscious you are of Siggy, and her ill feeling towards you. And in turn that seems to be resulting in more conflict between your identities, and more regular fugues.

EP: But that's exactly what I mean! That's why I don't want to come, because it's making me worse. It feels like what you're doing, you're trying to make me worse! Then I've been thinking about that book you said you were going to write, after the session last week, you know?

CC: Well, yes, I've been asked to contribute a chapter, but—

EP: But it's like you want me to be this really awful case so it makes you look good. I'm getting … it's getting worse, like my mum said it did before, when I was little and we did stuff like this before. It's like you're trying to give Siggy more control by bringing it all up. But I'm really, really scared of her, you know?

[pause: 49 sec]

CC: Ellie, look: about that book. I can take it or leave it. OK? All of what we do here is for you. My only interest is you. Look at me. OK? I am not trying to make things worse.

EP: But I am worse. She's … Siggy's there all the time now. I just want her gone and she's getting so … just getting more and more—

[crying]

[pause: 34 sec]

EP: I don't-I don't know what she's going to do.

57

Mae

The three of them sat listening, headphones on, staring at the waveform on the monitor ahead of them as if they expected visual accompaniment to the audio.

Ellie's voice came through, crackly but definitely her, the angles in her voice unmistakable. *'Mum, if you found something … '* Then Christine, the angles in her voice unmistakable: *'I didn't. It's nothing.'*

Ellie, saying: *'But it's not, is it? What if Siggy … what if it's happened again?'*

McCulloch listened with her eyes closed, her forefingers pressed into her temples and let her breath out in a long stream.

Later, Ellie: *'Mum. Tell me what's going on.'*

'I want to be prepared,' was Christine's reply. *'They're going to come here, aren't they? The police. And they're going to ask questions.'*

The sound dampened and McCulloch squinted away from the desk, trying to hear. When it was audible again, Ellie was saying, *'I'm calling the police,'* then Christine: *'No. No. That's not the right play. Not at all.'*

Mae hit pause, then shuttled through to the timecode he'd written down on the pad in front of him.

Watching, McCulloch said, 'And this is from the day he went missing, right?'

'Morning of,' Kit confirmed.

His finger ready on the play key, Mae said, 'And this is from yesterday.'

The recording was far from perfect, but Christine's voice was plenty clear enough. McCulloch and Kit dipped their heads to listen.

'Here's what's happened. We thought Siggy had stopped, but she hasn't. I thought, when you were little, that if we focused on being gentle and kind and letting you express whatever part of yourself you wanted to express, that Siggy would go away.'

Christine talked about trying to control Siggy, about the sacrifices they'd made, until she got to the part that made McCulloch's eyes go wide.

'I'm sorry, Ellie. But this is where we are. She has got bigger and badder than we thought she could get. Jodie is dead, because of her. And now Matt …' Christine said, and then the voice disappeared for a few seconds.

McCulloch took her headphones off and laid them down, arranging them just so. She pushed her chair back, and put her forehead on the desk.

'Jesus.' She straightened up, and looked at Mae. '*She* killed Jodie Arden. Ellie Power did?'

'The way they're talking about it, it sounds like it happened when Ellie was – wasn't Ellie.'

'Dissociative fugue,' Kit said.

McCulloch sighed heavily. 'OK. God, all right. Nothing yet from your patrol?'

'Christine and Ellie aren't at the flat but we're on it. Christine was there a couple of hours ago. They've been cooperative so far.'

McCulloch stood. 'Right. I want updates on the half hour.'

'Yes, Ma'am.'

Mae's phone rang as the door closed behind his boss. He conducted the call with minimum input, his tight mouth spreading into a grin as he listened, his eyes on Kit. He grabbed his jacket from the back of a chair, mouthed *let's go*. He shoved the door open and waved to her to follow.

'What we got?' she asked in the corridor the moment he hung up. She was jogging ahead of him now, through the double doors and out into the yard.

'Cox. His Corsa's been picked up by ANPR.'

'But we should be on Ellie and Christine, surely? That tape, it's as good as an admission of guilt.'

But it wasn't as simple as that. 'We're spinning plates. Ellie must have known about Cox's pictures. Possibly Christine, too. There's got to be a reason they're keeping his secrets for him. Sooner we can get to him, the better.'

The Focus they'd been using was still in its spot, and still smelt of her discarded churros when he buckled up beside her, taking the passenger seat so he could work on the way.

'Where's the ping?' Kit asked, sparking the ignition.

'Garage near Teddington.' He closed his eyes for a moment, summoning a mental map and trying to spot how it fitted in to what they knew of him.

Kit twisted in her seat for the A to Z on the back seat and started riffling the pages. 'Teddington ... OK, here,' she said, finding the page. 'So what's he doing there?'

Mae glanced over and it clicked straight away.

'He's doing yoga.'

'Yeah right,' Kit said, smirking.

'It's true: my CCTV guy said he'd logged the van in East

Molesey: same place that Lucy Arden said she'd followed Cox to. His mother lives there, she's got some kind of yoga centre.'

'Right then. Let's go.'

While Kit headed up to the flyover, Mae dialled Rod for the exact address he'd logged Cox at. Rod answered instantly, and within half a minute he'd brought up the postcode.

'It's not just one address though,' Rod said, accompanied by the sound of proficient touch-typing as he looked for what Mae wanted. 'Guessing wherever he goes, there's only on-street parking, but I can narrow it to a couple of blocks.'

Noting down the postcode, Mae thanked him, hung up, and wanged it into the satnav, taking the A4-then-South route instead of risking the rush-hour inertia of the smaller roads.

'Who covers East Molesey?' Kit wondered. 'Surrey force. Think it's Elmbridge nick?'

A quick check, and it turned out she was right. She put her phone into the holder and talked to the handsfree to find the right number. As it rang, she said, 'I'll get them to send round a uniform, shall I? Watch the place?'

Kit spent a few minutes talking Surrey command into sparing someone to keep an eye on the place until they got there, weaving north-west through the early-evening traffic as she spoke. While she spoke, Mae searched the internet for a definite connection between one of East Molesey's yoga venues and a Mrs or Ms Cox.

It didn't take long. On the homepage of the Gayatri Institute there was an image of a healthful, tanned woman in her seventies outside a handsome stone building, surrounded by a small handful of Lycra-clad devotees. Closest to her side, though, was a beaming, bearded Cox, taken maybe a few years previously.

He gave Kit the address just as the traffic miraculously cleared.

She accelerated hard onto the Great West Road, then straightened her arms against the wheel and flashed him a look.

'Tell me you're not going to bitch like a grandma about my technique the whole way there.'

But he wasn't complaining. 'Go for your life.' The way Kit floored it, they might even get there first.

58

Ellie

The tracks of the District line clattered beneath my feet. It was dark, and if the train was supposed to be heated it didn't seem to know about it.

At Hammersmith I changed for the Piccadilly line, sweeping up northwestwards. When the train emerged from underground it passed right beside the big yellow plastic-clad storage facility I was headed to. I got off at Hanger Lane and headed over, thinking how I'd need a whole load of the luck I was owed, just to get inside. People who used places like this wanted their stuff kept secure. My mother, if I knew anything about her at all, would be no exception.

From the street, the building was vast and overwhelming, but inside, the reception was just a greyscale office like any other. A faint smell of cigarettes came from the young man behind the desk who looked up briefly from his screen as I walked past. I lifted my hand loosely in a greeting but I didn't stop.

'Hold on,' he said.

Shit.

My heart thrashing under my ribs, I turned.

'Unit?' he said.

I made a *silly me* face and dug the slip from my pocket. 'Zero-

zero-three-twenty-seven,' I told him, flattening the letter onto the counter.

He put the number into his keyboard, didn't look up. 'Name?'

'Christine Scott,' I said without hesitation.

He held his hand out. I looked at it, then at him.

'ID,' he said.

The lifts were just ahead of me. Just there. Could I make a bolt for it? I could probably get a head start. But then what?

I leaned over the desk. I was going to do this. I could do this.

'Look, I've just lost my handbag. All my ID, everything.'

'I'm sorry, but—'

'Please. I know it's not the way we usually do things, but, please. Just this once.' I gave him a pleading smile.

He narrowed his eyes and tapped the end of his biro against his lip. 'Look, I'm not allowed to—' he started, but he was interrupted by the suddenly trill of the desk phone. 'Just hold on.'

As he went to answer it, I mouthed *please?* again and made a praying gesture. As he lifted the receiver he rolled his eyes, broke into a grin, and waved me on.

I climbed six short flights of steel steps, my footsteps reverberating all the way up and down the stairwell. I emerged onto the third floor. Sensing me there, the lights along the corridor flicked on, and I headed to the far end.

The little code box on the door of our unit asked for my four digits. Above it was a sign: *NEED HELP? SEE RECEPTION. 1-hour lock-out after 3 incorrect attempts.*

I blew out a breath. Three goes. OK.

My birth date. It seemed like the obvious one would be my birthday. I punched in the four digits, day and month, Siggy tightening with anticipation in my head when I pressed the green tick.

The line of asterisks encoding my digits disappeared and INCORRECT PIN flashed on the display.

I swore and walked away, then turned to watch the door from halfway along the corridor, biting the corner of my thumb. Whose birthday, then, if not mine? Not her own. Definitely not, too easy, too stupid. But it would be a date. She was big on anniversaries of events, the markings of years passed since landmarks in our lives. Because she was a journalist in more than just training, she kept records, she knew when things happened, and she worked out why.

I leaned against the opposite wall, eyeing that little box on our door, daring me to get it wrong again. It would have to be a big thing, something important.

That was it. I bounced myself straight and strode down the corridor, completely confident. It was the day everything changed. The event of our whole lives. The day Jodie died. I tapped the number in: 0211. Second of November.

INCORRECT PIN.

I smacked my hand against the cold metal door, then leaned in, my forehead squashed against it. *Come. On.* Siggy was still there, I could feel her like a coat, like a film on the inside of my skin, but she was passive. Watching me. Letting me do what I had to do.

I opened my eyes, thinking, *Siggy*.

I didn't even pause when I pressed the buttons. I'd been looking at it wrongly: the catalyst wasn't the day we became fugitives. It was the day we'd assigned to the thing that triggered all of it.

Cherry Tree Day.

An innocuous beep of acceptance from the box. The click of the door unlocking.

I was in.

59

Mae

They'd covered all of four miles before the fuel alarm beeped. Swearing, Kit swung across all three lanes and just made the slip road to Heston services before the chevrons ran out.

Mae got out on the forecourt to do the honours. As he stood there, turbulence from the motorway billowing at his shirt, she wound the window down.

'Shout us a can of pop?'

'Sure.'

The window started to rise again, then paused, backtracked.

'Buy you a proper drink when we finish, if you like.'

He made a vague shrug, not wanting to seem too keen.

'Unless,' she went on, 'do you actually ever *finish*, though? Or do you just plug yourself in somewhere under your desk for a few hours?'

He tapped the last few drops of fuel from the nozzle. 'I have a very healthy work-life balance,' he told her. She looked at him for a moment, smile bitten off to one side and eyebrows raised, then scoffed gently and hit the window button again.

Mae jogged in and paid. When he got back in the car, Kit was just hanging up on the handsfree.

'What was that?' he asked, then, remembering, added, 'The portrait?'

'What?' she said, turning the key.

'From Lucy Arden's. The painting of Jodie?'

'Oh, that – no. It's definitely signed Shevah but the only Shevah I can find is the rabbi at the synagogue down there. I've left messages. That,' she said, indicating the phone, 'was the hospital. You would not *believe* how fucking complicated their HR is.'

Mae narrowed his eyes. 'As in, Helen Williams?'

'No. She left. I'm on that too, actually. I think she was sacked, need to know why. But no, that was Christine's manager.' She pulled back out into the traffic. 'Turns out we were right: she's agency staff, and she does use a different name for work. Scott instead of Power.'

'Weird. Why?'

'Who knows.' She overtook a string of lorries. 'I had him check her shifts. She was working the night Matt disappeared.'

He cracked open the two-quid can of lemonade for her and handed it. She took it, frowning.

'What are you thinking?'

After a mouthful she said, 'Just something Ellie said. That she'd gone to see her mum at work, but it was in the middle of her shift, so she didn't know where to find her.'

Mae gave a low whistle. 'So she could have been anywhere.'

'Shame their upgrade of security didn't extend to actually keeping some kind of tabs on their staff. Might have avoided all of this.' She took her eyes from the road for a moment, struck by a thought. 'Corsham was new to the area, right?'

'New-ish. We should probably check with Police Scotland, see if they've got anything we haven't seen.'

But Kit kissed her teeth, dismissing it. 'But we've checked his records. He'd have needed to disclose anything major to be working in a hospital at all, surely. One of those checks, Criminal Records Bureau or whatever it's called now.'

Water bottle halfway to his lips, Mae froze. Looked at her. 'DBS.'

'Yeah.' Then, 'Why, what?'

'I wanted to go on Bear's school trip. My DBS has lapsed, so they said I couldn't. You have to have a DBS to work with kids.'

'That's what I'm saying—'

'No, look.' He twisted in his seat. 'Since she met Matt, Ellie started volunteering with the kids, in the hospital. She would have to have had a DBS to do that. But how?'

'You just apply, don't you? I don't actually know, I've never—'

'No. You need more than that. References, employers, background, traceable previous addresses, all of that. They can take months, especially if there are any gaps in the information. So when you bear in mind the Powers spent a long, long time hiding, after Jodie—'

'How do you know?'

Mae paused, realizing what he'd said. But there was no way he was going to explain this without coming clean. 'I tried to find them. More than once.'

'Why?'

'Just wanted to know Ellie was OK.' He was glad Kit was driving, her eyes occupied by the road ahead. 'The whole thing got under my skin. Badly, I mean, and—'

'I know,' Kit said, glancing over for just long enough to smile at him. 'You don't have to go into it.'

He looked away, out of the window. 'It makes sense now, why they did that. If they're really saying that *Ellie* killed Jodie, they've probably spent every day since looking over their shoulders. But the upshot was that they never had an official address. Ellie doesn't have an NHS number, DWP, anything. It would have been nigh on impossible for her to get cleared to work with vulnerable kids.'

'Unless someone helped her.' Kit twisted the can into the holder behind the handbrake and increased her speed. 'And why would someone want to help her get access to kids?'

Mae slowly rotated the cap onto his bottle. He was thinking about Cox. How only a few short hours before, he'd very nearly felt sorry for the guy.

'Same reason someone with a proven interest in child pornography wanted sedatives out of the hospital pharmacy.'

60

Mae

The Gayatri Institute was a well-kept, glass-fronted building on the corner of two smart streets near to East Molesey's well-heeled main drag. Gauzy white curtains obscured the floor-to-ceiling windows of what Mae guessed was the main studio downstairs. No lights on, and no sign of any furniture or anything else in there. If Cox was in the building, he wasn't advertising it. Turning around the side of the building it was possible to make out an empty reception room, neat and dark. Just up the road, with eyes on the only entrance, was a bright squad car sitting under an orange streetlight.

'I thought we said discreet,' Mae said as Kit pulled in bonnet-to-bonnet with it.

'We did.' She smiled sweetly. 'They wanted to know whether our budget stretched to a newspaper with eyeholes cut out, but I already had my eye on a chip supper after, so I said no.'

She flashed the headlights and the shaven-headed uniform in the driving seat of the squad car, whose face had been underlit with the tell-tale blue of a smartphone, suddenly straightened. He got out of the car and came around to lean in to Kit's open window.

Mae reached across her to shake the guy's hand, trying not to brush his knuckles against Kit's chest. 'No sign of our man presumably?'

'No one in or out, sir.' His eyes zipped between them. 'I offered to go down there and see if I could get an answer for you but—'

'Glad you didn't,' Kit said. 'I told your inspector we didn't want to alert him before we got here.' She was right: the last thing they wanted was Cox lawyering up before they'd even had a chance to say hello. 'Thanks though.'

'Any time.'

'And the car?' Mae asked. 'He's not been back to it?'

Two stiff shakes of his head. 'Nope. Only way out of the building is that door there,' he said, pointing, 'and the gate next to it goes round the back.' He gripped the edge of the rolled-down glass. 'You sure you don't want me to get in there for you? Got my big red key in the back,' he added, miming the two handles of the battering ram he was clearly itching to use.

Kit laughed and hit the window-up button. 'You're all right, ta.'

Leaving the constable with strict instructions to stay where he was, Mae and Kit got out and walked back down the hill. Still no lights, no movement. They found the narrow passage behind the building, an old stone wall standing between them and what was probably a small courtyard or garden out the back.

'Give me a boost?' Kit said. Mae did as he was asked, linking his hands together and dropping onto a knee. She stepped on his palms and sprung up, scrabbled to hook her hands over the top of the wall.

'Anything?' Mae asked, squinting up at her.

'Nope,' she said, dropping down again brushing flaked paint off her thighs. 'There's a door into the building but no lights back there either.'

Mae got no answer from the intercom at the front. He stepped back to check again for movement at the upstairs windows when he buzzed it for the third time, but if Cox was in there, he wasn't in the mood for guests. He motioned to Kit to follow him.

'Time for our eager friend to get his favourite gear out,' he said, motioning for Kit to follow him. 'See if he can't talk Cox into putting the kettle on.'

But after a few steps, he stopped. From inside, there was a series of electronic bleeps, an alarm being deactivated. Mae turned as the door opened, the prospect of a chase sending a leap of anticipation through his blood. But then he saw Cox's face. Every feature of it was hollowed out, exhausted, stressed to the damp marrow. He opened the door as wide as it would go, and gestured them both inside with a tired sweep of his arm.

'I don't know what you're looking for, and I don't know what happens next,' he said as Mae approached, 'but I'd like to think it will be noted that I have brought this to your attention without any resistance of any kind.'

'Brought what to our attention?' Kit asked from behind Mae.

Cox said nothing, just gestured resignedly for them to follow him into the studio. It was completely empty, except for some rolled mats and foam blocks stacked up along one side. The front door closed softly behind them, and a drift of a breeze followed them into the room, nudging the fabric of one of the thin curtains aside. A scrap of moonlight glanced across the floor and was gone. The three of them squinted into the darkness.

'This,' said Cox, kneeling by what Mae could now see was a large bag on the floor. The doctor unzipped it, and stood up. Took a step back and stuffed his hands in his pockets.

It was a blue holdall, loosely packed with what looked to Mae like the sorts of things someone, a photography enthusiast, would take on a trip. A few clothes, a camera, a telescopic tripod. Mae tipped his head, then realizing what he was looking at, he instinctively put his arms out to the sides, a barrier in front of Kit and Cox, preventing them from moving forward, touching anything. Because right on the top of it, there was a plastic Ziploc bag.

Containing two fat, neat, side-by-side stacks of bank notes. Pink ones.

And without counting it, without even taking a step closer, Mae would have bet the farm that it totted up to something just shy of ten grand.

61

Ellie

I went inside and the lights came on automatically. The unit was much bigger than I'd expected, the size of a small shed inside, maybe eight by six, with containers of various sizes stacked along one wall. Strip lights buzzed above me but there was no natural light.

I scanned the wall of unmarked boxes. had to fight the feeling I was being sidetracked: trying to discover what my mother was hiding instead of looking for Matt. But I had run out of leads. I had nothing else to pursue. I needed to join the dots. Everyone had secrets, something they had gone to great lengths to keep locked away: Matt, Cox, Mum. The whole thing, the common denominator, was me.

I slid the first boxes over to a space on the floor. Inside there were scripts, transmission documents from ITV and the BBC, sleeves full of research and notes in my mother's handwriting: 1983, 1987, 1990. All work from her heyday, folder after folder of it. Guerrilla warfare in Colombia, massacre in Kenya. Famine in Ethiopia. A whole load of photographs: all centred on her, the person she had been before me. I didn't know this woman at all. Mum grinning in sunglasses in front of what the note on the back told me was Ceaușescu's palace; Mum looking serious into the camera with a horrifically malnourished child on her lap; a close-up of Mum speaking into the round ball of a microphone, eyes on whoever it was she was interviewing, out of the frame.

I chose the next box at random. It was sealed more effectively than the others, and I had to tear at the packing tape with my teeth to get it open. But the very first thing I found justified the effort.

A padded envelope containing old passports. I glanced at the images in them, my mother at nearly sixteen, then a decade older, then another. That lightning intellect sparking behind her straight-ahead, unsmiling eyes in all of them.

There were the stamps indicating her trips to the war zones of the 1980s: the Falklands via Argentina and later, Uruguay; Iran, Turkey. Returned back into the UK when the war ended. The next one was issued in 1992, the year I was born. I turned the page, expecting blank sheets from then on because I'd never been abroad. But there was another stamp, from 1995.

Bosne i Hercegovine – Bosnia. But how? And where was I when she made this trip?

As I closed the little booklet, I saw something else.

My name, beneath hers. The passport had been issued in the days before children needed ones of their own, although I'd never been abroad.

A moment resurfaced.

Me, at ten. A library book about Spain thrown against the wall, my face slick with crying. Still panting from the dying throes of a tantrum I was too old for. Mum explaining how we could never go abroad. Her hands on my knees, telling me how Siggy would come, and I wouldn't cope with all the noise and the crushes and the crowds. There would be so many triggers on planes, we'd never get anywhere. I was too fragile to go on a plane; I always had been. It could never happen.

But here, on this document, was a contradiction. I flipped through it again, and yes, there it was under one of the stamps, in English. *Entry x2.* I'd been with her, on the way in, and on the way out. I would have been three years old. I let the thing drop into my lap and stared at the wall, trying to make sense of it. Was this the trip Mum had taken us on then, when she lost touch with Bernadette? Why Bosnia? Hadn't there been a war on? I scrutinized it again, then put it aside, my whole head tight with confusion.

The next box held some of my things. Despite my efforts not to be sucked in, as I flicked though the box there were things that transported me, pictures I had drawn, tickets to films and museums I remembered wholesale, instantly. Under that, box files. I brought the top one onto my lap and opened it. It was full of envelopes, the addresses hand printed.

My handwriting. Not grown-up me. Adolescent me. The hairs on my arms lifted, and the silence in that dead-air room tightened like a shroud.

I lifted one at random. Addressed in careful letters to the Centre for Anxiety and Trauma Disorders, London. Underneath, another, this time for the First Person Plural, a mental health charity. I dug deeper, recognizing every one of these names. Great Ormond Street Hospital. Hope for Dissociative Survival. Young Minds. A thick, elastic-banded bundle of letters to different NHS Child and Adolescent Mental Health Services: CAHMS east London, CAHMS west London, CAHMS East Sussex, dozens of them.

All of the letters we'd worked on together. Asking for help, offering to volunteer for trials, to try to make me better, to understand Siggy. To make her leave me alone.

And every one of them was unsent.

Numb and confused, I started to put everything back. I didn't even want to think about what it meant. Folders and boxes and binders, but there were too many and I hadn't been careful enough. I had to completely unpack one box and start again, anxiety making steady gains on my breathing. I dealt with the envelope full of passports last, but as I returned the stack to the envelope, something bunched up in the bottom of it. I pulled it out.

It was a handwritten sheet, no envelope.

Chris, it started, scrawled spikily in letters that got bigger and bigger until the words at the bottom of the page were double the size of those at the top:

> *wearever the fuck you are. I want you to no, your not getting away with this. Im going to find you both I dont care how long it takes. That kid needs its dad and were supposed to be a family and thats what were going to be. Were good for each other. You think you can live your life without me and you cant I'm going to*

Holding my breath, I turned it over. It was blank on the other side. That was it. Slowly, I folded it back up.

That kid needs its dad.

I dropped the letter, let it drift down on the top of the mess of files on the floor. Right then, from nowhere, a wave of fury swelled and broke in me.

I didn't care that he was obviously an arsehole. I didn't even care that he'd threatened her, threatened us.

She'd *lied* to me. I had trusted everything she said. And she'd lied. About her family, about the letters, about my father – about everything.

I kicked the whole pile. Papers and files cascaded up and against the opposite wall like a drift of dead leaves. Paper and files and all the pointless stupid bits and pieces of shit from a childhood I didn't even know any more.

I grabbed Matt's hoody, bundled my face into it, and screamed. Then, sobbing, I got up. Started stuffing everything into the boxes without any consideration of order. She'd come here and she'd know I'd seen it all. I didn't care. I grabbed her precious archive by the handful, the armful, shoving everything into a corner. When I finished, panting, I laughed. She'd be furious. The passport was still on the floor, open at the page with the Bosnian stamp. I stooped to collect it.

It was as if everything went quiet. There was a tiny shield I hadn't noticed before, next to the lettering. The same shape and stars design as the one on the paper I found in Cox's drawer. I was cold, suddenly, but not just cold. In my mind, at the very end of a long, dark corridor, a light went on.

Siggy's eyes flew open. She pinned me still, drilling something into my head. The answer was right there at the edge of my grasp, the cogs of it grinding so hard I could almost hear it. Bernadette and my mother, my mother and Cox, Cox and Matt, Matt and me, me and Jodie. None of the teeth fitting. Everything jammed up, the gears slipping and failing.

I leaned back against the wall, put my hands in my pockets, and closed my eyes. I gave myself a count of twenty, the way Dr Cox used to tell me to do. When I opened my eyes again, I had the answer.

I sniffed hard and wiped my face. Then, clearing a space in front of me and from my pocket I slid the folded, yellowing document from the envelope I'd taken from Cox's files, and although the words meant nothing to me, I studied the whole thing. Right down to the handwritten words on the scored line: names, possibly? *Mubina* above and *Idrizovic* below.

And then, from the zipped inside pocket, I pulled out my baby photo, the one Matt had in his boat. I placed the photo on top of the document, lining up their top left corners. Bright lights danced in front of my eyes, and I found I was holding my breath.

They both had rust marks, and the rust marks matched.

Once, a lifetime ago, they could have been stapled together.

62

Mae

Mae drove while Kit slept open-mouthed but silent, having talked him into driving her home. They'd left the local SOCOs on site after Cox had been cleared for transfer to Brentford. Now, under a smooth onyx sky, with open roads ahead of him and his veins full of caffeine, he had some time to think.

Item one was Cox. Although neither he nor Kit wanted to be the first to admit it, once he was bagged and tagged in the back of the squad car, they'd agreed that his performance when he'd let them in was serious Oscar material. So was he just an even better bullshit artist than Mae had thought? Or was he telling the truth?

Items two and three were Christine and Ellie. Neither had answered their phone since teatime. There was a uniform stationed outside their flat on strict instruction to alert him to any sight of them, but so far, not a peep.

And item four – item four was the handwritten note they'd found at the bottom of the baggie full of twenties.

On the inner orbital, things started to slow up a little, and Kit stirred, opened one eye and closed it again. She lifted her hand and wiped at the corner of her mouth with a knuckle.

'Where are we?' she croaked.

'Slight detour. Go back to sleep.'

It was gone one by the time he pulled up and killed the engine. He considered waking Kit, but decided to go this one alone. As near to silently as he could, he opened the door by degrees and closed it behind him with a click. Through the window he saw Kit frown in her sleep, then shift and settle.

The street was deserted. His breath steamed white as he pushed the little garden gate. A frame of light glowed around the curtained window in the front room of the house, and he rang the doorbell once, twice, then again. Inside, the sound of the TV fell silent, and there were footsteps, and then the door opened.

And there stood Helen Williams, her dishevelled hair in a backlit halo and her eyes smudged dark from half-shed make-up.

'Oh,' she said, sighing heavily as if she'd expected him hours ago. She stood aside to let him in. 'It's you.'

She studied the picture on his screen with a blank, haggard face, then handed his phone back and sank into her jumbo-cord sofa. 'I'll give you the benefit of the doubt,' Mae told her. 'I'm going to assume there was a good reason that you didn't tell me about this before.'

'I don't know,' she said finally, looking up at him.

'No?'

'No.'

Mae closed the photo of the note they'd found folded in half under the cash in Matthew Corsham's bag. Handwritten, black ballpoint on an NHS comp slip. A simple message:

> … *And I never even want to hear your name again, you piece of shit.*

'Is that standard wording, when you let someone go?'

She let her head drop back and screwed up her eyes, but she didn't reply.

'I mean, for example,' Mae went on, 'is that what they said to you when you got the sack?'

Her eyes flew open, but he raised a finger before she had a chance to reply.

'There were no *pastures new*. You did get the sack, Helen, we don't need to argue about that.'

She looked at him miserably. 'What did they say?'

He shrugged. 'I'll be talking to your boss in the morning. But I'm here asking you, now.' He put the phone away in his jacket pocket, and waited.

Tucking her slippered feet under her, she raked her fingers through her hair and laughed. Mae glanced at the bottle of wine on the table. A few inches from empty, one glass. Not that he blamed her. Judging by the label on her Sauvignon, this was a woman accustomed to the finer things: good wine, great clothes, a personal trainer, probably. As of that afternoon, she was probably staring a defaulted mortgage in the face. It was a bad day in Helen Williams's world, whatever way you looked at it.

'All right,' she said at last. 'I've got a reason I didn't say before. It's just not a very good one.' She slipped the rest of the wine into the glass, and told him all about it.

Six months earlier, the children's wing had had an inspection. There was nothing significantly wrong with the provision of care, Williams told him, and the medical side of what happened there wasn't down to her anyway.

'What they kept coming back to, again and again, was that the kids were bored. The long-term inpatients were falling behind socially, as well as all the rest of it. There wasn't enough for them to do, and their mental health was suffering.' She took a mouthful of white, suppressed a ladylike burp with the back of her hand, and placed the glass on the table, too near the edge. Mae's fingers itched to right it.

'And then all of a sudden everyone cares. Everyone's giving me grief about it, saying we have to boost activities, we have to offer enrichment and pastoral care and all this bullshit that no one wants to spend any money on.'

'How was that your job, though?'

'Ex-fucking-zactly,' she said, reaching for the glass again and tilting it at him precariously. 'Exactly the question. It's my fucking job because I'm the one who gets the free resources. The humans.'

'Volunteers.'

'But people don't want to do it, you know? They like the idea of helping little children, they like the idea of telling their friends that they're reading to the kiddies in the hospital, but when it comes down to it, very poorly kids give people the heebie-jeebies. We get people starting off with good intentions, then time wears on and they stop turning up, they find they can't commit the time they thought they could. Excuses, net result being that the issue persists. Kids are miserable. And I do *care*,' she said, waving a finger at him accusingly, 'whatever you might think of me. I've got a heart of gold. I have.'

She waited for him to concur.

'Go on,' he said.

A big sigh. 'So I was getting desperate, badgering everyone I knew. Word got around I suppose because after that we got a few people in.'

'Well done you.'

She eyed him blackly. 'Yeah well. Then there was the usual wait for the checks, and then we got another date for the interim inspection and the pressure just got ...' Trailing off, she sighed, shook her head. 'And then Matthew Corsham turned up in my office. Three, four months ago, I can dig out the date. He had someone for me. Ellie Power. She wanted to come and volunteer nearly *every day*. She'd already got DBS forms, so she could start right away.'

'And that was a problem?'

'It wouldn't have been any kind of problem if the forms hadn't been faked.'

Mae looked up. She met his eye.

'You didn't check?'

'I didn't. I absolutely did not suspect a thing, at the time. Then a few months later I got a call from this psychotherapist, not one of ours.'

'Do you remember his name?'

She screwed up her eyes, then shook her head.

'Dr Cox?' Mae ventured.

'Yes. Cox, that's right. He wanted to know about Ellie, how she was interacting with the children. I wasn't going to discuss her with him, it would have been massively against policy, so I said no, obviously—'

'Obviously.'

'Yeah, all right. I said I could pass his details to her if he wanted, but he made some excuse and hung up. So that was a huge alarm bell. I dug her forms out and pieced it together. Realized what I'd done. I went straight down to the lab, confronted Matthew about it because he'd set the thing up in the first place, and he said, he'd keep quiet about it if I would.'

'Meaning what?'

'Meaning I had more to lose. Yes, he'd faked the clearances, but I should have checked. It was my arse on the line.'

'So you buried it.'

'I didn't *bury* it. I slimmed down her shifts. Down to one a week, and I planned it so her last one would be this week. I really thought that would be the end of it. But then we got the tip-off, about the—' she paused, glanced away, 'the drugs. Then they dug everything up and then that was it.'

'But it wasn't just the drugs, was it?'

She reached out to upend the bottle into the glass, found it empty, shook it, and set it back on the table with a crack.

'Helen.'

'No. OK? You happy? No, it wasn't just the drugs. We had an anonymous email, someone telling us they knew Matthew Corsham had pornographic images on his computer, and they'd confronted him and he said he'd delete them. The caller said they wanted to be sure, so they broke into his locker, and found the drugs.'

'And it was *my* lookout, wasn't it, because I'd taken him at his word. I'd done my best to hide it, pretend the computer thing hadn't happened, but it wasn't enough. Now he's just disappeared, and I'm utterly fucked, all for the sake of a bunch of kids having someone play fucking snap with them.'

He tried to muster some sympathy, but he came up short. 'Did you know why he faked them?' Mae asked her, counting up the possible reasons as he said it.

She gave a little shudder and looked away.

'Did he use her to get on the ward himself, Helen? To get access to the kids?'

Almost inaudibly, she said, 'I don't know.'

Meaning with all the resources at her fingertips, the CCTV, the logs from keycards, the people she could have asked, she had chosen instead to turn her back and hope that she didn't get caught.

'Don't just stand there staring at me,' she told him, then she let out a groan and buried her face in her hands.

He could, at that moment, have made an attempt to make her feel better, let her know that anyone might have done the same, that it was an error made under pressure. But then he thought of Cox, and Jodie Arden, and all those pictures of other people's children. Those pictures of Ellie. So he stayed where he was.

63

Ellie

I awoke into pitch blackness, panic firing like Catherine-wheel sparks in all directions. The thin, rough carpet was doing a bad job of disguising a cold cement floor under my hip, but reminded me where I was. The storage unit. No windows, neither daylight nor moonlight. I'd fallen asleep.

I got to my feet, still dizzy from sleep, and waved my hands around to trigger the sensor for the lights. Squinting against the sudden brightness, I checked the door, first – shut and locked – then checked my hands, my arms. My shoes were still paired neatly by the door. No sign that I had been out. No sign that I had been up.

Siggy was silent and still, just a shuddering little crouch of something, balled up in my stomach. I had an urge to reach in and cradle her, and in the wake of that, a terrible sadness. How unbearably alone she was.

She had hardly stirred in the last couple of days, like an elderly cat. There, alive, but only just. A year ago, a week ago, I would have thought I'd be relieved, but there was no victory in it. She had always been there, and now I was ... alone.

And I missed her.

I opened the door for a moment to see if it was morning: the corridor outside was flooded with thin daylight. Then I turned my phone back on. Battery almost gone, but it was long enough to discover I had half a dozen voicemails.

Not Matt. Mum.

I think they know. Don't go to the flat.

We have to leave. I'm waiting at our special place. You have to come, please.

Where are you? I can't bear you being gone.

You are breaking my heart. Please call. I'm waiting for you.

You can't do this on your own.

I deleted each one of them, but when I came to the last I heard a different voice. It was Bernadette, a short message just asking for a return call.

She picked up on the first ring.

'I found something I need to show you. Photos.' Then, quickly, 'it's not going to be … like before. Nothing with the uniform.'

She was going to work in Ealing that morning, she said. It wasn't far from where I was. We agreed to meet in an hour, and I ended the call.

Kneeling, I lined everything up. The passports. My baby photo. Cox's document. The phone bill, the letter from my dad. I looked at it like that, spread out on the floor like a Kim's Game, until the idea took shape. I fitted the whole lot into an empty plastic envelope, buttoned it into a pocket, put the hoody and my shoes back on, and got out of there.

Bernadette was there before me. It was still early, not even half seven, and there were only a handful of customers. She was sitting at a small booth table stirring slow circles in her grey-looking tea. She straightened as I sat down opposite her, almost as if she hadn't expected me. If she had noticed my dishevelled appearance she didn't show it, but she didn't look as if she'd slept well herself.

'I wasn't sure you'd come,' she said with a weak smile, pushing the cup away and lifting a bag onto the table.

'Before you do,' I said, stopping her. I wanted her to see the letter: *The kid needs its dad.* I unfolded it and slid it across the desk.

She looked it over, biting her lip, then looked up at me.

'Is that his writing?' I asked her. 'My—' I paused, not quite able to call him *my dad.* 'Jim?'

'Jim Scott.' She nodded, then slid the sheet back.

'Scott?'

'Yes. Why, what?'

'Nothing.' I slid the sheet back and folded it. 'You didn't say he was an arsehole.'

'He was … troubled.'

'Troubled enough to batter us?'

She flinched.

'Did he?'

'Look, I don't—'

I stood up, pulled at the top buttons of my top.

'What are you – stop it, Ellie,' Bernadette told me, but I wasn't going to stop.

I turned my back to her and twisted my top round to show her the scarred skin on my shoulder. 'Did he do this?'

Horror on her face. 'Look, sit down, we can—'

I yanked the fabric down again, then faced her and lifted the top to expose my side and the rucked, ruined skin around my flank and onto my abdomen. The conversations around us went silent.

'This man you're talking about like he's some kind of victim here. Did he do this to me, do you think?'

She got up and put her hands on my shoulders. 'Ellie. Please. You need to sit down.'

'Do I? Is that what I need?' I was breathing hard, my teeth tight and furious. 'It's funny. Because everyone seems to have an opinion on what I should be doing. But I'm starting to get a bit tired of doing what I'm told.'

She didn't take her eyes from mine, even when the chairs beside us scraped back and the two guys in suits muttered their way over to a different table. 'You're angry. I'm not surprised. You've been lied to, and the people you thought you could trust haven't turned out to be that trustworthy. I get it. I do. But I don't know the answer to your question.' She gave my shoulders a gentle squeeze and dropped her hands. 'Can I show you what I brought?'

I sank back into my chair, the fight gone out of me.

Opening the bag, she slid out a brown envelope. 'To be honest, finding you has been … not what I'd thought. But anyway. Here.' She carefully upended the envelope and slid out a slim stack of photographs.

'I took these out of the albums when Mum was in the hospice, before she passed away. She wanted them in her room, in frames so she could see them.'

She placed the first one on the table. It showed a younger Bernadette holding a little blonde girl of maybe two on her lap, both of them grinning at the top of a playground slide. The next was the same girl standing on the driver's seat of a convertible, gripping the steering wheel, Bernadette beside her, hands around her waist. The next showed the girl again, a little older this time, on the shoulders of an older man. I studied the girl, being the obvious theme, trying to recall her. Was I supposed to know this child? Why?

'Dad,' Bernadette said quietly, touching the man's face.

She put the remaining two next to the others. One was of two women, startlingly similar, their hairstyles both in the exaggeratedly voluminous style of the eighties. Bernadette, and my mum. Sisters in their twenties, a night out.

The colours in the other image were slightly faded and the focus was off, but it was clear enough. It was my mother, her hair permed almost into ringlets, cradling a baby. She was leaning in to a man who could have been the soldier she'd shown me yesterday, though he was in a denim shirt this time. They formed the classic pose of the new family of three. I touched my fingertip to his face, the light smudge of an unshaven lip. The shaggy, ash-coloured hair. Blue eyes.

'And you've never seen any pictures like these before?'

I shook my head. 'There was a burglary,' I said vaguely, not taking my eyes from the picture. 'All our photos.'

'When?'

'I was two.'

The backs of his fingers were resting against the child's face, and he was pulling my mother in with the other hand. Their beatific faces gazing at the tiny, newborn child. Pink, blotchy cheeks as round as peaches; a puff of white-blonde hair.

'Ellie,' she said. I lifted my head. 'There wasn't a burglary. Not when you were two.'

'Yes. There was. We lost everything—' I insisted, but even I could hear the weakness in it.

Infinitely gentle, she said, 'Are you sure? Have you checked?'

I opened my mouth. Closed it. Didn't have room for what she was saying. I didn't have any room for any of it.

Bernadette touched my hand as I turned my attention back to the table. I could feel her eyes on me. 'This is Christine, you

can see that. It's the day of the birth. This man is ... well, you
can see. It's true he and Christine had their problems, and they
might well have called it a day even if she hadn't disappeared
but – look. This is him. He's alive here, and as far as I know, he
still is.'

I turned it over and read the faded handwritten date: 11th
June 1992. The day I was born.

'We lost touch a few years ago,' she was saying. 'I think he
went to Canada or ...' Bernadette trailed off, but I wasn't listening.

From my pocket I produced the Polaroid: my one surviving
baby picture, my tiny head taking up the whole frame, the edge
of a tanned hand holding my sleeping face to the camera.

'*This* is me.'

She met my eyes and then studied the picture, forehead tight
and lined. Then she blew out a long, controlled breath. 'I don't
understand what's happened, but I promise you, I've got no
reason to lie to you.' She put the Polaroid down and rested her
fingertip on the family scene. 'My sister, Christine. Jim. This is
their daughter, Eleanor. Ellie. All of these pictures are of her. My
niece.'

My eyes locked on that family picture, on the face of the man
who should have loved me, whose colouring should have
explained mine, who should have had the same eyes as me, one
green and one blue. Because that's what Mum had said, all my
life. His genes won; I was so like him.

But it was a lie.

There was no way the baby in the picture was me.

64

Mae

Kit came onto the CID floor, returning from the drinks-run she'd volunteered for after morning briefing.

'Ready?' she called over, waiting for him to nod before she went round distributing the half-dozen coffees among their colleagues.

He finished the sentence of the write-up he was doing about the previous night's trip to Surrey, then got up and fell into step with her, heading to the back stairwell. Halfway there, McCulloch joined them.

'You shouldn't have,' McCulloch said, accepting the cappuccino Kit held out to her. 'Not without a pastry, anyway.'

Without breaking her stride, Kit handed her a bag, a few spots of grease showing through the brown paper from the still-warm pain au chocolat inside.

McCulloch took that too with an appreciative chuckle. 'What have we got so far?'

'We had round one at 8 o'clock this morning,' Mae said, pushing a door and holding it open until everyone was through. 'Cox claims he's as much in the dark about Matthew Corsham's whereabouts as we are. Total denial on paying his rent as well.'

'Hold on, you thought Cox had paid Corsham's rent?'

'Someone did, and it doesn't look like it was Matt.'

'Why would he have done that?'

Mae shrugged. 'Buy him a bit more time?'

'Minimize suspicion,' Kit put in. 'If something had happened to Matthew, his car being abandoned and his rent lapsing would trigger a hike in the resources we throw at it. We figured that Cox was in the middle of this surveillance thing of his, and wouldn't have wanted the thing blown just yet.'

McCulloch looked unconvinced. 'So what's your theory now, then?'

Kit chewed her lip. 'We don't know. Cox could easily be lying.'

McCulloch gave it a minute's thought and asked, 'So he doesn't know where Matthew Corsham is, but he's admitting he knows him. Did he say how?'

'We're going to get into that now,' Mae said. He swallowed the last of his espresso and tucked the empty paper cup into the bin between the lifts, then hit B for basement. 'So far he's just said Corsham called him about Ellie, wanting to find out what he knew about her condition.'

'And so he blew his savings on kitting out a surveillance van?'

'Said he'd decided to get hard evidence before they worked out he was onto them.'

'Right, well that's a perfectly logical conclusion,' McCulloch said, rolling her eyes. 'What about the photos? You think he's going to cough for that?'

'We're coming to that next. I asked him about the child porn, why he deleted it from Corsham's laptop, and he says he didn't know anything about them until he saw them on the drive.'

McCulloch turned to Mae, one eyebrow arched high. 'Well, it wasn't his laptop.'

Mae had been turning that very question over in his head all morning. 'No. But we do know he sent Matt the pictures of Ellie, so there's context.'

'Hmm, I don't know ...'

'And there's also the context of Jodie Arden—'

'Who was over the age of consent, might I remind you,' McCulloch said through a mouthful of French pastry.

'... who was in the grey area between the age of consent and adulthood, and who had written a diary entry saying he'd bought her so much stuff that it was tantamount to paying her for sex.'

McCulloch paused and faced him. 'We're not going there again, Mae. CPS rejected that exact point five years ago.'

He couldn't argue with that. 'Yeah well. I'd still hope a jury would raise its eyebrows. Time will tell, I guess, once the tech forensics are done.'

She looked like she was turning this over. 'Thoughts, Catherine?'

'He was convincing,' Kit said simply, stepping into the lift as the doors slid open. 'And the fact remains that when the images of Ellie were taken, he was under the impression she was sixteen. No one disputes that. Even Jodie Arden thought she was sixteen.'

McCulloch screwed the paper bag up and handed it to Mae. He tutted but put it in his pocket, while she brushed crumbs off her chest. 'But he's claiming no knowledge of the bag and the cash, you're saying.'

'Flat out denial,' Mae said. 'Claims he's being framed.'

'What's his take on the vehicle, the burnt-out one?'

They'd arrived at the interview room. 'That'll be what I'm here to find out.'

'Righto. Good luck.'

Mae nodded and pushed open the door. 'After you, Kit.'

65

Ellie

Bernadette and I said goodbye outside the coffee shop. I walked without direction, a watery sun rising to my left and flaring in the higher windows to my right. I couldn't get the pictures out of my head. The baby had to be a sibling, I reasoned, but if that was so, where was that child now? And why had I never been told?

Eventually turning onto the Broadway I stopped, scanned the street until I saw an internet café, and crossed the road.

A little bell above the door sounded as I went in. There were posters everywhere advertising telecoms deals for calls to Africa, Europe, India, everywhere and anywhere. I paid for an hour and chose a booth in the corner.

The first thing I did was move the keyboard and the peeling mouse mat aside to make room for the envelope from Cox's office. I copied the words from across the top, and ran an image search.

I sat back, slowly pulled the cursor down the results. I clicked on one after another until I was sure I wasn't jumping to conclusions. Because it seemed to be telling me that what I had in front of me was a birth certificate.

'Hey!' The young guy behind the counter called over to me, making me jump. 'You want coffee? Cold drink?'

'No, I'm fine,' I told him, but as I glanced at him my eye snagged on a poster behind his head. A tariff. Costs per minute of a call Senegal, Serbia, Sweden.

After a frozen moment, I dug in the envelope again and pulled out Matt's phone bill. There, halfway down the last page: that international number. I'd tried it before, but I hadn't had enough credit to call, and I'd forgotten it. Checking each number, I typed it into a search. A whole load of hits.

The code was for a region of Bosnia, it said.

Tuzla. *Toos-la*, was how it was pronounced. I knew that name, and there was no reason why. At the back of my skull I could suddenly feel Siggy again, and she was holding her breath. I selected the top result on the search, the one that contained an exact match of the phone number from Matt's bill. The screen went white for just a second as the website loaded.

I brought a hand to my mouth, jolted away from the desk. The image at the top of the page. It was a building, terracotta-coloured against a cloudless turquoise sky, and there were people, dozens of them, standing outside with their arms in the air, posed but smiling.

I knew the building. Not a hospital, not a barracks. The number Matt had phoned – it was the number for that *building*.

It was the building that Siggy had been showing me my whole life.

66

Charles Cox Psychotherapy Ltd.	
Clinical audio recording transcript	
Patient name:	*Eleanor Power*
Session date:	*7 October 2006*

[recording resumes]

CC: OK Ellie. So we've got a nice, relaxed, empty mind right now. Every time you start to think about something, you just notice the thought and move it away, OK? Your mind is a big, big empty space. Any thoughts that come in, you don't need to worry about them, just let them drift on past.
EP: Mmm. OK.
CC: Great. And then, when you're ready, I'd like you to very gently, very slowly, allow just something small from the dream we discussed earlier to emerge. You don't need to try, just relax and tell me what you see.

[pause: 1 min 5 sec]

EP: A lot of people. Frightened ... everyone is frightened.
CC: What are the people frightened of? Can you take a step
  back from what you see and have a look around you?

[pause: 25 sec]

EP: Soldier. There's a soldier and he's got ... something in
  his hand. And ... dirty. He's very dirty and shouting.
CC: Is this ... the big building we've talked about, are we
  there?
EP: No.
CC: All right. Tell me more about this soldier.
EP: He's got soldier clothes on but his hair is all longish and
  dirty like he hasn't washed and it smells like cigarettes and
  – man smell.

[pause: 27 sec]

CC: So I saw you flinch just then, is there anything else you
  can tell me about what you see?
EP: Blood.
CC: Blood, OK. Where is the blood?
EP: On the floor.
CC: Good, right. Tell me about the floor. Let's see if we can
  get an idea of this room.
EP: Not a room. Outside. Blood on the ground. Stones. I'm-I'm
  scared.
CC: OK. Here ... all right, so keep your eyes closed but I'm
  just going to ask you to move your hands down, is that all
  right? Good, that's good. So you covered your ears then,
  what happened?

EP: A lot of noise.

CC: Can you describe the noise?

EP: Screaming. But … he's trying to cry but he can't.

CC: Who's trying to cry?

EP: Little boy. Bleeding. His throat – the soldier cut him and he can't. The little boy can't—

[pause: 20 sec]

CC: So just try to slow your breathing … just slow that right down if you can. So there's a little boy who's been hurt by a soldier. On his neck? Can you describe what happened?

EP: He says it's the little boy's fault. The little boy shouldn't have been crying.

CC: Do you know why the boy was crying?

EP: He was … he was hungry. He was really hungry and I was hungry too and the man said he won't be hungry anymore.

CC: The man said that? The soldier?

EP: Yeah but the little boy—

CC: All right, listen to my voice a moment. I want you to take some deep—

EP: The little boy is going to die.

CC: He's … all right, let's take these deep breaths together, all right?

EP: He's going to die and I want to help him but I'm too scared. I want to help but I can't because—

CC: OK I'm placing my hands on you now, you can feel I'm here, you're safe—

EP: He's going to die
[crying]
EP: There's so much blood. I can't help him. I can't—
CC: *OK, Ellie? I want you to open your eyes. Ellie. Open them now.*

67

Mae

Inside the windowless interview room, the duty solicitor folded her arms across her chest. It was, Mae noted, the one who always managed to have a rod up her arse about something.

'Was that your superior I saw outside?' she wanted to know. 'Because I'd like to ask her if there's a good reason it's *you* doing this. Given the history. Other than revenge, I mean?'

Mae ignored this and sat himself opposite Cox. Took the time to make himself comfortable. Crossed his ankles, leaned back, rolled his neck a few times. The light on the recorder told him he was all set, and while Mae fixed Cox with his best angle-grinder stare, Kit introduced the interview, repeated the formal caution. Cox, his hair dishevelled, shifted in his seat and looked around.

Kit waited for a beat, then dipped her head, trying to scoop Cox's eye contact away from Mae. 'Please confirm that you have understood.'

Cox blinked at her, nodded. Kit repeated her question firmly, gesturing to the recorder. 'You need to say it, Dr Cox.'

'I ... yes. I have understood, yes. Is that OK?'

Mae cleared his throat and leaned forwards, forearms resting on the table between them. 'How about we start with what you were doing driving Matthew Corsham's car from your little lookout spot on Abson Street to the derelict yard in Feltham.'

Cox looked from Mae to Kit then back again, confusion ruching his forehead. 'Genuinely and sincerely,' he said, enunciating every syllable with care, 'I have no idea what you're talking about.'

'We'll need the specific details of this accusation, please,' the solicitor said coolly.

'I was rather hoping you'd be able to fill us in on that.' Mae didn't take his eyes from Cox.

But the solicitor crossed her arms and huffed with indignation. 'We're not here for a fishing exercise. The charges you brought last night don't mention anything about—'

'OK then,' Mae said, shuffling the papers in the folder and pulling out a second bundle. 'Let's try ... oh yes. Matthew Corsham's NHS-issue laptop computer. The one you got your assistant to deliver back to the hospital when you realized they were getting itchy about it being missing.' He squared the sheets on the table and waited.

Cox bit his lips a few times, eyeing them both. Then he said, 'I stole it.'

The solicitor lunged forwards, looking like she'd just vomited in her mouth. 'Wait. Hold on, what—?'

But Cox put both his hands up. 'I did. I'm going to be honest here. I want you to know that. I have made some bloody ... stupid mistakes,' he said, like he was dragging the words out of a very dark place. 'But if I don't admit to the things I *have* done, you lot are going to think I'm responsible for much more. Much worse. So let's start there. I'm happy to admit that all of the recordings in the van are my doing, no one else knew about any of that. But I *had* to do it *that* way. The moment they knew I was around they would have raised hell, or disappeared, and I would never have got the evidence I needed. Honestly, I know nothing about any car. I knew Matt had one but nothing else. But the computer ... I can tell you about that.'

'Go ahead.'

'Matthew called me, a week ago. Said he'd been suspended, that he was going to get the sack. Someone at work had reported him for having indecent material on his computer. He obviously hadn't put it there himself. Well, I say *obviously*, but it was obvious to me. But he wanted to take the computer in, let them look at it exactly as it was, without wiping it or doing anything to get rid of what was on it. He said he had nothing to hide and that the best approach was to just go in and be absolutely honest. But he knew there were going to be questions asked, so he said I should probably pre-empt it. Get a lawyer. Talk to you lot.'

Mae folded his arms. 'But you weren't going to let that happen.'

'Not at the time, no. I knew how bad it would look, and you have to remember what happened the last time I found myself in a room like this,' he said, glancing at the cameras in the corner of the IR, then at Mae. 'I tried cooperation and honesty last time. Didn't serve me so well. So I begged him to just delete it all—'

'Because you knew there were images of yours on there that were going to be found,' Kit said.

Cox looked away.

Mae waited. 'So then what happened?' he asked eventually.

'I went to his boat, the day before he went missing, and I took it.'

'He knew you took it, you know,' Mae said. 'The moorings manager saw you do it. He told Matthew he saw you.'

'I'm aware of that.'

Mae sat back. 'See, there's something wrong there. If you stole my laptop, and if I knew you'd stolen it, I'd be round your house with a baseball bat faster than a coked-up Uber.'

'I'd ask you to refrain from threatening my client,' the solicitor said.

'He wasn't threatening me,' Cox said. Everyone turned to look at him: traditionally it wasn't the done thing for the suspect to take the side of the police during their interview. 'Well, you weren't,' he repeated. 'But the point is, Matthew knew what was on that machine. The obscene material involving children – which was *nothing* to do with me, and I'm certain was also nothing to do with Matthew, for the record – he wanted to just get the machine back without causing a fuss.'

This was a far cry from how Mae had expected the interview to go. He took his time making a couple of notes, then said, 'Let's go back a little way. Tell me about how you knew Matthew Corsham in the first place.'

Cox shifted in his seat, relaxing a bit with the new line of questioning. 'It was a couple of months ago. I just got a call. Out of the blue, really. I thought it was … I don't know, a joke, or something to start with.'

'Why would you think that?' Mae asked.

'Because I'd given up hope of finding her. I'd tried, many, many times after her suicide attempt, after she came out of hospital, but both she and Christine appeared to have vanished into thin air. Then I got this call from Matthew. He had some queries, he said, from a professional point of view, and could I answer them.'

'What sort of queries, exactly?'

'Regarding my initial diagnosis of Ellie.'

'Uh-huh.' Mae tapped the biro against his lip. 'Go on.'

'His belief was that there was more to Ellie's condition than it had maybe appeared.'

'And that rattled your cage, being undermined like that. Him, just a layman, thinking he'd spotted something you'd missed.'

Cox smiled but it wasn't goading. More just sad. 'But I *had* spotted it. I just wasn't able to treat it, because she disappeared.'

'You're saying you diagnosed ... you think it's something other than DID?'

'I'm of the opinion that while I was seeing her, there were elements of her history and ... home life which demonstrated a risk of ... other concerns.'

Mae frowned, laid his pen down in line with his notepad. 'Let me put this simply. You were found last night with a bag belonging to a missing man, containing several thousand pounds in cash. You previously stole a laptop belonging to this man, and attempted to conceal its return once you became aware we were looking for it. You are not in a position right now to be playing word games with us.'

Cox nodded. 'It's a long story,' he said.

'I'm all ears.'

He inhaled deeply, resignedly, as if preparing for a dive he didn't wish to undertake.

'Three weeks before Jodie disappeared I went on a conference trip to the Balkans. I'd been before: it was every few years, I'd got to know people out there. I added in an extra week to talk to a few colleagues about Ellie's case. What I discovered when I was out there shed significant new light on what I had previously thought about her case.

'Ellie had come to me, without her mother's permission, as you know, in 2006. She wanted to talk about her condition, her experience of what we call an *alter*. Dissociative Identity Disorder was something I had an interest in. We started with a traditional gestalt methodology: I was primarily trying to search for a way for her to speak about the underlying trauma.'

'The cause, you mean,' Kit said.

'After a fashion, yes. The problem was that she was very – closed off. She'd spent a long time living with her condition in absolute secrecy. It was almost cultlike, the level of betrayal she was feeling about talking about her history without her mother knowing. I tried some regression, a few other techniques. What I discovered was that her recall of events of her very early childhood was actually very revealing. It was,' he paused, sighed, 'incredible. It turned out she actually knew swathes of detail that she'd locked up.'

'We're talking recovered memory?' Mae said. 'Wasn't that stuff all debunked?'

Cox shook his head tightly. 'It's still hugely controversial actually, but that's not what we were doing. I wasn't looking to trigger the memories as such, it was just a matter of bringing the alter to the fore, to give that aspect of her personality a chance to be heard.'

Clearing her throat, the solicitor said, 'I fail to see how all of this can possibly be relevant to you.'

Cox waved it away. 'No, no I want to cooperate. I want it noted that I am cooperating.'

Mae and Kit swapped half a glance.

'Of course,' Mae said.

Cox poured himself a plastic cup of water from the jug on the table. 'I wanted to get to the bottom of the trauma, what happened that was so frightening to Ellie that she couldn't process it and retain full control of her identity. From what Ellie had told me, I understood that she and her mother had already sought help, but what concerned me was an enormous taboo between them around Ellie's early life. She didn't even know the name of her father, and she had these,' he gestured loosely across the back of his own body, 'these marks, scars that she had no good explanation for. Her dissociation seemed like a classic response to ...' he paused, tipped his head back to stare at the ceiling for a moment. 'Good god, the years I've spent protecting the confidentiality of my patients and now I'm telling you this without even asking her.'

Mae waited. Eventually, Cox's crisis passed and he continued.

'Her condition appeared to be a classic response to abuse. Fear is a major catalyst in cases of dissociation: a child may be so afraid of showing their true emotions that they essentially *split off* a part of their identity in a subconscious attempt to control or hide that emotion. These fugues, as she called them—'

Mae held up a hand. '*As she called them*? What do you call them?'

Cox met his eye. 'I don't call them anything.'

'Meaning what?'

'Meaning I see her condition differently.'

'So you saw something in her that went unnoticed by *all* of the other therapists she saw over the years?'

He considered this. 'But which therapists, exactly? Because I have never seen any evidence that she did see any therapists.'

'You think she's making them *up*?'

'I try to deal with evidence. Which is why I wanted to substantiate what I was hearing about the fugue states. I wanted to ask

Ellie's mother, but Ellie was against me contacting her. Vociferously so.'

Kit squinted at him, head tipped to one aside, confused. 'Why?'

'It's a good question. To my shame, it wasn't one I asked myself at the time. In retrospect, it was obviously for the same reason that she lied about her age. She didn't want Christine knowing I was treating her.'

'And that would have been because—?'

He shrugged expansively. 'You'll have to ask her.'

Kit flipped a new page of her notebook. 'You mentioned the Balkans.'

After a mouthful of water, Cox nodded. 'One of Ellie's prevailing fears was of men in uniform. We worked on this during one particular session and she very courageously agreed to confront this fear, really look at it. We found when we talked about it that it wasn't just generic uniform, it was the green or khaki you associate with infantry, armies. But we also found that the root fear involved a very scruffy soldier, very unkempt. It wasn't just one incident, it was a few different scenes that seemed to surface. That rang alarm bells for me: that sounded like someone – one or more people – acting outside of a recognized unit.'

Kit stopped chewing her thumb. 'So she's scared of guerrillas?'

'Let him finish,' Mae told her, lifting his hand. 'Go on.'

Cox looked at his hands. 'She had this recurring nightmare about the death of a little boy, a toddler. I wanted to see if there was a connection between this traumatic event and Ellie's injuries. I just didn't buy the official line that there'd been a domestic accident with a pan of water. All the time I was thinking, someone close to Ellie must have the information about where she got those scars. I became preoccupied with it: obsessed, almost.

'Anyway, when I was abroad at a conference, I mentioned this to a colleague who happens to be a Bosnian Serb involved in a childhood PTSD charity, very involved in reconciliation, that kind of thing. Obviously, I didn't initially concentrate on the details of the trauma itself but after giving him a few vague outlines he insisted I go into the details. What he told me was that this story of Ellie's – about a young boy being murdered by a soldier – was very like something that had been reported by a witness in The Hague, years later. He dug out the transcript, and we discovered that much of what Ellie talked about in this dream matched this ... event. It was a real-life thing that had happened.

'But there was no way Ellie could have seen it. Not only would she have been too young to process it at all – she'd never even left the UK. But I couldn't let it go, it was just too – the details were too similar.'

Mae pressed his fingertips into his forehead, his mind scrabbling for purchase on what he was hearing. 'I'm sorry, you're telling me you think Ellie's trauma came from ... what *are* you saying? That she heard about this thing in the news? That she *astral-projected* when she was a baby, or something?'

'No, that's not it. I had this friend help me track down the incident. I couldn't let go of the idea that there was some kind of link. It was laborious work, took days to get anywhere at all because so many place names had changed since the war, and people were still afraid of talking. But we tracked down the person who had given that evidence: she worked at a refugee centre on the site of an old technical college in another town from the incident, across what had temporarily been a border. It's a charity place now, or was last time I was in touch.

'I managed to get her – the witness – on the satellite phone. Rana Filipovic, her name was. Perfect English. So off we went to meet her, find out about it. I was excited about it, so I made a call back to England to tell Ellie that I-I don't know, that I thought I had found something. But when I rang, I got Christine instead.' There was a pause. 'And she was furious.'

Mae let his chair rock forwards, planting the front legs back on the carpet. 'Christine was?'

'Yes.'

'About what?'

'Me. The fact that I'd even spoken to her daughter. It was the first time I'd had any contact with Christine. That phone call, that was when I discovered I'd been deceived about Ellie's age. She'd told me she was sixteen and I believed her. Anyone would have. But she was two years younger, meaning I needed a parent's permission to see her.'

'What happened after that call?'

Cox gave his head a little shake, met Mae's eye.

'I hadn't realized before I spoke to Ellie's mother, but I saw a connection. She had been a war reporter. It occurred to me that Christine Power could have been *there*.'

'Right, but that still doesn't explain anything about Ellie, does it?' Kit said, shaking her head, eyes screwed up. 'Would she even have been born when it happened?'

Mae, though, was beginning to see a path through it. Reporters took photographs, footage. Could Ellie have seen this thing second-hand, this *trauma* that had affected her so badly? But was it even possible that her condition could be caused by that?

'Look, the thing was,' Cox went on, 'I had got so close. We'd found the woman who had given the evidence at The Hague, I'd planned to go and see her. But suddenly after speaking to Christine, the whole thing folded. Later the same day when I got over there, this woman Filipovic, just shut down. Wouldn't let me through the door. Said she didn't know anything about the evidence, told me to leave, and not to contact her again. I practically begged her, but.' He lifted his hands into wall in front of him. 'No dice. So I came home.'

'And what did Ellie say, when you told her?'

'I didn't tell her. I couldn't. I had Christine on my back saying that Ellie was getting worse, the stress of what she referred to as *digging everything up*. Lucy had—'

'Lucy Arden?' Kit interrupted, looking up from her notes.

He nodded. 'She'd started being suspicious about Jodie at this point, and Jodie was calling me all the time, wanting me to tell her everything. She had this mad notion that she'd go out there herself and finish what I'd started.'

'And then what happened?' Mae asked him.

'I couldn't get hold of Ellie, Christine wouldn't open the door, and then the next thing I knew, Jodie Arden was missing and Ellie ... well, you know what Ellie did, after that.'

Kit was scribbling notes. Mae waited for her to catch up, then went on.

'You took on Ellie's care after she was discharged from hospital after the-the suicide attempt.'

'Yes.'

'And you told her about this new information at that point?'

'No.'

'Why?'

'Because I was unable to continue treating her.'

Mae gripped his eyes shut, trying to process it. 'You're telling me her care was transferred specifically to you—'

'Which must have been sanctioned by her next of kin, given that she was still a minor,' Kit pointed out, looking up.

'But you were unable to carry out your responsibilities to her because ... because why, exactly?'

Cox looked him square in the eye. 'Because Christine refused.'

Kit rubbed her face with her hands. She gave a joyless, exasperated laugh, and linked her fingers onto a dome on the desk.

'OK,' she started. 'So, I've probably got this wrong, yeah, but if you've been legally designated as the provider of psychiatric care after a Mental Health Act section has expired or been removed, aren't you legally bound to either provide that care or alert the co-signatory of the discharge notice. Or failing that, whoever's the mental health lead at the relevant PCT?'

It was all Mae could do not to laugh out loud.

But Cox didn't look at all amused. 'You're very well-versed in my field, constable.'

'Detective Constable,' Mae corrected.

Kit jerked her chin at Cox. 'Is that a yes?'

'Yes.'

'So you allowed someone else's demands to trump Ellie's needs.'

'It wasn't just *someone else*. It was her mother.'

'Sure. But you let her come between the child whose care was entrusted to you, and their health, without reporting it? Isn't that, like—' she broke off, turned to Mae. 'What's the word?'

Mae made a show of recalling the term. 'Negligence, is it?'

'Yeah,' she said, snapping her fingers then fixing Cox with a look. 'That's the one. Medical negligence.' She paused. 'Or, criminal negligence. Dr Cox?'

The solicitor, cage rattled, flipped over a clean sheet of her legal pad. 'It's not my client's job to determine the charges for you.'

Kit conceded it with a tip of her head: like she'd been doing this for years. 'Tell me though,' she asked him simply, 'why was it that Christine Power managed to get in between you and your professional responsibility to this child?'

Cox's shoulders dropped, and he muttered something inaudible.

Mae leaned forward. 'For the tape, Dr Cox.'

'I said, because of the photographs.'

'We're going to need more detail than that, Charles.'

Cox drank the water slowly. All of it. Then he straightened his collar. This layering of little tasks, this series of gestures: this was a tell Mae knew well. It came before the gathering point of the interview, always, when the interviewee made the final step, and revealed the thing they knew they wouldn't be able to hide any longer. He could almost feel the air tighten around him.

'I photographed the marks on Ellie's body. My theory was that as she couldn't clearly remember the accident that had caused them, that it was likely to be connected to the trauma that triggered her dissociation. She thinks that the scarring was a result of burns, an overturned pan of boiling liquid. But – well, without going into the dermatology of it, I wasn't so sure. There were sections of the burns across her legs, for example, that looked to correspond more with contact burns, or exposure to flame.'

Mae shrugged. 'Right. So you took a picture of her legs. That doesn't seem so bad.'

Cox said nothing.

Mae poured himself a cup of water. Watched Cox over the rim. 'But it wasn't just legs.'

'No.'

'Her whole body.'

'Yes.'

'Including the extremely intimate parts of her body.'

'There were scars all around the very top of one of her legs. Across the pubic area.'

'Right,' Mae said.

'So I needed images of that area, too. I was going to consult an orthopaedic surgeon I know of. I took a total of fifty-five photographs of Ellie.'

'And these photographs were—'

'Ellie was naked, yes, and that would have been fine because Ellie gave permission, and, I believed, she was of age to give that permission. But then Christine became aware of the images, after I returned from my trip. I realized pretty quickly after that what had happened, and that what I had done – innocently – could be used against me.'

Kit said, 'Are you saying you were blackmailed, Dr Cox?'

'Christine demanded that I sever contact completely, not speak to Ellie ever again, not discuss any of my findings in Bosnia, or she would alert the police to what she called—' His eyes fluttered shut, and he took a breath before he finished it, his voice almost a whisper. 'The sexual abuse of her daughter.'

Quietly, Kit asked, 'And did you abuse her?'

Cox's eyes flew wide open. 'No! God, no! No. I did not.'

'Or sell those images?

'No. *No.* I would *never*—'

'Share them around?'

He looked as if he was about to cry. 'After making absolutely certain Matthew was who he said he was, I shared my file with him. The photos were in the file.'

Mae cleared his throat. 'OK, excuse my ignorance here but how is Christine Power blackmailing you if you've got nothing to hide?'

Cox shook back his hair, a note of defiance about him. 'We all know how it works, Detective. No smoke without fire.'

'Hold on, though,' Kit said, setting her pen down. 'You're telling us that it was Christine who wanted you to keep quiet about what you found in Bosnia?'

Cox nodded.

'And so that floppy disk you said you'd lost, the one with all of the information about what you'd discovered out there—'

'I destroyed it.'

This was too much for Kit. She groaned in exasperation and slammed her hand flat on the table. 'What was on it, though?! What was so bad that you couldn't share it with Ellie? That her own mother didn't want her to know?'

Cox seemed to shrink, deflate, like someone was bleeding the life out of him. 'It was a shameful thing to do. I lied to a patient, a child, who had been relying on me for the truth. I just couldn't forget about it. It followed me around. It was-it was just ...'

He trailed off, rubbed his eyes and huffed out a heavy breath, composing himself.

'Look, I don't expect your sympathy. But the guilt of it was just enormous. Being so close to the answers but being told to keep away from the person who needed them most. I don't know. There was this one evening at this family party, after I got back from my trip, I got drunk and ended up talking to Jodie about it. I'd been avoiding her, if I'm honest. Things had already started to cool, and it was so complicated with her mother.'

Complicated wasn't the word Mae would have used, but he let it go. His phone buzzed on the desk, and flipping it over he saw it was Nadia calling. He frowned – she never called him when she was at work – but silenced it anyway. Gestured for Cox to continue.

'I told Jodie I was worried about something I'd found,' Cox went on, 'and she wanted to know what, obviously, and I decided not to tell her the details of it and she was so angry, said I was monopolizing the information on Ellie's life. It was the last time I saw her. But then a few weeks later—'

'Wait,' Mae said. He didn't ordinarily interrupt the flow like this, but this was news to him. 'I don't remember you mentioning this argument between you and Jodie Arden.'

Cox frowned. 'No? I mean, you wouldn't call it an argument exactly, more of a disagreement—'

'Who knew about that disagreement?'

'No one, I don't think. But that's not what I wanted to—'

'Did Ellie know?'

'No, of course not—'

'Christine?'

'What? No, I don't think ... actually, yes. I think so, I think I mentioned it. I was calling her a lot at the time, trying to get her to reconsider, to let me speak to Ellie. But here's the thing, a few weeks later, I got a fax from Rana Filipovic, who I'd tried to meet when I was in Bosnia.'

Mae made a note. 'And what did she say?'

Spreading his hands, Cox said, 'She wanted to come clean. She did have some information: she sent over all the documents she had. But the big thing was ... do you need to answer that?'

Mae looked down at his phone. It was Nadia, again. He got up, suddenly aware that something was wrong. 'I need to take this, sorry. Stop the tape a second, Kit.'

The first thing he heard when Nadia's call connected was enough to tell him that this was bad news. Properly bad. It was an ambulance siren, and she was shouting over it.

'You need to get here right now,' she was saying. 'She's hurt, Ben. I mean, she's really hurt.'

'Slow down,' he said, 'Slow down,' he said, breaking into a run. Behind him, the door to the suite opened and Kit called out to him, but he didn't stop. 'Hurt how? What happened?'

'Just come. The hospital.'

Kit, shouting now, 'Sarge? What's happened?'

Without pausing to turn, he hollered back, 'Bear. She's in hospital.'

He flew out into the car yard, sending a score of pigeons airborne. He chose a car at random, shook the handle. Locked. He tried another, jamming the phone between shoulder and ear.

'Tell me what's happened.'

But the voice he heard next wasn't Nadia's. It was from further away, and it just said, 'Mama? *Mama?*' And it had to be Bear, but it wasn't possible because it was Bear's voice from five, six years ago, a little girl's voice, frightened and uncertain and very, very small.

'Mama? Whev babby?'

Mae stopped. Dead centre of the car yard, with one arm through a jacket sleeve, the rest of it hanging behind him.

'Why is she talking like that?' he said.

'He's coming, baby,' Nadia said, a sob catching at the end of it. Then, to him, 'You are coming, right? I can tell her you're coming?'

The double doors into the station swung open and Kit was there.

'Keys,' she said, holding them up as she ran. 'Bay 7.'

They slammed the car doors in unison and were out of there in seconds.

'We'll get you there,' Kit said as she flicked on the blues and twos and floored it up the Boston Manor Road.

68

Ellie

The woman at the school was called Rana. She had been businesslike when she came to the phone, summoned by the person who originally answered because she was the only person in the building who spoke English. But then I'd told her why I was calling, although I hardly knew: my boyfriend had called her, and I thought his call must have been about me, but now he was missing. I didn't even know what I was asking her: the whole story came out of my mouth in a tumble, disjointed and crazy-sounding. But she had listened until I stopped, then she asked me to Skype her instead.

She burst into tears the moment the video call connected.

And after that, across a crackly connection that cut out four times in the course of the five-minute call, her pace changed entirely. She wouldn't talk on the phone, she said: I must go, straight away, to see them. She had to show me what she'd shown Matthew. She looked up the flight then and there, insisted on paying for it. I just had to get to Heathrow for 12.25. I'd wanted to tell her I couldn't. Me, fly, alone? No way. I just couldn't. *You'd understand if you knew me*, I wanted to say. *It's not possible.*

But Siggy was there. She was listening. When I was almost too fearful to stay on the phone at all, she held my hand steady. When Rana told me what to do, Siggy fortified me. It was Siggy who agreed that yes, I could do that, I could go out there today, if that's what was needed. It was Siggy who raised me from my chair and lifted my feet.

We were going to find the answers. And we were doing it together.

My mother, who I trusted above all others, had lied to me.

I waited for my stop, eyes defocused, my mind returning again and again to a single point. Not to Matt, not even to the police outside my home, but to my mother's face in that picture of Bernadette's. Holding that baby. So obviously, utterly in love with that little child. The edges of the two of them so permeable, like their meniscuses could touch and that would be it, they would be consumed back like mercury into one pure, complete, perfect whole.

The tube went into a tunnel and the window I had been staring through became a black mirror. I looked away.

*

The noise, the activity when I emerged onto the concourse of Heathrow almost broke my resolve. Hundreds, thousands of people, rushing and queueing. Fast, bright, loud. I shrank, frozen. I couldn't do it. I couldn't *fly*, who was I kidding?

I turned on my phone, and two minutes later, Mum rang.

I let it ring, five seconds, and I saw the future. She would listen, she would explain. I would go back to her. I would stay the same.

I answered. 'Mum.'

'Oh thank fuck, Ellie! Where have you *been*? You have to come. We need to talk.'

'No.'

She let out a laugh, before she realized I wasn't joking. 'Ellie. I'm not asking.'

'Why didn't you send our letters, Mum?'

She was silent for such a long time that I thought she'd hung up. 'Mum?'

'Because there are things you can't understand, Ellie.'

'Try me.'

'We can talk about it. OK? If you really want to, we can. But you have to come. Now. I mean it.'

'Well, I mean it, too. I'm not coming. I have to go somewhere.'

'Go where?'

I didn't reply.

She sighed. 'OK. I'm going to tell you something and you're not going to like it.' She paused, and then, tenderly, 'Please Ellie, can you make sure you're somewhere quiet, for this? God! I really don't want to do this over the phone.'

I didn't know where she was, but I could feel that love, dense and enveloping. But it was a strange thing, like a thickness around my larynx, like concrete. I realized what I hadn't seen before: that I was the one with the weapon. I was the child, and that I would grow up, and I would leave. I could never love her back the way she loved me, and that inequality would trail around after us, smearing its indelible mark on everything. The ledger could never settle, because the love between a mother and a child has a grain, a natural direction of travel. Like a bayonet.

And I realized that it didn't sound like love at all.

'What is it you want to say?' I asked flatly.

'Ellie,' she said. 'My baby. I'm so sorry. I lied to you; I shouldn't have lied but I just didn't want to see you suffer. But if we've got to this, there's no other way.'

I watched a mother pulling a toddler along on a wheeled suitcase as he played a game on a screen, oblivious to his destination. The mother paused by the departures board and he jolted to a stop, and didn't even look up.

'When I went out, the morning we found the door broken, and your hand all hurt. I found something. I didn't tell you because I thought maybe we could ride it out, like we did before.'

I closed my eyes and braced.

'Baby, I did find him. I did, and I couldn't tell you, because it was like before, with Jodie. I dealt with the ... the evidence. To protect you, because I love you, and because it's my job to keep you safe.'

I said nothing at all, just waited to hear the thing I already knew. The thing I'd known right from the start, when she'd come home muddy and in shock.

'It was Siggy, my sweet lovely girl. Everything was like before, with Jodie. Strangled with a belt, exactly the same. It wasn't you, but he's dead now. He's gone.'

There was a silence. I wasn't going to cry. I would not do it with her there, even though my heart was breaking. I wasn't going to be that person for her anymore.

'But *I'm* here, sweetheart,' she said, when I didn't reply. 'I am here. I will always be here. Come home. I need you. We need each other.'

I took the phone away from my ear, and I turned it off. I walked to the security queue, and from there to the departure gate.

And whatever she thought I relied on her for, that I couldn't survive without: it turned out I could manage without it.

69

Mae

Bear was asleep now. It was late afternoon, about the time that, if things had been different, she would be on her way home from school. Somewhere there would be a sunset, but not through this hospital room window, which looked onto a brick wall. Mae sat, still and silent, on a folding chair beside her, his fingertips resting beside the canula in the back of her little hand. He was watching her breathe. Grateful for every rise and fall of her chest.

What they'd thought might be a collapsed lung was actually just a very sudden, very acute asthma attack brought on by the chaos of what happened in the school toilets. She'd lost blood and needed a hefty transfusion and they still had tests to run for internal damage, but the doctors were happy enough with her progress to let her sleep for a while. The damage to her face – the *split*, actually, the *trauma* to it – would heal. Everything else would have to wait.

A quiet click from the door behind him, and footsteps, not Nadia's, which stopped at the foot of the bed.

Mae looked up. Mike, thinner than Mae had remembered, back from dropping Nadia back home to sort out the toddler. He handed Mae a steaming, double-thickness plastic cup and Mae straightened, took it, and drank it mechanically even though it burned in his mouth and burned again as he swallowed it. He didn't care.

Couldn't say thank you. Couldn't say anything.

What Nadia had told him, in stilted, tear-soaked segments, was this:

Bear had been in the girls' loos when it happened. Another kid, younger, had watched the whole thing. Two girls and a boy had followed Bear in. They called things out to her while she was locked in the cubicle. Things about her dad being a Jap, an immigrant, and a pig. Things about her weight. At first she'd just shouted back at them, and then she'd lost it.

According to the friend, when Bear finally came out, she was screaming. Head down, barrelling out into the posse. After that, pandemonium. In the confusion, Bear had slipped, fallen hard, and there had been an almighty crash that caused all the teachers in the staffroom halfway across the school, plus half the kitchen staff, to come running. By the time the adults got there, Bear was unconscious on the floor, her lower lip and chin lacerated and bloody, the smashed remains of half a ceramic sink strewn around her like a debris field.

Under his fingertips, movement.

'A-ee?'

Daddy. He dropped the empty cup and stood, leaning over her, taking her face in his hands. A trickle of blood from the corner of her mouth had dried along her cheek, above the dressing on her lower jaw. Both lips were swollen tight and discoloured to a whole spectrum of angry purples, blues and reds.

She tried to smile, but immediately winced and abandoned the effort, winced, and let out a pitiful groan.

'Shhh, baby,' he told her, smoothing her hair. 'Shh, you'll be OK.'

But she wouldn't shush. The croaky sound from the back of her throat persisted as she kept trying to speak.

'Dominica, you need to rest—' Mike started, but Mae snapped round.

'Leave us alone. *Go.*'

Mike took a step back, as if on instinct, but he didn't leave.

'I'm her dad,' Mae told him, his voice breaking. 'OK? Me. She doesn't need you here.'

Mike, visibly hurt, chewed his lip for a moment before doing as he was told. 'I'll be outside, Dom, if you need me. Just outside, OK?'

She made a weak sound to confirm she understood, and Mike was gone.

Exhausted, Bear eventually quieted, her eyes fluttering shut. Seconds later, a soft knock at the door, followed by a careful click.

'Hey,' said Nadia.

He turned, expecting an earful about Mike's abrupt dismissal, but what he got was her hand on his shoulder.

'She sleeping?'

'Yeah.' He looked behind her to the door. 'Where's the baby?'

'Mike's sister's got her. But listen, I just saw the consultant. She says the X-ray looks OK. No fractures, nothing deeper than the ...' she cut herself off, gesturing vaguely to the mess of their daughter's face. 'So. Guess it could be worse.' That old exasperated laugh, an effervescent burst of optimism that she always managed to dredge up from somewhere.

He stood, faced her. Nadia blinked slowly, and gave him a small, sad smile.

And Mae saw a flash of who she had been at twenty, open-mic at the Troy Bar. Eyes closed, swaying like a willow to the Cassandra Wilson song she was covering, the only sober girl in the room. The whole place sat silent, entranced, and when her eyes had opened, they had been only for him.

For a while, things had been perfect.

Outside the door, a nurse rattled past pushing a trolleyful of medicines.

Mae gathered his strength, and he said what he'd known for ages – months, more than a year – but hadn't been able to admit. 'She's not happy.'

Nadia opened her mouth to reply, but then her hand was over her mouth, and her shoulders were making short jerks. When she got it under control, he handed her a tissue. She dabbed at her eyes and tried to smile. 'You could put it like that, yes. She hasn't really been happy for a long while.'

They stood together in silence for a while.

'I got that message from Mike,' Mae said. He nodded at the floor. Pressed his lips between his teeth. Said, 'About your plan. The move. I listened to it. A lot of times.'

'Okay,' she whispered. She dropped one handle of her bag from her shoulder and felt around in it with the opposite hand.

'I got a hardcopy of the prospectus, if you want to see.'

She held out a glossy, folded card booklet. Lake View Elementary, it said on the front. A hundred bright-eyed kids waving at the camera outside a sparkling glass-fronted school flanked by palm trees. A yellow school bus parked outside. Sky the colour of a tropical lagoon.

He looked, but he couldn't quite make his hands make the necessary movements to take what was being offered to him.

'What if she hates it? I mean, if they're going to give her grief here, what's to say it's going to be any better there?'

'Nothing. But what if she loves it?' Nadia countered. 'What if it's the best thing that ever happens to her?'

He sank back onto the chair, brushed away a stray thread of Bear's jet-black hair from across her nose.

'What if – I mean, what if there's a shooting?'

Nadia crouched beside him. Pleadingly, she held it out to him, closer. 'Ben, please. The facilities are incredible. Out of this world, compared to what we can give her here.'

'I know.'

'And her cousins go there, and she loves them. Every time we visit she asks if we can stay. Look,' she said, casting a glance at Bear, 'I know it's not perfect—'

'It's nowhere near perfect.'

'… but she's miserable here. It's been getting worse. And now this.'

On her bed, Bear started to move her lips again, soft vowels creaking out from her throat. Mae ran the backs of his fingers softly up and down her cheek.

'Just rest, sweetheart. Don't need to speak,' he said. He turned until the prickling in his eyes subsided, then gave her his best smile. 'All going to be OK. Daddy's here.'

There were things people said, Mae knew, at times like this. During his early days on Response he'd seen relatives arrive and put everything right with a single word. Or not even speaking, just being there. But Bear was still trying to speak, making vague sounds, frustrated, her eyes filling with tears.

'Baby, it can wait, just calm down.' He shot a look at the door, willing a nurse, someone to come in, put her at ease, because he couldn't think of anything to say. *I love you* was all he had, and what use was that going to be?

Nadia, from the other side of Bear's head, started to sing to her, but the distress was coming off their daughter in waves.

With no other ideas, he shushed her again, and thumbed her soft cheeks. She gave a shout, exasperation on her face. She looked exactly, *exactly* like him.

And he stopped trying to soothe her.

She didn't want soothing. She wanted him to listen.

And as if the charge in the room had just been spent, Bear stopped struggling. She took a deep breath, and she looked him right in the eye, and she said, 'O ore sool.'

'OK, baby,' Nadia said, 'I hear you. We'll talk it out, OK?'

But his little girl's eyes were still locked on his. '*O. Ore. Sool.*'

He looked to Nadia for help, and without a single degree of pride in her ability to translate for him, she met his gaze. 'She's saying, *no more school.*'

The tears in the corners of his daughter's eyes broke and tracked towards the pillow, pooling in her ears.

He sighed, and nodded, and a tiny crack opened at the side of his heart.

'OK,' he said.

Nadia blinked. 'OK? You mean—?'

'I mean, OK.'

Fact of it was, if she had a better chance of happiness somewhere else, only a complete arsehole would stand in their way.

'Just don't let her forget me completely, all right?'

And Bear understood. She squeezed his hand, closed her eyes, and after a few minutes her breathing had slowed into a rhythmic sleep.

As he stood, his pocket caught on the arm of the chair, and he thought of something. He reached inside, and brought out his mother's watch. He weighed it in his hands, then slipped it into Bear's half-open palm.

Nadia came round the bed, and hugged him.

'You deserved better,' she said into his neck. She didn't need to tell him she meant his mother. They'd spoken only the once about what had happened when he was young, about her decision to pack up and leave. The months and months of searching for her until she finally sent them that message telling them to stop, that she should never have had children. That she wasn't coming back. Nadia had been the only person he ever told about it, the only person he would ever tell.

As they disengaged, something Kit had said came back to him. About dealing with things. *Shit happens, and you move the fuck on.*

Nadia squeezed his shoulder and went out to join Mike in the corridor, and the two of them huddled there for a time, talking in whispers.

For a little while longer, Mae stayed where he was, thinking about the practicalities of it. It wasn't like they were talking about emigrating to Mars. It wasn't like she was lost forever.

He guessed there was always Skype.

When he left Bear with Nadia an hour later, he almost walked straight past Kit. Hours had passed since she'd dropped him off: it hadn't even occurred to him that she might still be there. But she was. Seeing him, she was on her feet in half a second, and then her arms were around him, tight.

Disengaging, she gave him a slap on the back. 'You did the right thing.'

It took him a moment to piece it together. 'Oh, so you've met my ex-wife, then.'

She grabbed his elbow and led him down the hall.

'You've got news?' he asked as they walked, glad of the distraction. 'Finish the interview with Cox?'

'Yeah, but look. The data dude who did the file recovery—'

'Guild of Thieves?'

She laughed. 'That's him. His name's Guy. Anyway, he went through all the images and categorized them. So we had the fifty-five images that must have come from Cox. But then he found two other things that are really interesting. Firstly, all of those other images were downloaded to the laptop in one sitting, about a week before Matt lost his job.'

Mae waited. 'And?'

'Come on. Matthew Corsham had the laptop for months, and there's no images like this at all on it. Then all of a sudden he gets a boner for naked little kids, and someone at work happens to *see* this stuff on his screen like two days later?' She drew in her chin, incredulous. 'Doesn't add up.'

Mae filled his lungs all the way down, and blew the air out in a thin stream. 'I don't know, Kit. Occam's razor, you know?'

'Yeah, sure, simplest explanation is that it's his machine, so it's his material. But at the same time ... And Cox said Matthew thought he was being set up. So, what if he was?'

'It's a theory,' he conceded. 'But we'd need a lot more than that. What's the other thing?'

'Ah!' she said, clearly trying to contain her excitement. 'The other thing is this.' She swung the bag she was carrying off her back and unzipped it, handing Mae a folder. Inside were printouts, a couple of scanned images. 'You remember that photography group he joined?'

'The social group thing?' Mae had given up trying on it.

Kit nodded. 'I hassled the guy who ran it and he eventually

called me back. He didn't have much to say about Matt socially exactly, but he did say they'd bonded a bit about the same kind of niche, they're both into analogue photography. But the interesting this is that Matt called him up a couple of weeks ago about a particular photo. He says Matt was agitated, wanted to meet up straight away. So they arrange to meet, right, and Matt's got this whole load of technical stuff, notes and everything printed out about a photographic format, this baby photo of Ellie's.'

'Go on.'

'The photo he's talking about – there's a scan of it, here – it's supposed to be Ellie, right? As a newborn. So we're talking 1992.'

'With you so far.'

'The format is a Kodak Instant. The old-fashioned ones that come straight out of the camera.'

'As in, shake it like a Polaroid—'

'Picture, exactly. But Kodak stopped production of that film at the end of the eighties, they lost a legal battle with Polaroid. But the stuff doesn't keep. If it's not used within a year, less, it basically goes off.'

'Meaning what, though?'

'Meaning that, for that film to have developed properly, for that picture to *exist*, it had to have been taken, like, a year before she was born? Two?'

'So it's *not* Ellie?' Mae crunched his face up, trying to twist out the implication of what Kit was telling him. 'A sibling, or something?'

'No. It's *her*. You can see from the eyes. Different colours, one green, one blue. And her face: it has to be her.'

Mae gave a slow nod, and without making it happen consciously, he felt his shoulders fall by an inch. There was a moment, in every investigation, where the fog gets almost so thick that you have to start striking out blindly. *Peak Bafflement*, he'd heard someone call it, or *Total White-Out*. It had many names. But the thing was this: that after that point, if you were lucky, all it took was one thing.

One little movement, like a key in a music box, to make the whole thing sing.

70

Ellie

I held on to the edge of the torn back seat, my body tight with adrenaline. Sarajevo was hours behind us, and we'd stopped only once for petrol and food. Rana's daughter Emina met me from the airport, and insisted we get in the car straight away, her mother was desperate for our return. Her English was clear but limited, so there was no chance of an explanation from her: of why Rana had seemed almost to have expected my call, to know who I was.

Emina shared with me the pastry she had stowed from her hastily curtailed breakfast meeting, but apart from that, she just drove. She kept checking on me, her wide, immaculately outlined eyes flicking up to the rear-view mirror whenever we swerved a pothole or rounded a corner. She drove fast, locking her arms intermittently to brace for another pothole under the wheels.

There were fruit trees, something Mediterranean about the landscape, but not like Italy, not like Spain. We passed a village, quaint and pretty at first with whitewashed, tiled houses on the outskirts giving way as we progressed to the hurried, brutal Soviet style of construction. A greying block of flats sat empty in the middle of the village, car-sized slabs of concrete missing from their exterior walls, their buckling steel veins exposed along one side. I knew almost nothing about the war here, but it showed me its face anyway, scarred and unblinking, in every derelict building and pockmarked road. Outside a skeletal petrol station, a Western couple sat on their backpacks, thumbing their guidebook and waiting fidgetingly for the bus out.

I rolled down the window and held my hand out in the air, rubbed the fine red dust between my fingers, tasted it. I wasn't afraid. I was hundreds of miles from the people I knew, hours from anywhere familiar. But this – this felt like coming home.

'You are smiling,' Emina said, and I pulled my gaze from the landscape.

'I suppose so.'

Outside a village, she turned hard onto a track between two cracked, cropless fields. I gripped the handle above the window and pressed my feet down into the footwell, lifting myself slightly from the seat for stability.

'Over there. See?' she asked, pointing out of the window. I squinted across the half-mile of scrubland, and I saw it.

'My god.'

It was of a long, low construction, two storeys at the far end reducing to one. A stable to the east of it, roofless. The whole place, somehow, caught in its own shadows. Three wide trees, which I knew were almonds even though the fruits and the leaves were all long gone.

The building from Siggy's dreams.

And then we had stopped, and the door was swung open, and I was helped out, a woman, her grey hair cut in a sharp bob, her green-framed glasses hanging from a beaded cord around her neck.

Miss Filipovic. Rana. She held my shoulder for a moment, shaking her head almost imperceptibly. Somehow, I knew instinctively that she was not a woman who cried easily or often, but her cheeks were wet now, her lips pressed tight in a sad, heart-felt smile.

And then her arms were around me. Her hand pressed against the back of my head; she stroked my hair as if I was an injured child.

'You've come back,' she said.

*

There was tea then, served in smoked glass mugs with thin milk. Inside the office, we sat for a moment on white plastic garden chairs. Rana, her daughter, and an elderly man spoke to me and each other in a tumble, continually slipping in and out of Bosnian. I didn't know these people, they didn't know me. But in that shabby room, with the paint peeling and the rattle of the wobbling ceiling fan merging with the purr of a single computer so ancient its glass screen was rounded at the corners, there was such warm, naked stability, such comfort. Their love knitted around me as if I was one of their own. For her part, Siggy was silent. She was there, but she was *calm*. As if we were friends. Even with the confusion and newness, I'd never known such peace.

Then we were on our feet, none of us able to sit. 'Come,' Rana said, taking my arm again.

She led me out into the cool hallway and into the big room at the back of the building. High windows, a huge, bright mural painted by children on the far wall. She saw me looking, and stood next to me, nodding slowly, then she led me through a glass door. We went outside, round the back of the wall I'd been admiring. We stopped a few feet from it. Ivy from the ground clung to the crumbling plaster, but had been cleared from a wide patch in the centre of the wall. Along the centre of that cleared area, a line of holes. Head height.

Rana took a step forward and bent her head. She muttered something I took to be a prayer before pressing her fingers to one of the indentations.

'Before we used this place for refugees, they used it as a prison. This was where the men were brought,' she said, stepping away, her arms folded, surveying it as one might a field of crosses. I followed the line across and noticed two, three, more holes lower than the rest. I stretched out a hand to touch one, a tight ball of sadness in my throat. A careful brush had layered paint in there, smoothing the ragged damage. I drew my hand away slowly, and dropped it.

Rana stood still. 'Boys of twelve, thirteen,' she said.

All the while Siggy watched, saying nothing.

We continued the tour in silence. Back inside, she took me up the stairs through a door. As I went inside, I gasped.

What I saw in front of me – and the connection I had with that small, bare-walled room – it wasn't possible. It made no sense. Because Siggy was just my alter. She was a part of my identity that I had somehow and for some reason *splintered* from myself: but she wasn't separate from me. Yet here was *her* room. This was somewhere she knew, somewhere that was nothing to do with me. This was Siggy's place, somewhere she had retreated to, where she had slept. I went straight to the corner, touched the place where her head would have been.

Rana was crouching, fiddling with a small, plasticky hi-fi. Suddenly the room was filled with music, something poppy and disposable from the nineties, too loud then turned down. She turned to me, her head on one side.

'We used to have music in here. You remember?'

I nodded, although I hardly knew what I was saying. 'The other children. Some of them had brought tapes from home.'

'Yes.' She smiled sadly. 'We tried to find ways for you to be happy. We had dancing up here sometimes, when people were getting too gloomy.' A sigh. 'But not you, poor girl.'

'Rana,' I said, almost in a whisper, 'I'm sorry, I don't understand what's happened but, I've never been here. I'm not – I think you've made a mistake.'

'What do you mean?'

I opened my mouth to speak, but I found I did not have the vocabulary, didn't even know where to start. Rana dropped her head to one side and reached out a hand, her thumb brushing at my cheek, at a tear. She smiled, and in that gesture, the gentleness of it, something folded in her and she was familiar, softer, younger, all of a sudden.

And I remembered her, this woman. I knew her.

Her hair had been a beautiful auburn brown the colour of foxes and she had smelled always like hibiscus and ashes. I knew the softness of her body as she rocked me, rocked *Siggy*, when she woke up screaming for her mother, for her little brother whose name was Huso, and finding only strangers in a dead place where she found she couldn't talk. I leaned against the wall and slowed my breath.

But *I* knew her. Not Siggy. Me.

An awful sadness had formed on Rana's face. She turned away, went back to the radio and bent to retrieve a box. Full of cassette tapes, mostly boxless, a few CDs. She rummaged in it until she found what she was looking for. Then she got up, smiled, and put it on. David Bowie. A song about a lonely messenger watching humanity from space.

The chorus started. I'd heard it so many times before but as

I looked around where I was, blinking and disorientated, something gave way. And suddenly, I was hearing that music as if it was coming from inside me. I knew that song from here – from *inside this room*.

'Do you remember?'

I was on the floor now, without having consciously sat down, my legs gone from under me. Everything swimming, my chest sparkling as if my heart couldn't be held. And Rana was there, next to me, looking into my eyes. Touching her finger just beneath my right eye.

Sometimes I think about that little wedge of time between not knowing and knowing, and what teetered on the fulcrum of it.

'Ziggy Stardust,' she said. 'Your eyes, two different colours, you see? Like the singer. David Bowie.'

Ziggy. Not Siggy. Because of her eyes.

Rana stayed crouched beside me and spread her hand out across my back.

'I was there too, do you remember? I saw what happened to the little boy. Your little brother.'

'I don't have a brother.'

'Not now. But you did.'

'I *didn't*,' I said, starting to panic. I tried to get to my feet, needing to get out of there, but my knees wouldn't take my weight. 'I've got to go. I have to go home. *This isn't real.*' But Rana held me firm.

'Listen to me,' she said. 'When we first came, you wouldn't talk. You had injuries from a fire: there had been a shelling in another part of the town, and you had hidden in a house that was on fire. There were militia soldiers. I suppose you thought it was safer to risk the fire, maybe. Later, they cleared the town

and I saw what happened to the boy, your brother. We didn't
know each other then but I saw it all, and I saw you. It was …
it was the worst thing I have ever seen. A soldier took him from
your mother. He had been crying and—'

She broke off, pulling her hands down her face. Then she
tried again, her voice stony. 'It will never leave me, not as long
as I live. Your brother, he was crying, and the soldier killed him
just like that in front of everybody. And then when we got here,
it was too late by then to work out who you were. You'd got
separated from your mother, somehow. It happened all the time.
You have to understand, people were arriving here in the middle
of the night, on foot, in awful conditions, barely alive. Many,
many people came here, their first place of refuge after crossing
the border. Some stayed, some passed through. Chaos.' She held
onto my shoulders. 'By the time we found your papers, someone
had given you the name, and although you stayed silent you
were at least responding to Ziggy. So it stuck.'

I tried to speak but I had to swallow first to get anything out.
'I think something's got confused,' I said, and I started to shake,
everywhere. My mind convulsing, unable to link what I had always
believed with what was forming in my head. It was an earthquake.
An inexorable, impossible rearrangement of who I was.

I forced myself to get to my feet. Went to the window. I laid
my hand on the cool glass and let my eyes drift across the
courtyard beyond it, out to where Emina was filling the water
in her car from a plastic bottle. Out to the scrubby field beyond.
There was a horse. A little girl talking to it, reaching up with
both hands to pull its muzzle close.

It was as if a page had been turned. Like the skin I had been
wearing every day of my life was stripped off in one piece,
revealing what was left, shivering and newborn and dropped

into existence from the far black reaches of the other side of the universe. Everything Siggy had showed me, all the nightmares, all the terror and pain and desolation, the awful, obliterating violence: they weren't visions. I hadn't made them up. They weren't the creations of a disordered mind.

They were memories. My memories, of my own family.

All of it, all of Siggy, was me.

71

Christine

Sana Plain, Bosnia, 1995

Look, Ellie.

On my lap there is a child. Sleeping now, though she fought it at first, just like you used to. My hand is over her ear to muffle the rattle of the jeep's window, and I'm taking up the broken suspension with my feet for her, softening the jars and the bumps. She is older than you were, than you will ever be. She has seen things that would make you turn your eyes from the world forever. Her hair is warm and sleek like a cat under my palm, and she twitches, her dreams strafed with what she thinks is real.

Our wheels whip the dust into a billowing wake behind us, but the air is pleasant, warm even, just before dawn. There are so many fruit trees here, Ellie, you can eat figs and pears and plums straight from the branch. We have to go just a little further now, heading north and then east over the border. I have contacts from working here, before, and they have helped. They are paid to move people and things and to do it without detection, without asking questions, without expecting any answers. Didn't I tell you we would have adventures? The snipers are behind us, but there is still the border. After that, there will be the rest of our lives. Start where we left off. Friends again.

Her eyes fly suddenly open. She looks up at me with these strange irises of hers, two different colours, like a wolf. I look away, I can't help it. A sob escapes from me like a pea from its shell. I miss you more than you can ever know.

I came here looking for another you, and I found her. Not in the rows and rows of babies, two to a cot, their bottles propped into their mouths. I found her down by a well, throwing in stones.

We threw stones, do you remember? Trips to the woods, following the path down to the river. The little mud beach we had to ourselves, hot chocolate from a Thermos then the stones, bigger and bigger ones, you hopping from foot to foot as I collected them in my hat so we could throw them all back in. Sunshine. Your voice.

Sleeping again, she slips from the vinyl-covered seat and I pull her gently back. I hold my fingers just away from her face, tracing the contours of her cheeks without touching, without waking. I've seen so many like her, a whole generation of children whose world has changed from bright and green and whole into a grainy monochrome, smouldering and hacked into federations and republics and safe-zones and sieges. Fearless children, their faces carved from rock. They come out at night in the fog to collect firewood. They can tell the direction of RPG fire as well and as instinctively as you knew the sound of the ice-cream van.

But even if it ends tomorrow, it will be years, generations, until this place can heal. War does not leave when the soldiers leave. The people, the children, are the echo chamber. All the death here has left the air slack. It climbs out of the earth and the buildings to greet you. More than just quiet: it is something stretched and released, like a womb just vacated.

I touch the tip of my little finger against the drying streak of a tear on her face. They said she saw her brother die; that she'd already survived her town being shelled. She doesn't speak, but I know she will. She'll forget whatever scraps of her language she knew, and soon she will speak just like you. I have freed her from a world that was not made for children. I am changing her course, and she is young enough. I can clean it out, redact it. She doesn't need to remember any of this. This is the little girl whose name I will scratch out, who will slip into the oblivion you left and fill it up, zip you up around her like a winter coat, ready-made, ready-warmed. I will trim out the cancer of her past and replace it, and she will love me, Ellie.

Shh, now, my darling. Shh baby.

She's mine now, and I'm taking her away.

I listen to her breath, and I hardly notice the other sounds, although they are much louder, more menacing. Checkpoint. Tanks outside, adjusting their barrels, an electronic sound, coming in long syllables. The punctuation from a distant fire-fight.

Dear god, let me keep her, and I will never hurt her. If I can keep her, I will never let her out of my sight. I will keep her safe from everything; I will give everything I have to keep her safe. I will feed her my own flesh before I let her feel hunger again. I will strip myself bare; I will give her my own skin if it will keep her from being cold. I will never raise my voice, not ever.

Please. Dear god. Let me take this child.

You said you hated me. It started with nothing – really nothing, a tantrum about toast – and I failed to control it, to put it right. Nothing I can say will change it, Ellie, and I don't even recognize myself in what I did. Turning the key in your bedroom as you screamed and screamed with tears and snot glossing your scarlet face, I remembered what I had read, about *showing the child the consequences of their behaviour*. I don't even know which book now. Or if the advice had been meant for three year olds. I remember telling myself as I locked you in that I was doing it for you.

'I hate you, Mummy. I hate you. You don't love me.'

You thought I'd left you in that room. You heard the mortice clunk and you thought I had left the house and abandoned you all alone, and that was the last thought you had. Your screams no longer in rage, but in sheer terror that you would never see me again.

I was right there, my back against the door, waiting for it to stop. My heart thudding so hard I could feel the pressure of it on my windpipe. I sat outside that door for hours, and you screamed until you ... until you stopped. I don't know why. Maybe your little heart failed.

No one ever died from crying. I read that somewhere, too.

I stayed outside the door after you had gone silent. I will never know if I could have saved you. But I stayed outside, so you could rest, not wanting to wake you with the click of the latch, the squeal of the hinge, even though you were already beyond hearing. But I ever-so-gently unlocked the door so you could come out when you woke. Knowing you would wake again before midnight, as you always, *always* did and that you would run down the dark hall with Bunny tucked into the front of your nightdress. Knowing you would crawl into bed with me and lift my arm over you and say *friends again now, Mummy*, and I would say it too. I even murmured it to myself as I padded down the hall to my own bed that night. *Friends again, baby girl.*

I didn't know, Ellie.

Hours later when I woke up, the first thought was of you, as it had been for the last thousand days. It was midnight, and you were not there.

You were in your room. The door was still closed. Unlocked, but it didn't matter anymore. You were still and cold, your little fists tight. Your eyes open, your mouth open. Your tongue blood-less and dry, resting on your teeth as I lifted you in my arms, as I saw what I had done.

I hate you Mummy.

I sat with you for the whole day. I washed you. I held you and I didn't let go. I saw my future unroll like a carpet. Police, a trial, prison, because it was my fault. After prison, if there even was an *after*: a life of absolute emptiness, and no chance of redemption.

And so when all the light was gone I took you to our woods, beside the Thames. You were wrapped in the blanket I made for you while you were still a part of me, and I dug into the earth. I sang to you and I laid you down, Ellie. I placed flowers around your little body, and it was so cold. But I left you there. What else could I do? I planted a cherry tree where you rested, so that you could live.

The nights after you were gone, I ran you your bath, I couldn't break the routine. I would crouch beside the tub, trailing my fingers in the water, my heart a formless mulch in my chest. Conjuring you in my mind, naked and smooth, your hair length-ened by the water, your little belly pressing out under your ribs. Bubbles sliding down your perfect shoulders. *One two three, out you get*, heavy and inert in a towel, your head on my shoulder, your yawn stretching out now in my memory, fossilized by your absence.

On my lap, there is a child. She is nothing like you, Ellie, but she will learn, just as she will learn English. She is young enough.

The world is changed by her being in it, the air parts when she moves through it, and vibrates when she makes a sound, quivers around her. She is *alive*.

She is mine, and she will love me. Just like you did.

Shh, baby. Shh, Ellie, my baby girl.

72

Mae

The call went straight to voicemail, again, but he left a message anyway. This time, after what he'd just found out, his tone was a little softer.

'Ellie. We've got developments here. Things you really, really need to see. Ring me back.'

He cut the call and pocketed it, turning back to the spread of photographs, letters, documents on the passenger seat, sent over by Samira Anand, who had found the originals. Rain drummed on the roof of the car. A shape across the carpark caught his eye, running towards him, something shocking pink held overhead. Kit. He leaned back and across to open the back passenger-side door, didn't want her sitting on the paperwork. She jumped in and slammed the door behind her, balling up what he could now see was a poncho. She sat panting, water clumping her hair into thick ropes.

'Well, today's going to go down as the most spectacularly mental day of my entire life,' she said, rubbing rain out of her eyes, 'I'll tell you that for absolutely fuck all.'

'Yeah? Snap.'

Kit hooked her forearms around the headrest in front of her and looked down at the passenger seat. 'What's all this?' she said, wiping her hands on her sides and taking the stack Mae handed her.

'Letters from Bosnia. This woman Rana Filipovic, the one who sent Cox packing when he went over there.'

He watched her face as she scanned them, watching it change as she took in what the letters said.

The first, written to Cox shortly after his book was published, was apologetic, professional. *I made a mistake*, Rana had written.

'"I was told to keep quiet about what happened",' Kit read, '"but I should not have been intimidated." Intimidated by who?'

Mae raised his eyebrows. 'Keep reading.' He passed her one particular letter that he'd marked with a paperclip. It was from three years ago, long after Cox and the Powers had apparently lost contact. 'This one.'

'"She promised me that once it was safe for the child to return, she would bring her back. There must be a way to find them. The birth mother tracked her down, and she calls me every month. She is desperate to see her."' Kit met his eyes. 'But why did this Filipovic woman keep it a secret for all that time? I mean, how come she lied to Cox, when he was so close to putting it all together?'

'Looks like she took a bribe. To the refugee centre. Christine turned up – fake name, obviously – made a big donation.'

'Christine *bought* Ellie?'

'Not exactly. According to this, Christine said she would keep her safe until the war ended, and keep in touch in case the mother got back in touch.' From under a stack of papers he pulled out a brown envelope. 'Pictures. Couriered from Cox's office. Have a look.'

Kit pressed rainwater from her fringe and peered at the images.

Her eyes widened, and Mae shifted in his seat to look at them again. Ellie as a baby. Ellie as a toddler, and from her clothes and the look of the house in the background, it was obvious this wasn't Britain. Ellie at maybe two, a baby boy swaddled on her lap, her eyes on him, her face beaming.

Then Ellie, a little older, three or so. A hospital bed, the window behind her glassless, sealed up with cardboard and tape. Her little body bandaged from the shoulder down, her eyes drilling through to the back of your own head as you looked at them. Blank.

'Jesus. So all this time—?'

'All this time, Ellie's been fed a whole crock of bullshit. She remembered being in Bosnia, but Christine must have convinced her it was … something else. Not her own memories. It kept her terrified, so she believed she couldn't manage on her own.' It hung there for a minute like a spectre.

'But what about the fugues?'

Mae shrugged. 'Christine's word against … well, it's just Christine's word. Ellie always says she never remembered them. Cox says he doesn't think they ever happened.'

And if Cox was right, there could really only be one explanation for the injuries Ellie sustained during the episodes. He held his breath for a moment as he thought that through to its conclusion: because as it stood, and because it had been so comprehensively engineered that way, right now Christine was all Ellie had.

Kit put the sheets she was holding down on her lap. 'Where does Matt come in then, in all of this?'

'I don't know. Maybe he got too close to blowing the whole thing open.'

'Meaning, on balance, we're not expecting to find him alive and well, are we?'

'He's already been bumped to high-risk. We've got a press call booked for later on.'

Kit slumped back against the upholstery and blew out her cheeks. 'Does she know? Ellie, I mean?'

Mae nodded towards his phone. 'Can't get hold of her.'

'So what now?'

He gathered the sheets and slipped them into a plastic folder. 'We put everything we've got into picking up Christine,' he said, gesturing for the photos. 'There's a team at the flat now. See how they're getting on, shall we?'

He cleared the seat and Kit climbed through to the front, strapped herself in. Mae flipped the visor down and slid a Roots Manuva CD from the pocket.

Kit slapped her thighs. 'So. You want my news?'

'Go on then.'

'Rabbi Samuel Shevah, Brighton Central synagogue.'

Mae killed the engine and the music. 'The Jodie portrait thing. You found the artist?'

She nodded once, slowly, eyes locked on his. 'Lucy Arden goes to Brighton Central, has done for years.'

'And?'

'The rabbi's wife is Lucy's best friend. Their daughter is an amateur artist. Does portraits for friends.'

He frowned. 'She has to be a professional though? Got some kind of age-progression software and done the painting from that. Surely.'

'Nope. She's like, seventeen, doing her A levels. And she only ever does them from life.'

Mae felt his face slip, like the muscles had come loose from their moorings. But Kit was beaming like it was Christmas morning.

'I had to get a bit shitty with him, but he told me in the end. Strong moral compass.' She started to laugh, but her eyes went oddly bright, and he realized she was about to cry.

'His wife and daughter went to Europe with Lucy Arden last year. Jodie was there.'

'Sorry, what?'

'She *sat* for it, Sarge. Summer just gone. She's alive.'

And just for a moment, Mae laughed too, but only until his phone rang. After that, the atmosphere took something of a nosedive.

73

Ellie

All the way back to Sarajevo from the school, I had tried to think of one true thing. Any one real moment that wasn't tarnished with what Christine had done. But there was nothing. Every memory, everything the woman I thought was my mother had ever told me. All of it lies.

'She meant to love you,' Rana had said, gripping my shoulders before she hugged me and sent me off through the departures gate. 'I do believe that. She wanted to take you and love you. Whatever happened after that, and whatever you decide about her, remember that. I am not a bad judge of character.'

She may have been right. She may not.

From the air, England was beautiful. I leaned my cheek against the thick plastic of the window and looked down, waiting for the landmarks of the city I had thought was my home. We dipped landwards and I felt myself pushed back into my seat. I didn't want to go back; I didn't want to see her: Mum, Christine – I didn't even know what I should call her now. I didn't want anything to do with that love of hers, the love I'd thought I could rely on, through anything. It was worthless.

The plane landed, the magic of its suspension suddenly broken like a cut rope, and we taxied along in the rain. When it stopped, the terminal building was still a hundred metres away, and there were groans when a voice on the intercom told us we were being held for a short while. I rubbed at my ears, trying to release the pressure from the descent, until something caught my eye.

A police car. Coming closer, slowing: stopping right underneath the wing. Someone else noticed, and within a few minutes everyone was craning over to see what was happening. Then on the other side of the plane a staircase was driven over and attached. There was some confusion, whispering between the uniformed staff towards the nose: passengers standing, craning to see what was happening, until one of them broke away from the huddle, went to the door. There was a clunk, and the pressurized door opened.

And in walked Ben Mae, his eyes raking over the waiting faces of the passengers, until he found mine.

'I'm going to need your passport,' he told me, glancing back at me in the rear-view mirror. We had driven straight off the runway through a gate held open by someone official. 'I thought it would be better for you not to have to go through customs with everyone else, but I had to promise I'd deal with the little issue of documentation.'

I handed it over suspiciously. 'What issue?'

We were out of the Heathrow complex now. Mae slowed into a lay-by where someone was running a caff out of the side of a van. He turned the car off, and angled himself around to face me.

'It's a false document. You didn't know,' he added quickly, responding to my shocked intake of breath, 'so no one's going to give you any grief about it. But there's going to be a whole load of ironing out for everyone to do. I just spoke to Rana Filipovic myself – she told me everything so – I'm up to speed. We'll get her over here at some point.'

I folded my arms and watched him.

'Ellie, I've got some really bad news.'

They'd found Matt lodged under a pontoon past Putney Bridge, he said. To start with they assumed he'd just fallen in.

But he hadn't just fallen in.

'The water in his lungs wasn't river water,' Mae said. 'I don't know if you want the details, or ...'

'I do.'

He nodded. 'The tests they've run so far show evidence of flora: this kind of mould that you get in stored water sometimes. Aspergillus, it's called. It's not common in the river, so they tested the water in the boat's tanks, and it matched. There were small amounts of detergent. Soap, residual chemicals you find in cleaning products.'

'I don't understand.'

Mae held my eyeline steady. 'It looks like he drowned in his shower tray.'

'You can't drown in a shower tray.'

He drew a long breath. 'There were traces of a powerful sedative in his system. Haloperidol: one of the drugs that they'd found in his locker at the hospital. We're going on the theory that someone put those drugs there in his locker to get him sacked, and probably put the indecent images on his laptop as well. Wanting to discredit him, in advance of anything he might say. Whoever that was probably drugged him, then drowned him, and then ...' he paused, searching for a way to put it, as if there was any way to soften what he was telling me, 'then put him in the river. They probably did it that way to keep the whole thing quiet, and to be certain he was ... he didn't wake up.'

There was more to come, I could tell from the way he paused, tapped his fingers on the steering wheel. But I didn't care. I didn't care about anything.

Matt was dead, then.

And now I had no one at all.

I asked for a moment on my own, and Mae got out, saying he'd fetch some tea from the van.

What I didn't know about grief back then was how random it could be, how moments that you didn't think anything of at all, at the time, will come back and floor you with the force of a tidal wave.

I sat in that car, utterly alone, and what I recalled, what played out in real time in my mind's eye with no conscious effort whatsoever was this:

Hyde Park, a month ago. Throwing chunks from the leftover heel of our baguette for the ducks in the Serpentine. Rain, fine as drifting ash, clinging in pinheads to the fine hairs of your face.

You turn to me, swing an arm across my shoulders, squeeze. You say, 'This is good.'

I say, 'Yeah.'

You throw a strip of crust at the water, and it splits the surface into rings.

'Matt,' I say, and I'm going to tell you I think we should call it off. Because this is the morning I woke to find the door of my bedroom kicked hollow from the inside, and Mum hurt and weeping.

But you look at me and I love you. So I don't say it at all. But I watch those rings spread and the ducks bobbing gently in the wake and I know I'm going to hurt you. I know I'm going to be bad for you.

But you smile, and squeeze my shoulder again. And then, like you have a direct line to everything in my head you say, 'It'll be OK, Ellie.'

So I leave it all unsaid. Instead, I let this happen, I let that small swell of joy rise, and break, and I turn and I kiss you.

Because I believe you. It will be OK.

I believed you Matt. And now you're gone.

There was movement, the car door opening, and Mae was back. He placed the two polystyrene cups carefully on the dashboard, lay his hands on his thighs, stared straight ahead, and told me the rest of it.

That Matt had been too close to the truth. About me, about all of it. She knew she'd lose me if I found out.

'It seems to me that she wanted you to believe things about yourself so that you stayed dependent on her,' he said after a silence. 'Does that seem ... possible, to you?'

I watched the steam curl and rise, fogging up the windscreen. There were a few moments when I could say nothing at all.

'His car,' I said eventually, hardly believing I was saying this out loud. 'His car was outside our flat. She took it away because she thought I ... I thought *Siggy* had driven it.'

He nodded. 'Well, we can't be sure yet, but my guess is that it was your—' he stopped himself, then adjusted it: 'it was Christine who put it there in the first place.'

He started telling me about the CCTV they'd found, but I wasn't listening anymore. She parked the car there so I would find it. She must have known I'd been having lessons. I tried to picture her doing it, and found it wasn't that hard to imagine, now. The woman into whom I had put my absolute, unquestioning trust, slipping outside when she knew I wouldn't see her do it. Setting the seat, adjusting the mirrors, planting my coat in there, all so I would think ...

So I would think I was a monster.

I lifted my tea, but my hands were shaking and it spilled.

Mae took the cup from me, set it down and pulled out some tissues.

'But she had an alibi,' I said, barely above a whisper. 'She was at work.' Where else could she have been? She never went out. She didn't have friends. All she had was me. That was the deal. Just us.

Mae folded the wet paper into a neat square and stowed it in the glovebox. 'Her story fell apart. As long as she got her tasks done every shift, no one kept tabs on where she was.'

I shook my head. He was telling me that Mum – *Christine* – had gone out there and *killed* him. Held his head under the few inches of water. Watched the light go out.

I drank the tea without tasting it. When I finished it, I remembered the pictures. Bernadette's little blonde niece.

'What happened to her daughter?'

'How do you mean?'

'Christine. She's not my mother but she did have a daughter, Ellie. The one she pretended was me. I saw pictures of her. I think,' I said, realizing how deep it went, 'that all my stuff, my passport and my birth certificate and everything, it must be all hers. What happened to her?'

He spread his hands. 'We don't know that yet. We'll find out, don't worry.'

For a moment, neither of us spoke. Then Mae said, quietly, 'Ellie, I'm sorry to have to ask you but we're going to need your help with something.'

'Like what?'

Releasing a slow breath, he reached for his tea, took a mouthful. Replaced it on the dash. 'We can't find her.'

I turned, wide-eyed. 'What?'

He shrugged apologetically. 'We've got half a dozen people

looking for her. She's not at home, she's not at work, she isn't anywhere else we know she has links to. She's good at hiding. I know how you must be feeling Ellie, but—'

'Do you? You're telling me she murdered him. She tried to make it look like it was me, so I'd be scared of myself, even more scared than I already am.' I shook my head, rage swelling around me like a rising tide. 'You know how that feels? Really?'

I brought my knees up and hugged them to my chest. Sat like that for a while, saying nothing, just the sound of the rain tapping on the metal roof.

Eventually he hauled a breath in and shifted in his seat. 'OK,' he said. 'You're right. I can't possibly know what that's like. I can't, I don't. But we need to find her. We can't do it without you.'

He reached over and took my hand, and squeezed it. I recoiled, crying out from the hot bolt of pain. I hadn't even unwrapped the dressing for twenty-four hours, and the throb was now a steady percussion up my arm and into my shoulder.

'You hurt?' he asked, releasing the hand.

'No,' I said automatically, covering the hand with my good one. But I paused.

My whole life had been held together by lies. Lies I was a part of, lies I thought were truths. Lies I knew were lies but that we talked about as if they weren't, and lies we admitted to ourselves. It was our default position: false until proven otherwise.

And I didn't have to keep her secrets anymore.

I held my hand out in front of me, pulled the sleeve back and took off the glove. Mae frowned, watching me unwrap the dressing. As I did it, another recalibration: if Siggy wasn't real, nor were the fugues. If the fugues weren't real, then I hadn't been outside that night.

And it wasn't just the hand. I touched the place on my hip where the bruising was still livid beneath the fabric of my jeans. 'I was covered in injuries that morning.'

He frowned at my hand, then looked me in the eye. 'Ellie, do you not remember getting hurt?'

I shook my head.

'OK. Then I think we're going to have to test you for the drugs we found in Matt's system, too.'

I realized what he was saying. The bandage pooled in my lap, and I picked at the greying glue at the edges of the adhesive pad, finding a way in and peeling it away to leave a rectangle of white, saturated skin framing the raw wound. Mae pressed his lips between his teeth, shocked at the mess.

'She said it was barbed wire. But it's not true, is it?'

I've never seen anyone shake their head as sadly as he did just then. I nodded, let the hand drop into my lap.

'She did this to me herself,' I said, and I breathed a long, long breath in, as if I'd surfaced from a life underwater.

74

Ellie

Mae wanted to take me to have the hand looked at before we did anything else, but I wasn't having it. Later, I said. After. I needed to find her first. I needed her to tell me what she'd done.

I knew exactly where to take him.

A mist hung through the trees, the kind that seems to sag earthwards, thickening under its own weight. Several times Mae asked me if I was sure we were going the right way. He couldn't see the trampled path through the brambles, or the track of her machete, the younger shoots from the branches she'd amputated on last year's visit, or the one before that. This place beside the river was the one constant thing, unchanging through all the moves we'd had to make, all the upheavals. Our secret place.

I bent a young branch away from my face, twisted it limp.

Mae hung back, and when we got close I put my arm out to tell him, *no further*. Because there she was.

Our Welsh wool picnic blanket folded underneath her, a flask lying on the damp leaves at her back. The crisp, spikey shell of a fallen beech nut crunched under my step and she straightened, smoothed back her hair. But didn't turn. The cherry tree was just beside her, to her right. Side by side, sharing the view.

As I got closer I saw that she must have been there a long

while. Her hair was soaked, and she was opalescent with rain. She smiled lightly without looking up.

'Here you are,' she said.

'Here I am.'

She patted the blanket beside her and reached behind her for the flask. 'I really, really hoped you'd come.'

*

It had never been her intention to make me afraid, she said. She wanted me to forget what had happened to me in Bosnia, but I wouldn't, and the only thing she could do was pretend that the memories were someone else's.

I listened to all of it, sitting beside her, her low, smooth voice punctuated with the soft splashes of stored rain slip from the leaves above us.

About how much she loved me. About how she'd done everything she could to stop Matt from finding out, because she couldn't bear the thought of losing me. Because I was all she had.

'And now you've got nothing,' I said.

She looked at me. 'Baby, no. We're going to find a way. I still love you. Nothing's changed.'

I laughed, a single bitter syllable. 'I have never been your little girl. There is nothing between us that I want to keep.'

She opened her mouth to protest it, but I hadn't said it for a discussion. I could see the finality of it settle on her. Recognizing how completely she had lost, that the door had closed: I had never seen her beaten, but right then, she crumpled.

'Ellie, please. I only wanted to help you. I wanted to love you and keep you safe and—'

'No. No, you didn't. That's not how loving someone works.'

'Don't you tell me what love is. Don't you *dare*.' Tears gathered in her eyes and she rubbed furiously at them. 'I gave *everything* for you. Do you not think I wanted anything else in my life? But you needed me. You were a mess. A total write-off, I'm not kidding. When I found you, you had zero chance of a decent life.' Her voice wavered with the effort of controlling it. 'You were a shell, you were just – *empty*. Couldn't speak a word. You'd shake like a blind little rat every time I started the car. But I didn't *ever* give up on you. Not *ever*.'

'But I wasn't yours to take!' I shouted, pointing a shaking finger at her. 'I wasn't *yours*.'

I stood up, walked a few paces off, putting space between us because even through the deafening rage, I couldn't bear to see what was happening to us.

She cleared her throat and called my name. I kept my back to her.

'Ellie,' she said again, softly. 'Please. I need to explain.'

'What?' I leaned against the smooth bough of a beech, my hands behind me to hide their shaking.

'I did an awful thing.' She lifted an arm towards me, palm up, wanting me to go to her. I stayed where I was. 'Come on, love.'

'No.'

'Please, Ellie.' A sob burst out of her. 'Don't do this. Don't make me lose you too.'

I watched her bend forward, pressing her fingers into the damp, leafy mulch of the ground. I saw a bone-deep, aching sadness pass over her face, slow and dark as a storm cloud.

As her eyes fluttered shut, the realization of where we were hit me like a glancing juggernaut. I moved my feet back instinctively, suddenly aware of what was beneath them.

My whole life, I'd thought we had come to this place for Siggy, to hold a space for her. But as this woman I hardly knew any more touched her hands reverently, desperately to the ground, I understood that we hadn't come for Siggy at all. We hadn't even come for me.

Our place in the woods was more than just a randomly chosen place of stillness. This was where she came to visit the child she had tried to replace with me.

'She's here, isn't she?' I asked. 'Your daughter. Ellie.'

I didn't get an answer, but I didn't need one.

All this time, we'd been visiting a grave.

She got up. 'I didn't mean for any of this to happen. I just wanted you to love me back.'

'I did love you back.' I held her gaze, but I had nothing else to give her. Not even here, where she had buried her own child. The heat in my eyes, the tears, they weren't for her. They were for Matt, for the little brother I could hardly remember, for my mother, the real mother I'd had and lost. For all the things I had lost because of her. But I wouldn't cry. I wouldn't let her believe that I would cry for her.

We were never going back. I watched the truth of that settle on her. Up to that point, there was still a part of me that wouldn't believe that she could have done what they said she'd done. Looking at her now, I realized I didn't know her at all.

'Good God,' she said. 'To think what I sacrificed. And for what? Look at you. You're broken. On your own you're nothing at all.' For the first time, I saw contempt in her face. 'I should have seen you for what you were. I should have left you where I found you.'

There was the sound of someone approaching.

'That's probably true, Christine.'

Mae. Hands in his pockets, looking past her, out towards the river. He brushed his hand across my shoulder as he passed me, before stepping across the broken branches and dead leaves, closer to her. 'She would probably have been better off, all things considered.'

For a moment she looked around as if she was going to run.

'You need to come with me, now,' he said, one hand towards her. Gentlemanly.

She glanced at me, the swagger all gone. Then she dipped to pick up the blanket and the flask, not a trace of emotion in her movements, and tucked them under her arm. Before she turned away, she lifted her hand towards the cherry tree, and let her hand trail along one of its branches.

Then she shook back her hair, and walked off towards the path.

75

Mae

Once Christine was booked in, Mae headed straight back up to his desk. Kit had been assigned to Ellie for the rest of day, sorting out somewhere for her to stay, and a first meeting with a specialist trauma psychotherapist.

McCulloch had told him to check in with her, but before he went to find her, he spent a few minutes at his desk, checking something out that he'd been putting off. He called Nadia. She cut him off the first time – he knew she would still be at the hospital where phone use was discouraged – but rang back a minute later.

'Bear's awake. Swelling's going down, and the antibiotics are working.' She sounded tired, but happy. 'She's asking for you, too.'

'Good. Does she remember anything more about what happened?'

'Kind of. She said she got really angry and she wanted to hurt them. But the collision with the sink was an accident. Seems like all of them agree.'

'She's not been forced to say that?'

'Don't see how she could have been, she was knocked out, and since then she's been in here.' There was a pause. 'She did say one thing though.'

'What's that?'

'Your friend. Kate, is it?'

'Oh, Catherine. Kit.'

'That's it. Well, Bear asked if she might come over to visit too, when you do.'

'Right,' he laughed.

'So, who is she?' his ex-wife asked archly. He could hear the little twist of a smile in her voice.

'Nadia, come on.'

'What? You're allowed to have someone in your life, Ben. It's been a long old while.' He tucked the phone between his shoulder and his ear, and on the screen in front of him he brought up the website he'd been looking at, one of those places that compares the prices of international travel for you. He put some dates into drop-down boxes and hit return.

'I don't think I'm her type, to be honest. We're really just colleagues.' Pretty much. Most of the time.

'No? Worth a bit of an effort though? Only, Bear's really taken with her. Says they're going to go to some roller-skating thing together?'

'Roller derby.' No one had mentioned it to him, but then again that sounded about right. Not that he minded. 'Talking of which, what size are Bear's feet? About a thirteen?'

'Ye-es,' Nadia said suspiciously. 'Why?'

A little circle spun on the screen, telling him the algorithm was running. 'DC ... Kit wanted to know. Getting her some skates.'

Now it was Nadia's turn to laugh. 'So she's just a colleague, but she spends a whole evening sitting outside your daughter's hospital room and wants to buy her skates? You sure you're not her type?'

The website processed his request and the result pinged onto

the screen. Two adults, long weekend trip to Florida. He turned
the corners of his mouth down.

Not cheap. But not eye-watering.

'I guess it's not impossible.'

Nadia laughed again, and they said goodbye. Mae flipped the
laptop shut and headed to McCulloch's.

He knocked on the frame of her open door and went in.

'Ah. Man of the hour. Take a seat, Ben.'

She took her glasses off and waved him into the chair opposite hers, then remembering something, she swivelled her seat
all the way around and ducked, opening what he guessed was
a box or a drawer behind her. When she twisted back again,
half a smile on her face, she placed a glass bottle and two plastic
cups on the desk. Champagne, and not a brand he recognized
from the supermarket, either.

After popping the bottle open, she poured and passed him a
cup, and raised hers to toast. 'To your solve. However grisly.' She
took a sip. 'I have to admit,' she said, blinking as the bubbles
went up her nose, 'I was actually about to pull you off this one.'

'I wouldn't have blamed you,' he lied, feeling the comfortable
blur of the alcohol as it spread through his blood.

She eyed him over the rim of her cup. 'I don't know about
that, Mae.'

He shrugged, put the cup down, and opened his folder for
the update. 'Data Forensics came back with the IP address, so
we can see where the laptop was when the rest of the images
were accessed.'

'Where the *laptop* was? But not Corsham himself?'

'It was in the hospital. Corsham's debit card was used in a
café ten minutes away as it was happening.'

'Someone else use his card?'

Mae took a sip, swallowed. 'Nope. Coffee shop has CCTV. It's definitely him using his card: cappuccino and a muffin, and he stayed in the café for the whole time the download took place. No way he accessed those images himself.'

DCI McCulloch leaned back. 'You're going to tell me Christine was on shift though, right?'

'That's exactly what I'm going to tell you, yes. Tip-off to HR was made before Matthew was back in the building. The missing meds had already been clocked by the pharmacy manager, so that ship had sailed. But Helen Williams paid Matt off anyway. Wanted him to go quietly: she didn't want to risk the images coming to light because it was down to her that he'd got away with those forged DBS documents for Ellie.'

She smoothed her forehead with her fingertips, unconvinced. 'But why, Mae? Why did he do that with Ellie?'

Draining his cup, Mae said, 'There's no evidence there was anything else to it: she just wanted to work there, and he wanted to help. Kit's gone over the whole ward – CCTV, interviewing the nurses, kids – no one's got anything remotely alarming to say about him. Ellie swears blind he never showed an interest in her work there beyond what you'd expect; he wasn't unduly keen on the kids, anything like that. There was a girl he'd bumped into when he'd gone to meet Ellie after her shift once, a teenager who seemed to have taken a shine to him, but apart from that, nothing at all.'

'And the bag? Is Cox coughing for that?'

'Nope. Traffic picked up an ANPR ping on Christine's car out in Surrey yesterday. East Molesey. Forensics think they have a partial on a shoeprint of hers at Cox's mother's yoga place, meaning—'

'She planted it.'

'Yeah. Knew we were looking at Cox, thought she'd throw us a bone and put us off the scent.'

'And let me guess – it was her who paid his rent?'

'Took it straight out of the twenty grand,' he confirmed.

'Slippery old cow.' She turned down the corners of her mouth and drank. 'Ironic really, considering how we're relying on his recordings for prosecution.'

'And it is admissible? The stuff Cox recorded from the van?' It had been playing on his mind: the rules could be a bitch about covert recording.

McCulloch raised an eyebrow. 'There'll be a way. Crown should be amenable. They're looking at the charges for him at the moment too. It's a toss-up though, considering how it turned out.'

'Perverting the course of justice?'

'Yep.'

Mae wasn't sure. 'I don't know if I'd trust a jury to convict. Considering motive, you know?'

'I guess we'll hear soon,' she said, chasing a bead of condensation from the bottle with a fingertip. 'Which brings us to the issue of the girl who came back from the dead. Or, *presumed* dead, let's say.' She meant Jodie Arden. 'Your views? CPS liaison says we've got a decent chance on a PCJ charge as well, but ...' she tailed off, weighing it with her hands.

Mae dipped the corners of his mouth in an approximation of apathy, like it was just another case to him. 'I guess we'll have to consult, but I can't see a public interest in prosecuting either of them,' he said. 'They've been through enough.'

He'd already spoken to Lucy and told her what he could, but it had been a short conversation. She'd pretty much burst into tears with relief.

McCulloch knocked back the last inch of her champagne. 'DC Heath'll be turning in his grave,' she observed, before crumpling the cup, and tossing it over Mae's head for a perfect shot on the bin in the back corner.

Mae agreed, closed his file and stood. Before he got to the door, McCulloch said, 'It's a shitty old thing, this one.'

'Yep,' he said. 'It is.'

'But I'm glad you could help her.'

He tapped the doorframe a few times, nodded, and headed to the lifts.

'You did help her, Ben,' she called out behind him.

And walking away, Mae raised a hand to acknowledge it, thinking, *actually: yes.*

I did.

76

Ellie

That first night after they arrested Christine, Detective Ziegler booked me into a hotel. Our flat and Matt's boat were both still being 'processed', as she put it, but she got me a bag of my things and saw me to my room.

'You've got my number,' she said when she'd laid the suitcase on my bed and checked I had money for a meal. 'You sure you'll be OK?'

'I'll be fine.'

I closed the door behind her, then put my hands on it. As well as the electronic keycard box that locked automatically, there was a double lock I could twist to lock it from the inside, and a chain bolt higher up. I looked at them both. Touched my fingers to the smooth metal shapes of them.

And I left them as they were.

Sleep came like sand in a sieve, catching for a moment then slipping away, and by 5 a.m. I gave up. I sat in the wicker chair by the window, scrolling through pictures of Matt and waiting for dawn.

I'd had the wounds on my hands looked at by the police doctor; she'd given me new dressings plus antibiotics to deal with what had become a low-level infection, and then drawn the blood they needed for the tests. The results would take a few days, but we all knew what they were going to find. The aches and nausea that came as side-effects of the sedatives she'd stockpiled from the pharmacy exactly matched what I'd been suffering for years whenever I woke up after a fugue.

Except there was never any fugue. Maybe Matt knew that, too.

I would probably never know why he hadn't told me what he'd found. On the screen, I stretched an image of him with my fingertips, zooming in on his eyes. Maybe he wanted to protect me from the worry, or maybe he'd wanted to have it all absolutely straight before he told me. What I did know was that he did what he did, all that research, all those phone calls, to try to help me find a way to the truth, because he believed in me. He knew I could be better than the person Christine had turned me into.

Or, more accurately, who she'd *tried* to turn me into. I let my eyes close for a moment. I felt myself in my body, from the roots of my hair to the soles of my feet. Just me. The psychotherapist I'd spoken to the day before said that I wasn't going to be better straight away, that what I had – aspects of post-traumatic stress, atypical dissociation, identity issues – they were all things that would take time. Christine had been so comprehensive in her creation of Siggy as a myth that, even though I knew the truth about my past now, shaking her wouldn't be a simple process. But what I did know was that I was more than my fear. I was more than any of the weak things she wanted me to be. And it was up to me to prove it.

On the dot of eight, a text from DC Ziegler. *Call me when you're up.*

I called straight back, and she answered immediately.

'Ellie. How're you feeling?'

'I'm OK,' I told her. 'I'm feeling OK.'

'Good. That's good, that's-that's great. Listen, there's someone who wants to see you.'

'OK, when?'

'Well, whenever you're ready. We're at the station now but I just need permission from you to bring them over,' she said.

She didn't need to tell me who she meant. I told her to come straight away, and I started getting dressed. Daylight diffused through the gauzy curtain and I was warm.

And half an hour later, DC Ziegler arrived at my door with Lucy Arden, her eyes red but smiling.

Lucy held out her arms, and I went to her. I was fourteen again, dissolving into her. Not letting go, she stroked my hair, said my name. Then eventually disengaging, she held me by the shoulders, and told me she had something to tell me. She glanced at DC Ziegler for reassurance, then drew a long breath.

'I want you to know that none of this is your fault. OK? None of it.'

I glanced at DC Ziegler and back to her. It hadn't even occurred to me until that moment that there could be more bad news.

'She's alive, sweetheart.' Lucy's voice choked, but the look on her face was one of joy. 'I didn't know. Not at the time. I want you to understand that, because I would never, never have let you believe that you had done what you thought you did.'

I opened my mouth, but found that nothing would come out.

'I know this is a lot to take in, Ellie,' DC Ziegler said, reminding me she was there. 'But while we were investigating Matt's disappearance we discovered what had really happened back in Brighton. It turns out that when Charles Cox came back from the Balkans he shared a few things with Jodie that made her suspicious of your m— of Christine.'

Lucy cleared her throat. 'And Christine had a lot riding on you not finding out the truth. So she followed her, looking for something she could use against her. It was her bad luck that Christine discovered, even before she had a chance to tell you, that Jodie was pregnant.'

My heart contracted, readying itself. There had to be a line somewhere that Christine would not cross, but I had no idea where it might be.

'She cornered Jodie outside the hospital where she'd just gone for her first scan. She didn't even wait until she'd got home.'

'What ... what did she do?' I asked, haltingly.

Tears broke over Lucy's cheeks and she pressed a flat hand to her mouth, still trying to smile, but unable to speak.

'She offered Jodie ten grand to disappear,' DC Ziegler said softly. 'She said that if Jodie didn't take it, she'd tell everyone that she was sleeping with Cox, and that Lucy would never speak to her again.'

I looked back to Lucy, who nodded her confirmation.

'But – disappear? How?' Jodie was resourceful, certainly, and determined: but she was also *seventeen*.

'She paid a lorry driver to hide her and went to Spain. Worked in bars and clubs ever since, she's just been scraping around. I've been going out there to see her whenever I can. I wanted to tell you, love, because I knew you were devastated about losing her. But I just couldn't.'

'Obviously, it all came out about Cox anyway,' DC Ziegler continued, 'in the investigation. Not about the pregnancy but about Jodie being with Cox. And she could have come back in theory, but by then she realized she'd basically conspired against Cox by taking the money and failing to come forward when the police were looking for her. Christine got messages to her telling her she'd be prosecuted for all kinds of things, so she just ended up staying where she was.'

'I tried to talk her into just going to the police to explain, hope for the best,' Lucy said. 'She wasn't having it: she was too afraid she'd be arrested. She didn't want to risk her child being taken away.'

DC Ziegler spread her hands. 'DS Mae and I are very much against bringing any charges. We're fairly confident it's not going to happen.'

Lucy wiped her eyes. 'I tried to find you, put the record straight for you, but even then ... I don't know, I was too afraid what would happen if I did tell you. But when Matt contacted me, I took legal advice about what would happen if we just came clean, and I really was going to—'

I held my hands up, stopping her, incredulous. 'So you're telling me ... you're saying there's—' I started, but a noise from the corridor answered my question. A laugh – a high, full-bodied hoot. A sound that belonged to a child.

DC Ziegler and Lucy exchanged a look and Lucy said, 'We understand if it's too much for you, Ellie, but if you feel ready ...'

I didn't let her finish the sentence. I was at the door, and then the door was open, and then Jodie was there.

She held my shoulders, then her arms were around me, saying my name, laughing with tears on her cheeks. A child, her daughter, pulling happily at her clothes.

It would take time. But what I did know was that Christine Power, who was not my mother, was wrong.

I wasn't broken. I could be fixed.

Epilogue

Weeks passed before everything was in place for the dig. When presented with the evidence – from Ellie, from Christine's sister Bernadette, from Cox and the Ardens and the people she'd been in contact with in Bosnia – Christine had offered little resistance, and had told them what they wanted to know. She insisted she'd do whatever was asked of her, only would they please, please try to bring Ellie again. They had to let her apologize, she said: they had to let her explain.

So far, Ellie was refusing, but she wasn't ruling it out forever. Things were going to be on her terms. Not even Christine could begrudge her that.

But the investigation was a long way from over. On the second Saturday in December, Mae and Kit were on site at six in the morning, helping to lay the trackway down from the base plant where the team were assembled, all the way down to the spot beside the river where Christine had been arrested.

When all the track was laid, the machinery went down. And afterwards, the team did what they could to save the cherry tree, so it could be replanted.

Because underneath the roots, they found the body of a child. It would be a few days before the tests came back, but they would only confirm what was already known. That the bones were all that remained of Christine's daughter, who had died sixteen years before, two weeks past her third birthday.

High above the dig, at the moment that the tiny skull was

being lifted from the earth by the lead forensic officer, three women and a little girl were ascending to a cruising altitude of 32,000 feet. Along with three dozen other passengers, they were on their way to Sarajevo. Two of the women, Jodie and Lucy Arden, sat portside, with Jodie's daughter between them. The little girl, whose pink tongue poked out of the corner of her mouth as she concentrated on the sticker book she'd been bought at the airport, had been named Eleanor, after her mother's best friend.

The third woman in the party sat apart from the others. She rested her head against the thick plexiglass, watching for the first sign of the land of her birth as it expanded into focus beneath her.

In her hands was her new passport, held open at the thickest page, the one with her photo. It was a good thing she had allies now, people with clout fighting her corner, because this had not been an easy document to get hold of. Everything had to be changed: her place of birth, her nationality. Her next of kin. Even her age. A week ago, she had thought she was nineteen years old, but today, as she watched the fractals of ice form on the outside of the window, she was closer to twenty-one.

For a brief day, she had thought she'd found an aunt and a father, but the girl they'd been looking for was long, long gone now. But she was making this journey to find her own family, and to mourn the death of those who'd been claimed by the war that had started before she was born. Her father, Faruk, who had been killed in the first months of the conflict; her infant brother Huso, whose murder had to this day gone unpunished.

She tucked the passport away in her bag, next to the folder full of information collected about her by the man she had loved.

They'd let her print all of it out, and although he was gone, she would be forever grateful to him for every word of it.

It was an almost unbearable injustice that he would never know what he had done for her. But she would be forever grateful to him for trying to show her the truth: her past, and with it a path forward to her future. He had helped her find her way to who she really was, right down to her name.

Because she wasn't Ellie Power. She never had been.

Her name was Mubina Idrizovic. And thirteen hundred miles away, in a village rebuilt over time but still healing from the horror of what had befallen it, her mother was waiting for her.

Acknowledgements

Some considerable years ago, when I was filming officers at Oldham Police cut a dead man down from a tree, it occurred to me that my career in TV wasn't quite turning out the way I'd hoped. So I did what only a few of us on this planet are lucky enough to do, and phoned Charlotte Cox, who told me I should be a writer instead. So that's what I did. Thanks, Auntie Charles.

Because it took such a long time to pupate into a published author, there have been many, many patient friends who have given feedback and encouragement. A comprehensive list would just be silly but Louise King, Nic Gunning, John Moyes, Tanya Cowan, Jo Fielding, Rob Stevens, and Helen Williams all deserve special mentions. Mum, Dad, and Faye: thank you for your love and support.

Writing is a very isolating job, and I wouldn't have got this far without an army of writers standing in as ersatz colleagues. We're talking *legions* of nerds and oddballs here, but special appreciation goes to Jess Mitchell, Harriet Tyce, Trevor Wood, Garry Abson, and Anne Corlett for help with this book, and also to Emma Shevah, Jen Faulkner, Kerry McKeagney and Harriet Kline for general writerly support. Thanks to Celia Brayfield, Fay Weldon, Maggie Gee, Henry Sutton, Tom Benn and Laura Joyce for showing me how it should be done. Late-night graduate-bar glasses should also be raised to fellow UEA alumni Marie Ogee, Stephen Collier, Merle Nygate, Suzanne Mustacich, Jenny Stone, Caroline Jennett, Geoff Smith, and Shane Horsell.

Massive thanks to my boundlessly enthusiastic agent Veronique Baxter, and to Stephanie and Jane at Gregory and Company for early support. Kathryn Cheshire and the team at HarperCollins have been a dream to work with.

Much of the police procedure in this book was learned by osmosis during my work on Crimewatch UK and other police shows, but specific advice came from DCI Steve May of Merseyside Police, the best-read copper I've ever met and whose surname I shamelessly appropriated for Mae; DCI Matt Markham of West Midlands Police (whose demonstrations of J-turns still give me nightmares); and DI Gary Stephens of Avon and Somerset Police. Thanks also to Albinko Hasic of bosnianhistory. com.

But above all else, thanks to my gang. Prize-winning author Mo Kennedy isn't allowed to read this book yet (because of Very Bad Words that no ten-year-old should know) but has championed my career since she could say, 'my Mum writes stories about people murdering each other.' Expert right-arm spinner and ship-builder Sid Kennedy has waited patiently (ish) for attention when my head has been in my laptop (though he would probably rather this book had a higher body-count). And then there's Tom. Thank you, Hound, for the absolute and unwavering belief in me, especially when I'd had enough and decided it was all a waste of time. I bloody love you bunch of weirdos.

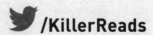